Neil Cross is the creator and sole writer of the international hit BBC crime drama series *Luther*. He was previously a lead writer for *Spooks* and continues to write widely for TV and film. He is also the author of several acclaimed novels, including the recent thrillers *Burial* and *Captured*.

LUTHER: THE CALLING

DCI John Luther has an extraordinary clearance rate. He commands outstanding loyalty from friends and colleagues. Nobody who ever stood at his side has a bad word to say about him. And yet there are rumours that DCI Luther is bad — not corrupt, not on the take, but tormented. Luther seethes with a hidden fury that at times he can barely control. Sometimes it sends him to the brink of madness, making him do things he shouldn't; things way beyond the limits of the law. And as we delve into Luther's past and into his mind, the case is revealed that tore his personal and professional relationships apart and propelled him over the precipice. Beyond fury, beyond vengeance. All the way to murder . . .

Books by Neil Cross
Published by The House of Ulverscroft:

BURIAL
CAPTURED

NEIL CROSS

LUTHER: THE CALLING

Complete and Unabridged

CHARNWOOD
Leicester

First published in Great Britain in 2011 by
Simon & Schuster UK Ltd.
London

First Charnwood Edition
published 2012
by arrangement with
Simon & Schuster UK Ltd.
London

British Library CIP Data

Cross, Neil.
  The calling. - - (Luther)
  1. Police- -Great Britain- -Fiction.
  2. Detective and mystery stories.
  3. Large type books.
  I. Title II Series
  823.9′2–dc23

  ISBN 978–1–4448–1262–6

Published by
F. A. Thorpe (Publishing)
Anstey, Leicestershire

Set by Words & Graphics Ltd.
Anstey, Leicestershire
Printed and bound in Great Britain by
T. J. International Ltd., Padstow, Cornwall

This book is dedicated to the memory of Gwen Kooznetzoff.

1

John Luther, a big man with a big walk, crosses the hospital car park, glistening with night rain. He strides through sliding doors into Accident and Emergency, approaches the desk and badges the Filipino triage nurse.

'I'm looking for Ian Reed?'

'That's the police officer?' She glances at her monitor. 'He's in cubicle eighteen. Over on the far side.'

Luther marches through the waiting area, weaves through nurses in rubber clogs. He ignores the moans of the binge drinkers, the beaten women, the self-mutilators, the overdosers.

He sweeps aside the heavy curtain to cubicle 18 and there's Ian Reed, sitting tieless on the edge of the bed.

Reed is blond and lean, tense by nature. The blood on his white shirt has dried in patches. He's wearing a soft surgical collar.

'Blimey,' Luther says, shutting the curtains.

'Yeah. It's not as bad as it looks.'

Reed's got a couple of stitches in his scalp, a torn ligament, bruised ribs. Bruised kidneys too; he'll be pissing blood for a week or two.

Luther pulls up a plastic chair. 'What about the neck?'

'Sprained. They had me in a headlock. Dragged me out the car.'

'Who did?'

'Lee Kidman. Barry Tonga.'

Luther knows Lee Kidman; he's a bodybuilder, a doorman, a debt collector. Does a bit of porn. He's not familiar with the second name.

'Barry Tonga,' Reed says. 'Samoan bloke. Shaved head, tattoos everywhere. Size of a truck. Does a bit of cage fighting.'

Luther lowers his voice to a murmur. 'So why'd they do it?'

'You know Julian Crouch? Property developer. Used to run a few nightclubs — House of Vinyl, Betamax, Intersect. And a recording studio down in Camden. But he's on the downslide.'

'Aren't they all?'

Reed explains that Crouch owns half a terrace in Shoreditch; six houses. He's got a buyer lined up, some Russian who wants to develop the site, turn it into a gym in time for the Olympics.

Crouch is servicing massive debts. And he's divorcing. He needs a buyer; but only five of the six terraced houses are available to sell.

'So,' says Luther. 'Who lives in house number six?'

'Bloke called Bill Tanner. Old sailor.'

Luther groans because Reed is sentimental about old servicemen. It's landed him in grief before.

'And what?' Luther says. 'This bloke Crouch is trying to force him out?'

'Yeah.'

'So why doesn't he just move?'

'Because it's his *home*, mate. He's rented it

2

since 1972. His wife died in that house, for fuck's sake.'

Luther holds up his hands. Okay, okay.

Reed outlines a campaign of intimidation; threatening phone calls, hoodies shoving dog shit through the old man's letterbox, smashing his windows. Breaking in, covering the living room in graffiti.

'He call the police?'

'Thing about Bill Tanner,' Reed says, 'he's a game old bastard. He's got heart.' This is Reed's highest compliment. 'He takes photos of these hoodies, hands them in as evidence. He's shit scared, he's an old man living by himself, being harassed every night. So uniform goes round, picks up the hoodies. They don't mention Crouch. And they're out before the sun's up. Next day, maybe the day after that, Bill gets a proper visit. Two heavies.'

'This'll be Kidman and Tonga?'

Reed nods.

Luther crosses his arms and stares up at the strip light, dotted inside with the desiccated carcasses of dead flies. 'So what did you do?'

'What do you think? I went to see Crouch. Told him to lay off Bill Tanner.'

Luther closes his eyes.

'Oh, come on,' says Reed. 'It's not like we haven't done it before.'

Luther concedes with a shrug. 'When was this?'

'A couple of days ago. Then tonight I'm coming home, I'm about to park, when this Mondeo rear-ends me. Before I can get it together, two blokes get out, run round, drag me out my car and give me a right kicking.'

Luther glances at the neck brace. 'And this is at your place? Your flat?'

'On my own doorstep.'

'It was definitely Kidman and Tonga?'

'I know it was Tonga because he's the biggest fucker I ever set eyes on. Plus the tattoos. And I know it's Kidman because, well, I know Kidman. We've had dealings.'

'What kind of dealings?'

'He's just around. On the edge of things.'

'You reporting this?'

'Nope.'

'Why not?'

'Can't prove it was them. And even if I could — so what? Crouch rolls out another bunch of cunts to lean on poor old Bill Tanner. Bill won't move. They'll end up killing him, one way or another. He'll have a heart attack. A stroke. Whatever. Poor old sod.'

'But there are better ways to do this stuff,' Luther says.

'That old man served his country.' Reed is clenching and unclenching his jaw. 'He was there at D-Day. He's eighty-five fucking years old and he tried to do things the right way and his country let him down.'

'All right,' Luther says. 'Keep your hair on. What are you asking me to do?'

'Just pop in on him. Make sure he's all right. Take him some milk and a loaf of bread. A few tins of dog food. Not the cheap stuff. Meaty chunks in jelly. He loves his little dog.'

'What is this thing with old people?' Luther asks. 'They'd rather freeze to death than feed cheap food to their pets.'

Reed would shrug, if he could.

★ ★ ★

The killer walks the empty nocturnal streets: avenues lined with plane trees, Victorian terraces, concrete local authority buildings, belts of local shops with darkened windows. Stone churches with faded, desperately jaunty signage: *Life is Fragile. Handle with Prayer!*

The killer is a compact and muscular man. Short hair, neatly parted. Dark pea coat. Jeans. A laptop backpack.

The backpack does not contain a laptop.

On Clayhill Street, a Smart car reverses into a small parking space. The driver, a young Asian woman, gets out and hurries to her door clutching her handbag. She looks at the killer in passing, but doesn't really see him.

The killer walks on. He turns onto Bridgeman Road with a sense of magnitude.

He marches along the frost-buckled pavement until he comes to number 23.

Behind the rusty gate and the overgrown hedge, number 23 is a handsome, double-fronted Victorian house.

The killer opens the gate. It squeaks, but he doesn't mind: it must squeak every night and every day.

He stands in the front garden, which is a small paved area sheltered by high hedges. A green

5

wheelie bin in one corner.

He lingers in the shadow of the house. It seems churchlike, pregnant with the future.

He thinks of standing underneath a great railway bridge as a locomotive shrieks overhead, the shocking power of it. That's what the killer feels inside him, now: the shriek and rattle and thunder of a great engine.

He snaps on the latex gloves he's kept rolled in one pocket of his pea coat. Then, from the other pocket, he removes a pair of needle-nosed pliers.

He walks to the side of the house. His legs are trembling. He follows the vertical line of the drainpipe until it meets the small, square drain around which grows sparse London grass.

He kneels to snip the telephone wire close to the ground. Then he pockets the pliers and returns to the front door.

From his pocket, he removes a set of house keys.

He grits his teeth. With great care, he inserts the Yale key into the lock and slowly turns it. The door snicks open as he leans a shoulder into it. Quietly, so quietly.

When the gap is wide enough, he slips through like smoke.

Into the wall near the door is set a plastic keypad. A small red light flashes. The killer ignores it, and sharks through a haze of the Lamberts' scent: their clothes, their deodorants, their perfumes, their cleaning products, their bodies, their sex.

He enters the dark living room and sets down his backpack.

He shrugs off his pea coat, folds it and lays it on the sofa. He unzips the backpack and removes a pair of painter's bootees. He slips them over his shoes.

Then he wriggles into a pair of paper overalls. He pulls up the elasticated hood. He stands there in the white paper jumpsuit and the thin rubber gloves.

He reaches into the backpack and removes his tools: a taser, a silvery roll of duct tape (one corner folded over for easy access), a scalpel, a carpet knife.

At the bottom of the rucksack, rolled into a sausage, is a small polar fleece blanket with satinette edging.

He lays the blanket on the sofa. Looks down at it, a pallid rectangle.

The killer's spirit balloons and seems to leave his body. He hovers above himself.

He watches himself head upstairs: gently now, gently.

He avoids the fifth step, slips back into his body, and proceeds into darkness.

★   ★   ★

Luther kills time in the waiting area by flicking through a tatty old *Heat* magazine.

In the far corner, a tramp with ash-grey dreadlocks bellows at God, or perhaps that he is God. It's difficult to tell.

Reed limps out around 3.15 a.m. Luther takes his coat and helps him through the doors, through the main entrance, blazing bright.

7

They cross the wet car park to Luther's decayed old Volvo.

Luther drives Reed home — a top-floor, one-bedroom rented apartment in Kentish Town.

The flat is bare and disorderly, as if it were temporary accommodation, which it is. All Reed's flats are temporary accommodation.

Reed yearns for a big house, a big garden with a trampoline in it, a horde of kids to bounce on it — his own kids, their friends, their cousins, their neighbours.

Reed dreams of community, of pub lunches on Sunday, of street parties, of wearing comedy aprons as he cooks sausages at well-attended barbecues. He dreams of being adored by his children, adoring them in return.

At thirty-eight, he's been married four times and is childless.

He hands Luther a buff folder.

Luther leans against the wall and flicks through the file. Sees arrest sheets, mugshots, surveillance reports.

The top sheets detail the kids who were arrested, remanded and released for harassing Bill Tanner: dead-eyed ratboys, English white trash.

Beneath the arrest sheets are more detailed reports on Lee Kidman, Barry Tonga and their boss Julian Crouch.

Luther slips the folder into a carrier bag and checks his watch.

It's late. He thinks about going home. But what would be the point? He thinks about the

8

dead and can't sleep. He lies there boiling like a star about to explode.

So he drives to Crouch's place, a townhouse overlooking Highbury Fields.

He parks and sits at the wheel. He wonders what he's going to do to Julian Crouch and how he's going to get away with it.

At length, he pops the boot, walks round the Volvo and pulls out a hickory wood pickaxe handle. He feels its satisfying weight.

He marches across Highbury Fields and waits in darkness, the pickaxe handle clenched in his fist.

Shortly after 4.30 a.m., an immaculate, vintage Jaguar pulls up.

Julian Crouch gets out. He's got riotously curly hair, thinning on top. Suede coat, paisley shirt. White Adidas.

He opens his front door and hits the lights — but lingers on the threshold, backlit by the chandelier. He sniffs the air like prey at a waterhole. He knows someone's out there, watching him.

He frowns and shuts the door, squeaks across marble tiles.

Luther stares at the house, breathing.

Lights come on.

Crouch comes to his bedroom window. He looks down like a troubled king from his high castle, peering into blackness. Then he draws the curtains and turns off the light.

Luther stands sentinel. His heart is a furnace.

At length, a fox scurries down the centre of the empty road. Luther can hear the quick, prim click of its claws on tarmac.

He watches the fox until it disappears, and he heads back to his car.

He waits until the winter sun begins to rise and the first joggers pass by. Then he drives home.

2

Luther walks through the red door before 6 a.m.

Zoe's already up. She's in the kitchen making coffee, bed-headed and lovely in silk pyjamas. She smells of sleep and home and that scent behind her ears, the scent of her skin.

She takes a carton of orange juice from the fridge, pours herself a glass. 'So did you tell her?'

'Babe,' he says, taking off his coat. 'I'm sorry. I didn't get the chance.'

She drinks almost a whole glass of juice, then wipes her mouth with the back of a hand. 'What does that mean, exactly?'

Luther nods at the floor. It's his tell, a signal that he's lying. He knows it. He says, 'It's just, the timing was wrong.'

'The timing's always wrong.' She puts the juice back in the fridge. Then she crosses her arms, silently counts down from five. 'Do you actually want to do this?'

'I do,' he says. 'I absolutely do.'

'Because you look like death, John. You actually look ill. When's the last time you slept?'

He doesn't know. But he knows his mind's not right. At night his skull cracks open and spiders crawl inside.

'When's the last time you did anything,' she says, 'except work?'

Zoe's a lawyer, specializing in human rights and immigration. She earns good money; they've

11

got a nice Victorian house with a red door. A little shabby inside. Scuffed skirting. 1970s heating. No kids. Lots of books.

She turned to him in bed one morning, propped her head on the heel of her hand, her hair mussy and chaotic. Winter rain peppered like gravel against the window. The central heating was on the fritz: they'd slept in their socks. It was too cold to get out of bed.

She said, 'Sod it. Let's go somewhere.'

He said, 'Go where?'

'I don't know. Anywhere. Wherever. When did we last have a holiday?'

'We went on that boat thing.'

He was referring to a holiday they'd taken with Zoe's colleague and her husband. Photographs showed four smiling people propped near the rudder of a barge, raising wine glasses. But it had been a disaster: Luther alienated and withdrawn, Zoe brittle and blithely make-do.

Luther said, 'That can't have been the last holiday.'

'Where then? Where have we been?'

He didn't know.

'We made all these promises to each other,' Zoe said, ending his silence. 'About how it would be. We'd travel. We'd spend time together. So how come none of it happened?'

He lay on his back and listened to the icy rain. Then he turned, propping himself up on an elbow. He said, 'Are you happy?'

'Not really, no. Are you?'

His heart hammered in his chest.

'We go days and days,' she said. 'We hardly

speak. I just want to see a bit more of you. I want it to actually be like we're married.'

'Me, too,' he said. 'But look — if our biggest problem is that we'd like to spend more time together then, well . . . that's not so bad, is it? Not when you look at other people.'

She shrugged.

Luther loves his wife. She's the straw at which he clutches. It mystifies him that he needs to tell her this. When he tries, she gets embarrassed: she laughs and makes a humorously appalled face.

Propped up in bed on that cold morning, he banished thoughts of the dead kid and said, 'So what are you thinking?'

'We take a year off,' she said. 'Rent out the house to cover the mortgage.'

'I don't want strangers living in my house.'

She batted his upper arm, impatiently. 'Let me finish? Can I at least finish?'

'Sorry.'

'Well, actually there's not much more to say. We just, we pack and we travel.'

'Where?'

'Anywhere. Where do you want to go?'

'I don't know.'

'There must be somewhere.'

'Antarctica.'

'Good,' she said. 'Let's go to Antarctica. You can fly there from South America or New Zealand. I don't even think it costs that much. Not really. Not in the scheme of things.'

'Can you actually do that?'

'Apparently.'

He sat up, scratched his head, suddenly taken

13

with the idea. 'I've always fancied New Zealand,' he said. 'I don't know why.'

'Turkey's on my list,' she said. 'Turkey's good. Let's do Turkey.'

'I'm not big on beaches.'

He didn't like to sit in the sun, having people nose at what he was reading.

'You can read in the hotel,' she said. 'We could meet for lunch. Have a siesta. Make love. Theatre in the evening.'

'You've really thought this through, haven't you?'

'Yep. We'd need to update your passport.'

'Do we?'

'It ran out.'

'Seriously? When?'

'Two and a half years ago.'

He rubbed his head. 'All right. Fuck it. Let's do it.'

She laughed and hugged him and they made love like they were already on holiday.

That was nearly a year ago.

★   ★   ★

Now he's standing exhausted in the kitchen at just gone six in the morning, dazed by lack of sleep, placing two bowls of muesli on the breakfast bar; a late night snack for him, breakfast for her. He says, 'I was going to ask her today.'

He means his boss, Detective Superintendent Teller.

Zoe makes a mouth with her fingers and

14

thumb: yada yada yada. Heard it before.

Luther picks up a bowl of muesli, turns his back to her, shovels cereal into his mouth. 'The thing is, Ian got hurt.'

He allows her a moment. Ashamed of himself.

'Oh, God,' she says. 'How bad?'

'Not too bad. I picked him up from A and E, took him home.'

'What happened?'

'He was cornered somewhere. We're not sure by who. But they gave him a pretty good kicking. So we're a detective down.'

'Okay,' she says, relieved that Ian's all right. 'But that doesn't mean you can't tell her, does it? Whatever happens, she'll need a few weeks to arrange cover for you. You know that. Ian being in hospital is not an excuse.'

'No,' he says. 'It's not. You're right.'

'So tell her?'

'I will.'

'Seriously,' she says. 'Tell her.'

She's imploring him. But it's not about the holiday. It's about something else.

Zoe sometimes has flashes of what she believes to be psychic insights. Many involve him. Two nights ago, she cried out in her sleep. 'Marked!' she said.

He'd meant to ask what that meant. What was marked? What had she been seeing in that secret time behind her eyes?

He says, 'I will. I'll ask her. I promise.'

'Or else, John,' she says. 'Seriously.'

'Or else what?'

'You can't go on like this,' she says. 'You just can't.'

15

He knows she's right.

He's trudging upstairs to the shower when his phone rings. He checks out the caller display: *Teller, Rose.*

He answers, listens.

Tells her he'll be there as soon as he can. Then he washes his face, brushes his teeth, puts on a clean shirt. He kisses his wife.

'I'll ask her today,' he says, meaning it. 'I'll ask her this morning.'

Then he heads out to the crime scene.

3

He's forced to park some way off and walk to the scene.

The morning is damp and chilly; he feels it in his knees. He thinks it's all the bending over, all the ducking through doors and under tape; half a lifetime spent cramming himself into spaces that aren't quite big enough for him.

It's sunrise, but already plain clothes and uniform are conducting a house to house. Curious neighbours stand blinking in doorways, huddled in sweats and nightgowns. Some will ask the police inside; none will have heard or seen anything. But all will sense their deliverance from something sombre and profound, something that passed them by like a hunting shark.

The house is behind tape. Two and a half storeys, double-fronted Victorian semi. Probably a million and a half.

Luther shoves through the rubberneckers, the citizen journalists hoisting iPhones, not drowning but filming; he shoulders aside the real, old-fashioned journalists. He badges the Log Officer, who signs him in, then he ducks under the tape.

Detective Superintendent Rose Teller steps up to greet him. Five foot four, fine-boned, hard-faced. Teller's grown into the pinched expression she first adopted as a younger woman who sought to accommodate superior officers,

17

men who saw frivolity in grace. She's wearing a forensic suit, bootees.

He says, 'Morning, Boss. What've we got?'

'Nasty piece of business.'

Luther claps his hands, vigorously rubs them. 'Can you give me a minute, first? I need to ask a favour.'

She gives him the look. They don't call her the Duchess for nothing.

She says, 'You really choose your moments, don't you?'

'Later,' he says, taking the hint. 'Whenever you've got a minute. Won't take long.'

'Okay. Good.'

She clicks her fingers and DS Isobel Howie hurries over, trim in her white forensic bunny suit; strawberry-blonde hair worn short and spiky. Howie's a second-generation copper, doesn't like to talk about it. Some issue with her dad.

She nods good morning to Luther, hands him a manila file.

'Victims are Tom and Sarah Lambert. He's thirty-eight, she's thirty-three.' She shows him photographs: Mr Lambert dark, handsome, fit-looking. Mrs Lambert blonde, athletic, freckled. Stunning.

'Mr Lambert's a youth counsellor. Works with troubled kids.'

'Which means a lot of people with emotional and mental problems,' Luther says. 'Mrs Lambert?'

'She's an events manager; organizes weddings and parties, that sort of thing.'

18

'First marriage?'

'First marriage for both of them. No jealous exes that we know of, no restraining orders. Nothing like that.'

'Point of entry?'

'Front door.'

'What? He just let himself in?'

Howie nods.

Luther says, 'What time is this?'

'The 999 call came in around 4 a.m.'

'Who made the call?'

'Male, walking his dog, didn't leave his name. Claimed to hear screams.'

'I need to hear the recording.'

'We can do that.'

'Neighbours? They didn't report any screams?'

'Didn't hear a thing, apparently.'

'No cars? No slamming doors?'

'Nothing.'

He turns back to the open door.

'So who's got spare keys? Neighbours, babysitters, mothers, fathers, cousins? Dog walker, house-sitter, cleaner?'

'We're looking into all that.'

'Okay.'

Luther nods to the interior of the house. Howie follows the line of his gaze, sees a plastic keypad set into the wall. A small red light is flashing. Yapping like a silent dog. A burglar alarm.

Howie beckons Luther with a nod, leads him along the stepping plates that SOCO have placed along the side of the house.

Near the drainpipe, Luther shoves his hands

deep into his overcoat pockets; it reduces the temptation to touch things. He squats heel to haunch, nods at the point where the phone line has been snipped. Then he takes one hand from his pocket and mimes a pair of scissors. The cut is close to the ground, half hidden by the spindly city grass that grows round the bottom of the drainpipe.

'So he's got a key. He also knows they've got an alarm. And he knows how to disable it.' He stands, rotating his head to loosen a stiff neck. 'Let's find out who installed the alarm. Start with the contractor, the actual bloke who fitted it. I've seen that before. If you don't get any joy with him, go to the security company that employs him. Check out everyone. Invoicing department, IT department, the boss, the boss's PA. The sales force. All of them. If you don't get anywhere, go wider. Look at employee spouses. And hope that comes up trumps. Because if it doesn't . . . '

He lets that dangle, looks at the snipped wire in the pallid grass, feeling that feeling.

Howie tilts her head and looks at Luther in a strange way. She's got a smattering of freckles across her cheeks that make her look younger; her eyes are green.

He looks over her shoulder and there's Teller, giving him the same look.

'Okay,' he says. 'Let's have a look inside.'

Howie gathers herself, takes a breath, holds it for a second. Then she leads Luther back along the stepping boards, past the SOCOs and the uniforms and into the house.

It's a prosperous, middle-class home: family photographs, occasional tables, stripped wood flooring, vaguely ethnic rugs.

There's a hot, black zoo stink that doesn't belong in this bright clean place.

He walks upstairs. Doesn't want to go, but hides it. Trudges down the hall.

He enters the master bedroom.

It's an abattoir.

Tom Lambert lies naked on the seagrass matting. He's been opened from throat to pubis. Luther's eyes follow an imbroglio of wet intestines.

Mr Lambert's eyes are open. There are forensic bags on his dead hands. His penis and testicles have been sliced off and stuffed into his mouth.

Luther feels the ground shift beneath him. He scans the blood spray, the blood-glutted carpet.

He stands with his head bowed and his hands in his pockets and tries to see Tom Lambert, thirty-eight, counsellor, husband. Not this cluster of depravities.

He's aware of Howie at his shoulder.

He takes a deep, slow breath, then turns to the bed.

Upon it is spread the carcass that until recently was Sarah Lambert.

Mrs Lambert had been eight and a half months pregnant. She's been popped like a tick.

He forces himself to look.

He wants to go home to his clean house, to shower and slip under a crisp duvet. He wants to

21

curl up and sleep and wake up and be with his wife, in sweats and T-shirt watching TV, amiably bickering about politics. He wants to make love. He wants to sit in a sunny, quiet room reading a good book.

Mrs Lambert still wears the remains of a baby-doll nightie, probably bought as an ironic gift from a young female workmate. Her ballooned belly must have stretched it comically before her, lifting that high hem even higher.

She had good legs, traced with pregnancy-linked varicose veins.

Luther thinks of Mr Lambert's fingertips tracing the soft brown stripe that had run from Mrs Lambert's pubic hair, over the hemisphere of stomach, right to her protruding belly button.

He turns from the enormity on the bed, buries his hands deeper in his pockets. Makes fists.

On the floor not far from his feet, marked out with yellow evidence flags, lies Sarah Lambert's placenta. He stares at it. 'What happened to the baby?'

'Guv, that's the thing,' Howie says. 'We don't know.'

'I prefer Boss,' he says, frowning, mostly absent. 'Call me Boss.'

He turns from Howie and makes his way downstairs.

In the kitchen, his attention is caught by a magazine page that's been torn out and stuck to the fridge with a magnet in the shape of a teddy bear dressed as a Grenadier Guard.

Ten Mistakes That Stop You Being Happy

1) If you really want to do something, don't wait 'until there's time.' If you wait, there never will be!
2) When you're unhappy, don't seclude yourself. Pick up the phone!
3) Don't wait for things to be perfect. If you wait until you're thin enough or married enough you could be waiting for ever!
4) You can't force someone else to be happy.
5) But you can help them along.

He looks at this list for a long, long time.

The door that leads to the little back garden is open, letting in the cold and the wet.

Eventually he steps through it, ducking his head as he goes.

Teller's outside, sitting on the low garden wall and sipping a large takeaway coffee. She looks tired and raddled. Pale morning sunlight gleams through her spectacles; he can see a thumb-print on one of the lenses.

She finishes the coffee and calls out, '*Oi!*', catching the attention of a young detective constable. 'Bin this, Sherlock.' She tosses over the empty cup.

Luther sits next to her, hunched up in his coat. Looking down on the crown of her head, he feels a rush of tenderness. He loves Rose Teller for the defiant stride she takes through the world.

She says, 'So what did you want to ask me?'

'Nothing.'

'You sure?'

'It'll keep.'

'Good.'

She stands, grinds a fist into her lower back. Then she leads him to find the medical examiner.

Fred Penman's a hayrick of a man in a three-piece pinstripe. Grey mutton-chop sideburns, white hair in a ponytail.

He should be puffing on a Rothman's, but isn't allowed, not any more. Instead, he's chewing on a plastic cigarette, rolling it round his mouth like a toothpick.

Luther's feeling the cold as he shakes Penman's hand and nods hello. It's the adrenaline wearing off. He needs to eat soon or he'll start trembling.

He says, 'So what are the baby's chances? Worst case.'

Penman takes the fake cigarette from his mouth. 'What does 'worst case' mean, in a situation like this?'

Luther shrugs. He doesn't know.

'You've got a healthy, late-term foetus,' Penman says. 'You've got a nutjob with an idea what he or she's doing: they cut through Mrs Lambert's belly layer by layer. He used clean, sharp instruments. So I'd say the baby may have been extracted successfully.'

'By 'successfully' . . . '

'I mean 'alive', yes.'

'So how long does it live?'

'Assume it's given adequate nourishment and warmth. This is finger in the wind, you do know that?'

24

Luther nods.

Penman looks mournful. He's a grandfather. 'We think of babies as weak,' he says. 'Because of the instincts they evoke in us: preconscious, very powerful. Actually, they can be tough little buggers. Fierce little survival machines. Much tougher than you'd think.'

Luther waits. Eventually, Penman says, 'Give it eighty per cent.'

Luther stands without speaking or moving.

Penman says, 'Ding-dong. Anyone home?'

'Yeah. Sorry.'

'Thought we'd lost you for a minute.'

'I'm just trying to work out how I feel about that answer.'

'Just pray to God the child was taken by a woman.'

'And why's that?'

'Because if a woman took it, at least she wanted to care for it.'

He trails off. Can't finish.

'It wasn't a woman,' Luther says. 'Women don't target women at home in bed with their husbands.'

Penman lets out a long, slow whistle. 'We've seen too much,' he says. 'We shouldn't have room in our heads for thoughts like this.'

Then he pops the plastic cigarette back in his mouth, chews on it, passes it from side to side. He claps Luther on the arm and says, 'You'll be in my thoughts.'

Luther thanks him, then goes to join DS Howie.

She's waiting for him at the tape.

They pass through the thinning crowds, the people at the back reduced to standing on tiptoe.

They reach the tatty Volvo. Luther throws Howie his keys.

The car is cold inside, smells a bit of fast food and rotten upholstery.

Howie starts the engine, works out how to operate the heater. Sets it to full blast. It's loud.

Luther belts himself in. 'Any dirt on the victims?'

'It's early days yet, but no. From what we know, they seemed to have been devoted. The only dark cloud seems to have been a problem with fertility.'

'So, what? They used IVF?'

'That's the funny thing, Guv.'

'Boss.'

'That's the funny thing, Boss. Five years of IVF. No luck. Then they give it up as a bad lot, start thinking about adoption. Mrs Lambert stops the IVF twelve or thirteen months ago. And then — bingo. She's knocked up.'

'They religious?'

'Mrs Lambert's C of E, meaning no. Mr Lambert seems to have had some interest in Buddhism and yoga. Tried out a macrobiotic diet for a while.'

'His dad die young?'

Howie checks the paperwork. 'Doesn't say.'

'Men get close to the age their dad was when he died, they start thinking about diet and exercise. Mr Lambert was in pretty good shape.'

'Better than pretty good. Played tennis. Squash. He liked to fence, ride mountain bikes. Ran a marathon or two. He was pretty ripped.'

26

'Anything else?'

'We looked into the alarm,' she says. 'Tom Lambert used it extensively the first year it was fitted, then gradually his usage dropped off. That's a pretty typical behaviour pattern, probably applies to four out of five people who've had them fitted. His usage drops off almost to zero. Then four or five months ago, he starts using it again.'

'That might not mean anything,' Luther says. 'Mrs Lambert was pregnant. Sometimes men get extra vigilant when their partner's expecting. It brings out the caveman in us.'

'Or,' Howie says, 'maybe he was nervous about something specific. Something he'd seen or heard.'

'At work, you mean?'

'You said it yourself: the people he deals with every day.'

Luther gives her the nod. Pleased, she enters the coordinates into the satnav.

As she drives Luther says, 'Can I hear the 999 recording?'

She makes a call, passes him her phone.

He listens.

Operator: Police Emergency.

Caller: Yeah, I'd like to report something really weird. I was walking my dog down Bridgeman Road. I heard, like, a noise. And I saw something really weird. (*Sound of typing*)

Operator: And what's your name?

Caller: I don't want to say. Do I have to say?

27

Operator: Not if you'd prefer not to. What did you see?

Caller: A man. He was, like, sneaking out of this house.

Operator: You saw a burglary in progress?

Caller: I don't know. He didn't look like a burglar. He was too old to be a burglar.

Operator: How old was he?

Caller: Forties? I don't know. Like a man in his forties. (*Typing*)

Operator: Okay. Calm down. What was he doing?

Caller: I don't know. He had something with him. He had like a bundle. He had blood all on him. Blood on his face and that. He sort of ran down Crosswell Street, carrying the bundle. It looked really bad. It looked really, really bad.

Operator: Okay, officers are on the way. Can you hold the line?

Caller (sobs): No, I can't. I can't. Sorry. I have to go. I've got to go.

Luther listens to it three times. 'Have we traced the number?'

'Number belongs to a mobile phone reported missing by a Robert Landsberry of Lyric Mews, Sydenham. Two days ago.'

'Mr Landsberry have any idea who nicked his phone?'

'We'll re-interview this morning. But not really. He's not even sure exactly when it was taken.'

'So what do we think? The caller's a burglar on

28

the prowl, maybe? Or someone trying to put a deal together, shift a bit of weed?'

Howie shrugs.

Luther chews his lip as they drive. He says, 'And this is our only witness?'

'If he hadn't called,' Howie says, 'the Lamberts would still be lying there. Nobody would even know.'

Luther closes his eyes and runs through the checklist: look deeper into friends and family. Extra-marital affairs. Was the child conceived with donor sperm? Were there money worries? Workplace rivalries?

If they don't get a quick result, the problem won't be the absence of information but an exponentially increasing superabundance of it.

He sighs, and places a call to the best technical forensics officer he ever worked with.

'John Luther,' says Benny Deadhead down the line. 'As I live and breathe.'

His real name is Ben Silver, but no one calls him that. Not even his mother.

'Benny,' says Luther. 'How's Vice?'

'Depressing. The things people do to each other.'

Luther lets that one go by. He says, 'Listen, how's your workload?'

'Insurmountable.'

'Anything urgent?'

'Well, that depends how urgent you mean.'

'I mean, I need your help with a really bad one. If I get my guvnor to ask your guvnor if I can borrow you, how's that going to go?'

Benny says, 'I'm already packing a bag.'

4

Until yesterday, Anthony Needham was Tom Lambert's partner in a small, two-man counselling practice near Clissold Park.

Needham's in his thirties, in wine-coloured shirt, tailored, and grey trousers, neatly gelled hair. He's tanned, fit and sporting. Expensive watch. He doesn't conform in any way to Luther's notion of a therapist. He makes Luther feel grubby and unhealthy.

The room is designed to be agreeable: three comfy chairs arranged in a semi-circle, low bookshelves. A desk, bare but for a laptop and some framed photographs of Needham taking part in an Ironman Triathlon — scowling in muddy agony, running with a mountain bike slung over his shoulder.

Needham opens the window; it's stiff and doesn't come easily. Sounds of the city insinuate themselves in here with them, the smell of traffic and the smell of winter.

Luther crosses his legs and clasps his hands in his lap; something he does to constrain nervous energy. Howie observes Needham with silent gravity. She has her notebook in front of her and a pen in her hand.

Needham opens the lowest drawer in his desk, takes out a flattened, mummified pack of cigarettes. He roots around until he finds a disposable lighter. Then he perches on the windowsill, lights a cigarette and takes a puff.

He discreetly dry retches, leans on the windowsill with the cigarette held between two fingers.

He grinds out the cigarette after that one puff, comes back queasy and moist-eyed. He sits in the third comfy chair, hands laced in his lap.

Luther lets him work it through. Turns over a page of his own notebook, pretends to consult an earlier entry.

'Holy Christ,' says Needham at length. He's Australian.

'I'm sorry,' Luther says. 'I know it's a lot to take in. But I'm afraid these first few hours are critical.'

Needham gets himself together. Luther likes him for it.

Needham swallows, then unlaces his fingers and gestures, meaning: *ask away.*

'Well,' Luther says. 'You deal with some very troubled young people here. Violent people, presumably.'

'You do know this is covered by doctor-patient privilege?'

'I do, yes.'

'Then I don't know what you want me to tell you.'

'Non-specifically — do you know if Mr Lambert was concerned about any of his patients?'

'No more than usual.'

'What does that mean?'

'Like you say. We deal with a lot of disturbed young people.'

'Can I be honest with you, here? This wasn't a random attack. This was a very violent, very personal crime.'

Needham shifts in his chair. 'All I can tell you is, Tom had some raised levels of anxiety about some of his patients.'

'What kind of anxieties?'

'Would counselling actually help them? Could he actually stop them victimizing? Would one of them lose his temper once too often?'

'That happens? They lose their temper in here?'

'These are angry young men. Introspection isn't in their nature, but we encourage them to confront difficult personal issues. It can be hard.'

'Issues like violence?'

'And usually the history of abuse that led to it.'

'A lot of kids are abused,' Luther says. 'That doesn't give them licence to hurt other people.'

'Nobody said it did.' Needham has the infinitely patient air of a man who's answered this indictment a thousand times. 'Life's about choices. We try to give them tools to make better choices.'

Luther refers to his notes to break the eye contact. 'So, no specific worries? No threats, no funny phone calls?'

'None that he discussed with me.'

'He wasn't drinking a little more? Maybe self-medicating some other way? Sleeping pills? Cigarettes?'

'Nope. None of that.'

Howie steps in. 'What about young women?'

Needham turns to her. 'Not Tom.'

'I mean, do you treat young women at this practice?'

'You think a woman did this?'

'It's possible,' Luther says.

'Tom's a strong man. He's very fit. A woman. It just . . . '

Silence falls. The clock ticks. 'We do treat women,' Needham says. 'But I don't know. It seems strange. Why a woman?'

'We're just trying to cover all the possibilities.' Luther tucks his notepad into a pocket. 'Just one more thing. Do you know anyone who may have a key to the Lamberts' house?'

'I'm afraid I don't. I'm sorry. Their cleaner, presumably. But that's all I've got.'

Luther thanks him and stands. Howie is half a beat behind him.

Needham leads them out. At the door, he says, 'Are you going to catch this man?'

'We're doing all we can.'

'Well, sorry to be rude, but that sounds like generic police speak to me.'

Luther hesitates, lets Howie take the lead.

She says, 'Mr Needham, do you have any reason to be worried for your own safety?'

'Objectively, no more than usual I suppose. But I do have a wife and children, y'know. I'm only human.'

'Then you can help us. Let us see Tom Lambert's patient records.'

'Obviously I can't do that.'

'We know,' Howie says. 'Absolutely. But do you really think it's ethical to gamble with your children's safety?'

33

Needham gives her a measured look.

Howie returns it.

Quietly, Luther says, 'Whoever did this, they let themselves into the house while Tom and Sarah were sleeping. They cut off Tom's genitals and choked him with them. They cut open Sarah's belly and they took her baby. The baby may still be alive. We both know what Mr and Mrs Lambert went through to conceive that child. If you want to help them, Dr Needham, then help me find it — before whoever took it does whatever they're planning to do.'

Needham glances at his hand, still clasping the door handle. It takes him a moment of concentration to make the hand let go. Then he wipes it on his shirt. He says, 'Like I said, I suppose the cleaner must have a key. She must, surely?'

'It stands to reason,' Luther says. 'Did Mr Lambert keep details of people who may have access to the house? Cleaners, builders, that kind of thing?'

'He did,' Needham says. 'Tom's very diligent when it comes to record keeping.'

'Where did he keep these records?'

'On his work computer.'

'Do you have Mr Lambert's password and log-in details?'

'I do. But you do understand, I'd be trusting you not to access his patient database or his work diary. Those items are subject to doctor-patient confidentiality.'

'Absolutely,' Luther says.

'Then I don't see a problem.'

Needham leads them to Tom Lambert's office, similar to his own. Tom uses an older IBM ThinkPad. His chairs are comfy dark leather. Needham sits at Tom's computer, logs on, then pointedly checks his watch. 'I need to make some calls, cancel Tom's appointments and so on. I'll be back in about fifteen minutes?'

'That's plenty of time,' Luther says.

'Excellent,' Needham says.

There's a moment. Then Needham backs out of the room like a servant, leaving Howie and Luther alone with Tom Lambert's computer.

Luther says, 'Okay. Get on with it.'

Howie shrugs off her jacket and hangs it over the back of Tom Lambert's chair.

She gets on with it.

* * *

They leave without seeing Needham again. They nod goodbye to the receptionist, who sits at the desk wearing the raw, blank expression of the recently bereaved.

Luther makes a note to have her interviewed. But not today.

As Howie negotiates the traffic, chewing her lower lip and cursing under her breath, Luther consults Tom Lambert's diary and patient records.

Finally, he calls Teller.

She says, 'What've you got?'

'A few possibles,' he says. 'People worth having a look at. But right now, one name's leaping out: Malcolm Perry. Made a number of death threats to Lambert over the course of a year, eighteen months.'

'Any particular reason?'

'Lambert was trying to help him with his paraphilia.'

'What paraphilia we talking about?'

'Sex with corpses.'

'Nice. So he was angry enough to threaten Mr Lambert. Was he angry enough to follow through?'

'According to Lambert's notes, Perry's the reason they started setting the burglar alarm every night.'

'What a world,' Teller says, down the line. 'So where do we find this charmer?'

5

Clive, Zoe's boss, has cancelled a longstanding community outreach engagement. So a day that started badly soon gets worse; Zoe finds herself addressing a gaggle of sixth formers about the work of Ford and Vargas, and about the nature of human rights legislation.

She tells them about Lisa Williams, twelve years old when she was killed in a hit-and-run. This was back in 2003. The driver was Aso Ibrahim, an Iraqi asylum seeker already on bail for driving while disqualified.

Lacking clear evidence that Ibrahim had been driving dangerously, the Crown Prosecution Service charged him with Driving While Disqualified; the more serious offence of Causing Death While Disqualified didn't become law until 2008.

Ibrahim served two months in prison. Since his release, he's been appealing against his deportation.

Zoe tells the class that over the course of nine years, Aso Ibrahim cost the taxpayer several hundred thousand pounds in legal aid for lawyers and interpreters. There were immigration hearings and trials, at which he was convicted variously of harassment, possession of illegal drugs and, three years after Lisa Williams's death, Driving While Disqualified.

Then she asks the sixth formers what they'd do about him.

The consensus, as she'd presumed it would be, is — *send him home.*

'But he's entitled to stay,' she tells them, 'because he's the father of two children with a British woman. Though he doesn't actually live with those children, taking him away from his estranged girlfriend and those kids would breach his rights under Article Eight of the Human Rights Act.'

She asks them what they think about that.

She sits back and listens. The kids debate the danger Ibrahim would be in, back in Iraq. They talk about his two children and their right to a father. They talk about the bereaved parents of Lisa Williams, and their right to a daughter.

Zoe lets them discuss it for a bit, then tells them about how the British National Party had used Lisa Williams's death as a propaganda tool during local elections in Barking.

She tells them how Lisa Williams's father, a good and broken man, had made a public appeal for the people of Barking not to vote BNP because this injustice had nothing to do with the colour of his daughter's skin.

One of the sixth formers, a good-looking, supercilious kid called Adam, suggests that Aso Ibrahim should be hung.

Zoe says, 'Now you sound like my husband,' and everyone laughs.

Then she tells them about Article Three of the Universal Declaration of Human Rights: Prohibition of Torture, Inhuman or Degrading Treatment or Punishment, dictates that Ibrahim should be granted asylum in the United

Kingdom, because rejection of torture is a moral and legal absolute.

She asks if there are any questions.

There are always questions. Adam tries to hold her gaze, but Zoe's been an expert at that game since before this kid was born.

'No questions?' she says. 'Come on. There must be one. Who's got a question?'

The quiet girl sitting off to the far side raises a timid hand.

'Yes?'

'Stephanie.'

'Yes, Stephanie?'

'Do you, like, get a clothing allowance?'

Zoe looks at her, deflating.

Stephanie says, 'Because your clothes are really nice and everything.'

Her classmates perform a lot of exasperated eye rolling, sucking air over their teeth.

Stephanie blushes, and suddenly Zoe's fiercely on her side. It's in her nature.

'Good question,' she says. And as she's saying it, she begins to believe it. 'No, we don't get a clothing allowance but we're expected to meet a required minimum standard of dress every day. And when I say *minimum*, I mean — going to a royal wedding.'

Stephanie smiles, seraphic. Zoe smiles back, wanting to help her, wanting her to come away from this pointless little forum with something of worth.

'It's easier for men,' Zoe tells her. 'The dress thing. Their wives buy their ties.'

'Racist,' says Adam.

'I beg your pardon?'

Adam withers a little, not much, crosses his arms, slumps in his chair, looks her in the eye. 'That's racist against men.'

Zoe feels the corner of her mouth twist. She knows the futility of engaging this kid. After all, he's here because he wants to be; he's just trying to make the kind of obscure, self-defeating point adolescent boys seem compelled to make. But he's still a prick.

She says, 'Sorry, what's your name, again?'

'Adam.'

'Okay, Adam. I'll tell you what. Why don't we step outside this room and conduct a spot poll. We'll see how many men in this office — that's about sixty-five per cent of the personnel by the way, and about eighty per cent of the senior partners — bought their own tie.'

Adam grins like the triumph's his. Zoe's torn between giving up and laying into him.

Then there's a discreet tap at the door and Miriam, her PA, pops her head into the meeting room and mimes a phone call with thumb and little finger. She mouths the words: *It's John.*

Zoe thanks everyone for coming, gathers her notes, gives Adam a withering look and Stephanie an encouraging smile, and leaves.

She hurries to her office and dials John's number.

'Zoe,' he says.

She can tell he's outside. 'Where are you?'

'Right now? Next to a canal.'

'What are you doing?'

'Looking at a dead pigeon trapped in a shopping trolley.'

'Lovely.'

'How're you doing?'

'Clive had me speak to the sixth formers.'

'I told you he would.'

'Well, he did. Arsehole that he is.'

'Any progress on the Hattem thing?'

The Hattem thing is Zoe's biggest current case. She says, 'I've got that bloke coming round later today, tomorrow maybe, wants to liaise about it.'

'What bloke?'

'Mark thingy. From Liberté Sans Frontière.'

'Hippy?'

'Trustafarian,' she says, hating herself. 'All ganja and yeah.'

Luther laughs. 'You'll get through it.'

'I hope so. I'm sorry I ever said yes to it.'

She runs a hand through her hair, becomes aware that she's dying for a cigarette.

She holds her fringe in a bunch and tugs slightly, just enough so it hurts a bit.

She'd been doing this since she was seven years old. It relieves stress. She doesn't know why. Sometimes she worries she'll get a bald patch, like one of those stressed parrots that yanks all the feathers from its body except the ones it can't reach, so in the end it sits on its perch like an oven-ready chicken in a Halloween mask.

She says, 'Did you speak to Rose?'

'I did. I did, yeah.'

And now she knows why she's tearing at her

hair. It's got nothing to do with the Hattem case. It's John and his inability to say no to anyone except his wife.

She says, 'What happened?'

'It's difficult to talk about,' he says. 'Too many people around. But I can't ask her today. I just can't.'

John knows when anyone else is lying, usually at a glance. The speed and conviction of it gives her the creeps sometimes. But he never knows when he's lying to himself.

'It's a pretty bad one,' he says.

'They're all bad ones,' she says. 'That's the point.'

Zoe's ashamed as well as angry. And she's resentful that John can do this to her — make her feel guilty for wanting a marriage.

And here they are, like nightwatchmen patrolling the same ground, the same route, night after night after night.

'I have to do this,' he says. 'Then I'll talk to her.'

'No you won't.'

'Zoe.'

'You won't, John. Because after this one there'll be another one, and after that one there'll be another. And then another one after that and it just goes on and on and on.'

There's a long silence.

'Fucking Rose Teller,' Zoe says. 'That woman's managed to fuck over more marriages than anyone I ever met.'

'Zoe — '

She hangs up.

Her hand is shaking.

She grabs the tin of tobacco from her drawer and sneaks outside, to the CCTV blind spot on the corner.

She calls Mark North. 'You were right,' she says. 'I give him chances. I give him chance after chance and he just *lies*. He just lies and lies.' She tugs at her hair and says, 'Christ. You were so right.'

Mark doesn't say anything.

Zoe smokes the roll-up, picks a bitter thread of tobacco from her tongue. She says, 'I'm shaking.'

'Why are you shaking?'

'I've never done this before.'

'Done what?'

'Harrington Hotel,' she says. 'Ten minutes.'

There's a silence. 'Are you sure?' he says at the end of it. 'Because you need to be sure about this.'

'No,' she laughs, 'I'm not sure. But I'm done with it. I'm finished. I've had enough.'

Mark doesn't hang up and neither does she.

She can hear her own breath feeding back down the line, ragged with anxiety and arousal.

Zoe calls Miriam and tells her to cancel her meetings until after lunch.

Miriam's worried — Zoe's never done this before.

'It's a personal thing,' Zoe says. 'Don't worry. I'll see you about two.'

She walks to the Harrington, a boutique place on Tabernacle Street. She hasn't brought a coat and it's raining. She hugs herself for warmth.

When the hotel is in sight she breaks into a

jog. Click click click go her heels.

Mark's already booked a room and checked in.

He's sitting in the over-designed lobby, pretending to read the *Guardian*. He's holding a white key card with a black magnetic stripe.

They don't speak. Just step into the waiting elevator.

Inside, they stand shoulder to shoulder.

Zoe can hear her heart.

6

The squat consists of eight derelict council flats knocked into one. It's occupied by artists, students, anarchists, junkies and the mentally deranged.

There's no heating. Crumbling walls are hidden behind graffiti, tie-dyed and screen-printed bed-sheets, posters.

Malcolm Perry only stirs when he hears the shouting downstairs. It's still early, and shouting like that usually involves Random Andy, the schizophrenic often to be found huddling in one corner of the farthest flat, indulged by the dreadlocked art insurgents to whom intolerable mental anguish is a valid form of self-expression.

The shouting is louder than usual this morning, but Malcolm has been up for three days straight on a dirty form of amphetamine called Pink Champagne, washed down a few hours ago with some Temazepam.

Which is why he's still in bed when the police kick down the door and surge into the room like spawning salmon, a big black copper in a tweed overcoat bringing up the rear, stomping into the room with a sneer of contempt for Malcolm's posters and his screen-printing equipment.

Malcolm is a skinny man with long, fine hair and a scrubby beard. He's naked from the waist down, his dick shrivelled by the cold and by the

45

Pink Champagne into a nub of wrinkled gristle.

He's wearing hiking socks on spindly legs, and one of his own T-shirts.

The big copper stalks up. He looms over Malcolm, looks like he's about to rip his head off. Instead, he leans close and reads aloud the words printed on Malcolm's T-shirt.

'Work Obey Consume,' he says.

'That's right,' says Malcolm, belligerent and confused.

'Search this place,' says the big copper. 'Nick everyone in here. Interview them all.'

The big copper squats with a look of distaste. With finger and thumb he tweezes a pair of greasy tracksuit bottoms from a pile of clothes near the foot of the bed. He throws them and a pair of rubber flip-flops to Malcolm, completely ignoring Malcolm's Para boots. 'Put these on,' he says.

'Where are we going?'

'To my house,' says the copper. 'It's not much. But it's better than this shithole.'

★   ★   ★

Luther orders a search of the squats and immediate surroundings.

A second team make a number of arrests based on drugs offences, parole violations, receiving stolen goods, outstanding warrants, suspicion of this, suspicion of that.

And they rush Malcolm to Hobb Lane under blues and twos.

Howie stops off for Luther to pick up a

46

burger. He eats it upside-down in waxed paper.

He's wiping his mouth on one hand as they walk into the station at the corner of Hobb Lane and Abbadon Street.

The building is a brutish old monstrosity: a utilitarian 1950s construction crudely grafted onto a Victorian frame. It's a chimera, and thus born to be a police station.

And it smells, like every police station Luther's ever been in, of linoleum, floor polish, armpits, printer toner, dust on radiators.

Balling his paper napkin as he mounts the stairs three at a time, he passes through the doors into the Serious Crime Unit.

Furniture filched from other departments; ratty office chairs and fire-sale desks crammed into a space that demands to be three times as large.

He strides to his office, a narrow, undersized workspace he shares with Ian Reed.

Benny Deadhead's waiting for him at the door, holding out a skinny white hand. He and Luther shake.

Luther says, 'You all right there, Ben? Thanks for coming.'

'Where do I sit?'

They step into the cramped, disorderly office. Luther gestures to Reed's desk.

Benny perches his skinny arse on the very edge of it. He is gangly and bearded, wearing a washed-out *Chrome* T-shirt.

Luther says, 'You're all over the paedo forums, right, Ben?'

'In a manner of speaking.' Luther leans in to

47

catch his Belfast mumble. 'Those little corners of the internet where the kiddie-fiddlers share their vibrant fantasy lives. That's where I spend my working day.'

'You been briefed about this case?'

'I've been told as much as there is to tell.'

Luther closes the door. 'How are you? Really?'

Benny's had some mental health issues, work-related. It's not uncommon in people who do his job. It's the things they have to see.

'I'm all right. I'm actually pretty good. Fighting the good fight.'

'Because I'm going to ask you to hang around until this one's sorted. You know about this stuff.'

'I wish I didn't.'

'But you do.'

'Have you squared it with the Duchess, me being here?'

'No, but I will.'

'Because I'm not sure she approves of me.'

Benny tends to leather jackets and patchouli oil.

'It's not you,' Luther says. 'She hates everyone.'

'Fair enough, then. Do we think the bairn's alive?'

'We're scared it might be, Ben.'

Benny plonks his ballistic nylon briefcase on the desk, unzips it, hauls out his laptop. 'Where do I plug myself in?'

★ ★ ★

48

Malcolm Perry waits in the interview room. His breath tastes rank. He can feel the cold floor, linoleum over concrete, through the thin rubber of his flip-flops.

Eventually the big copper and his pretty, green-eyed DS walk in and take a seat. They introduce themselves, go through all the rigmarole with the tapes.

The DCI sits back, spreads his legs. Just sits there, watching Malcolm, vaguely amused, as the woman begins the interview.

'Malcolm Perry,' she says. 'In 2001, aged fourteen, you happened across the obituary of Charlotte James, who'd died a week previously in a motorcycle accident. You set off for St Charles's Cemetery equipped with,' she frowns a little, refers to her report, 'digging tools and a tarpaulin, which you apparently stole from a neighbour.'

Malcolm meets her gaze through long, centre-parted hair.

'You were arrested trying to dig up Miss James in order, apparently, to have sex with her corpse.'

Malcolm shrugs one shoulder. Tucks a lock of hair behind his ear.

'Since you were a juvenile, and since sexual interference with a human corpse was only made illegal under the Sexual Offences Act 2003, you were let off with a caution for minor offences. And an order to undergo counselling.

'But in 2005, while working in a funeral home, you were caught in the act of sexually molesting the body of a twenty-eight-year-old female victim of a road traffic accident. You sucked

49

blood and urine from her, bit her buttocks, then sodomized her. For which you served four months of a six-month sentence. Released with an order that you attend a bi-weekly counselling session.'

Howie closes the file, lays the flat of her hand on it and turns her green eyes on Malcolm.

'So,' she says. 'How's the counselling going? You making progress?'

'Well,' says Malcolm. 'That depends what 'progress' means.'

'It means, do you still want to have sex with dead women?'

There's a long silence.

'All right,' says Howie. 'When did it start? These special feelings of love?'

'When I was little,' he says. 'I used to hold funeral services for my pets. I had a little pet cemetery. It's all in the file, I expect.'

'How do you choose them? Your victims.'

'Lovers.'

'Whatever.'

'You want a job in a funeral home, a hospital, a graveyard. Obviously, a morgue's your best bet.'

'So you like them fresh?'

'As the moment that the pod went pop.'

She gives him a neutral look. 'But of course that's difficult for you, isn't it. Seeing as you're banned from working with or anywhere near the dead.'

'I'm not practising,' he says. 'I'm not a morgue rat any more.'

'And why's that?'

'I've got no interest in being a political prisoner.'

'It's a political stance, is it, raping corpses?'

'A corpse is an object. You can't rape an object.'

'And what about the families?'

'The dead don't belong to them.'

'It's all the same to you, isn't it, Malcolm? You take what you want from the dead. Forget about the families and how they might feel. You live rent-free. All this peace and love bollocks you print on your T-shirts — '

'It's not bollocks.'

'Peace and love is about mutual respect. And you've got no respect for anybody.'

'That's not true.'

'So you're not a morgue rat any more. What are you? I mean, I don't think the counselling's helped you one little bit, has it? I think you know enough to say the things they want you to say. But all the time, you were still fantasizing. Masturbating to the thought of dead girls.'

'Of course I fantasize, *Mein Herr*. I'm allowed to think about what I want when I wank. This isn't a police state. Not yet.'

'That's true,' says Howie. 'As long as no one gets hurt.'

'What are you getting at?'

'What are your feelings about Dr Tom Lambert?'

'What, my counsellor?'

'Yes,' says Howie. 'Your counsellor.'

'He's a sanctimonious prick. Why?'

'Sanctimonious in what way?'

'A hundred years ago, fascists like him were lobbying to castrate homosexuals.'

'Is that why you threatened to kill him?'

'Is that what this is about?'

'I don't know. Is it?'

'Because I didn't say that. He's lying.'

'See,' Howie says, 'I'm not sure that's actually true.'

'Did he tell you this? Because if he did, he's a fucking liar.'

'What about his wife?'

'What about her?'

'Did you ever meet her?'

'No.'

'That's not true either, is it?'

'What are you getting at?'

'We'd show you the crime-scene photos,' says Luther, his first words since the interview began, 'but we don't want you getting excited.'

Malcolm's eyes flit from Luther to Howie. 'What crime-scene photos?'

'So what was it?' Luther says. 'You've had enough of him? He doesn't believe all the crap you give him during your sessions?'

'What do you mean?'

'What about the baby?' Luther says. 'What does a man like you do with a baby?'

'Honestly,' says Malcolm, much more quickly, 'what has he said? Because he's a lying prick.'

'Where's the baby, Malcolm?'

'What baby?'

'Do you have any idea what prison will be like for you?' Luther says. 'Being a weirdo's one thing. Hurting kids is another. They're a sentimental lot in Wandsworth. They'll do to you what you did to Mr Lambert.'

'Wait. What did I do? What are we talking about?'

'Where's the baby?'

'What baby?'

'Where is it?'

'He's lying about the baby. It wasn't a baby.'

There is a moment.

'What wasn't a baby?'

'He's not supposed to fucking tell you this stuff. He's not. He's a fucking hypocrite.'

Luther doesn't move. Neither does Howie.

At great length, Luther says, 'Malcolm, what wasn't a baby?'

'I'd never touch a baby. If he told you I did, then he's a fucking liar. I like girls. Women.'

★ ★ ★

Outside the interview room, Howie makes a disgusted face, shakes her hands as if she's touched something contaminated.

Luther claps her on the back, tells her well done.

Then he approaches Detective Sergeant Mary Lally: thirty, curly hair kept short and practical.

Lally's a methodical and insightful detective, creative in interrogations. But she's also gifted with a particular, scornful look. Sometimes Luther applies her as a secret weapon, just to sit there and employ that peerlessly judgemental stare.

They call her Scary Mary.

She looks up from her computer, sets down her phone. Gives Luther a look, like she knows what's coming.

Luther says, 'How d'you feel about getting out into the fresh air?'

★   ★   ★

'Scary' Mary Lally meets the Dog Section van outside the squat at Hill Park Crescent. She greets Jan Kulozik, a uniformed patrol handler.

A stately German Shepherd waits at the leash. Kulozik encourages Lally to kneel and greet the dog.

Then Lally pulls all personnel out of the squat, leaves them hunched and carping in the drizzle.

She follows Kulozik and the dog inside, Kulozik droning words of encouragement. The animal's obvious joy makes Lally smile despite herself.

In the farthest, dark corner of the farthest, darkest flat, the dog becomes agitated. It scrabbles and paws at the floor under Malcolm Perry's grey mattress.

Kulozik pulls the dog back and murmurs low encouragement, pats it, as Lally kicks the skinny mattress aside.

Her foot finds a loose floorboard. And then another. Lally scowls, then kneels and pulls aside the loose boards, exposing a small cavity.

In the cavity is a black bin liner.

She removes the bin liner.

In the bin liner is a grey woollen blanket.

Wrapped in the grey woollen blanket is a woman's head.

54

7

Henry is surprised by how well the baby slept on the way home.

She is in the back seat of the car, wrapped in the soft blanket with satinette lining. The street lights pulse above her as Henry's son, Patrick, drives fastidiously under the limit.

Every now and again Henry glances at her over his shoulder and feels a warm surge of fulfilment. A tired, happy grin spreads across his chops.

Patrick pulls over near the park; he wants to pick up some rabbits. So Henry slides over and gets behind the wheel.

Soon, he is chasing the headlamps through the electric gates at the end of the long gravel drive.

The house is very large. It overlooks the park. It's worth somewhere in the region of two and a half million pounds, but Henry has far too many secrets buried in the garden to consider selling it.

He's lived here for twelve years. Elaine, his elderly landlady, has been five feet down in the garden for eleven and a half of them. He catches himself talking to her sometimes. Doesn't really know why.

The neighbour to his left is a banker with a young family; they moved in two years after Elaine died. As far as they're concerned, Henry is Elaine's son. That's fine by Henry.

Elaine's real son is another of the secrets

buried in the garden.

The neighbours to the right are foreign, Arabs probably; he sees them rarely and has never spoken to them.

Henry parks, gets out of the car, looks around at the morning, then opens the back door and reaches inside. The baby turns her black eyes upon him.

She's surprisingly warm. She's scrawny and has that weird, dark purple colour, almost beetroot in places.

Henry's hand is dirty, still carrying traces of blood, but he didn't think to bring a pacifier. So he offers his thumb to the baby. She accepts it into her hot, gummy little mouth. Under a soft rubbery layer, the gums are surprisingly hard. The sensation is not displeasing.

He's decided to call her Emma.

He bundles her into his arms, lifts her gently from the car seat and tucks the blanket around her, nice and tight. This is called swaddling.

'Welcome home,' he says. 'Welcome home. Would you like to see your bedroom? Yes, I bet you would. I bet you would, baby girl.'

Henry is interested and strangely moved to note that although he's speaking quietly, and although there is no danger of being overheard, he speaks to the baby in the babbling, glissando intonation known as *motherese*.

'Youwannaseeyourroom?' he says, delighting in it. 'Do you do you do you? Yes you do! Yes you do want to see your room! You do!'

He carries her through the front door into the wood-panelled hallway. It's old-fashioned, of course; Elaine was in her eighties when Henry suffocated her. She hadn't remodelled for at least a generation. But Henry quite likes it. He thinks of it as timeless.

The baby is in his arms, still bite-sucking his thumb. 'Are you hungry?' he says. 'Are you hungry, baby girl? Yes you is! You is a hungry liddle girl.'

He takes her up to her room, the nicest room in the house. Inside is a brand new cot from John Lewis, a brand new changing table and mat from Mothercare. Her new clothes, many still displaying price tags, hang from a chrome rail. (There is a second rail, which contains boy's clothes, but Henry pretends not to see it. When Emma's asleep, he'll take the boy's clothes away and quietly burn them. There's a wood-burning furnace in the basement. It comes in handy.)

On the wall are prints of Pooh Bear and Piglet. Henry has waxed and polished the oak floor and laid down pretty rugs. The only item that isn't new is a manky, one-eyed teddy bear, bald in patches. She's called Mummy Bear. She's Henry's.

He lays the baby on her back. Her loose purple skin is streaked with blood and other ochres. But Henry's read that babies don't like to be clean: the smell of sweat and shit and sebum comforts them. So he tucks Emma tight under the blanket and gazes down upon her with tear-pricked eyes.

She opens and closes her mouth like an animatronic alien. And she has a curiously extra-terrestrial look of absolute wisdom in those ebony eyes. She has a perfect nub of a nose with finely etched little nostrils so pink they seem faintly illuminated. There's the trembling, downturned rage and sorrow in her mouth, the balled fists on spindly arms. And her bowed legs! It's funny, that her mother should have such good legs, while the baby's should be like a wishbone! He expects they'll straighten.

The baby begins to mewl as Henry steps back from the cot. Her cry is low and warbling, wet in the throat and not as loud as he'd feared it might be. But it's piercing, a depleted sound that seems to cut through walls like a wire through cheese.

'Don't worry, iddle baby,' he says. 'Don't oo worry.'

He leaves the room. His heart is thin and anxious in his chest. He hurries down to the kitchen. It has recently been scrubbed down so thoroughly the stink of bleach stings his eyes and he's forced to open a window.

He reaches into the fridge. Inside are lined up twelve or thirteen sterilized bottles containing formula milk.

Henry takes a bottle and warms it slightly in the microwave. He tests its temperature against his forearm, then hurries upstairs through the faltering but gathering squall of his new daughter's crying.

★   ★   ★

Luther goes to find Benny, who's set himself up at Ian Reed's desk.

Reed's spare suit jacket, tie and shirt hang

58

from the back of the door, still in dry-cleaner's cellophane. In Reed's desk drawer is a wash and shave kit: soap, disposable razors, deodorant, moisturizer for sensitive skin.

Benny's already surrounded by empty cans of energy drink, takeaway coffees, bottles of multivitamins, half-eaten protein bars.

Luther says, 'How's it going?'

'Slowly,' Benny says. 'I've been checking the Lamberts' phone accounts, work email accounts. No extra-curricular flirting that I can see. Nothing of real interest.'

Luther pulls up a chair. 'No old loves popped up on Facebook?'

'We're checking out all the friends,' Benny says. 'Right now.'

'Yeah, but that's what . . . '

'Nearly three hundred people.'

'Nearly three hundred people. We need to find this baby today.'

'So what do you want me to do?'

'If we're looking at a sex crime, normally we'd look for precursor offences in the area, right? An uplift in peeping Toms, knicker-sniffers, under-wear thieves, flashers. But there's been no uplift.'

'Okay . . . '

'So somebody this sexually confused,' Luther says, 'somebody who did what this man did to the Lamberts, you'd expect him to be known to us already, most likely a local schizophrenic. But that doesn't feel right, does it?' He fiddles with the beige keyboard of his computer. Types QWERTY. 'People put so much of their lives out there. On Facebook and wherever. There's so much information on who we are, how we're feeling, what we're doing. I don't know. I just want to be sure.'

Benny nods, turns to his screen.

Two seconds later, Howie knocks and enters, a folder in her hand.

'Womb raiders,' she says, closing the door. 'Women who snatch other women's children from the womb.'

'Yeah, but this was a man.'

'Just bear with me, Boss.'

Luther makes a gesture: *Sorry*.

'Usually, womb raiders are female. Average out at thirty years old. Generally no criminal record. Emotionally immature, compulsive, low self-esteem. Looking to replace a lost infant or one she couldn't conceive.'

'Right,' says Luther. 'But they also go for low-hanging fruit. Vulnerable and marginalized women. Not middle-class event organizers.'

'Totally. But I've been going through Mr Lambert's work diary. Every Thursday night, 7.30 p.m., they had an appointment at, quote, ISG.'

'What's ISG?'

'Well, we know Mrs Lambert was taking fertility treatment for a long time. Mr Lambert's a counsellor, so we also know they're into therapy and whatnot. So I'm thinking — ISG: *Infertility Support Group?* So I go back to the first instance, call the number he listed — '

'And?'

'And I get through to the Clocktower Infertility and IVF Support Group. I've googled it. It's less than a mile from the Lamberts' home.'

'So we're saying what?'

'You look at the catchment area, it's well above national-average income. That's probably true of the support group, too. But an infertile woman can undergo a psychotic episode if she's middle-class or not.'

'I still don't think it was a woman.'

'Totally,' says Howie. 'But it's a group for couples. Plenty of men.'

Luther reads her smile and knows there's more.

She passes him a photocopied printout, taken from Tom Lambert's diary.

He scans it. 'What am I looking for?'

She takes the printout from his hand, points to a blocked-off appointment. 'They last attended the group three months ago.'

Luther grins, seeing it.

'She kept attending the support group,' Howie says. 'Even when she was visibly pregnant. Imagine it. All these desperate couples — '

'And here are Tom and Sarah Lambert,' Luther says. 'Gorgeous. Well off. In love. Blooming with it. Good work. Get your coat.'

Beaming, Howie leaves the office.

Luther grabs his overcoat. Pauses halfway through putting it on.

Benny looks at him.

'Lust for power,' Luther says. 'Lust for money. Jealousy. All the things we do to each other. It all comes down to sex in the end. But sex comes down to babies. You look at a baby, it's the purest thing in the world. The best thing. Totally innocent. So how do you square that? All this wickedness, in the name of creating innocence. Doesn't that seem wrong to you?'

Benny looks at him for a long time. Then he says, 'If you don't mind, I'm going to make myself forget what you just said.'

'Good,' says Luther. 'Good.'

Buttoning his coat, he walks out to meet Howie.

* * *

The Clocktower Infertility and IVF Support Group is run from a small private hospital in North London.

The group is led by a GP called Sandy Pope. It seems to Luther she's a little forbidding and severe to be running a group like this. But what does he know?

Luther and Howie sit in her surgery; it has a faint camphor smell.

'The group's run on a drop-in basis,' she tells them. 'So there's no database, no list of phone numbers. Some people come for years. Some come once and find it's not for them. Most are somewhere in between.'

'But on average?'

She's reluctant to answer. Luther knows her type: well-educated, middle-class, left-leaning liberal. A good-hearted roundhead. Doesn't care for the police, not least because she's never had cause to need them.

'There's no such thing as average,' she says.

'But often they'll stay for a year or two. Which doesn't mean they come every week. It'll be every week for three or four months. Then twice a month, then once a month. Then they just stop.'

'And there's no list of attendees?'

'People don't even have to give their real names.'

Howie takes the baton. 'How did Sarah Lambert's pregnancy go down with the group?'

'I'm not sure I understand where you're heading with this.'

'We're trying to establish why the Lamberts kept attending the group, even after Sarah was pregnant. It seems unusual.'

'Not really. It can be difficult; a couple comes to identify themselves as infertile, then suddenly they face this whole new challenge. They turn to a support group.'

'So how did Sarah deal with her pregnancy?'

'During the first trimester, her anxiety levels were very high. She had bad dreams.'

'What kind of dreams?'

'Of something happening to the baby.'

'What kind of thing?'

'She never specified. It's actually not uncommon.'

'So she wasn't happy?'

'She was non-ecstatic. That's not the same as unhappy. She was damming up her happiness. Scared she was going to lose the child.'

'And Mr Lambert?'

'He was supportive. Possibly more supportive than most male partners.'

'So how are most male partners?'

She gives Howie a meaningful look and says, 'Men who've come to define themselves as infertile can feel detached from a pregnancy. It's a kind of safety mechanism. Plus, they feel the need to be strong for their wife. Just in case something goes wrong.'

'So,' Howie refers to her notes, cycles back a step or two, 'the rest of the group. How did they take it when they learned about the pregnancy?'

'I'd say the reaction was mixed. On one hand, pregnancy provides hope . . . '

'And on the other?'

'Well, obviously it can lead to envy.'

'Did it make anyone in the group feel like that?'

'It would be surprising if it didn't. Women often find this aspect of it all, the apparent randomness of it, to be very difficult. They see it in terms of fairness — or unfairness, however you choose to look at it.'

'And the men?'

'Their response is often — ' She breaks off, looks at Luther. 'The male reaction can be very primal. Potency and fertility can be central to a man's sense of gender identity.'

Luther thinks of the timid people in the support group: the shocked women, grieving for children who would never be conceived, would never be born, would never die. Sad people in Gap jeans and Marks and Spencer's blouses sitting in a circle on plastic chairs. The shabbiness of the room. The hairs on their forearms, the freckles. The intimacy of their sex organs. Hair sprouting from unbuttoned collars. Men seeking to lose weight, lose their guts to increase their fertility, looking one to the other, pondering who was potent and who was not, cuckolding each other in the imagination.

And Sarah Lambert, terrified to tell of her good fortune in case the baby didn't latch on to existence but instead let go, allowing itself to be carried downstream by time: a bundle of cells, a tumbling ball of life.

He thinks of a small piece of plastic he once found behind the bin in his bathroom.

'I can't go into details,' he says, 'but there are special circumstances surrounding this case. This was a crime of rage. And about as personal as you can get. The best lead I have right now is this support group.'

'Then I really can't help you.'

'I know. But perhaps you'd be willing to ask members of the group to come forward, allow themselves to be eliminated from the enquiry?'

'I can do that,' she says. 'Absolutely. Happy to.'

He makes as if to leave. Then he says, 'There's just one more thing.'

She waits.

'There may have been a couple you didn't feel right about?' Luther says. 'They could have been regular attendees. Or one-offs.'

'Didn't feel right about in what way?'

'Well, that's something you can tell us. I'm not asking you to judge. But you're familiar with every kind of behaviour that goes hand in hand with infertility. So did one couple maybe strike you as being, I don't know — atypical? Outliers? Was there anyone, maybe you couldn't put your finger on it, but they were wrong somehow?'

'That's not really for me to say, is it?'

'Just for once, it might be.'

'Well, there was Barry and Lynda,' she says.

Luther sits back. He crosses his legs. Smooths his trousers over his knee. He knows this is a tell, the sign of a man trying not to show agitation. He's working on it. 'Who are Barry and Lynda?'

'They came once or twice. Didn't say much.'

'When was this?'

'I don't know, three or four months ago?'

'So — during Sarah Lambert's pregnancy?'

'I suppose so, yes. It must have been.'

'And what about them made you feel uncomfortable?'

'They were just — wrong. As a couple. He was very trim. Wiry. Like a marathon runner. Suit and tie. Overcoat. Short hair, worn very neat. Side parting.'

'And the woman? Lynda?'

'Well, this is what struck me as strange. She was obese.'

Luther nods. Waits for more.

Howie says, 'We know it goes against the grain to judge people in any way but this is so important. If this couple had nothing to do with what happened, they'll never know that you pointed us in their direction. If they did then believe me, you want us to catch them.'

Pope laughs. She's uncomfortable. 'We have so many training courses,' she says. 'So many awareness sessions.'

'Us too,' Luther says.

Pope laughs, a bit more openly. 'I suppose you must.'

'You wouldn't believe it,' Luther says. He smiles and tells her, 'They want to put a tea vending machine in the station because they think we'll electrocute ourselves if we're allowed to have a kettle in the workplace.'

Pope opens her drawer, takes out a mint and unwraps it.

'They just seemed wrong,' she says. 'For one member of a couple to be that fit and the other . . . Well, the other to be that fat. It struck me as odd, like a couple on a saucy postcard. Besides which, if you're obese and having problems with conceiving, you're told to lose weight. A lot of IVF clinics refuse treatment to obese patients until they've reduced their body mass index.'

'So you were surprised by this woman's size?'

'I think we all were.'

Luther makes a note to check all applications to the IVF programme, see who's been rejected for obesity. It'll be a long list, but it could take them somewhere.

He says, 'What was their story?'

'In what sense?'

'I mean, what did they tell you about themselves?'

'This isn't Alcoholics Anonymous. We're a drop-in centre. We don't pressure new couples. For a lot of them, just coming along is a giant step. If they want to sit in silence, fine.'

'So how did they behave, Barry and Lynda?'

'She was . . . sweet.'

'When you say sweet,' Luther says, 'you say it with certain emphasis.'

'She was . . . she was very pretty, in a strange way. But there was something grotesque about her. I don't mean in terms of her weight. I mean there was something — Shirley Temple-ish. She wore very girly clothes, pinks and ribbons. Knee-high socks. And she had this teeny, tiny, little mousey voice.'

Luther's heart is hastening. He says, 'And him?'

'He was — '

'Dominant? Submissive?'

'Neither. He was distant. They just didn't feel like a couple.'

'So he wasn't paying attention to his partner?'

'No. They sat next to each other. She was smiling at everyone. Little rosebud lips.'

'And he was . . . '

'Smug and over-assertive. Sat there like this, with his legs splayed.'

'I'm sorry to be vulgar,' Luther says. 'But a crotch display like that, a certain kind of man thinks it's a turn-on. He's sitting with his legs wide apart, advertising the goods. So were there any innuendos, any double-meanings, off-colour remarks? Joking offers to get women pregnant, maybe?'

'None of that,' Pope says. 'Besides which, I know how to tread on that pretty quickly and pretty efficiently.'

Luther bets she does. He nods, once, in professional recognition. 'So I wonder — did Barry pay any particular attention to any member of the group?'

Pope's eyes head up and to the right. She searches her memory.

Then she looks at Luther.

She considers her answer for a long time.

'He sat there,' she said, 'leering at Sarah Lambert like she was a ripe peach. He made them both uncomfortable. Tom and Sarah. I think that's the last time they came to the group.'

* * *

Luther and Howie walk into the blaring London noise, the grit and filth.

Luther says, 'You ever think about it? Kids?'

Howie shrugs. 'What about you?'

'Nah,' he says. 'My wife and I had a pact. When we got together.'

'Seriously?' Howie says. 'Whose idea was that?'

'Both of ours, I think.'

'And it still stands?'

'Apparently.'

She flashes him an enquiring look.

'Who knows,' he says. 'The stupid things you say when you're twenty-one.'

Howie says, 'Are you okay, Boss?'

He snaps out of it. 'Sorry,' he says, 'miles away.'

* * *

Detective Sergeant Justin Ripley, curly hair and a trusting face, has been seconded to the Lambert

69

investigation. He drives to Y2K Cleaning. He's partnered with Detective Constable Theresa Delpy.

Y2K Cleaning is run out of an office between a newsagent and a dry cleaners on Green Lanes.

Ripley badges the elderly receptionist. He and Delpy wait for ten minutes, sipping cups of water from the cooler and reading trade magazines — *Cleaning and Hygiene Today, Cleansing Matters* — until the owner appears: a short, bearded, fat man in a plaid tank top.

He shakes Ripley's hand, asks what the problem is.

Ripley asks about Tom and Sarah Lambert's current cleaner.

The owner comes back in five minutes. 'Her name's Sheena Kwalingana. I can show you a file copy of her visa if you like.'

Ripley declines. 'How long has Sheena Kwalingana been working for the Lamberts?'

'Three years, four months. No complaints.'

Ripley thanks the owner and drives to Finsbury Park Road, where Sheena Kwalingana has a weekly appointment to clean a graphic designer's basement flat.

He parks on the corner of Queen's Drive.

The hookers are still out, pale girls with corned-beef legs offering blow jobs to men on their way to work.

Ripley and Delpy walk to the door of number 93, ring the bell and wait. Inside, they can hear the sound of vacuuming.

Delpy rings the mobile number the Y2K owner gave them.

No answer.

They wait until the vacuuming's stopped, then ring the doorbell again. There's a change in the quality of the silence; a sense that someone inside the flat has become aware of their presence.

There's more silence, then footsteps in the hallway, the shiny black door opening.

Behind the door is Sheena Kwalingana, a short, elderly black woman with very high hair. She wears an old-fashioned nylon tabard with her firm's logo embroidered on the breast. She's wearing flip-flops; she's laid her shoes outside the flat, neatly arranged next to the welcome mat.

She's brought the vacuum cleaner to the door with her. She stands in the doorway holding the hose.

Ripley badges her. 'Sheena Kwalingana?'

'I don't live here, son. I'm just working.'

She's got an accent, pleasantly sing-song. Ripley has to strain a little in order to understand it.

'I know you don't live here,' he says, endlessly polite. He badges her again. 'I'm DS Ripley, from the Serious Crime Unit at Hobb Lane. This is DC Delpy.'

'I'm sorry, what?'

'I wonder if we might step inside?'

Sheena Kwalingana looks at Ripley with great anxiety, glances back over her shoulder. 'It's not my house,' she says. 'So no. No, you can't come in. It's not my house.'

'Well, we could talk out here . . . '

71

'What's the problem?'

'Mrs Kwalingana, you're not in any trouble.'

This only seems to increase her vigilance.

Delpy sighs. Less polite than Ripley. 'We're investigating a burglary — '

'I don't burgle people.'

'We're not suggesting you do. You're honestly not in any trouble here, Mrs Kwalingana. Really.'

Sheena Kwalingana nods, but says nothing. Her hand is palpating the ridged tube of the vacuum hose; squeezing it, loosening it.

Ripley says, 'You clean for Tom and Sarah Lambert of 25, Bridgeman Road.'

'Yes?'

Ripley says nothing for a while, waits for Mrs Kwalingana to speak.

Eventually, she says, 'Why?'

'As my colleague mentioned, we're investigating a break-in at that address.'

Kwalingana squeezes the hose.

Ripley says, 'Mrs Kwalingana, would you be more comfortable speaking to us at the police station? It's more private there.'

She stares at Ripley for a long time. 'Can I have two minutes to finish off?'

'Two minutes,' says Ripley. 'No problem.'

Mrs Kwalingana makes a move to close the door. Very gently but very firmly, Delpy pushes out a hand to hold it open. 'We'll wait here.'

Sheena Kwalingana turns her back, mutters to herself.

Then she goes back inside to finish doing the bathroom.

Henry's son Patrick is twenty years old. He's lean and delicate-looking, half wild in jeans and a drab, olive combat jacket.

He's caught eight rabbits in the park. They're in his special backpack now, writhing and squealing. Leave them long enough, they'll chew through their bags and start biting on each other like baby sharks in the womb.

Patrick passes through the electric gates and into the huge, overgrown garden. The gates close behind him.

In the quiet there's the nice sound of drizzle on leaf-fall, fat water dropping from heavy trees, distant traffic. Under it all he can hear the low, miserable squall of a crying baby.

He walks round the back of the house, to the most sheltered part of the garden. He opens heavy corrugated iron doors and steps into the twilight of the long, concrete-floored garage.

He passes the treadmill on which they exercise the dogs, increasing their cardiovascular fitness and their endurance.

He arrives at the wire kennels. The silent dogs wait; stocky, muscular terriers with broad heads, exaggerated occipital muscles and frog-wide mouths. Each has a heavy chain wrapped around its neck. The chains build neck and upper-body strength.

The dogs greet him in excited silence. Henry has excised tissue from their vocal cords.

The dogs worship Henry as a capricious God, but they know it's Patrick who feeds them

— and that in the morning he often brings live bait; sometimes puppies or kittens advertised as 'free to a good home'. Sometimes rabbits or rats caught in the park.

As he lifts the bag of rabbits, the dogs follow him with eager, idiot eyes.

Patrick upends the bag into a wire cage and watches the carnage that follows. The rabbits are smarter than the dogs, possessed of glinting intelligence and a self-evident desire to live.

He's watching the dogs rip them to moist wet rags when the garage doors scrape across the concrete and Henry enters, looking baffled.

'Emma won't take her bottle,' he says. 'I don't know what to do.'

Patrick follows Henry into the house and upstairs.

He washes his hands in the sink, using liquid soap that makes them smell of oranges.

Then he goes through to the infant's bedroom. Once again, he's struck by her toad-like ugliness.

Once, Patrick found a tangle of baby rats. This was in the days when he was a young boy and sleeping in the soundproof basement. The rats were crammed between a loose chunk of plasterboard and Henry's bodged soundproofing; blind and mewling pups, a pink fist of them plaited and knotted by their reptilian tails, tugging each other through all points of the compass.

Patrick had wailed in panic and hammered at the solid door with his little fists. He cried and cried, but of course nobody came. Henry didn't come down until teatime. He had Patrick's bowl of warm milk and a couple of slices of white bread.

Seeing the rat king, even sleek, rapacious Henry stepped back in horror.

Sometimes Patrick chuckles to remember how he and Henry had reacted, that far-off day. If Patrick were to find a rat king behind the baseboard these days, he'd consider himself fortunate. They're a rare phenomenon.

He'd scoop it up with a shovel — still blindly mewling — and deposit it into a demijohn of alcohol. He'd keep it on a shelf in his bedroom.

Part of him feels hate for this angry helpless creature wriggling on a plastic mattress decorated with teddy bears. But he feels pity, too.

'She's coughing,' Henry says.

'Then take her to a doctor.'

'I can't.'

'Have you tried feeding her?'

'Of course I've tried feeding her,' Henry says. 'For fuck's sake.'

'Is the milk too hot?'

'No.'

'Too cold?'

'No. She's just — she seems weak. And she's sleeping a lot. Do you think she's sleeping too much?'

'I don't know.'

'She should wake long enough to eat, shouldn't she? Babies get hungry.'

'Is she hot?'

Henry reaches into the cot, arranges Emma's limbs so that he's able to take the temperature under her armpit. Patrick is revolted by how lifeless and doll-like she seems.

'Ninety-four,' says Henry. 'It's low. Fuck.'

'She seems really shaky.'

Henry has noticed Emma's quivery chin and shaky hands. But now her entire body seems to be shivering.

'A bottle isn't the same,' Henry says. 'We need a wet nurse.'

There is a silence.

'Could you do it?' Patrick says.

'Me?'

'Please, Dad. Yeah.'

'Why me?'

'Because I'd be embarrassed.'

Henry's not a big man but he's well-groomed and vicious as a mink. 'And how do you think it would look if I did it, eh? You chinless little spastic. How would that fucking look?'

'Please,' says Patrick.

Henry shushes him through his teeth, then shoves him onto the upstairs landing.

He gently shuts the bedroom door.

Then he grabs Patrick's hair and rams Patrick's head into the wall.

Patrick staggers around. He's confused. Henry cuffs him round the face a few times, then tosses him to the floor.

'Just take some of the money,' he says, 'and fucking do it.'

8

Zoe and Mark met just over a year ago. He works for Liberté Sans Frontière; he was her designated liaison on the Munzir Hattem case.

Mark's handsome; slightly bohemian in tweed and cords; laid-back and sincere; a little earnest sometimes.

The fourth time they met, he offered to buy her lunch. They sat somewhere outside, watching people go past.

She talked about John.

She always talks about John.

In the end, Mark gave up and joined in. 'So how did you two get together?'

'How does anyone get together?'

'I dunno,' he said. 'My ex-wife and I were childhood sweethearts.'

'No!'

'Yes!'

'That's so *sweet*.'

'We went to primary school together,' Mark said, 'Stockwood Vale Primary. Emily Edwards. She had a ponytail. She could climb trees. All of it. The full package.'

'So she was your first and only?'

'Oh, God no. No, no, no. We went out for about, I don't know, three years? Four years? Split up when sixth form came along. She got a bit political. Ban the Bomb, Socialist Workers. Greenham Common.'

He laughed to remember it.

A flicker of shared sadness passed between them. Zoe wanted to reach out and touch the back of his hand, to give comfort and to take it.

Instead, she flicked back her hair, stirred her latte. 'So what happened?'

'Oh, we met again. This is years later. By coincidence really, some New Year's Eve bash in Brighton. And when we saw each other it was just like old times. She'd gone through her phase and out the other side. And I'd gone through mine.'

'And what phase is this?'

He shrugged, sheepish. 'Echo and the Bunnymen, basically.'

'Echo and the what now?'

'Bunnymen. You don't know the Bunnymen?'

'To my knowledge, I've never even set eyes on a Bunny Man.'

'You ever hear of Eric's?'

'No.'

'It was a club,' he said. 'In Liverpool, this was. Elvis Costello, I saw him there. The Clash. Joy Division. The Banshees. The Buzzcocks. You never heard of the Buzzcocks?'

She shook her head.

He sang her a few bars of 'Ever Fallen in Love With Someone You Shouldn't've'.

Realizing, he trailed off. There was an awkward moment.

'It's a good song,' he said.

Zoe got the bill and they stepped into the autumn, bundled up in their coats.

Mark said, 'I don't feel like going back yet.'

She said, 'Nor me.'

So they walked to the park, found a bench and sat down. She perched on the edge, spine straight. Mark sprawled, took tobacco from a flat tin in his pocket and began to roll a cigarette. 'Do you mind?'

'Not at all. Blow the smoke my way.'

'You a smoker?'

'Occasional.'

'I can roll you one, if you like.'

They sat in silence while he rolled her a cigarette, then passed it to her. She placed it in her mouth. The faint burn of unlit tobacco.

He produced a lighter and she leaned into him, smelling him, then sat back, puffing on her first roll-up since she was a student. She liked the taste and the smell of it, wondered how it went with these clothes, these shoes, this hair.

'So how long did it last?' she said, picking a thread of tobacco from the tip of her tongue, aware that he was watching her do it.

'What, me and Emily? Eleven years, all in.'

'Kids?'

'There's Stephen. He's sixteen. Chloe's nine. They live with their mum. You?'

'Me and John? God, no.'

'What does that mean?'

'What does what mean?'

'That tone.'

'I don't know. Did I use a tone?'

'You definitely did. There was definitely a tone in use.'

She snorted, then covered her nose with the

back of her hand, embarrassed. Mark was grinning at her.

She said, 'The thought of it. Me and John with kids.'

'What's so mad about that?'

'We agreed not to. Back when we were kids ourselves.'

'Really? How long have you known him?'

'Since the Big Bang.'

It was supposed to sound funny, but it came out sad. She watched the pigeons for a while. Then she said, 'We met at university.'

'Same course?'

'No. I was doing law, obviously. He was postgrad in English.'

She tucked her chin into the warmth of her coat and smiled to think of it, just as she sometimes did when flicking through old photographs.

'We only met because we were both doing this elective course in comparative religion. I sat next to him in this tiny little lecture theatre. Everybody there already knew each other except me and John. I knew him by reputation.'

'And what reputation was that?'

'He's very tall,' she said, self-conscious as a schoolgirl. 'Very strong. Very handsome. And very, very intense.'

She laughed out loud, delighted and liberated to be talking about it. 'And it was like, all the girls fancied him and he didn't even notice them, y'know? And the more he didn't notice them, the more they fancied him. He used to make girls do the stupidest things around him, really clever,

80

brilliant young women who should have known better, behaving like idiots to get his attention. And he never noticed.'

'Everybody notices.'

'Swear to God. It wasn't even arrogance. It was a kind of . . . myopia.'

'And you liked that?'

'I thought it was endearing.'

'Not, like, a challenge?'

'God, no.'

This time, they both laughed.

Mark said, 'So how did you . . . y'know. Get together?'

She smoked the roll-up to its last quarter-inch, then squeezed it between her fingernails.

'There wasn't like a *moment*,' she said. 'We met in that lecture and kind of drifted out for a coffee afterwards. Neither of us asked the other. Or that's how I remember it. We just sat in the café and chatted. I told him everything there was to tell about myself — which at the time wasn't all that much.'

'How old were you?'

'Twenty? So girls' school, sixth form, gap year, university. It felt like a lot of life experience at the time. So I tell him this, all about myself. Then I ask him about himself and he tells me about books. As if he's made up of all these books he's read, or was going to read. And later on, he walks me home. I didn't question it for a minute. And I'll tell you one thing about John: if you're a twenty-year-old girl and you're not that knowledgeable in the ways of the world and you live in a dodgy area, walking home with him, you never felt so safe. And he stops outside my door and says, *This is you, then?* And I say, *This is me.* And I'm thinking, *Kiss me you arsehole, kiss me or I'm going to die on the spot.*'

'And did he?'

'No. He just slouches and gives me this nod — he's got this shaggy-dog nod he does sometimes. Then he digs his hands in his pockets and walks off.'

'Well played, that man.'

'Except it wasn't,' she said. 'It wasn't a tactic. I swear! It was just him. That's who he was. Is. Whatever.'

And then a melancholy descended on her — as it always did when she thought of that boy and that girl. The thought of John Luther, twenty-two, slouching off without kissing her. And the lightness in her heart that night; how she couldn't sleep and couldn't believe herself: serious, level-headed, hard-working Zoe, who'd slept with two men in her entire life, one long-term school boyfriend, as a kind of parting gift, and one slightly older man she met on her gap year.

It wasn't in her nature to lie in bed wondering what a boy might be doing right *now*, right this second. But she spent the whole night like that.

And she spent the next few days pretending she wasn't trying to manufacture ways to bump into him in the corridor, the English department, the refectory.

Sprawled on that park bench, looking at the pigeons, Mark said, 'Are you okay?'

'Yeah,' said Zoe. 'Sorry. Miles away.'

82

He stretched his arms. 'Best be getting back.'

'I don't want to go to work,' she groaned, stretching her neck. 'I want to take the day off. I'm tired.'

'We could play hooky,' said Mark. 'Go to the pictures or something. I haven't been to the pictures for ages. Especially not in the afternoon.'

'Me neither.'

'We should totally do it,' he said. 'Say we're in a meeting. Go to the pictures. Grab a Chinese afterwards.'

'I'd love to,' she said. 'But no.'

So he slipped his tobacco tin into his pocket and they strolled back to work.

In her memory they were arm in arm, although of course that can't be right. Not yet. Not then.

★   ★   ★

That afternoon, she'd been distracted and clumsy. She spilled a cup of coffee over her desk.

Just by sitting there, laughing at the past, she'd felt that her John, that boy, was nothing more than a memory.

He'd catch her sometimes, after one glass of wine too many. She'd be tearful, going through their old photos again.

'Look at my hair,' she'd say. Or, 'Christ, look at those boots. What was I thinking?'

Or she'd say, 'God, remember that flat? The one on Victoria Road?'

And Luther would oblige her by flicking

through the albums, unaware that the man looking at the photos was not the boy they pictured.

Somewhere along the line, that boy had joined the dead and Zoe had spent years waving to him from a far shore, trying to call him back.

★ ★ ★

And now it's not even lunchtime on this strange day a year later and she lies naked on a hotel bed with Mark North in the warm afterglow of orgasm.

She nuzzles his neck, kisses him. He turns, kisses her.

She knows she'll feel guilty. She'll get up and walk naked to the shower and walk back and dry herself and Mark will watch; of course he will — he's going to watch her do these everyday things because here and now everything she does is fascinating, vertiginous, magical. Just as everything he does is fascinating and magical to her.

She'll towel herself in front of this man who has just come inside her, twice. And she'll dress: underwear and tights and shirt and suit and shoes, and she'll toy with her hair and reapply her make-up. She'll make an appointment with the doctor to pick up the morning-after pill because neither of them had been planning this and neither had thought to pop into the chemist and buy condoms.

The morning-after pill may give her a headache and sore breasts and it may nauseate her; she'll have to think of a good lie and practise it over and over again until she no longer thinks of it as untrue. That's the only way to lie with any success to the man she married.

She'll kiss Mark goodbye and because she knows now that their bodies fit, there'll be no awkwardness between them. She likes his smell, the hint of fresh tobacco in his sweat; the few grey hairs on his chest, the scar on his upper arm.

She can feel it all, like the faint foreshadow of tomorrow's hangover throbbing through the bright white glare of dancing drunk.

But all she feels right now is the satisfaction of being fascinated. And of being fascinating.

When, reluctantly, she gets out of bed and walks naked to the shower she doesn't cry and she doesn't laugh. She just washes herself and tries not to think.

* * *

Paula's been on the game more than twelve years, during which time she's sold pretty much all she has to sell. But she didn't truly find her niche until she fell into the erotic lactation game. That was a few months after Alex was born.

Now she trades under the name Finesse. Compared to some of the crap she went through when she was younger, it's easy money; she gets to spend her working hours in a clean little flat, and most of her lactophiliacs are long-term customers, middle-aged men who like to engage in what they call Adult Nursing Relationships.

Sometimes they like to go the whole hog and assume the role of a breastfeeding infant, complete with nappies.

Some men like to have breast milk sprayed onto them as they masturbate. One or two like her to express into a manual pump as they watch and wank themselves off. They take the milk home to drink it or cook with it or do God knows what with it. Paula doesn't really care; what harm can a little bit of milk do to anyone?

A very small minority of her clients are lesbian. She even has a lesbian couple. They like to latch on to a nipple each and nurse before doing their thing.

Paula doesn't judge. She just gets on with it; takes her Domperidone, her Blessed Thistle, her red raspberry leaf, and counts her blessings.

So she's surprised to see this sweet-looking young man standing in her doorway, telling her that Gary Braddon's recommended her.

Braddon's one of these tough-looking men, all tattoos and shaved heads, but he's a gentle soul really, a softy. Loves his dogs, loves his milky boobs to kiss and nibble and suck.

Paula assesses the kid. He's skinny, nervy. He smells not unpleasantly of fresh earth. She can see how he might be a friend of Gary's. So she asks him in.

He looks at the prints she's hung in the little hallway, faintly erotic Christian art showing the Lactation of St Bernard, in which the Saint receives milk from the breast of the Virgin Mary.

Paula paid her downstairs neighbour, who's studying interior decorating, to do it for her at cost. He's a nice straight boy, her Chris downstairs, so above the cost of materials she paid him in kind and everyone was happy.

Along with the subdued lighting, the prints add the right touch of reverence to the proceedings. Unlike most apartments providing related services, this is a place of nurture and worship.

Now this kid looks her up and down. His eyes can't meet hers, but they never can at first. A lot of the younger ones never had a mum. The first time they look her in the eye is when they're laid out on her lap, suckling away. Sometimes she strokes their hair and murmurs gentle words of encouragement. Sometimes they cry when they come, spunking all over her tummy.

Finesse doesn't mind that. She's pleased. It seems to help.

This kid digs into the pocket of his army surplus coat and brings out a wad of tenners. He tries to foist it on her — a fistful of greasy money in her lovely clean hands with their lovely manicure.

She says, 'There's no need to do that now, love.'

He blinks at her, embarrassed and confused.

She says, 'Why don't you come in for five minutes, take off your coat, sit down, have a little chat?'

But the kid won't relax. He looks nervous, shifting his weight from foot to foot as if he needs the loo.

He follows her into the little front room. There's a nice vibe in here, too, like a boutique hotel in earth tones and artifically aged wood. Paula does all right for herself, but that's not the point of this display: the point is to suggest that she doesn't *need* to do this — that she's essentially an altruist, a therapist providing a service.

She invites the kid to sit.

He perches on the edge of a chair. Wipes his palms on his thighs. He jiggles his leg. He twists his hands in sweaty knots. He look at her, he looks away.

She crosses her legs, shows a bit of thigh, and leans forward. And there's the cleavage. Boom. 'Would you like some tea?'

He shakes his head once, looks away.

'I've got some herbal blends,' she says, in her smoky voice. She's been doing it so long now, this voice, that she hardly thinks about it any more. She got training from an acting coach. He wasn't a straight boy, so it was payment in cash. 'Peppermint's very relaxing,' she tells the kid. 'And chamomile.'

He shakes his head, looks like he wants to cry.

Paula sits and waits. Sometimes that's the best thing.

Looking at the floor, the kid says, 'It's my dad.'

'Oh, love,' she says. 'What about him?'

'He sent me. He wants you to come round our place.'

'Does he have a disability?' Paula says. 'Because that's not a problem. The building's got wheelchair access.'

'It's not that.'

She makes a concerned face, and the real emotions follow. This was taught to her by an acting coach too, and the funny thing is, it doesn't make her feel like a fraud. It makes her feel like a better person. 'Is he bedridden?'

'No.'

She waits for more, begins to doubt it's ever going to come. Fighting the urge to look at her watch she says, 'Then what is it, love?'

He taps his foot, plucks at one of the sparse blondish hairs on his spindly forearm.

'We've got a baby that needs feeding.'

There's a silence. Paula hears cars go past, like the sound of blood in her ears.

As a girl, working the streets, the first sign that something was wrong was your hearing suddenly got very clear. It was your body, getting ready to react before your brain knew anything was amiss.

Hearing the traffic now, she knows she should have followed her first instinct and not invited this young man in. But he'd sounded gentle and personable on the phone, and she didn't see the harm in starting an hour or two early; she could always take a nap afterwards.

None of this shows in her voice or in her body language. She just says, 'I'm not sure what you mean.'

'We've got a baby,' he says. 'It needs feeding.'

'A little boy or a little girl?'

The kid hesitates, as if thinking about it. 'Little girl. Emma.'

'Can't her mum feed her?'

'Her mum's dead.'

'Oh, I'm so sorry, love.'

'That's all right. She wasn't my mum or anything.'

The kid squeezes his eyes shut as if silently rebuking himself for something. He blushes.

Paula says, 'How old is she? Little Emma?'

'Very young. Just a baby.'

'What do the doctors say?'

'My dad doesn't trust doctors. He says a baby needs proper milk. From a woman.'

'Well, there's a lot of people who'd agree with him,' she says. 'My special friends think that's true later in life, too. There's something about a woman's milk.'

The kid nods.

'But formula milk's safe for a baby,' she says.

'She won't take a bottle. She just spits it out.'

Paula smiles, tenderly. 'They do that. You've just got to be patient.'

'Dad thinks she's sick.'

'Then he should go to the doctor. I think it's lovely that you've come to me: it shows that your dad loves your sister very much. I'm touched. It's a special bond, nursing a child. And it's wonderful to think we could share that together. But it's not the right thing to do. The right thing would be to go to the doctor's. Then maybe contact your local breastfeeding support network. You might find some young mums who offer to help. They call it cross-nursing now, but that's just a newfangled way of saying wet-nursing. That's what I think you should do.'

The kid grows more agitated. He digs in his other pocket, produces another fistful of money. 'This is all I've got.'

'This isn't about money, darling.'

'Please. He'll kill me.'

'Tell you what,' Paula says. She's aware that her palms are damp. She needs to get this kid out of the flat. She's angry at herself for letting him in, but she hides it.

'Please,' says the kid. His face is grey with wretchedness and fear.

'Give me your dad's phone number,' she says. 'I'll have a little chat with him.'

'I can't.'

'Then why don't you call him yourself and pass your phone to me? I'll have a word with your dad, tell him how great you've been.'

'He'll kill me.'

'Come on. Don't cry.'

'I mean it,' he says. 'I mean he'll actually kill me. He's done it before. Please.'

Now Paula can't hear or see anything except the abject, unhinged kid at the end of her tunnel vision.

In a false back of the left-hand drawer in the small dresser is a pepper spray and a taser. On top of the dresser, next to the landline, is a small pad of scented paper.

The kid says, 'Where are you going?'

'I'm going to write your dad a little note.'

The kid leaps to his feet. Shrugs narrow shoulders.

'Come on,' he says, 'please. Just once. Just come to our place for one time.'

'I can't love,' Paula says. Her voice is still calm, a little firmer now. But her hand is shaking as she pretends to look for a pen. She makes a face. She tries to underplay it but her features feel grotesque and exaggerated. 'I'm sure when he reads the letter, you'll be okay.'

The kid paces, muttering to himself. Paula doesn't dare look back, but she thinks he might be tearing at his hair.

'Please,' he says, 'please please please.'

She opens the drawer. Takes out the little can of Mace and turns to him.

'Now,' she says. 'I've asked you nicely and I'll ask you nicely one more time. Please leave.'

The kid looks at her, aghast.

He backs away, trips over the furniture.

'Get out,' she says.

The kid scrambles to his feet, reaches into his other pocket. It takes her a moment to recognize what he draws from his pocket.

It's a torque wrench.

The kid draws back his hand, still snivelling.

No, Paula thinks, Not like this.

★   ★   ★

Luther and Howie step into the interview room.

Sheena Kwalingana sits behind a dilapidated desk, holding a cup of milky tea.

Luther slows down, makes himself relax. He nods at a chair. 'May I?'

Sheena Kwalingana says yes.

Howie cracks open fresh audio tapes, loads them into the recorder, switches on the machine. Makes sure Mrs Kwalingana knows the interview is being recorded.

Mrs Kwalingana gives her permission.

Gently, in a voice designed to calm the witness as much as give information, Luther repeats his name and rank. He asks Mrs Kwalingana to confirm her name, address, and date of birth, which she does after clearing her throat and sipping stewed tea.

Knowing her throat is dry with nerves, Luther gets her a cup of water from the cooler on the other side of the door. She takes it with a look of bashful gratitude.

Then, just as gently, Luther says, 'Can you tell me what happened on January seventeenth of this year?'

'I already told you.'

'For the record. Just once more, please. It could be very important.'

'I don't see how.'

'Please,' he says.

'I was burgled,' says Mrs Kwalingana. 'A man broke into my flat. He took a few things and ran away. No big one.'

Howie steps in. 'But that's not quite it, is it?'

'How do you mean?'

'Please, tell us everything you told the other officers about what happened that night.'

She sighs. 'I turned off the TV. I went to bed.'

'What time would this be?'

'I don't know, usual time. I work early. I'm up before the dawn. So not too late, ten-thirty, maybe?'

'You live alone?'

'Since my husband died.'

'No children, grandchildren?'

'In Manchester. Apparently it's fancy.'

'And you live in a flat in a local authority development, that's right?'

'Nice place,' she says, 'modern, very clean. Nice neighbours. Old-fashioned.'

'You're very lucky.'

Mrs Kwalingana sniffs to indicate she knows it.

'So what happened?'

'I wake up,' she says. 'I hear someone moving around.'

'Someone in your flat?'

Mrs Kwalingana nods.

'What time was this?' says Howie.

'Not so late. Quarter past eleven? Quarter to twelve?'

'You were still awake?'

'No. I was very tired. I work hard, love, I get up early. So when I woke up, I thought I was dreaming. But no.'

'What happened then?'

'I must have moved, because he heard me. Whatever he was doing, I heard him stop. Then he walked into the bedroom.'

'That can't have been very nice.'

'It was a lot worse than not very nice. I'm looking round for something to whack him with. Then he comes in. Stands in the doorway and he's — '

'What's he doing?'

'Breathing funny.'

'Excited funny? Or lots of exercise funny?'

'Excited,' says Mrs Kwalingana, 'in that way. The way men get.'

Luther writes a note.

94

'I just lay there,' Mrs Kwalingana says, 'and watched him through a crack in my eyelid.'

'What was he doing?'

'Playing with himself.'

'Excuse me,' Howie says, 'I have to ask. Was he exposing himself?'

'No. He was rubbing it through his trousers. Very slowly. Not' — she looks at the table — 'not up and down, but round and round. And he was smiling. Making these breaths.' She mimes it. 'And rubbing himself all in circles.'

'You saw his face?'

'I saw him smile.'

'Anything else you noticed about him? Did he have long hair? Short hair?'

'I don't remember. Short, I think. He wore a hat.'

'He was a white man?'

'White, skinny. Young. But muscles, you know?'

'How did you see his muscles?'

'In his forearms as he . . . jiggled it around.'

'Did he wear a watch, maybe? Jewellery?'

'No watch. No jewellery.'

'Did you notice a tattoo?'

'He was a thin young man. Quite strong.'

'Clean shaven?'

'Yes. None of these goatees.'

'And while he was . . . playing with himself, did he say anything?'

'No.'

'And he didn't touch you?'

'No. I pretended to be asleep and in a minute he went away.'

'What did he take?'

'Just my bag. My keys.'

'Your own keys?'

'Yes, my own keys.'

'And only your keys?'

'No.'

'What other keys did he take?'

'Keys from people whose houses I clean.'

'Mrs Kwalingana,' says Howie. 'This is important now. Did those keys have the address on them?'

'Do I look stupid to you?'

'No, you don't look stupid to me.'

'Good. Well, I'm not.'

'Do you keep a computer at home?'

'Whatever for?'

'Never mind. Do you keep your clients' addresses written down anywhere?'

She taps her head. 'No need.'

'And in the morning, you reported this theft to the police?'

'Yes.'

'What happened?'

'I put the kettle on and sat round waiting. And sure enough, they turn up eventually. I tell them what happened, they give me a crime number for insurance. I tell them — *these keys, if my boss finds out they're gone I'm sacked. There's nothing we can do,* the police lady says. I call her a name and she leaves. I never see them again.'

'And how did your employer respond,' Luther says, 'when you told him about the lost keys?'

'I never did.'

96

'All those keys were stolen, and you never told anybody?'

'Nope.'

He glances at his notes, knows he's missing something. 'You need those keys to get into the houses you clean, right?'

'Right.'

'Did you have a spare set?'

'No.'

'So?'

He sits back. Crosses his arms. Waits.

'So,' she says. 'The keys were stolen on Friday. No cleaning on Saturday. Sunday morning, I get out of bed — can't sleep, you know. Have to keep checking windows and the doors.'

'And?'

'And in the hallway, there's an envelope.'

'What's in the envelope?'

'My keys.'

Luther glances at Howie.

'What?' he says. 'All of them?'

'All of them.'

'He gave you back your keys?'

'Yes.'

'Did you ever wonder why?'

'Many times.'

'Any ideas?'

'Because they're no good to him?'

'So why didn't he just throw them away?'

'Perhaps deep down he's a good boy.'

'Could be,' Luther says. 'Did you tell the police about this?'

'Yes. They told me they'd get the SAS onto it.'

Luther laughs, liking this woman. He says,

'I'm sorry you weren't treated better.'

'Not your fault. The young gentleman this morning was very nice. He had a kind face. What was his name?'

'I'm afraid I don't know.'

'DS Ripley,' says Howie.

'I've never met DS Ripley,' Luther says. 'But if I do, I'll be sure to pass on your kind words. Are you sleeping better now?'

'A little. I'd like a dog.'

'That's a good idea.'

'I'm scared to get one in case I take a fall and can't feed it.'

Luther tucks away the notebook. 'You didn't happen to keep the envelope the keys came in, did you?'

'I don't know. I don't think so.'

'You may have kept it, though? To reuse, pay a bill, send a Christmas card?'

'It's not impossible.'

'Would you mind if I sent an officer home with you to take a look?'

'He'll drive me home?'

'It'll be a she. And yes.'

'Then fine. Good.'

'From memory,' he says, 'were there any marks on the envelope? Any words or drawings, or — '

'I don't think so. Sorry.'

'That's okay. You've been very helpful.'

Luther and Howie stand, head for the door.

Mrs Kwalingana says, 'Do you have any ideas?'

'About what?'

'Why he gave me my keys back?'

Luther hesitates. He wonders what to say.

The burglar needed a set of keys to copy, he thinks. So he took them from you. But he didn't want you to tell your boss. Because your boss would have to tell the people the keys belonged to. And they'd have changed the locks.

He can't say that. But he can't think of anything reassuring to say either.

He gives Mrs Kwalingana a smile and an encouraging nod, and leaves the interview room.

★   ★   ★

Patrick gets home to find Henry sitting on the lowest step with his head in his hands.

He looks up when Patrick walks through the door. He rubs his eyes. He's been awake for hours. He says, 'So where is she?'

Patrick steels himself. 'She wouldn't come.'

'So why not fucking *make* her come?'

'I couldn't, Dad.'

Henry stands. He advances on Patrick. 'Couldn't? Or wouldn't?'

'I'm sorry, Dad.'

Henry twists his lip and leers. 'I'm sorry, Dad,' he mimics.

'I really tried,' says Patrick.

'I really tried,' repeats Henry.

'I did.'

'I did.'

Henry slaps Patrick.

He grabs a fistful of Patrick's hair and bends him double. A flurry of rabbit punches to the ear

99

and cheek, then Henry spins Patrick round and throws him into the wall. Four vicious little jabs to the kidneys.

Then he bites Patrick's scalp.

Patrick cries out. He pleads and begs.

Henry spits away a coin-sized chunk of hair and skin.

★   ★   ★

Once — a long time ago, years and years — Henry made Patrick torture a dog. It was a German Shepherd, an intelligent and noble beast. Henry tied it up in the garden and gave Patrick a chain to beat it with.

At first, as Patrick thrashed the dog, it snapped and snarled, bared gritted teeth, snapped and lunged. But near the end, when it had shat and pissed everywhere, smearing Patrick with its excrement and its blood, it dragged itself towards him on its belly, using its forepaws. Its ears were pinned back. It was whimpering and trying to wag its tail.

'See?' said Henry. 'Now it loves you.'

Henry spent years beating love into Patrick. But this isn't a love beating. It's just a beating. Patrick knows the difference.

When it's over, Henry stands over him. His hair is sticking up. His face is pale with loathing. Two pale tributaries of snot run from his nostrils into his mouth.

'Well, what the fuck do we do now?' he shouts. 'What the fuck am I supposed to do? Everyone's going to think I'm a fucking kiddie-fiddler.'

He kicks Patrick one more time. Then he retreats to the kitchen, head in hands.

Patrick curls into a ball on the floor. He lies there and doesn't move.

9

Maggie Reilly is fifty-one and supremely well groomed — even in the studio, where nobody but her producer and the engineer can see her. Grey trouser suit, cerise shirt, glossy high heels.

Maggie took a roundabout and now obsolete way to get here: *Bristol Evening Post* at eighteen, straight out of A-levels. At twenty-five she made the move to television, working as a reporter on *Westward!*, an early evening current-affairs programme. Two years later she moved to television news in London.

There were some award shortlistings, including one for rear of the year. She was named as a correspondent in a reasonably high-profile divorce case. There were some unflattering photographs in the papers, most famously of Maggie leaving the 'love den' looking frumpy and hungover; a trick of light and shadow added twenty years and several chins. There followed a year or two in the wilderness during which she wrote a newspaper column, renting out opinions she didn't really hold, or not that strongly.

And now here she is, born again, enjoying solid but unremarkable ratings on the Talk London Drivetime slot, 3 p.m. to 7 p.m. Yesterday, an elderly immigrant woman was hit and killed by a bendy bus just round the corner from Camberwell Art College; there's nothing like a bendy bus death to make Londoners irate. Maggie's taken three consecutive calls on the subject and the subject's getting old. Keen to move on, she hits the dump button, goes to line four.

'Pete Black from Woking,' she says. 'You're through to Maggie Reilly on London Talk FM.'

'Hello Maggie,' says Pete Black from Woking. 'First-time caller, long-time fan.'

'Well,' she chuckles, checking out the monitor on the corner of her desk, 'a girl can't have too many of them.'

'Since '95, actually,' says Pete from Woking. 'I used to live in Bristol.'

'Did you, my lover?'

He chuckles at the exaggerated accent. 'I remember that thing you did,' he says. 'The thing about little Adrian York.'

Maggie laughs that near-famous cigarette laugh. 'Well, if I was feeling a bit blue round the edges, I'd say that dates you. So what's got your back up today, Pete?'

'Okay. Really, I'm calling to say that I'm the one who killed Tom and Sarah Lambert. It was me.'

There are two full seconds of dead air during which Maggie glances up and makes eye-contact with Danny, her producer. He's already reaching for the phone to call the station boss.

The engineer, Fuzzy Rob, is already Tweeting.

Holding the phone, Danny makes a gesture: *Keep going.*

Maggie swallows. Her throat is dry. She says, 'Are you still there, Pete?'

Detective Sergeant 'Scary' Mary Lally finds Luther making himself an instant coffee and eating cream crackers from the packet.

She hands him a thin file. 'The head we found at the squat. The owner's a Chloe Hill.'

Luther flicks on the kettle then glances through the file.' 'Owner',' he says. 'Do you own your head?'

'Whatever. It belongs to Ms Hill. She was nineteen. Died in a motorcycle accident. Canvey Island.'

'So it's not just dead girls he goes for. It's dead girls and motorbikes. Blimey.'

'Her grave had been interfered with,' Lally says. 'This is seven or eight months ago. We're thinking either he dug her up himself or maybe paid a friend to do it for him.'

'So where's the rest of her?'

'Still in the grave, presumably.'

'We can only hope, eh?'

'Should I order an exhumation?'

'Let's start the process, yeah. So this has nothing to do with the Lambert murder?'

'I don't think so, Guv.'

'Call me Boss.' He massages his brow, hands back the file. He's about to say something else when the door bangs open and Teller steams in.

She says, 'Do you ever listen to London Talk FM?'

'No,' says Luther. 'Why?'

'Come with me,' she says. 'You'll enjoy this.'

Luther follows her across a weirdly silent and

watchful bullpen, wondering what's going on.

Teller slams her office door, gestures for him to shut up and listen.

She stabs a finger onto her keyboard, unmuting the volume on a streamed radio broadcast.

'Pete,' says the husky-voiced woman on the radio. 'I'm asking you on bended knee. Please. Whether this is true or not, you need help. You need to give yourself in to the proper authorities.'

'Tom and Sarah Lambert sexually abused my daughter,' says the caller. 'They weren't fit to be parents.'

Luther glances at Teller.

She doesn't respond. She's pacing the office, arms crossed, head down.

Luther bows his head. Shuts his eyes. Listens.

★ ★ ★

'They seemed a nice couple,' the caller says. 'They loved kids. One night we let them take care of our little girl — '

'Pete, I need to stop you there.'

'Okay. I get you. All I'm saying is, there were reasons.'

'Whatever your reasons,' says Maggie Reilly, 'right now we're talking about a helpless baby. So where's baby Emma, right now?'

Luther mouths: *Emma? Since when?*

Teller shrugs.

'I can't tell you that,' says Pete Black.

'A newborn needs medical attention, Pete. You must know that.'

'She's fit and well. She's happy. She's a very contented little baby. She's lovely.'

'You do know you can't keep her? You have to hand her in to the proper authorities.'

'That's why I'm calling. I want her to be well looked after. I want her placed with a loving family that can care for her properly.'

'So what are you saying?'

'I'll drop her off tonight. At a hospital. Something like that. A convent or something.'

'Don't wait for tonight. Do it now. Do it as soon as you can, Pete.'

'Yeah. But I need an assurance, don't I.'

'What assurance? From whom?'

'The police.'

Teller braces herself against the desk. *Here it comes.*

'What kind of assurance?' says Maggie.

'I want the police to promise me, in front of London, that they'll let me drop off Emma safely. They won't be watching the hospitals.'

The strength goes out of Teller and she sits.

'All I want,' says Pete Black, 'all I want is for little Emma to be safe and sound. I need the police to help me with that. I'll call back later.'

There's a click and the line goes dead.

Three endless seconds of dead air.

'Okay, London,' says Maggie Reilly. 'Your reactions in a moment. First, let's go straight to the news.'

★   ★   ★

106

After a moment Teller says, 'So what do we think?'

Luther dry-washes his face. Rasp of skin on stubble.

'It's him.'

It's in the self-justification, the moral blankness. The need to control.

He tugs at his weary eyes. Looks at the ceiling. 'Holy shit,' he says.

★ ★ ★

London Talk FM is run from a corporate office building on the Gray's Inn Road. Grey and chrome, smoked glass. Luther and Howie arrive early in the evening; they're obliged to edge through a scrum of media already gathered outside.

There's a uniformed security guard at the front desk. He asks Luther and Howie to sign in, gives them each a badge, directs them to the lifts.

They go up five floors, then step into an anonymous reception. A few promotional posters have been framed and mounted.

They're met by a pretty and energetic young intern, who leads them to a glass-fronted conference room. Danish pastries on the long table.

On the other side of the table sit a scruffy man and a good-looking woman in early middle age. Danny Hillman and Maggie Reilly.

The four shake hands across the table, cordial and watchful. Hillman takes two business cards from his wallet and slides them across the table

107

to Luther and Howie.

Luther glances over the card. 'I'm sorry to cut to the chase,' he says, 'but obviously we're against the clock here, so . . . '

Maggie Reilly gives him the smile. 'Ask away.'

'Obviously,' Luther says, 'our first priority is to request that you don't give this man any more airtime.'

'Seriously,' says Hillman. 'How could we ever justify doing that?'

'Because he's not who he says he is?'

'You don't know that, any more than we do — unless you've caught and arrested the real killer. Have you?'

Luther shrugs, tucks the business card into his wallet.

'I'm not going to discuss open investigations with you, Mr Hillman. You'll have to take my word for it.'

'If you knew who he was,' says Danny Hillman, 'you'd have released his name to the media by now.'

'You think what you want. But I guarantee you this: if you cooperate with this man, nobody will ever see that baby alive. People like Pete Black only ever contact the media because it serves their agenda.'

'And can we quote you on all this?' says Maggie, with a warning grin. 'Senior Investigating Officer warns London Talk FM not to help find little baby Emma?'

Hillman steps in, speaks over Luther's visible irritation. 'Look,' he says, 'there's a very clear public interest here. We've run it past the

108

lawyers. They're happy. If you try to gag us, we'll go to air with it, treat it as a story. And once it's discovered the police tried to stop us helping save a child's life — what happens then?'

Luther sits back. 'I can apply for a D-Notice.'

He means a Defence Advisory Notice, an official request to news editors not to publish or broadcast certain stories.

Hillman says, 'We're not releasing any information that pertains or relates to national security.'

Luther sidesteps that. 'So how are the ratings?' he asks. 'Sky-high, right? Killer calls. You Tweet, you put it on bloody Facebook, it goes viral. You amplify that new interest by running the call as a news headline every what, fifteen minutes? Killer Calls London Talk FM! Other news outlets pick up the story. These things spread like an explosion. In a few hours, you're sitting on the biggest story in Britain. Which makes you, this station, the biggest story in Britain. We've seen them downstairs. The hyenas.'

'This is a commercial operation, absolutely,' says Hillman. 'But believe it or not, we actually do have the interests of our listeners at heart. And our city. Not to mention baby Emma.'

'Her name's not Emma. She hasn't got a name yet. Her parents died before she was born.'

'She's got a name now,' says Maggie. 'For better or worse.'

'All right,' says Hillman. 'Let's all calm down.' He stands and goes to the window. Peers out on London at night; unreal city. He turns to face them, leaning on the windowsill. 'When you came in here,' he says, 'you knew we'd never kill the story. You had to ask, but you knew. So what are you really asking?'

Luther won't answer, so it's Howie who says, 'We're asking you to help us catch him.'

The intern walks in with their coffees. She places them almost reverently on the conference table and slips away. When she's gone, some of the tension has drained from the room.

After successfully defending editorial principle, Hillman agrees without caveat to the covert deployment of a police intelligence and surveillance crew. They'll arrive in plain clothes, and monitor and trace all calls to the station. (They'll also be surveilling the surrounding area, in case Pete Black shows up in person. But Luther doesn't feel the need to share this detail.)

The meeting is concluded cordially enough. Luther and Howie button their coats. Then Luther pauses in the doorway. 'One more thing,' he says.

'Ask away,' says Hillman.

But Luther is speaking to Maggie. 'There's a lot of journalists in the world,' he says. 'Why did he come to you?'

'None taken,' she says. 'Obviously, he listens to the show. When you're in the public eye, people imagine they've got a relationship with you. So, yeah. He trusts me.'

'But he was pretty specific.' Luther checks his notes and recites: 'That thing you did. Adrian York.'

'Ah,' she grins. '1995. My annus mirabilis. My one and only ever report for *Newsnight*. Passion piece. Got nommed.'

'Nommed?'

'Nominated. The Margaret Wakely Award for Contribution to Awareness of Women's Issues in Television Journalism.'

'You win?'

The grin widens. 'Always the bridesmaid.'

'I'm sorry,' Luther says. 'I don't mean to be rude. But the name — Adrian York. It doesn't ring a bell.'

'That was kind of the point,' she says. 'It was an outrageous case, really. Still makes me angry to think about it.'

Luther and Howie take their seats and let Maggie tell it the way she wants to.

'Basically,' she says, 'decent working-class woman makes a bad marriage. Chrissie York. She's got one child, Adrian. The marriage breaks down. The husband's got an Australian passport. Chrissie begins to worry he plans to kidnap the child, take him back to the old country.'

'It happens,' Luther says.

'Too right it happens. Meanwhile, the son makes certain allegations about his father. Drug use, prostitutes and so on. The mother reports the allegations. Some court-appointed psychologist decides she's coached Adrian to lie in order to discredit the father. She's therefore causing him what they call 'emotional harm', which is a meaningless catch-all phrase if ever you heard one. And when Adrian actually *does* go missing, police are slow to respond because they assume the mother's loony tunes and the father's done it for the kid's own good. So the father's their

111

prime and only suspect, if suspect's the right word.

'Eventually, and this is like eighteen months later, they track the father down to some shithole in Sydney. He denies all knowledge of snatching his son, wants nothing to do with him. Denies the kid is even his. But by then the case is cold and the story's old. Never found any traction with the media. Or the police. No offence.'

'None taken. Do we know where the father is now?'

'No idea.'

'But he definitely wasn't Pete Black?'

'He was Aussie. Pete Black sounds pure London to me.'

'Me too. What happened to the mother?'

'Last I heard, she was in hospital. Overdose. But that's a long time ago.'

Luther shakes his head.

Howie mouths the word: *Blimey*.

'Chrissie York never saw her son again,' says Maggie Reilly, with more than a hint of the old anger; the feral ghost of the news journalist she used to be, wishes she still was. 'She never had any idea what happened to him. Well, she had lots of ideas, obviously. But no proof. And nobody seemed to care. It was an ugly little story. All there was to show was this woman who'd tried her best, who'd been let down by everyone — because she married badly, because she was working class, because she sounded like a hysterical woman. And because there were sexier stories around. Easier stories.'

'And this is what your piece was about? The

piece Pete Black mentioned?'

'Yeah. It was the best piece I ever did.'

'Can I see it?'

She gives him a brittle grin. 'It's on my website. Click on Archive.'

He nods that he will. Then he says, 'Anyone ever call you about it? Show undue interest? Write letters? Whatever?'

'Never. Remember, you're talking about a long-ago abduction that nobody remembers.'

'Except Pete Black from Woking.'

'Apparently.'

'And he's never been in contact before?'

Maggie gets her fair share of funny phone calls. Do a quick google and there she is: her dimpled, smiling face photoshopped onto some younger, bustier and definitely more naked woman's body.

'I've had my issues,' she says. 'Restraining orders and all the rest of it. It comes with the territory.'

'Do you have a list of names?'

'No, but my agent does.'

'And they'll be happy to pass it on?'

'More than.'

She gives her agent's details. Howie writes them down.

Then Maggie says, 'Actually, there was one person who kept showing an interest.'

'Who?'

'Police officer in Bristol. Pat Maxwell. A few months before Adrian York, there'd been an attempted abduction. Just a few miles away. A little boy called Thomas Kintry.'

'She thought they were linked?'

'She seemed pretty positive. Apparently no one else did.'

'When's the last time you spoke to Pat Maxwell?'

'Gosh, this is years back. She'd be retired now, I expect. Assuming she's even still around.'

★ ★ ★

Luther and Howie walk silently through the office, back to the lift. The doors open. They step inside.

Howie presses the button for ground.

The doors close.

She says, 'So what do you think?'

'About what?'

'Pete Black?'

'Either he's a stalker,' Luther says, 'some freak who's genuinely been a fan of this woman for fifteen-odd years. In which case, you'd expect some kind of prior communication.'

'Or?'

'Or he's the man who kidnapped and killed Adrian York. And maybe tried to abduct that other little boy.'

'Kintry. So why does he make this call?'

'Maybe because Maggie was the only one who ever paid attention to what he'd done. But I don't know. It doesn't feel right. Does it feel right to you?'

'No.'

'Good. Because it's not right, is it? It's not right.'

'You think he's serious about giving back the baby?'

'I don't know. I don't get him. I can't see him.'

The doors open.

They step out of the elevator, pass across the bright lobby, shove through the news crews and pass on, into the rainy night.

Then Luther stops.

Commuters, shoppers and tourists flow round him like water surging round a boulder.

'Adrian York,' he says. 'That's an abduction that nobody even knew was an abduction. Right?'

Howie nods, knowing not to interrupt.

'So. Victimology one-oh-one: what if that's *why* he chose Adrian York? The other abduction, the Kintry kid, if they really are connected . . . it sounds like an unplanned snatch and grab gone wrong.'

'A trial run,' Howie says.

'Exactly. So, say he was learning. Refining his methods. He tries brute force in broad daylight. That doesn't work out. Maybe he's closer to getting caught than we realize. So he decides to go another way.'

'I don't get you.'

'I'm saying, what if he knew about the complaints the mother made.'

'Chrissie York.'

'What if he knows about the complaints Chrissie York made to social services? What if he knew they treated her with contempt? If he knew *that*, he knew he could snatch the York kid right off the street. And if he's fast enough, and

115

nobody sees . . . nobody would believe it had even *happened*.'

'Which makes it the perfect abduction,' Howie says. 'But that doesn't alter the fact that he's completely silent about it for fifteen years. So why start phoning radio stations now?'

'I don't know,' Luther says. 'Maybe because the Adrian York thing went well and the Lambert thing didn't?'

'Didn't in what way? He got the baby.'

'Depends what he needed from it. But maybe he's feeling embarrassed. Feeling the need to justify what he did.'

'But why does he feel that need now?'

'Because he's a psychopath. He doesn't feel shame or guilt. He's superior. He's unique. He looks down on us. He detests us. But it matters to him that we *know* he's better than us. He needs our admiration.'

On the way to the car he calls Teller. He asks her to call Avon & Somerset, get them to bike over the Adrian York and Thomas Kintry cold case files.

He asks for the contact details of Detective Inspector Patricia Maxwell, probably retired.

He calls Ian Reed at home and asks him to look over Maggie Reilly's old news report to see if anything strikes him as relevant or odd.

They're all long shots: the York case is sixteen or seventeen years old. But the ground has to be covered.

Then he phones Zoe and asks her to meet him.

10

Luther walks through a night swarm of briefcases, umbrellas, pinstripe suits and taxis, then steps into Postman's Park. He walks through the icy rain until he reaches a long wooden gallery that shelters a wall decorated with ceramic tiles.

Waiting, he reads some of the tiles. Takes strange comfort from them:

Elizabeth Coghlam, Aged 26,
Of Church Path, Stoke Newington.
Died saving her family and house by carrying
blazing paraffin to the yard. Jan 1 1902

Tobias Simpson, Died of exhaustion after
saving many lives from the breaking ice at
Highgate Ponds, Jan 25 1885

Jeremy Morris, Aged 10,
Bathing in the Grand Junction Canal.
Sacrificed his life to help his sinking
companion, Aug 2 1897

It's called 'The Memorial to Heroic Self Sacrifice'. They knew how to name things in the Victorian era.

He turns and Zoe's there, shivering wet in her coat and holding a takeaway coffee in each hand.

'I saw the news,' she says.

'Yeah.' He takes a coffee. 'Bad day.'

They stand next to each other, read the tiles. Sip coffee.

She says, 'Is the baby alive?'

'I don't know. Part of me hopes not.'

'Will you be home tonight?'

'I can't. Rose has asked me to stay on.'

In fact, Teller has ordered him to go home and get some sleep.

He's not needed: they're pulling people off sick leave. Specialist surveillance units will be monitoring hospitals and late-night surgeries, drop-in centres. There are hundreds of coppers out there right now, waiting for Pete Black to show up somewhere on the sombre face of London; a baby bundled in his arms, alive or dead.

Luther says, 'Will you be okay?'

'I'll be fine,' she says. 'Glass of wine, catch up on work. I spent two hours today with those sodding school kids.'

'Lock the doors and windows,' he says. 'Set the alarm. Put on the deadbolts. Front door and back.'

'I always lock the doors and the windows.'

'I know.'

'So why say it?'

'To make me feel better.'

'That's the problem with all this,' she says. 'You spend all day in it. You see it everywhere.'

'I know.'

'It's not everywhere.'

'I know.'

'When we were kids,' she says, 'when you'd

just started out, you went to this flat. An old woman had died alone. She'd been dead in her chair for about two years. She'd mummified.'

'Irene,' he says.

'That's her. You came home. We had that little flat on Victoria Road, that tiny little place with the shared bathroom and that weird couple downstairs. Wendy and Dave.'

He smiles sadly, remembering.

'I fell asleep before you got back,' Zoe says. 'You came in, sat on the edge of the bed. I watched you drink a pint of whisky in about ten minutes. It was the first time I ever saw you really cry.'

He shrugs. 'It was sad.'

'I know it was sad, it was really sad. I still think about her sometimes.'

'Me too.'

'But that night, when you were drunk, you were angry. I mean, really angry. Scary angry.'

He turns to her, not remembering. 'Angry about what?'

'The jokes they told. The police, the medical examiner, the ambulance crew. The lack of respect. You said they objectified her exactly like a killer would. And you got so angry at yourself, for not saying anything to them. Telling them to have more respect.'

'I was a kid.'

'And you wondered if you'd made a terrible mistake — done the wrong thing by joining the police.' She brushes wet hair from her eyes. 'That was the first time you talked about leaving the police. Sixteen years ago. And you've been

119

talking about giving it up ever since.'

'I know.'

'But you never have.'

'I know.'

'And you never will.'

He doesn't answer that. How can he?

She steps closer. They stand side by side, looking at the tiles. She says, 'Have you ever heard of Bipolar Two Disorder?'

He laughs.

'It's under-diagnosed,' she says. 'I looked it up. Hypomania often presents as high-functioning behaviour.'

'I'm not manic. I'm exhausted.'

'But you can't sleep.'

'That's not the same thing.'

'I mean, you don't sleep *at all*. Not at all.'

'So I'll get pills.'

'You say they cloud your thinking.'

'They do.'

'People with Bipolar Two are at a high risk of suicide.'

'I'm not suicidal.'

'Seriously? Not ever? It never crosses your mind?'

'It crosses everyone's mind. Now and again.'

'Not mine.'

'It's just a thought pattern,' he says. 'Suicidal ideation: *if I had to do it, how would I do it?* It's not an intent. It's a game. Sort of.'

'Hypomania in Bipolar Two Disorder manifests as anxiety and insomnia,' she says.

'Don't do this to me now,' he says. 'Please. Not now.'

'If not now, when?'

'Soon. We'll talk about it soon.'

She laughs, and he catches the magnitude of her bitterness.

'I promise,' he says.

'You always promise. It's all you do.'

'Then I don't know what to say.'

'Maybe there's nothing to say. Because we've both said it all, a hundred times. I'm as bored of saying it as you must be of hearing it.'

He doesn't answer.

She says, 'Look into my eyes, John. Look at me.'

He turns. He looks at her. She's wet. Elegant. Drenched in London rain. He loves her inexpressibly.

She says, 'What do you see?'

'I don't know,' he says. 'Just you.'

'And there's your problem.'

She gives him a look, years of weary love in it.

He watches her walk away; perfectly poised and perfectly lost to him.

★ ★ ★

When she's gone, he drains the coffee and scrunches up the cup, then bins it and goes to meet Howie. She's sitting behind the wheel on a meter, reading the *Standard*, late edition: Maggie Reilly on the front page looking grave and glamorous. A smaller insert shows the Lambert crime scene.

'London awaits,' Luther says.

Howie grunts, folds the paper and jams it

121

down the side of her seat. She's left the engine and the heater running. The car's uncomfortably warm.

'Twitter's going mad,' she says. 'Facebook. Dead Tree Press is running with it on their websites. Maggie Reilly's all over the place. She's doing the overnight show, apparently. She wants to be,' she checks the interview in the *Standard*, 'on hand when he calls.'

Luther leans over and tunes the car radio to London Talk FM. He and Howie listen to the lonely and the lost and the mad rage about bringing back the death penalty.

He stares ahead, at the constant snarl of traffic, the rainy lights shining red, amber, green. He looks at the people. Flitting by too fast to identify. A river of flesh, ever changing, never changing. The commuters with their briefcases and laptop bags, the kids in their jeans and urban coats.

Eventually, he says, 'You got a boyfriend? Girlfriend? Husband? Whatever.'

'Yeah,' she says. 'Robert. Website designer. Bless him.'

'When's the last time you saw him?'

'Don't ask.'

'When's the last time you actually slept?'

She doesn't answer that. Just looks at the windscreen as she drives.

'Go home,' Luther says.

'I can't, Boss. Not tonight.'

'There are hundreds of coppers out there looking for this man,' he says. 'Go home. Be with Robert. Sleep. Come in early tomorrow, take a look at the York and Kintry files. You'll need a fresh eye for that.'

Howie smiles as she drives. Looks like she wants to hug him.

11

Reed sits at the table, opens the laptop, accesses Maggie Reilly's website. He navigates to ARCHIVE, then scrolls to 1995, clicks on a file called: SOCIAL SERVICES, 'EMOTIONAL HARM' AND FAMILY JUSTICE.

In the clip, Maggie Reilly wanders in front of some dilapidated council houses in a place called Knowle West.

She looks pretty good, even doing a walk and talk, addressing the camera with exaggerated gravity:

'A court-appointed psychologist, whom we cannot name for legal reasons, decided that the mother coached her son to lie, and was therefore causing her child 'emotional harm'.

'What all these cases have in common is the belief that mothers are putting their children at risk of what's called 'emotional harm'. Last year, more children were placed on the at-risk register for this so-called 'emotional harm' than for sexual or physical abuse . . . '

The doorbell rings.

Reed pauses the footage and limps to the door.

He opens it on Zoe Luther.

He smiles. Then his face falls. Zoe's a mess.

She says, 'Can I?'

'Yeah,' says Reed, stepping back. 'Yeah, of course.'

She steps over the threshold. Reed shuts the door. She follows him down the hall to the living room and drips on the parquet.

He says, 'Tea?'

'Tea would be great.'

'I've got something stronger, if you'd like it?'

'If I start drinking now, I'm not sure I'll be able to stop.'

'Tea it is, then. So what's wrong?'

'Bad day.'

'For everyone, apparently. What can you do?'

'I don't know, Ian. What can I do?'

She hangs her head and starts to cry.

Reed steps up. He embraces her. 'Hey,' he says, 'Hey, hey, hey.'

She says, 'Can you call John?'

'Why?'

'Because I need you to make sure he's all right.'

'He's all right,' Reed says. 'He's okay. He's stressed, but he's okay, I think.'

'He's not. He's making himself ill.'

'Shhh,' says Reed. 'Shhh.'

'Talk to him,' she says. 'He loves you. He'll listen to you.'

'He loves you, too.'

She laughs as if that were a bitter joke.

'Zoe,' says Reed. 'Hand to God, I never knew anyone loved his wife half as much as John loves you.'

There's a moment of embarrassed intimacy between them, almost normal enough to make them laugh and pretend this isn't happening.

Zoe fills a glass with water. 'Have you got any aspirin?'

'There's Nurofen in the drawer,' he says. 'Or I've got some codeine. You should try it. I'm a convert.'

She opens the drawer and palms a couple of painkillers.

Reed says, 'Okay. Look. This thing, the thing that's happening today. It's pretty bad. You're right, he's probably wound up a bit tight by it. The first chance I get, I'll take him to one side. Have a word.'

'He's going to kill himself,' she says. 'He can't carry on the way he is.'

He takes her shoulders, holds her at arm's length. 'Listen,' he says. 'I'll never let that happen, okay? Because you two, John and Zoe, you're the ones who give the rest of us hope.'

'God help you then,' she says.

★ ★ ★

Bill Tanner lives in a two-up, two-down, end-of-terrace in Shoreditch.

It's worth a lot less than it was three years ago, but it's worth a lot more than it was when the original landlord, George Crouch, acquired it in 1966.

Luther rings the doorbell. Inside, a small dog erupts in a spasm of yapping. The floral curtains part a little.

Aware that he's being watched, Luther raises his arms, two Tesco Metro carriers in each hand. 'I called. I'm a mate of Ian Reed. John.'

The curtains close and the hallway light comes on. At length, Bill Tanner opens the door.

Although he's shuffling and hunched, Tanner still carries the air of the powerful man he used to be: broad in the beam with immense, knobby fists at the end of meaty forearms. He's got a thick head of white hair, pinkie bald only at the crown. More white hair erupts in great tufts from his nostrils and ears. He's wearing a brown cardigan.

At his foot is a skinny, moist-eyed Yorkshire terrier. It continues to yap as Tanner digs in his pocket with a shaking hand.

He excavates a wadded-up five pound note and tries to give it to Luther — who waves a hand, still with the heavy bags in it. 'Don't worry. It's on the house. All part of the service.'

Bill nods his old lion's head and stuffs the fiver back into his pocket. 'Cheers, son. Do you fancy coming in for a cuppa, then?'

Luther hesitates. Then he says, 'Go on then. Just the one.'

He steps into the hallway.

The carpets, curtains and furniture are old, carefully maintained for many years but now grubby in the way of the old; Luther spots more than one tiny dog turd in dark corners, one under the music centre.

Yorkies are prone to it. Luther knows, because his nan had one.

He follows Bill to the kitchen and pulls up a

vinyl chair. It has a bright sunflower print, the kind of thing coveted by Shoreditch hipsters. Bill could sell them at Spitalfields market and make some decent cash.

Bill puts the kettle on and dumps a Tesco Value teabag into a mug whose interior Luther does not wish to glimpse.

He opens the fridge, takes out a carton of milk, dumps it on the worktop. 'Sugar?'

'One, please.'

Bill begins to shake. Luther stands, taking the old man's elbow. Helps him sit.

Bill Tanner sits with his head low. He's still holding the carton of milk. Luther can smell it.

'What's wrong?'

'I've got no sugar in the house.'

'That's all right,' Luther says. 'I'll have it without.'

'I hate tea without sugar. It's piss without sugar.' He's trembling. 'I'm too scared to go down the fucking shops, that's the trouble. Imagine that. A grown man, and I'm too scared to leave my own fucking house. The doorbell goes at night, I nearly have fucking heart failure.'

'Everyone feels like that when the doorbell goes at night,' Luther says. 'You sit there. I'll make the tea.'

When the tea is drunk, Luther empties out the carrier bags and catalogues what he's bought: bread, milk, some proper teabags, instant coffee, tins of beans, tins of Irish Stew, tins of soup, toilet paper, toilet bleach, lamb chops, tissues, a buttercream gateau, some bourbon biscuits, some custard creams. Then, at the end, he lays

128

out twelve cans of Caesar dog food in tiny cans. 'Show me where all this stuff goes,' he says. 'I'll put it away.'

'You don't have to do that.'

'You're a mate of Ian's,' Luther says. 'I promised I'd make sure you were looked after. He thinks a lot of you.'

'He's a decent lad, that Ian,' says Bill Tanner. 'He is.'

When Luther's put away the shopping, he asks for the dog's lead and takes the doddery old Yorkie for a walk round the block. It pisses on every third lamp post, finally squats to shit on the corner.

Luther takes automatic note of everyone who chuckles as they pass him; a young couple, hand in hand; a bunch of white kids hanging round outside a Chinese takeaway.

The kids give him the evil eye, call out a few insults. He's embarrassed by the little dog with its prim little feet skittering along next to him. But he gives them the passive eye, the eye that tells them he isn't afraid, and their eyes slide silently from his.

He walks the dog back home and lets himself in.

He helps the old man upstairs and into his musty bed.

Then he pads downstairs. He sits in the armchair and tunes the portable radio to London Talk FM.

He listens. But he can't sit still. He can't stop thinking. His head is a city. He paces the floor. He rubs at his crown with the palm of his hand.

The dog trots joyfully at his heel, showing the tip of its tiny pink tongue.

The radio murmurs.

★   ★   ★

Howie lets herself through the front door, trudges up two flights of stairs and opens the door to her flat.

Robert's asleep and she doesn't want to wake him. So she sneaks to the tiny second bedroom, rolls a polar fleece into a tube to serve as a pillow and sleeps in her clothes.

Around 5 a.m. she cries out, loud enough to wake Robert. He comes padding through. He stands half naked in the doorway, wondering whether to wake her or not.

He decides not to. He goes back to bed. He doesn't sleep for the rest of the night.

★   ★   ★

Zoe takes a long bath, ignoring that she's already showered twice today, then lies on the sofa in pyjamas and thick socks, her hair tied back. She lets News 24 flicker silently in the background and keeps Maggie Reilly low on London Talk FM while she reviews case notes, drinks half a bottle of wine and grows weepy.

She checks her phone every five minutes.

Around 1 a.m. she gives up. She wraps herself in a soft fleece blanket, sets aside the papers, turns up the radio and scans the news websites: COUNTRY HOLDS ITS BREATH FOR

BABY EMMA. TENSE WAIT FOR BABY EMMA. LONDON HOLDS ITS BREATH IN 'BABY EMMA' DRAMA.

She slips into sleep, and straight into a dream in which she and Mark are fucking. He is shoving his fingers into her mouth and she is biting them. All the while, John searches for something in the wardrobe.

She wakes before hitting the ground and turns back to the news.

The same two photographs of Baby Emma's mother and father. The same audio of the man claiming to be their killer. The same sober newsreaders, the same grave, gleeful trepidation.

She flashes back to yesterday afternoon, the way she and Mark writhed around each other, in her head, it seems that their legs had intertwined like snakes. She thinks of Mark's mouth at her breast and between her legs, his tongue between her lips, his cock in her mouth, and she wants to be sick.

She falls asleep sometime after 3 a.m.

At 4.17 she jolts awake from another dream, worse than the first.

She sits there until just after 5, gummy-eyed and with a crick in her neck, listening to the low, demented murmur of talk radio and refreshing the BBC News homepage every few seconds.

★   ★   ★

Danny Hillman sits in the narrow production room, monitoring the newsfeeds, RSS feeds, Reuters.

131

But mostly, he's waiting for Pete Black to call.

Just before midnight, Lucy phones to see how he's getting on. The girls are sleeping okay, they send him kisses. Danny's dad had called to ask about Christmas. Danny's dad is in a home and calls to ask about Christmas eight or nine times a week. After Christmas, he'll start worrying about Easter. But that's all the news Lucy had. She hoped he was okay.

Danny tells his wife he loves her. She tells him she loves him back. And good luck, she says. Fingers crossed.

★ ★ ★

Maggie sits at the microphone, taking calls. She is exhausted and exhilarated.

The news cameras are waiting downstairs. The station itself is news. The show is news. But Maggie is the real news.

She's dressed for the occasion — for the impromptu press conference she hopes to take before the day is out. But the crisp clothes and new shoes feel wrong against her tired body.

The clock ticks.

The light seems bright and glares on white walls.

She looks into the corner and there are her new shoes, and it seems strange to her to be doing this in bare feet. A call like this, you want to be ready when it arrives.

★ ★ ★

Luther sits in the upright chair, wrapped in his coat. He closes his eyes and listens to the low murmur of the radio.

In the darkness, he hears Bill Tanner snoring upstairs.

He tries not to think about where the Lamberts' baby might be and what the man who calls himself Pete Black might be doing to her. He tries not to think about the things he's seen. This twenty-year skid of blood and bone and marrow.

He does what he always does when the train in his head won't stop: he thinks of his wife. He thinks of the first day he saw her. Her gypsy skirt and flat shoes, her smile. Her voice, which sent tingles up his spine. It still does.

He scrolls through his memories of her — his personal koan. Her graduation day, the day they moved in together. The week she nursed him through flu. Their wedding day. Watching TV cuddled up on the sofa. Her nudity. Shopping in supermarkets together. Her forbearance as he stalks the fragrant rows of second-hand book-shops.

But the memories are like recordings of recordings. He searches them for something recent but good — something that belongs to him, here and now.

All he finds is Zoe tonight, in the park, kissing him on the cheek and walking away.

Luther's heart pumps queasily in his chest. He thinks about calling her. He doesn't.

★   ★   ★

Benny Deadhead goes home, gets changed, puts on some sweats. He thinks about getting it all out of his head by watching some TV, maybe one of the Korean horror DVDs he's been stacking up for about two years and which challenge him, still unwatched, from the middle shelf.

Instead he thinks *fuck it*. He racks up a couple of lines, sniffs them back, logs on to *World of Warcraft*.

He steps for a few enchanted hours into a better and braver world.

★ ★ ★

Teller wanders the Serious Crime Unit. The tired personnel under bright lights, the flickering monitors, the filing cabinets with their terrible secrets. The peeling plaster and the smudged glass bricks.

Downstairs, in the ringing bowels of the building, the drunks and the gang members and the burglars and the junkies shiver under strip lights.

She thinks of the people out there in London tonight, the plain clothes and uniformed coppers waiting on roofs and in cold cars. Men and women who've been up for forty-eight hours straight: the people who've come in off sick leave and off their holidays.

She's tired and she feels sick and she's worried about her daughter, fourteen years old and sleeping at the neighbour's house.

★ ★ ★

Via laptops and cellphones, memes propagate and bring forth:

. . . someone just told me that her friend heard a crying baby in her garden last nite!!! and she called the police because it was late and she thought it was weird the police told her WHATEVER YOU DO, DO NOT OPEN THE DOOR!!! WE ALREADY HAVE A UNIT ON THE WAY DO NOT OPEN THE DOOR!! He told her they think it is a SERIAL KILLER!! The man has snatched 2 girls in Manchester and is now in London and has a baby's cry recorded, he uses it to coax women out of their homes thinking that someone has left a baby. He said they have not verified it, but have had MANY MANY CALLS BY WOMEN SAYING THEY HEARD BABIES' CRIES OUTSIDE THEIR DOORS WHEN THEIR HOME ALONE AT NIGHT. Please pass this on!!!!! And DO NOT open the door for a crying baby!!!!!!

At 10.56 p.m. two newlyweds in Finsbury Park hear a baby screaming in their back garden. They call the police. No baby is found.

Attending officers believe the anxious couple may have heard the mating cries of urban foxes, which are often mistaken for babies in distress.

★   ★   ★

135

At 12.52 a.m. Claire Jackson, who lives in Wandsworth, calls 999 claiming that 'a tall black man' tried to lure her into opening her door late at night by using a recording of a crying baby.

Ms Jackson claims to have heard 'bumping sounds' outside. She got up to see what was going on. It was then she heard a baby crying from her front garden.

She and her husband saw the 'tall black man dressed all in black' outside their home, walking quickly away.

★ ★ ★

At 1.03 a.m. three young sisters, including a baby, are rescued by a neighbour from a smoke-filled house.

Left alone by their mother, who has gone speed dating, the two older children — aged six and eight — are trying to bake cakes. They inadvertently turn on both the grill and the oven.

Hearing a crying baby, Mo Sullivan, who lives two doors down, calls 999 before running out to pound on her neighbours' door.

The house is filling with smoke when the front door is opened a crack by eight-year-old Olivia. She's been told not to open the door to strangers.

Mrs Sullivan convinces Olivia to call 999 and obtain the police's 'permission' to leave the burning house with her sisters.

Mrs Sullivan, a Christian, will later tell the papers it was a miracle. She was only watching TV at that time of night because she was so anxious about dear Baby Emma. Any other night, she'd have taken her pill and gone to sleep.

Mrs Sullivan has been taking the pills since her husband died. They'd been married thirty-five years and were never blessed with children.

'Jesus led me by the hand to save this little tot and her sisters,' she says. 'All praise to him.'

★ ★ ★

At 1.42 a.m. Matthew Alexander, a motorist, is forced to escape the scene of a crash after being attacked by the men who had at first tried to rescue him.

Mr Alexander, returning from a dinner party, crashes his Ford Mondeo into a central reservation near Manor Fields in Putney.

Spotting Mr Alexander's baby son strapped into a car seat, the group — led by Graeme Kershaw, 23 — begin asking Mr Alexander questions about 'Baby Emma'.

Mr Alexander's protestations about the gender of his child are ignored by the gang, who become violent when Mr Alexander suggests they confirm what he's saying by checking inside the child's nappy.

Mr Alexander sustains moderate but not life-threatening injuries.

★ ★ ★

Police are accused of being heavy-handed after four officers storm a young couple's house at

3.54 a.m. because a 999 caller claims their baby is 'crying non-stop, like something's wrong.'

Lab Assistant Sean Scott and his girlfriend Becky Walker, wake up to find two police officers in their bedroom demanding to see their two-month-old daughter, Frankie.

Police reduce Becky to tears by threatening to call social services, but leave after confirming Frankie is safe and well.

★   ★   ★

At 5.12 a.m. a man is seen approaching Homerton Hospital carrying 'a suspicious bundle'.

He is apprehended and set upon by a large group of young men and teenagers. The youngest of the attackers is three weeks short of his thirteenth birthday.

The victim is Olusola Akinrele, a hospital worker on his way to an early shift. The 'bundle' was his gym bag.

Fortunately for Mr Akinrele, who loses the sight in one eye, the attack takes place less than a hundred metres from the Homerton Accident and Emergency department, which is where he works as a nurse.

★   ★   ★

At 5.47 a.m., Maggie Reilly comes to the microphone and announces that Pete Black has at last called back to London Talk FM.

'Pete,' she says. 'Is that you?'

Luther stops pacing. He snatches up the portable radio and holds it close to his ear.

'I've driven all over London,' says Pete Black, tearful with self-pity. 'There's police *everywhere*. I just want London to know that. I want London to know what the police are doing. I try to help, and this is what I get.'

'You can't blame the police for doing their job.'

'Yes I can. Because if it wasn't for them, Emma would be with the doctors now. But she's not, is she?'

'So where is she, Pete? Where's Baby Emma?'

'I've put her where I could. I hope she's safe.'

'Where is she, Pete?'

'If she's not safe, it's not my fault. I wanted you all to know that. I tried my best. I was only trying to help.'

'Pete, where is she? Where's Baby Emma?'

'They're tracing my call,' says Pete Black. 'They'll know.'

★ ★ ★

Luther turns off the radio and shrugs on his coat. He dials Teller.

He says, 'Where?'

She says, 'King's Cross.'

Luther's already out the door.

139

12

They seal off a two-kilometre area around King's Cross, concentrate the search on the Joy Christian Centre, at Saints Church of England, St Aloysius Convent, the Crowndale Health Centre on Crowndale Road, the Killick Street Heath Centre, the New Horizon Youth Centre.

Luther elects to join the squad searching the grounds of St Pancras Old Church, on the edge of the search perimeter.

It's the largest green area in the parish, and one of the oldest sites of Christian worship in London. Ancient trees. Ancient graves.

He arrives at an archaic ash tree ringed by a rusty fence. Around the tree's root-base, time-worn gravestones have been crammed together. They stand like weird fungi. Over the years the roots of the tree have grown between the stones, knocked them off-true, seem to be in the process of consuming them.

A baby has been jammed between two of the stones, sprinkled with handfuls of soil and leaf humus.

Luther reaches down.

He takes the baby from the earth.

Then he lays her back. She's cold.

★ ★ ★

Luther steps outside the evidence tent. Eyes pass over him. Coppers, onlookers, paramedics.

Outside the gates, misery lights flash blue. Uniformed officers erect crowd barriers.

The media are here, of course: there is a scrum of faces, all colours and ages, the mass homogenized by their eagerness to catch a glimpse.

There's a helicopter overhead.

He buries his hands deep into his pockets and strides through wet grass to a far, secret corner of the churchyard.

He puts his back to the Victorian brick wall. It crawls with evergreen climbing plants. It's shockingly wet.

He puts his head in his hands and cries.

When he's finished, Teller's there, half sitting, half leaning on a gravestone.

Luther's eyes are raw and wet. He wipes them with the back of the hand. He's embarrassed.

Teller doesn't say a word.

For something to do, they walk to the church.

Inside, they find cool stone and heavy silence. The sweet, dusty fragrance of old incense.

Teller sits on the pew in front but turned to face him, resting her chin on her forearm. She watches him.

He says, 'Fuck.'

'I know,' she says.

Outside is the crime scene, the tape, SOCO, the medical examiners, and beyond them the church gates that lead back into the city, the crush of people, the cameras, the journalists, the

141

mobile phones, the love songs on the radio of passing cars.

At the entrance to the church, a recently added marble stone is inscribed: *And I am here/in a place/beyond desire or fear.*

She touches his forearm.

He nods at his lap. Then he dry-washes his face to massage some life into it. He stands. Claps his big hands.

She watches him walk outside, through the big doors and into the morning. A big man with a big walk. The world turning like a wheel beneath him.

13

Henry buys the *Mail*, the *Mirror*, the *Sun*, the *Independent* and *The Times*. But not the *Guardian*. Henry detests the *Guardian*.

Then he goes to the café and orders a full English. He shrugs off his overcoat and scarf and, still trembling, sits at one of the red plastic moulded tables, bolted to the floor in an ungenerous manner that has become the norm.

It saddens him. But proper cafés, cafés like this, are closing by the dozen every week, winking out of existence like fairy lights. So he'll take what he can get.

He adds sugar to his tea, stirs it with a dirty teaspoon, stained by years of daily immersion in tannin.

Then he can't put it off any longer. He opens the first newspaper.

They tell the story the same way: LONDON HOLDS ITS BREATH. PRAYERS SAID FOR BABY EMMA. THOUSANDS OF PEOPLE PLEDGED LAST NIGHT ... HUNDREDS OF POLICE CANCELLED LEAVE LAST NIGHT ... WE ALL PRAY ... IN DARK TIMES ...

Henry burns with rage and embarrassment.

He looks through the window at the damp city coming alive: the market owners setting up stalls, selling organic veg and Indian food and knock-off Caterpillar boots and cheap polo

143

shirts. The women walking to work at the local Tesco, the taxi drivers stopping outside the newsagent to pop in for a paper and a packet of fags.

Then he turns back to the paper — to the photographs of the smiling Lamberts, the woman he sliced open like ripe fruit to remove the fresher fruit within. He'd slit the throbbing blue umbilicus with a folding knife he'd owned since he was a boy.

He'd been sure the Lamberts were ideal; he stuck with them through the years of IVF because he never doubted their fertility. They were too exquisite not to be. Two bodies like that, they were breeding machines.

Simple genetic principles implied their child would be ideal, too. But it wasn't. It was a mewling little runt.

It's not Henry's fault she died. And at least London knows that now. People know that the man who took Baby Emma wasn't a pervert.

*   *   *

Zoe goes downstairs and turns on the TV, sees the affable morning newsreader pulling her grave face.

' . . . an update on this still-developing story,' she says. 'Acting on a tip-off from the man who claimed to have kidnapped baby Emma Lambert, visibly devastated police officers reportedly found the body of a baby at St Pancras Old Church in central London early this morning. Simon Maxwell-Davis is at the scene.'

144

Zoe watches live footage of a London churchyard. A dizzying zoom — and there's John, stomping away from an evidence tent. Rose Teller is a beat behind him, like a terrier at his heels.

It's followed by helicopter footage of John leaning against a wall and apparently weeping.

Zoe's hand goes to her throat.

Cut back to the young man with the microphone. Blond and ruddily handsome, a little chubby.

'Well, Lorna,' he says, to the anchor, to the viewers, to Zoe, 'this must be the moment all police officers dread. Although I should stress that we've yet to have official confirmation, our sources do tell us that, following the dramatic call made to a London radio station early this morning, police have indeed found the body of a baby here at St Pancras Old Church in central London. Details are very sketchy at this time — '

Zoe snaps off the TV and calls John.

She gets voicemail.

He never answers his fucking phone. It's one of those things about him. It drives her insane. He says if you go around answering your phone, all it does is ring.

'John,' she says, 'it's me. I don't know what time it is. It's early. I've just seen the news. Give me a call as soon as you can. I just want to know you're okay. Please. Just — y'know.'

She hangs up. Tucks a strand of hair behind her ear. She puts her face in her hands. She says her own name like a mantra: *Zoe, Zoe, Zoe.*

Then she cranes her neck and looks at the ceiling.

Her phone rings. She snatches it up. It's Mark. He says, 'Have you been watching the news?'

'I'm watching it now.'

'Jesus Christ, Zoe. Are you okay?'

She doesn't know.

Mark says, 'Have you heard from him?'

'No.'

'Do you think he's okay?'

'I don't know,' she says, testily. 'I really don't know who's okay and who's not.'

'Listen,' he says, not rising to the bait. She loves him for it. 'Whatever you need me to do, I'm here. If you want me to come over, I'll be right over. If you want me to stay away, I'll stay away. Just let me know.'

She says, 'Look. Thanks. I appreciate it. I really do. But we had a row last night. A pretty bad one. And then, here he is on TV, crying. That's not like him. And . . . I just don't know. I don't know what I'm going to do. I've got to go.'

'Go where?'

'To work.'

After a moment he says, 'Is that a good idea?'

'What else am I supposed to do?' she says. 'Hang around the house all day, watching the news? If I did that every time John was up to his neck in something horrible, I wouldn't have a job to go to.'

★ ★ ★

146

Howie gets in about two minutes before the police courier arrives from Bristol. She hasn't even taken off her coat when he hands over the Kintry and York files, taped up in a second-hand Jiffy bag.

Howie thanks him, lays the Jiffy bag on her messy desk.

The courier is a young PC with a heavy West Country accent. She offers him a cup of tea. He prefers one of the Cup a Soups he sees next to the water-spotted kettle. He's been up all night and he's hungry.

He drinks the soup. They chat about the case in very general terms. Then he rinses the cup, wishes her good luck and leaves.

Howie takes a coffee to her desk, slips on a pair of noise-reducing headphones, opens the Jiffy bag and digs out the files.

★　★　★

Luther's barely through the heavy doors of the buzzing unit when Benny grabs his elbow and drags him into the office, Ian Reed's dry cleaning still hanging there behind the door.

Benny's twitchy, wide-eyed, washed-out.

Luther says, 'Christ, Benny. How much sleep did you get?'

'Not that much. It was niggling at me. It's difficult to sleep when you know you could be doing something useful — in case things didn't work out.'

'Well, things didn't work out.'

'I heard that. You okay?'

147

'Tickety-boo. What've you got?'

'Facebook.'

'I thought we'd done that.'

'Well, yes and no,' Benny's rushing now, eager to tell him something. He reins himself in, takes a breath and says, 'What's the golden rule of social networking?'

Luther hangs up his coat. 'Don't do it?'

'No. The golden rule is — only put up information or images you're happy for everyone to see and are happy to put your name to. And the Lamberts seem to have done that, by and large.'

'But?'

'But the problem is, when I say *happy for anyone to see*, it really does mean *anyone*. The problem with social networking, the internet in general, is it's easy for someone to pretend to be someone they're not. For instance,' he stands, 'do you mind?'

Luther gets out of Benny's way, lets him access the old beige computer with 15-inch monitor he's got tottering on his desk — brought here when Traffic had a refit, got themselves some nice flatscreens.

Benny logs on to Facebook, taps a few keys.

Then Luther's looking at his own Facebook page. Except Luther doesn't have a Facebook page.

Benny says, 'I set this up in your name last night.'

Luther looks at it. 'How?'

'Easy. I know your birthday, right? I know where you went to school, uni, blah blah blah.

148

You can easily get these details online. What I didn't have to hand was a photograph of you. But I happen to know you like David Bowie, right? And I know your favourite album.'

'*Low*.'

'Right. So I dig up the cover image for *Low*. Use that as your profile picture. Anybody who knows you, sees it and thinks: *Typical John Luther! Bowie fanatic!* So nobody's got any reason to think this isn't you. Now all I have to do is look up a few old friends of yours. Again, that's easily done because I know where you went to school. I send out a bunch of friend requests.'

'Tell me you haven't done that,' says Luther.

'No way. I value my ability to walk. But listen, the point is, I knocked up this page in ten minutes — for educational purposes only. Just to show you how easy it is, to be someone else online.'

'Okay. Point made. Internet bad. So?'

'So I combed through all the Lamberts' online 'friends'. Sarah Lambert's got 250-odd, Tom Lambert's got 70. He's a very occasional user. So let's put him to one side for the moment, come back to him if we need to. Let's concentrate on Sarah. She's got 253 friends: of those 253 friends, 185 post once a week or more. Of the remaining 68, most are occasional users. What happens a lot is, people start up a new account and go posting happy: what they had for breakfast, funny things the kids have said. But that loses its appeal pretty quickly, and their postings get fewer and fewer as the weeks go by. Some people sign up, make one or two postings, decide it's not for them and are basically never seen again.'

'How many of those we got?'

'About half a dozen: Tony Barron, Malcolm Grundy, Charlotte Wilkie, Ruby Douglas, Lucy Gadd, Sophie Unsworth.'

Luther nods, feeling something now — something coming down the line at him.

'I contacted them all this morning,' Benny says.

'What do you mean? Officially?'

'No chance. I rang round, pretending to be from a charity. Phoned their workplaces. That kind of thing.'

'You're in the wrong job, mate. So how'd it play?'

'Tony Barron, Malcolm Grundy, Charlotte Wilkie, Lucy Gadd, Sophie Unsworth — all of them check out — or seem to at a first pass. It wouldn't be a bad idea to do a bit more due diligence on them, belt and braces.'

'All right, consider it done. But the last name?'

'Ruby Douglas.'

'Who's Ruby Douglas?'

'Ruby Douglas went to the same prep school as Sarah Lambert. Moved away when she was thirteen. So you're talking about a very loose, very old acquaintance — if you can even call her that. Someone Mrs Lambert may remember, but hasn't actually seen for more than twenty-five years.'

'Okay.'

'This 'Ruby Douglas' joined Facebook three

years ago, befriended the Lamberts and a few others the same day. Then didn't make one post. Not a single post, until — '

'Until?'

'Until Mrs Lambert announced she was pregnant.'

Luther's heart is loud in his chest now.

He says, 'Let me see the post.'

Sarah Lambert:
We've been on tenterhooks for weeks and weeks, dying to tell you. Tom and I are pregnant! Four months gone!

'There are fifty-nine comments and thirty-eight 'likes'. One of those 'likes' was posted by Ruby Douglas. That's the only posting she ever made. To anyone. Ever.'

At length, Luther says, 'You tried to contact her? Ruby Douglas?'

'Oh yeah. No deal.'

'We don't think this is actually her, do we?'

'Not a chance.'

'So we're saying Pete Black stalked the Lamberts on Facebook?'

'It's so easily done,' Benny says. 'Seriously. People have no idea of the kind of person who's out there, watching them.'

Luther's sense of triumph fades. He sits. Thinks about it. 'So the announcement of the pregnancy is what got them killed? He was *waiting* for it.'

Benny says nothing. Knows there's nothing to say.

'Can we trace the user back?' Luther says. ' 'Ruby Douglas', find him that way?'

'Whoever it was used a free webmail address to sign up. Not traceable. Posted from different public ISPs.'

'The ISPs any use?'

'One of them's a public Wi-Fi hotspot. The other's a café in East London.'

'The chances of getting security camera footage?'

'After all these months? Pretty small.'

'Worth a try, though. I'll get someone on it.'

But there's more. He can see it in Benny's eyes.

He forces himself to sit still.

Benny says, 'The thing about cyber-stalking, it's not like the real-world equivalent. To someone like this, the internet is like a dessert trolley. He could be watching any number of people. I mean, he could be watching *dozens* of people. Or hundreds. He'd know when they were sick, when they're well. When they were on holiday. When they're at meeetings, out of town. He'd know what their kids look like, what their pets are called, what they watch on TV. He might as well be in their house.'

Luther thinks of Pete Black, out there, omniscient, full of jealousy and hatred.

Waiting for the next child. And the child after that.

Then Teller comes to the door.

He says, 'Boss?'

'The day's not getting better,' she says.

She leads him to her office, where the news is

152

playing on her computer.

On a rolling news channel, Maggie Reilly is being interviewed by a slim young Anglo-Indian woman in Armani and killer heels.

Maggie looks severe and focused, a solemn presence; not at all like she spent a sleepless night waiting for a madman to call and make her famous again.

'Whatever the facts of the matter may be,' she says, 'the man who calls himself Pete Black, the alleged killer of Tom Lambert, Sarah Lambert and now baby Emma Lambert, very clearly blames the police for the tragedy that took place overnight.'

The interviewer leans forward. She has a thin sheaf of papers in one hand. 'But surely no one can blame the police for doing their job?'

'No one's blaming the police,' Maggie says. 'They were doing a difficult job in what were clearly very difficult circumstances. It's just that, in this once instance, perhaps blindly following procedure wasn't the optimum strategy.'

'Are you suggesting the police should have met 'Pete Black's' demands and guaranteed not to stake out the hospitals?'

'Of course, it depends on the police service's operational priorities: catching a killer or saving the child. All I'm saying is, perhaps it's an option they could have explored.'

'But as you know, police are refusing to comment on operational details. They simply won't say whether they had officers posted at hospitals and churches.'

Maggie Reilly laughs. 'I've been a journalist too long to trust a 'no comment' from the police, no matter how prettily it's dolled up.'

'Maggie Reilly, we'll leave it there. Thank you.'

Luther rubs the flat of his hand in slow circles around the crown of his head.

He says, 'This is all such bullshit. The baby was long dead. She's been dead since yesterday. He's mortified by that. The baby dying wasn't part of his plan, whatever his plan was. He can't accept the blame, so it must be someone else's fault. He's passing the burden of guilt on to us.'

'I know that. You know that. Whether people out there,' she gestures, meaning the wider world, 'actually want to believe it. That's a different matter.'

Luther tugs at his ear, considering. He says, 'I don't think I can do this.'

'Do what?'

'This.'

She gives him the Duchess look.

'Things aren't good,' he says. 'At home. Between me and Zoe.'

'I see. She's being a madam, is she?'

'It's not that.'

'It's always that. You're not the first copper to marry a spoiled cow. You won't be the last.'

'Boss, that's not fair. She just — '

Teller gestures with open palms: *Just what?*

Luther rubs his face, exhausted. He needs to shave and change his shirt. 'I'm not right,' he says. 'In myself.'

'So what are you suggesting we do?'

'I've been meaning to ask about leave of

154

absence. Stress leave. Whatever you want to call it.'

'And whose idea was this? Yours, or Princess Tippietoes?'

'Both of ours.'

Teller removes her spectacles, blinks at him like an owl. 'If we take you off this now, it looks like an admission of guilt. It's like declaring we did something wrong.' She puts the glasses back on, shoves them up the bridge of her nose. 'They'll crucify the fucking lot of us.'

Luther practically folds in on himself. Crossed arms, hunched shoulders. 'We shouldn't react to this bullshit anyway,' he says. 'You can't run a case via the media.'

'You can't run a case like this any other way,' she says. 'That's the truth of it. If Pete Black controls the story, he controls everything. We look like the Keystone fucking Cops. That's why we've called a press conference, and that's why you're going to front it.'

He can't speak.

'Welcome to the world of modern policing.' She points to the TV, the endlessly cycled image of Luther in the graveyard, weeping. 'Like it or not,' she says, 'this little Kodak moment makes you the caring, sharing face of the Metropolitan Police Service. People might be quick to stand in judgement where the Met's concerned. But everyone loves a big, tough man who can cry over a baby. Which makes you the public face of the investigation. Congratulations.'

'I'm not competing with this psychopath to make people see who cares the most.'

Teller pinches the bridge of her nose as if she's got the worst migraine in history. 'You need to get out there,' she says, 'and do whatever needs to be done.'

'What else?' he says. 'You want me to cuddle a puppy?'

'This isn't my idea.' She looks pointedly at the ceiling. 'And it's not for negotiation. And don't suggest the puppy thing to Cornish, because he might go for it.'

She means her boss, Detective Chief Superintendent Russell Cornish.

Teller hands him a printed statement. He folds it and slips it into his pocket.

'Doing this,' he says, 'all it's going to do is feed his ego. To see us running around like headless chickens.'

'His ego's not our concern right now.'

Luther thanks her automatically, and shoves the press conference to the back of his mind. It's another thing to deal with later. He crosses the bullpen, finds Howie at her desk.

'Anything in the York or Kintry file?'

Howie swivels on her chair, massaging her neck. She passes him the Adrian York file. It's pitifully thin. 'Not really.'

She tells him that Adrian was out riding his new BMX while his mother, Chrissie, watched from the bedroom window. Chrissie had a clear and uninterrupted view of the park.

The phone rang, a landline. Mobile phones weren't that common in 1996. The caller was Adrian's grandmother, asking when she could bring round his birthday cake. When Chrissie got

156

back to the window, no more than three minutes later, Adrian had gone. She saw his bike lying in the grass and went out to look for him. Ten minutes later, she called Avon and Somerset Police. Attending officers immediately began to search for Adrian's father, David York. The senior investigating officer was Detective Chief Inspector Tim Wilson.

As far as Howie can see, no serious attempt was ever made to rule out a stranger abduction.

Luther glances over the file. 'Where's David York now?'

'In Sydney, Australia.'

'And the Kintry abduction?'

'If this is the same man, you're right. It looks like a first attempt, and a bit of a botch job. There were many more witnesses. Mr Pradesh Jeganathan, a local shopkeeper, apparently witnessed a white male leading a black child towards a small white van. He challenged the driver. There was an altercation during which the alleged abductor actually bit Mr Jeganathan on the ear and cheek.'

'Bit him? They get DNA?'

'Mr Jeganathan suffered a heart attack at the scene. They rushed him to the Bristol Royal Infirmary before he could be forensicated.'

'Bite imprints?'

'Poor quality, but on file.'

'That's something. But teeth can change a lot in fifteen years. Other eyewitnesses?'

'One more. Kenneth Drummond, freelance illustrator. Claimed to have seen a small white van cruising past the Kintry boy a few minutes before the attempted abduction.'

'He give a description of the driver?'

'Nothing that contradicts what we've already got.'

'But nothing to add to it either?'

'Sorry, Boss. It's pretty slim pickings.'

'Fifteen-year-old cold case,' he says. 'It's going to be a long shot.'

'It's more than a cold case. Maggie Reilly was right, actually. It's a scandal.'

'What about the senior on the Kintry case? Pat something. Did we contact her?'

'Inspector Pat Maxwell. Retired. I made a few calls. She died a couple of years back.'

Luther takes that in. Old cases close up like wounds, knit together.

He thanks Howie and heads towards the door.

He hesitates, thinks again, turns back to her. 'Pete Black,' he says. 'Obviously that's not his real name. So why'd he choose it? Of all the names available to him, why that one?'

Howie shrugs. 'It's a pretty *blah* name,' she says. 'It doesn't give much away. There must be a million Pete Blacks in London. They're being eliminated as we speak.'

'Did it mean anything to you, when you heard it?'

Howie shakes her head.

'It did to me,' he says. 'It meant something.'

'Like I say. It's a pretty common name.'

'Yeah,' Luther says. 'But he *chose* it. And our choices reveal us, don't they? So do me a favour, look into it. Not at the files. Go a bit wider.'

'Wilco, Boss.'

Howie sets aside the cold case files and turns to her computer.

★ ★ ★

Luther doesn't know what he's expected to say at the press conference until he's sitting flanked by Teller and her boss, Detective Chief Superintendent Russell Cornish, addressing the media.

'The murder of the Lambert family and the kidnap of baby Emma Lambert is a tragedy for all concerned,' Luther recites. 'For the victims, for their families, for the police, for the country as a whole. The Metropolitan Police would like to extend a plea to the man who has identified himself as 'Pete Black',' he pauses, and his eyes take in the room: the journalists, the cameras, the lights, 'to please contact us on the number listed below. Pete, we know you're in a great deal of emotional turmoil, and we want to help you. We want to talk to you and we will make every effort to do so. But we cannot communicate via the mass media. So please, call the number listed below. Be assured that we'll know it's you we're talking to.'

He looks at the desk, fighting his embarrassment and shame.

'We would also like to appeal to the family of the man who calls himself Pete Black. His voice is being made available to you on many news websites, on the police's own website, and also on a Facebook 'tip' page we've established for this purpose. Somebody out there knows who

Pete Black is. He's a husband or a son, a brother, a friend, a colleague. So we're asking members of the public to please listen to the recording of his voice. Is this someone you know?

'We urge you to bear in mind that 'Pete Black' is in a great deal of pain and that by helping us you will not be betraying him, but helping him.

'Once again I say to the man calling himself Pete Black: we urge you, for your own sake, to please get in contact.'

As he reels off the phone numbers one more time, he surveys the crowd. Then he says, 'No questions at this time. Thank you very much.'

He gathers up his papers and leaves the clamouring journalists, the shifting HD cameras. The void compound eye.

In the corridor he leans against the wall and closes his eyes.

He waits for his heart to slow, the nausea to pass, the anger.

★ ★ ★

All Julian Crouch wanted to be was a rock and roll star.

His dad, George, was the entrepreneur — property and secondhand cars, mostly. He made all the money; married an ex-Miss UK when he was fifty-eight.

That was Julian's mum, Cindy.

George had the rugged Brilliantine looks of a B-movie hero. George had a Soho tailor and wore handmade shoes. He claimed to have played cards with the Krays and exchanged

160

Christmas cards with Nipper Reed. He drank whisky and smoked cigars and fucked Soho hookers and was apparently loved by all who ever set fucking eyes on him.

George was an old man by the time Julian went to the London College of Music, of which George volcanically disapproved. Julian and George barely exchanged a word for eleven years.

Julian was thirty when, in 1997, George had a fatal aneurysm on the toilet during a long weekend in Portugal. He was reading the *Daily Mail*, his dead hairy fists closed around it.

By then, Julian knew he'd never be a rock and roll star. He was too old. But his ambitions had shattered and reformed; he could still be a kind of Simon Napier Bell figure, a manager, a bon viveur, a club owner, an entrepreneur.

So he stepped in and took over the family business. The cars and the properties ticked along nicely, essentially looked after themselves. He left that side of it to his mum.

He moved into recording studios, nightclubs, dotcoms. And fair play, he made a fortune. In 1998, he invested in, then quickly sold, tookool.com, an online store and delivery service for funky urbanites.

Tookool's primary attraction, its free delivery, also proved to be its undoing. It went bust in 2000. But by then, Julian had already sold it, making somewhere in the region of ten million pounds. Not much, as dotcom fortunes went, but not bad.

That was pretty much Julian's entrepreneurial

high point. Over the years, asset after asset turned to dust in his hands. The recording studio, Merciless Inc., failed to attract a single major artist and shut its doors in 2004. The nightclubs bumped along the bottom, did okay, never really caught on.

Julian married Natalie. She wasn't a Miss UK and she never stopped traffic. She did, however, slow it on occasion.

Natalie's divorcing him. Julian estimates that she's about to cost him approximately two and a half thousand pounds per orgasm. Probably the first fifty orgasms were worth it. Probably not enough to fill a can of Red Bull.

Then Cindy died and the world economy fell over and the property empire began to subside beneath his feet.

There was a biblical metaphor in there somewhere, something about sand, but Julian had been too busy trying not to sink to look it up.

He'd been able to shrug off the failure of the nightclubs and the recording studio. His timing had been off, that was all.

The collapse of the property empire, however, was vertiginously alarming.

'Capital,' George had taught him, 'is what you don't spend.'

Julian's capital was spent.

And now Lee Kidman and Barry Tonga stand dripping in his hallway, the hallway he is shortly to lose if he doesn't sell that fucking terrace in Shoreditch to that flash fucking Russian from Moscow on fucking Thames.

Basically, they're here to ask for their money. But Julian's not really listening.

His eyes drift, as they often do, to Lee Kidman's crotch. He finds himself contemplating the animal furled in there, that thick and lazy beast.

Julian is not by inclination homosexual, he's seen Kidman perform in quite a few pornos, pornos of the British variety: middle-aged hookers pretending to be housewives, women who look like they've hastily trimmed their snatches with Bic disposables and no foam, ostensibly offered twenty-five quid for a fuck in the back of a van then — ha ha! — left stranded by the side of the road.

Julian recognizes these films for what they are, comforting fantasies of availability, they're all whores in the end, blah blah blah. He doesn't, in and of themselves, find them erotic or stimulating, not beyond the occasional animal twitch in his crotch for a pleasured moan or an animal groan, or a pale jiggling breast.

But *Lee Kidman's cock!*

Lee Kidman doesn't use a disposable Bic. He looks depilated and smooth as an Action Man. His cock is as thick as Julian's wrist. Julian is fascinated by the laziness of it — the way it's too big to point upwards. It just kind of dangles there. The women stuff it into whatever orifice like half a kilo of uncooked sausages.

Lee Kidman's cock has started to insinuate itself into Julian's dreams. It's not like he wants to do anything with it, let alone have it *inside* him: the thought fills him with a shudder of biological terror — imagine trying to get that thing in your *mouth*!

And it takes Kidman so long to *come*. Although, to be fair, Julian expects it wouldn't take as long with a man. But still.

Kidman is aware of Julian glancing at his crotch. There's a kind of half-smile for it.

Julian says, 'Is the old man still in the house?'

'Yeah,' says Kidman. 'But that copper's not hanging round any more. Which was the point.'

'And you did it right? He got the message.'

'He got the message.'

'And there'll be no comebacks?'

'Nah.'

'Because I don't want to go to prison, Lee.'

Julian is terrified of prison. His therapist calls it cleisiophobia: the fear of being locked in an enclosed space. But it's not that. It's the fear of being locked in an enclosed space with men who have cocks like Lee Kidman.

'Seriously,' Julian says. 'This is an old man living alone in a shitty little house. How hard can it be?'

Kidman and Tonga have the grace to look embarrassed.

Julian says, 'I'm not giving you a fucking penny until you've got that old cunt out of my fucking house. Jesus Christ. You're unbelievable. Coming round here with the job half done. Have some pride.'

Kidman gives him a mock-innocent look.

Barry Tonga just looks blank, stands there with his massive arms crossed, judging him. And Julian doesn't like to be judged. It makes

164

him uncomfortable.

He dreams of just getting out from under this shit, just getting on a plane and flying away.

He's been thinking of moving to Thailand, perhaps opening a little bar. He can see himself in cut-off jeans and flip-flops, generally hanging out.

Of course, if Julian were to get into the Thai bar business, there'd be another tsunami and he'd be left with flotsam and jetsam.

But even that seems better than this: shitty London, shitty properties, shitty old people standing between him and liquidating assets. And the shitty fucking knowledge that George, his dad, would probably know exactly what to do.

★　★　★

Patrick has slept in the park. He's done it before, when Henry's in a mood.

It's the largest open space in London. It's like being in a different epoch. There are bogs and bracken, archaic oak trees. There are herds of red deer, a population of badgers, even parakeets: birds with incongruous, bright feathers and rosy red beaks.

Patrick walks back to the house. He brings a sack of rabbits for the dogs.

Before moving here, he and his dad lived all over. They even lived abroad for a while, he thinks, possibly in France. But it's difficult to be sure. Patrick was very young and not permitted to speak to anybody but Henry.

They were long years but not unhappy; there was always so much to do. And there was just him and Henry; the blinding spotlight of Henry's love, the cold light of Henry's rage.

Now Patrick walks through the front door and there's Henry in the living room. Patrick can almost smell his depression.

When Henry's unhappy you can see the thing inside him, the twisted thing that Patrick thinks of as a demon. It's ill-knit and crooked, full of hate and wrath.

Patrick lingers in the doorway, in case another beating is imminent. He says, 'Dad, what's wrong?'

Henry looks up. He's not a big man and his hair is dark and neat. His eyes are all wrong.

Henry picks up the Sky Plus remote and rewinds to a recorded news broadcast. 'Look at this,' he says. 'Just fucking look at it.'

On TV, Patrick sees a black police officer with broad shoulders. He's sitting behind a long desk, flanked by uniformed officers whom Patrick presumes to be of a higher rank.

'Here he goes,' says Henry. 'Here he fucking goes. Listen.'

On screen, the policeman is saying how sorry he feels for Henry.

'*We know you're in a great deal of emotional turmoil, and we want to help you. We want to talk to you and we will go to every effort to talk to you.*'

Patrick goes cold from his feet to his head.

'Those cunts,' says Henry, blinking and tearful. 'Those fucking cunts. Look at them. Who the fuck do they think they're talking to?'

Henry watches the press conference twice more, mouthing along with it. Patrick doesn't move from his position in the doorway.

'They feel *sorry* for me?' Henry says. 'They're trying to fucking embarrass me. They're trying to fucking show me up. Who are they, eh? Who are these cunts to feel sorry for *me*?'

'I don't know,' says Patrick.

'I'll do them,' Henry says. 'I'll fucking do them. The fucking cunts.'

Henry goes to the cabinet and takes out a disposable mobile phone, still boxed. He opens the box, takes out the phone, takes off the bubble wrap and fits the battery. He puts all the bits of cardboard in a Tesco Metro carrier bag, ready to be thrown in someone else's bin.

All the while, he's muttering to himself. *I'll do you, you cunts. I'll fucking do you. Fucking show me up. I'll do you.*

When Henry's got the phone, then his wallet, he stands waiting in his neat grey coat with the black suede collar, his square-toed Church's shoes. He looks almost small, like an angry bantam. It hurts Patrick to see it.

Henry tells Patrick to drive to Hyde Park. There are few CCTV cameras there.

Henry hates CCTV cameras. He sometimes talks about moving away, moving to a country where it's more difficult to be seen.

Patrick and Henry drive to Hyde Park and sit on a bench.

Henry calls the radio station and rages.

14

Pete Black: 'Are we on air?'

Maggie Reilly: 'You're live on the air to London.'

'Good. I saw what that policeman said about me on the news. The press conference. He was lying about me. That policeman. So let me tell you this. I want him to *apologize*. Properly. I want him to say sorry for the lies he told about me.'

'What lies did he tell? As far as I can see — '

'That I'm pathetic. That I'm in pain. I'm not in pain. I was trying to help. I wanted to help that little baby. And he comes on TV and *insults* me. Well, I've had enough. More than enough. I've had it up to here with scum like that, pricks who think they can talk to me any way they want to. I want an apology. A public apology.'

'I don't think that's going to happen, Pete. I don't think the police will apologize to you.'

'Well, they'd better.'

'And what does that mean?'

'I want you to get a police officer on the line and I want an apology. I know they're listening. I know they're tracing this call. They think they're so clever. They think they're so smart. They think they're whiter than white. Well, I've had enough.'

Silence.

'Either they apologize — or what happens next is their fault.'

168

'What does that mean, Pete? What's going to happen next?'

'That's not for me to say. All I want is for the police to come on here, on the radio, on your show, and say sorry for what they said about me.'

'Pete, you've freely admitted to killing two people.'

'What about all the hookers and all the dealers, eh? What happens to them? All the vandals and all the hoodies and all the dole scum? All these lowlifes, all these generations of parasites living in shitty, dirty, horrible council flats. They get away with murder. The police turn a blind eye to them, don't they?'

'Pete, I'm not sure — '

'If they don't apologize, I'll do it again.'

'Do what again?'

'I think you know what I mean.'

'No, I think London needs you to be very clear here. I think London needs to know exactly what you're saying.'

'I'll tell you what I'm saying. I've got keys to all your houses. I've got keys to all the houses in London. If they don't apologize to me, then I'm going to come for all the mummies and all the daddies and all their little babies. I'm going to let myself into someone's house tonight and I'm going to open them up and I'm going to gobble on their insides and I'm going to fuck them and I'm going to fucking *eat* them, all right? Do you understand me now? Do you fucking feel sorry for me now? Do I sound like I'm in pain now? You lying cunts. Do you understand me? Do you understand what I'm going to do?'

Teller clicks a mouse to stop the playback. 'That's enough of that, I think.'

Luther sits back in the chair. His eyes flick to Cornish. 'There's more?'

'Another minute or so. They killed the live feed, of course.'

'Another minute of — '

'Just ranting,' Teller says. 'Cunt this, cunt that.'

'I need to hear it.'

'You can hear it at your own desk. I've heard enough.'

'We get a location?'

'Hyde Park. Two and a half square kilometres of open parkland. Limited CCTV coverage. Thousands of people moving in thousands of different directions. He might as well have called from the moon.'

Cornish rolls up a sleeve. Doesn't seem to like it. He unrolls it again and buttons the cuff. 'Will he make good on this threat?'

'Yes,' says Luther. 'He's like the rest of them. He's grandiose, self-important, ego-driven. He can't stand to be thought of as weak. He'd rather be hated than pitied. And he'd rather be feared than either.'

'Well,' Teller says. 'If we had a PR problem before, we've got a humdinger now. Can we find him before tonight?'

'How?' says Luther. 'Tell me how, I'll do it.'

'I don't know. Sprinkle some fairy dust. Do your thing.'

'Okay. Then let me do what he's asking. Let

170

me go on TV, on radio, whatever, and apologize.'

'That's not going to happen,' Cornish says.

'There's a family in London who won't see the sunrise tomorrow if it doesn't. You can bet he's already picked them out.'

He outlines what Benny told him about the likelihood of Facebook stalking. Cornish and Teller listen, increasingly despondent.

Then Cornish says, 'But if we give this prick what he wants today, what does he ask for tomorrow? Do we give him that, too? And if we do, what does he ask for the next day? And the day after that? And the day after that?'

Luther sags, knowing he's right.

'Take me off the case,' he says.

'I beg your pardon?'

'It may be enough to appease him.'

'We already talked about this. We don't give in to blackmail. More importantly, we can't be *seen* to give in to blackmail.'

'With respect, Boss, we've got to react somehow. We've got to give him something.'

'And if we do,' Cornish says, 'we give a green light to all the loonies that come after him. Psychopaths don't get to use the media to control the investigation of their crimes.'

'Long term, absolutely. Short term, it's the best tactic I can think of. Release a statement saying you've suspended me, pending investigation into my running of the case. Hang me out to dry.'

'Holy Christ,' says Teller. She leans over, digs in her drawer, removes a bottle of aspirin with a tamper-proof lid. Struggles to open it.

'You can absolutely do this,' says Luther. 'You say the police don't respond to a criminal's demands. But you can imply I did something wrong, say I mishandled the chain of evidence. Say I'm emotionally incapable. God knows they're showing footage of me crying about every ten seconds. That might be enough to assuage him, mollify his ego.'

Teller doesn't answer.

Neither does Cornish.

'If we don't do this,' Luther says, 'he'll make good on what he said. Tonight. And he knows what he's doing. He's been doing this stuff for a long time without us even noticing him. He's probably got a pool of possible targets. Families like the Lamberts. Houses he knows inside out. We can't just sit back and let it happen. We can't do that, can we?'

There's a long silence. Then Cornish says, 'John, I understand. I honestly do. But we can't grab our ankles and let this psycho have his way with us.'

'Sir,' Luther says. 'Seriously.'

Teller warns him with a glance: *Shut. Up.*

'It doesn't matter how we dress it up,' Cornish says. 'We'd be sending a clear message. We'd be telling the entire world that we're running scared of this prick, that he gets exactly what he wants from us. We can't have that. We just can't. For the precedent.'

Luther walks out of Teller's office. He can feel the eyes on him. All the coppers in the bullpen. He must have been shouting.

Howie lifts a file from her desk and waves it to

catch his attention. It's a shy, defiantly jaunty little gesture, and in that moment he loves her for it.

He approaches. 'How we looking on that thing?'

'Fine,' she says. 'Actually, Boss, can I borrow you for a minute?'

'Of course. Bring those.' He nods at the files.

Howie scoops up the York and Kintry files, neatens them, follows Luther to his narrow office.

She nods to Benny and shuts the door. Luther closes the blinds.

'Is it just me,' Benny says, 'or is this actually getting pretty bad?'

'It's actually getting pretty bad,' Luther says.

Howie and Benny give him a sympathetic look. He shrugs it off; he's been getting them all day, since weeping at the churchyard.

He takes off his jacket, hangs it over the back of his chair, loosens his tie.

He sits and rubs his face. Takes a series of long, slow breaths. Closes his eyes. Keeps them closed. 'Okay. Talk me through it. Where are we?'

'Well,' says Howie, 'we know we're dealing with a very particular animal here. We also know this isn't his first offence; he's far too confident. Too self-important. He's narcissistic with an over-developed sense of grievance. And to judge by his voice, word selection, intonation, he's in his late twenties at the earliest, more like mid-thirties plus. Put all that together, you're looking at a likely serial offender.'

'But it's definitely his first time with this MO.'

'With this MO, yeah. But MO and signature are two different things. MO consists of everything he requires to carry out the crime: type of crime, victimology, the setting of the crime, method used. MO changes. Signature doesn't. So what was he doing before he cut open the Lamberts? We've been looking at one credible prior offence, maybe two: the abduction of Adrian York and the attempted abduction of Thomas Kintry. This is Bristol, mid-nineties. So we're talking fifteen, sixteen years ago. And these were slightly older children. Adrian York was six. Thomas Kintry was twelve.'

'That's abnormal for a start,' Benny says. 'These men, they usually have a very specific preference — age, sex, ethnicity, hair colour.'

'Okay,' says Howie. 'So he abducts children. We don't know what criteria apply because, even if we assume these cases are genuinely linked, victimology seems inconsistent. At best, he's working from a radically different MO after an apparent fifteen-year silence. During those fifteen years, we can imagine that either he's resisted the urge to offend, he's been in prison, or — '

'Or he's been offending under the radar,' Luther says. 'So where are we on the name? Pete Black?'

'Well,' says Howie. 'I'm getting to that. That's actually what I wanted to talk about. It could be a coincidence, but . . . '

'But what?'

She dry-swallows, excited and nervous. She slips a note from the thinnest of the files and reads from it. 'In the Netherlands 'Zwarte Piet', meaning Black Pete, is a servant of Sinterklaas. He delivers presents on the fifth of December and . . . ' She looks at Luther.

He's opened his eyes. He's looking at her.

'He takes naughty kids away in the empty bags,' she says. 'In some stories, the Zwarte Piets themselves were kidnapped as kids, and the kidnapped kids make up the next generation of Zwarte Piets.'

'Which fits with the Adrian York abduction,' Luther says. 'Which was a child abduction nobody even *believed* was an abduction. Not until it was too late.'

'So what if, during the last fifteen years he *hasn't* been inactive, or in prison? What if he's just been *quiet?*'

She begins laying documents on Luther's desk. Doing so, she tells him that numerous cultures have a mythical bogeyman who's portrayed as a man with a sack on his back, a man who carries naughty children away.

'There's *El Hombre de la Bolsa*, meaning the Sack Man. In Armenia and Georgia it's the Bag Man. In Bulgaria, it's *Torbalan*. In Hungary it's *zsákos ember*, 'the person with a sack'. In North India, he's the *Bori Baba* or 'Father Sack'. In Lebanon he's *Abu Kees*, that's literally 'The Man with a Bag'. In Vietnam, it's Mister Three Bags. In Haiti, it's The Gunnysack Man.'

Luther looks at the images: trolls and ogres and twisted fairytale things, scrawny, beak-nosed old men bearing away bawling children.

He stands. His legs won't let him sit. He paces the room.

He says, 'I think this is good. I think this has meaning. Benny, I need you both to trawl records, look for a link to any of these characters. Black Peter. The Gunnysack Man. Father Sack, whoever. Anything pops up, anything, let me know straight away.'

★   ★   ★

At 4.07, Cornish and Teller front the second hastily convened press conference of the day.

DCI Luther is not present.

Cornish reads the following statement:

'As you know, the Metropolitan Police Service is investigating a very serious offence and has no comment to make regarding any threats made by the man who calls himself Pete Black.

'I'd like to remind you at this time that whoever committed this atrocity against Mr and Mrs Lambert and their child, nobody made him or her do these things. He or she perpetrated these horrors of his or her own free will. If the perpetrator of these crimes is indeed the man calling himself Pete Black, then the Metropolitan Police Service once again extends its heartfelt wish for him to hand himself over to the proper authorities. He can be assured that he will be treated in full accordance with the law.

'We believe that the phone calls made to a London radio station are in fact a cry for help from a very desperate man. And we're keen, if he'll let us, to give him the help he needs.

'However, given the danger to the public this man represents, let me reiterate that we're asking members of the public to help us identify and apprehend him. Someone out there knows who he is. In order to hasten this process, the Metropolitan Police Service has authorized a reward of one hundred thousand pounds for information leading to the arrest and conviction of the man calling himself Pete Black.

'That concludes the statement. I will, however, take one or two questions. Let's keep it orderly please, ladies and gentlemen.'

Here they come, in a flashing, overlapping babble:

'Will you be making an apology to Pete Black?'

'I refer you to my statement, which you should consider the last word on this matter.'

'Will Pete Black kill again if you refuse to do as he says?'

'That would be entering into unwarranted realms of speculation.'

'How big is the threat?'

'That's impossible to gauge at this time.'

'If Pete Black does kill another family, will heads roll in the police service?'

'I'm not entirely sure I understand what that question means.'

'Who takes responsibility for signing off DCI Luther's tactics?'

'I do.'

'Has DCI Luther been removed from the case because of tensions inside the investigation?'

'DCI Luther has not been removed from the case.'

'Are you willing to back DCI Luther?'

'Absolutely.'

'Have you drawn up a psychological profile?'

'No comment.'

'What do we know about the killer? Has he done this before?'

'No comment.'

'Should you have known earlier?'

'Once again, I don't understand the question.'

'Do you have faith in your senior investigating officer?'

'I have absolute faith in my senior investigating officer.'

'Then where is he?'

'You'll appreciate that he's busy.'

'Is he off the case?'

'No.'

'Shouldn't he be?'

'No.'

'Did you make a mistake by not giving Pete Black an apology?'

'No. We did not.'

'How many Londoners are in danger tonight because of questionable operational decisions taken by DCI Luther?'

'If any Londoners are in danger tonight, and I stress the word 'if', then it's because of a man calling himself Pete Black. Once again, I urge Londoners to search their hearts and their consciences. If you know who this man is, please contact us on the hotline. That's it. Thank you, ladies and gentlemen, and good afternoon.'

While Cornish and Teller address the mobbed press room, Luther and Howie huddle at Benny's desk.

'I trawled the records,' Benny says. 'Looked at everyone on the sex offenders' register. I went through the list of names.'

'Anyone we like?'

'I'm not feeling it. So I looked off-register a bit, followed my nose.'

'How far?'

'I get to thinking, what if, during his years off the radar, our Pete's *not* abducting kids. Maybe he's *buying* them.' He shows Luther a mugshot. 'This is Vasile Sava. He's a child broker. He arranged the illegal adoption of babies from all over Eastern Europe. Anybody tried to buy or sell a baby in London, chances are he'd know them.'

'And why do we like him exactly?'

'Because when they arrested him and trawled his database, a 'Mr Torbalan' was included in his list of clients. That's one of the names for the guy who steals away the bad kids.'

Luther claps his shoulder. 'Nice work, Ben. Where does he live?'

Benny hands him a printout.

'Take disinfectant,' he says. 'Plus maybe garlic and a crucifix.'

*　*　*

Bill Tanner watches the lunchtime news, because he always does.

He's surprised to see the copper who came

round the other night sitting hunched behind the desk at some press conference or other, looking trapped and uncomfortable.

Bill feels for him; he's a decent bloke, and it's always a sad thing to see a big man made to look small.

Bill turns the telly over but there's nothing else on. He tries a bit of Radio 2; it's the same story. He catches snippets of it, knows it's horrible — a story he doesn't want to hear, more evidence that the world's going to hell in a fucking handbasket.

Dot's better off out of it.

Thinking of her gives Bill that trembly feeling in his shanks. He supposes it's loneliness, but loneliness is such a silly word, a pop-song word, a Herman's Fucking Hermits word. It's got very little to do with the awful feeling in his guts and in the top of his legs. If he sits still, he knows it'll sweep up his spine and round the back of his head and he'll start to cry like a fucking baby. In moments like this, he sees that the house stinks of cold and dirt.

He grabs the lead and collar from the hook on the back of the kitchen door. Little Paddy goes mad. He always goes mad for a walk.

Bill shuffles over to grab his grey windcheater and his Hush Puppies. He zips his windcheater to his chin and puts on the bobble hat Dot bought for him.

Then he and Paddy step outside.

It's all a bit awkward. Bill needs a walking stick and one hand's still in plaster. So he has to slip the loop of the lead over the plaster and kind of hook it there. Luckily Paddy's got a bit of arthritis in his hips, Yorkies get that, and he's happy to trot at Bill's heel, stopping every now and again to cock his leg. He's a fearless little thing, and Bill admires that.

Time was, he'd have been embarrassed by little Paddy. He was Dot's dog, really. He wasn't a man's dog; a man wants a companion, not one of these ridiculous fierce fuckers all the young ones have these days, the mean little ones with the tiny eyes and the puffed-out chests and the bandy legs. When Bill was a bit younger, the dogs you were scared of were German Shepherds and Dobermans.

Working on the bins in the sixties and seventies, you'd swap stories of fierce dogs. The dogs you swapped stories about were always black and tan.

But those dogs were intelligent and handsome; even a ratty and half-fed Alsatian had understanding in its eyes, that's why the police used them. And Dobermans were used as guard dogs for good reason. These muscular little things, all jaw and chest, they looked like fucking idiots, like wife beaters.

Bill and Paddy wander along, a bit shaky but doing all right.

He pops into Mr Patel's to pick up a copy of the *Racing Post* and twenty Benson & Hedges, then wanders down to William Hill. Even the bookie's not what it was.

A bookie's used to have a sorry, collegiate air about it, all the labourers and the cabbies and the alkies. He'd pop in after his shift ended, it was still early. Dot would be at work. He'd spend a pound or two, go home and have a nap. Then he'd tidy round a little bit: Dot always came home to a clean house, although that wasn't something you talked about down the pub.

But Bill was brought up in the navy, he knew how to keep things neat and tidy and everything in its place — and Dot worked long hours and came home footsore.

Bill never did the laundry, and he never cooked a meal in his life except sometimes a bit of egg on toast for the kids when Dot was poorly. (More often, he'd send them down the chippie and they'd eat a nice bit of cod in front of *Nationwide* — that Sue Lawley and her legs.)

But he'd happily do a bit of hoovering, wash up the breakfast things, have a tidy round, do a bit of dusting, make the bed (he got satisfaction out of making the sheets drum-tight). He'd clean the windows, have a potter round the garden if the weather was nice. Then he'd spend an hour at the allotment and be home in time for tea.

It seemed to him that that whole world, black and white, three channels, Sue Lawley and her legs, a decent shabby bookies, fried egg sandwiches, a pub without horrible fucking music blaring in your ears all day, it was all gone, like men wearing hats.

Bill bets a few quid, watches a few races, doesn't make a penny but enjoys himself anyway.

Then he goes out. Poor little Paddy's tied to a lamp post. His little legs are shaking with cold and the terror of abandonment and he's looking up at Bill with a kind of pleading relief. Bill feels a bit guilty. He says, 'Sorry there, boy. Was I gone a long time? Was I?'

He doesn't care who's listening. He's an old bloke with an old dog, fuck them all.

It takes him a long time, but he stoops and lets the dog jump into his arms. Little Paddy cringes into his barrel chest, like he's trying to push inside Bill.

A Sikh kid, the first softness of dark beard round his chops, eases up to him. 'You all right, mate?'

When Bill was this kid's age, he'd never in a million years, a hundred million years, have considered calling an elder 'mate'. He'd have been clipped round the ear. But the kid doesn't mean any disrespect, in fact he means the opposite of it. Bill responds by saying, 'Yes, I'm fine thank you, mate.'

A twelve-year-old and an eighty-five-year-old calling each other mate. There's got to be some good in that, hasn't there?

The kid says, 'Are you sure?'

Bill says, 'I'm a bit stiff, but I'm all right.'

The kid nods, a bit embarrassed Bill thinks, and walks on.

Bill makes his way home. He's knackered now and his legs hurt, he needs to pop a couple of pills. But he's glad he got some fresh air. Paddy's light as a bird and, cuddled to Bill's chest, he radiates a kind of desperate satisfaction, a bliss just to be there.

Bill's nearly home when the two big blokes step out of the alley between the blocks. The big white one, Lee Kidman, in his leather jacket and his dyed hair, the fat Asian-looking one, Barry Tonga, in his baggy shorts and oversized white trainers, a fucking handkerchief or something tied round his head.

The first thing that happens, before Bill can open his mouth is that he pisses himself in fear. He hardly knows it's happening — there's a big, warm spread across his pants and down his leg and then straight away it goes cold. It's probably been more than seventy years since Bill wet himself but he knows the feeling straight away and it makes him want to weep in rage and shame. He cuddles the little dog to his chest because he doesn't want it to see. He knows how stupid that is, except Paddy's the last part of Dot that he's got, she loved the little fucker and the little fucker loves Bill, and he's a weak little thing really, all skin and bone.

The thugs chest-push Bill into the alley.

'You silly old cunt,' says Kidman. He looks like he fancies himself; one of them blokes who thinks he's God's gift, but who actually gives women the creeps.

The other bloke, his big moon head on massive shoulders, he's a mystery. He's got tattoos all up his arms and down his legs. He's wearing three-quarter-length shorts. In this weather.

Kidman grabs Bill's bad wrist and a jolt of agony shoots up his arm. He says, 'Take his offer. Take his money. Look at you. Pissing yourself. You should be in a home.'

'You fucking prick,' says Bill, and is horrified to note that he's weeping. He doesn't want to but he can't help it. And he can't think of anything to say. He's lain in bed for hours planning what he's going to say to these geezers, should they come for him again. He'd rehearsed it again and again, the withering contempt, the dignity he'd stand on. But now all those words are gone and he's standing there dripping with his own piss and he's crying; the words are flown straight out of his head. He cuddles the little dog. It cringes there. It shakes and shivers, feeling Bill's fear.

Kidman shoves Bill into the wall. Bill staggers back. Kidman plucks the skinny dog from Bill's arms, holds it to his face, makes queer little kissy-kissy noises.

'Who's this, then?' he says in a mincing poof's register, horrible coming from such a big man. 'Who's this liddle thing, this little precious thing, then?'

'You leave him be,' says Bill. 'He's only a dog.'

Kidman doesn't address Bill directly. He speaks to the quivery, wet-eyed Paddy, tickles him under the wishbone chin with a great spatulate finger, manicured and pink-nailed.

'I am going to fuck you up,' Kidman says to Paddy. 'I am going to fuck you up, liddle doggie, yes I am.'

'Don't,' says Bill. 'You leave him alone.'

'Because your daddy didn't listen to my daddy,' says Kidman, 'no he didn't. He didn't, did he? And now I'm going to fuck you up, little doggie. I am going to fuck you up. Say bye bye now. Say bye bye to daddy!'

He raises Paddy's paw between thumb and

forefinger, makes Paddy wave to Bill.

'You fucking bully,' says Bill. 'You horrible fucking bully.'

'I am,' says Kidman. 'I am a horrible bully, aren't I, liddle doggie? I am a howwible, wowwible, liddle bully.'

He takes Paddy's neck in one hand, Paddy's hips in the other, then he twists like he's wringing out a towel.

Paddy yelps as his spine breaks. He voids his bowels and his bladder. Kidman laughs and skips backwards to avoid it, dropping Paddy to the ground.

Paddy makes a horrible noise of a kind Bill has never heard before. He wouldn't even know what to call it.

Bill howls. He draws back what used to be a feared fist, a great hammer of a knuckle sandwich, but now it's freckly and tremulous. He takes a step anyway.

But Tonga waddles in and grabs him in a full nelson. Bill can smell his sweet aftershave.

'Stop now, Poppy,' says Tonga, almost kindly. 'Stop now.'

Bill flails and windmills, he tries to stamp on Tonga's feet. He howls again.

Kidman looks down at Paddy, then looks at Bill and winks.

'You fucker,' says Bill. 'You mean fucker. You horrible fucker.'

Kidman cackles. Then he draws back his great foot and kicks Paddy fifteen feet down the alley.

Paddy's still alive when he lands. Bill can tell because his wet eyes are looking at him with adoring incomprehension, as if Bill could stop this happening with just a stern command and a point of the finger. Because Bill is God to little Paddy, his Dot's Yorkshire terrier.

Kidman saunters down the alley, grinning and self-conscious. He puts his big, handsome, horrible face to Bill's and says, 'Where's your wife buried?'

Bill doesn't understand.

'I said, where's your wife buried?'

'That's none of your business.'

'It is if I want to dig her up and fuck her.'

Bill struggles, but Tonga holds him until all the strength is gone. When Tonga lets go, all Bill can do is sag to the ground, sit with his back to the alley wall, his legs out before him.

Kidman and Tonga watch for a bit without speaking. Kidman is grinning ear to ear. Tonga looks a bit more sombre. But then, he's got a sombre face.

Then Tonga checks his watch and chin nods. Places to be.

They walk away.

⋆　⋆　⋆

Zoe leaves work the second she can. She takes the glass lift to street level and steps outside, belting her coat.

She walks. She takes a right, then a left. There's a little road at the bottom, a crooked lane. And that's where Mark's car is waiting; a tired-looking Alfa Romeo. Mark is at the wheel. Her heart swells to see him.

187

She slides in next to him, the smell of old vinyl and leather and roll-ups. The ashtrays overflow with crushed cigarettes.

They drive to his place, a big double-fronted Edwardian in Camberwell. They light candles and sit at his kitchen table in the remodelled basement. The table is scarred, antique, beautiful.

He pours them each a glass of wine, then concentrates on skinning up a joint.

She sips her wine and says, 'What am I going to do?'

'What do you want to do?'

'I don't know.'

'I could take you there. To the police station.'

'If he's not answering his phone, it's because he doesn't want to talk.' For half a minute, she concentrates on tearing a cigarette paper to shreds, flattening the pieces in front of her, making them neat. 'This is it, see? This is what happens. When things are fine, it's fine. But when things go bad, he just ups and disappears. Surely if he's going through all this, surely this is the time he should need me around?'

'Maybe he doesn't want to worry you.'

'I'm worried enough. I'm frightened for him. I'm tired of being frightened for him. I don't know.' She looks at her lap, the shreds of paper. 'I don't know.'

'It's pretty intense,' says Mark. 'Everything he's going through.'

'So you're defending him now?'

'Christ, no. But I didn't come here to bury him, either. I feel for the man. I watched him cry

188

over a dead baby today. And here I am, sleeping with his wife.'

She gives him a flirty smile. 'Don't be presumptuous.' She moves her wine glass around on the table like a planchette on a Ouija board.

She bites her lower lip, thinking it over. Then she says, 'Can I tell you something?'

'Anything you want.'

'My worst confession? It's pretty bad.'

'Is it something you did?'

'Shit, no. I've never done anything. I've been good my entire life.'

Mark doesn't comment in the way that most men would, working in a double meaning, an undercurrent of sex. He just holds her gaze for a moment, scratches at his short beard, lights the joint.

'Do you ever get these thoughts,' Zoe says, 'these feelings, that go round and round your head at three in the morning and you're ashamed of feeling them?'

'Everyone does.'

He takes a few puffs, then passes the joint to Zoe. She hesitates before accepting it.

'Sometimes I actually wish he was dead,' she says. 'I lie in bed and fantasize about him actually dying. Because it just seems so much easier that way. My problems would be solved — I could mourn John, and be free, and not hate myself for it. And everyone would feel bad for me, instead of thinking I'm a total bitch.'

She inhales, holds her breath for as long as she can, then exhales a thin plume of smoke. Passes the joint to Mark.

'Thoughts like that don't make you a bitch,' he says. 'They're just an escape fantasy. We all have them. The same thing happens with the spouses of terminal patients. It doesn't make them bad, either. It's just one of the ways we cope.'

They smoke for a while. The candles flutter, throw black dancing shapes on the wall.

'I'm leaving him,' she says. 'I've had enough of this bullshit. I'm leaving him.'

'Good,' Mark says.

He reaches out, takes her hand. They finish the joint and go upstairs.

15

Vasile Sava, the baby broker, rents a basement apartment in Maida Vale.

Howie and Luther take the short steps down to the front door, check out the grilled windows.

Howie knocks. She's got a good police knock. They wait.

It's 5.37 p.m.

At 5.38, Howie knocks again.

At length, Sava comes to the door. He's barefoot in an old muscle T-shirt and faded Levis, a little ragged at the cuffs. He's pumped up like a bouncy castle, brown hair waxed into a vaguely military flat-top. He looks like he should be forcing ethnic minorities to kneel before shooting them in the base of the skull and rolling their bodies into a ditch.

Actually, he runs a company called Primo Minicabs.

Luther and Howie badge him, ask if they can come in and talk.

They spend a few moments doing the dance: *What about? We'd just like to ask you a few questions.* Then Sava gestures with his head: *Follow me.*

Sava looks like he's doing okay. It's a nice flat, somewhat gloomy with dark wood and Turkish-looking rugs. A 46-inch widescreen with hi-gloss bezel.

The open-plan living room and kitchen has a

humid smell, not quite unpleasant. Across the longest wall are arranged a number of large glass terrariums.

Luther digs his hands in his pockets, ducks down to look. 'What've we got here?

'Death's head cockroaches,' Sava says. His English is good, just the hint of an accent. He's been here for eighteen years.

'Blimey,' says Luther. 'They're big sods.'

'Scary big. But easy to care for.'

'What's this?'

'Chilean centipede.' Sava kneels, points out a segmented, multilegged blue horror the length of Luther's hand. 'These over here, they're red-kneed tarantulas. Over here, that's a Mexican black king snake.'

Luther meets the impassive yellow eye of the black snake. He casts a glance at Howie.

She's over in the kitchen, arms crossed, trying not to look grossed out.

Luther considers the iguana in the largest tank: a sand-coloured creature, dewlapped and spiny, on a bone-pale branch. Then he ambles over to join Howie while Sava fusses like an old maid round the kitchen, making coffee. He says, 'So why are we here?'

'Because we need advice.'

'On what?'

'Stolen babies.'

Sava's busy grinding coffee beans. The machine makes a high dentist noise.

'We're not here to go digging up old allegations,' Luther says. 'We honestly just need some guidance.'

'So I guess this'll be the baby that was taken. The crazy radio guy. The dead lady, whatever.'

Luther nods.

'Then you're talking to the wrong man,' Sava says. 'The baby trade goes in the *other* direction. Babies move from Eastern Europe to England. Not the other way round.' He reads Luther's expression, the curled lip. 'What? You don't like that?'

'Not much.'

'Of course! Human rights activists are outraged! It's *wrong* to buy or sell a person! Traffickers are interested only in money. They're scum. Where were you born, DCI Luther?'

'London.'

'Right. Your parents?'

'London.'

'Their parents?'

'What's your point?'

'My point is: if there's one thing worse than a bad home in a rich country, it's no home in a poor country. So an unwanted child finds a happy home in London or Barcelona — '

He's building up quite a head of steam. Luther wonders briefly about roid rage, the aggressive hypomania associated with steroid abuse. He fingers the pepper spray in his pocket, moves it round and round in his palm.

'Is it such a bad thing,' Sava says, 'to find out your parents want you so badly they're willing to pay money for you? To break the law? Put themselves at risk to give you a loving home? How can that be a bad thing? I don't understand. Please explain.'

'You don't sell people,' Luther says. 'They're not cattle.'

'No?'

'No.'

'Twenty years ago,' Sava says, 'the news in England shows terrible conditions in Romanian orphanages. Kids are naked, starving, covered in shit. Dying. So thousands of Western families decide to adopt these orphans, okay? Save them from these terrible shit lives. But alongside the legal market, a black market springs up. Romania's a failed communist state, remember. Everywhere you look, pockets are being lined, palms are being greased. The usual story. So because of this corruption, the European Union puts pressure on the Romanian government. Not to sort out the illegal adoptions but to *stop foreign adoptions altogether.*

'All these babies, all these young kids. They've been approved for adoption to rich Western families! Officially approved! Rubber stamped! They're living in filth and squalor, like dogs, but soon they're going to get out, get away, move to Brighton, Amsterdam, Madrid. But no. This ban means they have to stay in Romania. They don't get a family. They don't get nothing. They're left behind to freeze and starve and be fucked in the ass and in the mouth. Have you ever seen one of these places?'

'No.'

'But you think you've seen some pretty bad things, right? All coppers say that. It's part of the image. *Oooh, the things we've seen.* Well, fuck you. And do you know the real irony?'

Luther ponders the malignant pets in their muggy glass tanks, their unblinking eyes under pale grey rocks. One tank is full of crickets. They struggle to crawl over each other like passengers escaping an underground fire. Hundreds of them.

He says, 'I don't know. Tell me.'

'Who goes on to abuse, eh? Who goes on to fuck kids in the ass? People who were fucked in the ass when *they* were kids! On and on it goes. So fucking high-minded pricks like you with all your morals and all your distaste, telling me it's wrong to sell people. It's *you* who leaves these kids in these terrible shitholes because it's so *dirty* to buy and sell a human being. Well, when you go to bed tonight I want you to think about all those kids who didn't get adopted back in 2001. I want you to think of them being fucked in the ass by men in blue uniforms. Then I want you to imagine those kids going on to rape the kids who were born *since* 2001. And in ten, twenty years, I want you to imagine the kids born since 2001 raping the kids being born today. And on and on it goes. Because of assholes like you.'

He takes a breath. His hands are shaking. Cables of vein running up his arms. He drains his dainty little coffee.

'The people who want to do this,' he says, gesturing to the air above him. 'English people desperate to adopt children. They're not monsters. The people they buy the children from aren't monsters either — not for the most part. And people like me, people whose only crime is to introduce supply to demand, I'm not a monster either. So if you're looking for someone who'd indulge a man who wanted to cut a baby from its mother's womb, then fuck you for looking in the wrong place.'

'Okay,' Luther says. 'I can see this means a lot to you. But you need to calm down, okay?'

'I'm calm.'

He's not.

'We're not looking at you,' Luther says. 'But we may be looking for someone you turned away. Somebody who came to you, made the mistake you think I'm making. A monster who thought he was coming to see a monster. Maybe used the name Torbalan.'

'These men, I don't deal with them. Not ever.'

'But you know of them. These men.'

'If I did, what would happen?'

'I don't know what you mean.'

'The reward. I saw it on TV. A hundred thousand. Is it still available?'

'Yes.'

'Do I have to sign anything?'

'You'd have to make an official statement and put your name to it, yes. If the information you give leads directly to a successful prosecution, the money's yours.'

'But there must be other channels, right? Faster ways.'

'I'm not playing this game. Two minutes ago, it was all about the kids.'

'No. Two minutes ago it was all about hypocrisy. People like you, who pretend to care — but who don't really give a shit.'

'I'm asking nicely,' Luther says. 'If you have a name, give me a name. Please.'

'No.'

Luther looks at Howie and laughs. He says, "No'?'

'Bring me money, I'll give you a name.'

'What name?'

'The name of the man who sent Mr Torbalan to me.'

'You could be saving lives,' Luther says. 'Instead, you're going to do this?'

'I could have spent the last six years saving lives. And making childless people happy.'

'I know you're bitter.'

'I'm not bitter. I'm poor.'

Luther thinks. He says, 'Okay. I'll see what I can do. DS Howie, would you mind stepping outside and calling our commanding officer? Please enquire if it's possible to arrange an urgent cash payment to Mr Sava?'

Howie produces her mobile, waves it. 'Will do, Boss.'

Luther and Sava wait in silence until Howie's gone.

Then Luther loosens his tie.

'The worst of it is,' he says, slipping the rolled-up tie into his pocket, 'you made a pretty good argument back then. Not one I'd agree with, but one I'd be obliged to think about if I was trying to refute it. You're obviously a smart man.'

'A smart man who has something you want.'

Luther acknowledges this with a gesture of the hand.

Sava smiles, shrugs.

Luther punches him in the face; a short jab with the weight of his shoulder behind it.

Sava falls to the floor. Luther kicks him in the ribs, then grabs his collar, hauls him to his feet and rams him headfirst into the wall of glass terrariums.

Tanks crash. Liberated crickets dance on Sava's head and shoulders. They flit and skip across the floor.

The black snake glides down Sava's arm, onto the carpet.

In one upended tank, tarantulas stir.

Luther drags Sava to his feet and throws him into the iguana tank. It doesn't break: it's made of heavy glass. But the impact throws it to the ground.

The floor hops with crickets; it crawls with spiders. A huge cockroach scuttles over Luther's shoe as he jams Sava's wrist between his shoulder blades and gives it a twist.

He presses Sava's face into the hardwood floor. For a moment he's driven to keep pushing until Sava's skull fractures then collapses under the weight of his hand.

Luther bends, puts his lips to Sava's ear. 'You don't understand,' he says. 'I really, really need your help.'

★　★　★

Howie waits outside in the cold, hands in pockets, stamping her feet for warmth, wishing she still smoked. But no one smokes any more,

198

it's one of those things. You smoke and people make you feel all weird about it.

She hears the sound of shattering glass, a muted bellow.

She glances nervously left and right.

She remembers being nine years old, a good girl who already wanted to be a police officer. A girl called Isabel dared her to steal something from the corner shop. Howie took a packet of Batchelor's Super Noodles. For weeks she privately wept, believing a thief could never be a police officer; not even after she slipped back into the shop and quietly replaced the Super Noodles on the shelf.

Now, in the cold of a Maida Vale cul-de-sac, she thinks for a bit, listens to the sounds of muffled violence and wonders if she should call for backup.

She decides probably not.

She walks to the corner, where she's out of earshot but can visually monitor the entrance to the flat.

She's only there for a minute before Luther walks out, buttoning his coat. He walks towards Howie, silently challenging her to say something.

Howie doesn't say anything.

Luther nods. 'We need to speak to a man called Steve Bixby,' he says. 'He's the man who put 'Mr Torbalan' in contact with Sava.'

'Okey dokey,' she says. 'Just point me in the right direction.' Her voice is shaking.

Luther walks to the car.

Howie spots movement on his wide back. She half jogs a couple of steps and squints.

It's a huge cricket, the hooks at the ends of its chitinous legs hooked into the weave of Luther's overcoat.

'Boss,' she says.

He glances over his shoulder. 'What?'

'Big bug.'

He brushes at it. Can't reach.

Howie steps up, hesitates, then brushes the cricket away in a sweeping motion. It lands on the pavement and plods towards the shelter of a wheelie bin. The cold will kill it soon.

Howie opens the passenger door for Luther, then closes it behind him. She jogs round to the driver's seat and gets in.

★   ★   ★

Henry began to think about other people's babies after all the other ways of growing his little family had gone variously and unpredictably wrong.

He began watching people on the streets, in shops, on buses, on the tube. Envious of their lives, he fell in love with them, with these perfect couples, these perfect little families.

Then, as now, he dressed to blend in. On winter evenings he liked to wear a business suit and a three-quarter-length overcoat in charcoal grey. A muted tie, Church's shoes, tortoiseshell spectacles and a discreet, slightly old-fashioned leather briefcase.

On summer evenings he wore cargo shorts and Nikes, carried a ballistic nylon laptop bag that didn't contain a laptop — it contained the same murder kit he carried in his discreet, slightly old-fashioned briefcase: a balaclava helmet, a length of nylon rope, a Leatherman multitool, a roll of duct tape, a small jemmy, a screwdriver, an awl, syringes, scalpels, a roll of medium-sized kitchen bin liners, a serrated hunting knife.

Henry liked to follow them home. Usually, something was wrong; they lived in a flat with a downstairs security door, or with security cameras. Sometimes he couldn't define what it was; a house had a vibe, an aura. It might have something to do with the architecture, perhaps, or the precise angle at which a bedroom window intersected with a street corner.

But he still recalls with a thrilling tingle in his testicles the first Perfect Time.

She was small, olive-skinned. She wore a short skirt that made her legs seem long. She had short hair in a feathered pixie cut that appealed to him. And she was wearing trainers with no socks. Her brown ankles in the soft lining gave Henry a powerful erotic charge.

She got out at Tufnell Park, barely aware of his presence. She was on the phone the minute she emerged into the summer evening. The low sun and the traffic and the hot concrete smell, London late in June. A perfect moment. He had an erection so rigid it hurt.

She met her boyfriend outside a pub called the Lord Palmerston. He was tall, blond, broad-shouldered, and he moved with a certain masculine assurance that Henry associates with Oxford and Cambridge — perhaps wrongly.

He hung back while they embraced on a street

201

corner, then kissed. He was rapt, watching their tongues slide over one another.

He nearly orgasmed when, disengaging from the kiss, the man brushed the palm of one hand over the tip of the woman's breast.

Henry followed them home and watched them through the windows.

Later, he broke in.

He promised himself he'd go home if they'd made it difficult for him — but it was a hot night and they'd forgotten to latch the kitchen window.

He clambered in and tracked around the small flat. He watched them sleeping. It was such a hot night. They lay on opposite sides of the bed, the sheet between them, plaited into a thin rope from the vigour of their fucking.

The man lay curled and naked, his cock shrivelled into a nest of pubic hair, a smattering of acne across his wide shoulders.

She lay on her back with a forearm thrown across her eyes. Naked, she wore the pale outline of a bikini. It seemed a little less pale across her breasts and he wondered if she'd done some topless bathing recently.

He watched them from the bedroom door. He didn't worry about being seen.

When he'd looked for long enough, he got on his hands and knees and searched among the discarded clothing on the bedroom floor. She'd been wearing a pair of pink and white Hello Kitty briefs. He picked them up, sniffed them, then masturbated into them. After two or three voluptuous tugs, what he experienced was less of an orgasm than a purging, like he was being turned inside out.

He knew he was taking a risk by leaving the underwear behind — but the thought excited him. The semen would be dry in the morning, he thought. She'd wake and bundle the Hello Kitty underwear into her handbag. She'd take them home and wash them, and then she'd wear them again. She'd wear them again and again. Henry loved the power this gave him over the secret folds of her cunt.

So he left the underwear where he'd found it, soaked in the gusset with his semen, and left the flat the way he'd come in.

It was a summer romance. Henry developed an addiction for the couple, whose names were Richard and Claire. Richard worked in the city, and Claire worked for a little production office in Soho; actually, what she did was man reception and make tea, but she was ambitious and cheerful and popular. Henry admired her for this.

He was on Claire's train twice a week, enough for them to develop a silent, nodding acquaintance. One or twice they were crammed together in the rush hour, holding the straps, and he smelled her and felt the intensity of his secret knowledge — the pale bikini shape she wore on her skin, and the way she orgasmed. (First her feet would arch and then the muscles in her legs would tense and the tension would rise up her body and into her neck and head and face. Then there were flutters in her belly and she bit down on her lip. She bucked her hips and made small, private, strangled noises and sometimes when it was over she laughed the way people do when disembarking a roller coaster.)

Richard and Henry never even made it to the nodding acquaintance stage, although Henry contrived to be on Richard's train just as often as Claire's.

The more he got to know Richard, the more he grew to accept that he'd made a mistake. Claire was perfect but Richard wasn't. He was like a crisp green apple that, when bitten, reveals its flesh to be floury and dry.

Richard was just a bloke. He had nothing of interest to say. He had no opinions that wouldn't be held by any randomly selected man of his age, class and ethnicity.

Richard was a bore. Even the way he fucked quickly grew boring. When he buried his face in Claire's holy cunt he'd sometimes look up to the ceiling, resentful of time spent bringing her off.

One evening, Henry followed Richard to a bar in Soho and saw him meet with another woman. He watched them get drunk. He watched Richard's hand on her knee. He watched them kissing across the table.

Henry still walks down Claire's street sometimes, and now and again, if he's in the area, he might pop into one of the local pubs or Soho wine bars that Richard frequented.

He often wonders what happened to them; if they found happiness with other people. Sometimes he thinks of another man's hands delving into those Hello Kitty briefs and slipping up inside her. He feels a warm glow of nostalgia.

But Richard and Claire had been an instructive exercise in the search for perfection; first impressions can dazzle, but you have to get over that wonderful exhilaration, the intense infatuation that feels like a kind of madness. You have to know all their moods, all their habits, good and bad.

As of today, Henry is actively watching sixteen couples in London; some childless, some not.

In a strongbox downstairs, he keeps a key to each of their houses. He likes to let himself in and walk around while they sleep. He likes to photograph them, film them. He likes to masturbate, although of course he no longer leaves his DNA behind him.

Henry knows how to be in a house and not be seen. He's been doing it for years, since long before Patrick was born.

Now he digs out the laptop from its hiding place and boots it up. He and Patrick sit on the sofa as Henry scrolls through the list.

Patrick is reluctant, churlish; perhaps resentful of the beating Henry doled out earlier.

Henry makes his decision quickly. The Daltons. Handsome dad. Delicious mum. Perky, pretty little daughter.

Actually, he'd made his decision long before opening the laptop. But he likes the sense of ceremony and ritual.

He sends Patrick out, to get things ready.

16

At thirty-two, Caitlin Pearce has been a Samaritan for five years — since a few months after Megan Harris committed suicide.

Megan wasn't a close friend, just someone Caitlin knew from uni; they saw each other mostly at weddings and birthdays, the occasional hen night, dinner parties. They spent a week in Faliraki as part of a group of seven or eight.

Caitlin didn't even know Megan was unhappy. If anything, she'd been a little in awe of her, for Megan seemed as carefree as she was lovely.

After the funeral, Caitlin began to wonder if Megan had in fact been tired-looking and withdrawn at some of those boisterous girls' nights out. Or perhaps that was her own guilt talking. Caitlin knew that survivor guilt taints memories of the suicide, that people left behind look for signs that simply may not have been there.

One evening, Megan had gone home from work and taken an overdose. Her flatmate found her in bed the next morning. Eight days later, Caitlin was sitting on a hard church pew in brand new funeral clothes and brand new funeral shoes that pinched her feet. And she sat dazed, looking at the coffin.

The instant permanence of it hit her hard; the fact that somebody could simply pop out of the world like a bubble.

It made the world seem less real. Caitlin slipped into what she now recognizes as a mild depressive illness. Everything felt like a film set; everyone she knew seemed like an actor. She looked through the rainy window of her fifth-storey flat, out at the London cityscape and thought: *That looks really realistic.*

After a few dismal months, she decided to do something about it; to do something good. So here she is, answering calls to the Samaritans, three volunteer shifts a month.

Right now it's 5.38 p.m., and at the end of the line a young man is sobbing. When Caitlin asks what he wants to talk about he says, 'It's my dad. I want to kill him. I want to fucking kill him.'

'What about your dad makes you feel like this?'

There is a long silence on the line. At the end of it, the caller says, 'He took the baby. Emma. It was my dad.'

Quite often, you get a crank call. In your bones, you know it for what it is, but you have to take it seriously — because what if you were wrong?

'Baby Emma?' she says.

'I was waiting in the car. I called the police, but they were too slow. She was all purple and wriggling. And then she got sick, like really sick, and he wouldn't take her to hospital.'

Caitlin controls her voice. 'And how did you feel about that?'

'Fucked up. All fucked up in my head. I want to kill him. I honestly do. It would be so much easier if I could just kill him.'

Caitlin's hands are cold.

'There's this family,' says the caller. 'The Daltons. He likes them.'

'Likes what about them?'

'Their little girl. They've got a daughter. He wants her to make babies for him. He says he's never tried it with a virgin. She's only little. She's only eleven.'

Caitlin's scared of flying, and she's got the feeling now that she gets when boarding an aircraft, like her blood sugar has crashed. Her hands and feet are cold. Her voice is weak.

Samaritans never call the police, no matter what a caller might say; it would transgress their code of absolute confidentiality. And you categorically cannot offer advice. But it's not advice Caitlin wants to offer; it's an instruction.

Whether the caller is telling the truth or enumerating a strange fantasy, she wants to tell him to stay where he is and wait while she dials 999 and has him picked up for his own sake.

She casts around, looking at the other desks, all the bowed heads.

'I hate him,' says the caller. 'I hate him. I don't know what to do.'

'What do you think you'll do?'

'What he says. Cut them up.'

'You'll cut them up?'

'Yes.'

'Why?'

'Because I have to.'

'Why do you have to?'

'Because he's my dad.'

Caitlin glances over her shoulder. Her shift

208

supervisor, Matt, is there. A short man with wispy hair and a prominent facial mole.

He pulls up a chair and just sits beside her. Offering his support, just as a presence. Suddenly, Caitlin knows she's way out of her depth.

'I don't want to do it,' the caller says. 'I don't know what to do.'

Don't do it! she says, but only inside her head.

She looks into Matt's calm eyes.

'I have to go,' says the man on the line. 'I'm in the garage with the dogs. He's coming. We're leaving now.'

Before Caitlin can speak, he's hung up.

He leaves behind an atmosphere on the empty line. You get it sometimes, when something really bad has happened. It spreads like a cloud.

Matt takes Caitlin to a little office upstairs. She clasps a mug between two hands, blows on the surface of her tea.

She says, 'How can we do it? How can we not tell someone?'

'Because it's not our place to do that. Our promise to our callers is that everything they say is confidential.'

'But what if he's telling the truth? What if there's a family out there tonight, the Daltons or whoever? And he's going to cut them up?'

'Cate, I understand how you feel.'

'All the respect in the world, Matt, but I'm not sure you do.'

Matt tells her about a time he answered a call from a woman who'd taken an overdose. She just wanted someone to be there on the phone with her as she died. Matt had to respect that. So he sat and listened as she slipped away.

Years later, the suicide troubles his dreams. In his dreams he sees her clearly, although in life he never saw her face. He sees her so clearly that sometimes he thinks she's actually a ghost. In the dreams, he asks her name. She tells him a different name every time.

'If you break one confidence you break them all,' he says. 'And then being a Samaritan stands for nothing.'

Caitlin nods.

Then Matt says, 'Would you like to speak to somebody?'

She laughs because — well, because that would be ironic.

She says no, she's fine. And by then her shift's over, so she puts on her coat and says goodbye to everybody.

She pops to the loo and fiddles with her make-up. Then she goes to get drunk.

17

The Hallissey estate was built in 1964. The design was influenced by Le Corbusier, who admired ocean liners and believed them to be the perfect model for housing estates.

The estate went up quickly and not well. Shabby concrete citadels are accessed via dank passageways, dark stairwells and concrete walkways. Grimy curtains hang at rotten window frames.

Steve Bixby lives on the fifth floor of Milton Tower. He's a lanky man in a Hawaiian shirt and combat trousers. Small eyes, heavily bagged, and thinning hair in a fuzzy crew cut.

He lingers in the doorway, stuttering slightly, asking why Howie and Luther want to come in.

It's 5.51 p.m.

Howie tells him they just want to ask some questions.

She glances down. At Bixby's ankle lurks a tan-and-white pit bull terrier. It looks at her with close-set, moronic eyes.

Bixby clocks her wariness. 'Don't worry about Lou,' he says. 'He's a sweetheart, aren't you, boy? Aren't you?'

Luther says, 'Do you mind?'

Bixby doesn't. So Luther drops to one knee and summons the dog by sucking his teeth and rubbing his thumb across his fingers. Lou lumbers warily towards him. Luther pats its

211

bony, muscular head, mutters to it in a low, comforting voice. He looks up at Bixby. 'Nice dog.'

'You a dog person?'

'The more I learn about people, the more I like dogs,' Luther says, straightening. 'Lou's got scars down his flanks. He been fighting?'

'He's been in a lot of fights,' Bixby says. 'They found him down by Waltham Forest. They reckon he'd been a bait dog.'

'Bait dog?' Howie says.

'Old dogs that've lost the will to fight,' Luther says. 'They chain them down. Let other dogs practise on them.'

Howie looks at the dog's wide triangular head, its beady little eyes, its absurdly muscular chest. She feels a twinge of pity for it. Its hot tongue lolls in the corner of its mouth.

'Are we okay to come in?' Luther says. 'He's not going to bite, is he?'

Bixby shakes his head and steps aside. 'He's got no bite left in him, have you, boy?'

He means it literally. Most of the dog's teeth have been removed.

They enter a cramped flat; floral curtains and psychedelic carpet that surely belonged to the previous occupant; the kind of armchair usually destined to be garnished with antimacassars, now blackened and greasy. A fat TV on a spindly coffee table. Canine kitsch: porcelain dogs, plastic dogs.

Bixby sits with his hands writhing between his bony knees. He asks why Luther and Howie are here.

Luther says, 'Your name's been mentioned in connection with an investigation. And we'd like to speak with you about it.'

'What investigation?'

'What investigation do you think?'

'I don't know. That's why I'm asking.'

Luther watches Bixby's fretful hands. 'You must be thinking something, Steve. It's difficult not to think something.'

'I haven't done a thing.'

'Well, like I say. Your name came up.'

'Then someone's lying to you. Speak to my supervisor, go see my probation officer. Speak to my shrink; I'm in counselling — group counselling and voluntary one-to-one. I accept full responsibility for my previous offending. I stay away from high-risk situations. I'm really trying here.'

'Trying to what?'

'Get better.'

'Do men like you actually get better?'

'Do you know what it's like, being me? Do you think I like it?'

His eyes search Luther's face, then Howie's. See nothing. No judgement. No pity.

'I used to drink,' Bixby says. 'To blank it out. I'd see a picture of a girl who'd been kidnapped and all I could think was *yeah, I could see why he took her. She's lovely*. I'd go to family birthday parties and I'd be singing happy birthday and the whole time I'm thinking: *I'd love to take your daughter away and fuck her*. What do you think that feels like?'

Howie looks at the shelf of DVDs. *Top Gear*.

213

Bear Grylls. The Matrix Trilogy.

'I don't know,' Luther says.

'I'll tell you. It makes you hate yourself and want to die.'

'Yet somehow, here you are. Not dead.'

Bixby looks at Luther as if he's been slapped. 'Fuck you,' he says. 'Fuck you.' He wrings those skinny hands at the end of bony wrists. 'Have you ever tried to be someone you're not? Hating every thought in your head, having them go round and round and round like a fucking train, and you can't stop them?'

'I know exactly what that's like, Steve. But you don't have to act on those thoughts, do you?'

'I didn't,' he says. 'I never even touched a child. Not once. Are you gay or straight?'

'Straight, if it matters.'

'Then can you imagine what it would be like, never to touch a woman? To have craved it since you were ten or eleven years old, to see women every day, beautiful women, sexy women? And never, ever, be able to lay even a finger on them, let alone make love to them? Not ever. To die a virgin. To know that your most loving touch would *ruin* them.'

'No,' Luther says. 'I can't imagine that. But then, I can't imagine trading in child pornography either.'

'I did that, yeah.'

'So you hurt kids second-hand. Did it ever occur to you that the kids in those photos would never have been hurt if there wasn't a market of people like you waiting to buy the pictures?'

'I think the people who took those pictures might have thought twice about selling them,' Bixby says. 'Not taking them.'

'So,' Luther says. 'You ran a network. People would come to you. You'd put people in contact with other people. People with similar interests.'

'Not any more.'

'I know. But we're looking for a man who may have come to you. A while ago maybe.'

'When?'

'I don't know. But he'd be a man who wanted something very specific.'

'They all want something very specific. That's their curse.'

'You love children, right?'

'Yes.'

'Do you watch the news?'

'Sometimes.'

'Did you watch it today?'

'I think so. I don't know. Why?'

'I think you know why.' Luther leans forward. Speaks low, the same way he did to the dog, forcing Bixby to lean in closer.

The dog shifts uneasily on the carpet. Whines low in its throat.

'Night before last, somebody cut a child from its mother's womb,' Luther says. 'A man like that, a man who'd do that sort of thing — I think you'd know him. Or know of him. I think part of you's been waiting for a knock at the door since this happened. Because you know who this man is.'

Bixby blinks. He pats his lap. The old dog struggles into the chair. Bixby strokes it.

215

'Yeah, I knew a lot of these men,' he says at length. 'But the thing about them, about us, you have to remember, there's no such thing as a 'paedophile'. Same way there's no such thing as a 'straight man'. Some straight men like high heels, or underwear, or bondage, or being submissive, or dressing as babies — whatever. I don't know. Sexuality is a broad church, okay?'

Luther nods. Lets him talk.

'It's the same with men who want sex with children,' Bixby says. 'There are a million and one variations — heterosexual, homosexual. Men who want to kill children. Men who idolize them, who honestly can't accept that it's impossible for a child to feel sexual desire for them. That was my problem, and I'm working with it.'

'And babies?'

'It's rare, but it exists. But for all that I've seen, I never, ever, in all the thousands of hours I spent communicating with these men, not once did I hear anybody fantasize about cutting a baby from a mother's womb for the purposes of sexual gratification.'

'So what are we saying?'

'That the man you're looking for isn't a paedophile.'

Luther takes a moment. 'So you *do* know him?'

Bixby looks away. Luther looks at his frantic hands, tickling the dog's sternum, scratching its angular head. Every now and again he leans in to nuzzle its neck.

The dog stares at Luther.

Luther says, 'DS Howie, would you mind waiting in the car?'

Howie doesn't look at him. She says, 'I'm okay, Boss. It's nice and warm in here.'

Bixby reads the vibe between them.

Luther says, 'Steve. It's important you tell me what you know about this man.'

'I don't even know it's the same man.'

'But you've got a feeling it might be, right?'

Bixby bites his lower lip and nods.

Luther says, 'Then I don't understand your reticence.'

'Aiding and abetting.'

'Did you help this man in some way?'

'I think I may have.'

'And you're worried about going back to prison?'

'I'd honestly rather die.'

'We'll see what we can do to avoid that. If you help us, right here and right now.'

'I want immunity. From prosecution.'

Luther laughs. It startles the dog. It gets down from the sofa. Stands in front of Bixby's spindly legs, protecting him.

'Everyone wants something,' Luther says. 'Except a dog. A dog's just happy to be here.'

'Do you know what happens in prison?' says Bixby. 'To men like me?'

'I don't know. Poetic justice?'

'I see. So rape's all right as long as you hate the victim.'

The dog barks — or tries to. Its throat has been damaged. It glares at Luther with its good eye.

'This man, your friend, is going to kill someone,' Luther says. 'Maybe tonight. You know that. You saw it on the news, you listen to the radio. Been on the internet.'

'I'm not allowed on the internet.'

'Whatever. But you know what he says he's going to do. And you can help me. If you like, I'll get on my knees and beg you to tell me what you know. But I'm in a hurry here. The clock's ticking.'

'Then I can't help. I'm sorry.'

'Steve,' says Howie. 'We don't need to tell anyone where this information comes from.'

Bixby looks up at her, his eyes widening in transitory hope. 'Would that work?'

'Absolutely it would work. We do it all the time. We'd log you as an 'anonymous source'. If it helps us catch a triple murderer before he kills again, trust me — no questions will be asked.'

'But you can't guarantee that, can you? I mean, not absolutely.'

Luther tugs at his thumb, hears the joint pop. He sits back in the armchair as if it's a throne or an electric chair. He says, 'Do you know when I last slept?'

'No,' says Bixby.

'Neither do I. And I don't mind telling you, Steve, I'm having a bad day. A really, really bad day. I pulled a dead baby out of the earth this morning. And I've got this stuff going round in my head. Bad stuff. Right now, it's telling me that if this man kills someone else tonight, it'll be my fault — for not trying hard enough, for not pushing hard enough to catch him, for saying those things at the press conference. You get me?'

Bixby nods.

'Okay,' Luther says. 'So the way I see it, you've got two options. Option one: you take DS Howie's advice. Which is good advice, by the way.'

'What's option two?'

'You sit there while I order DS Howie to leave the flat.' He lifts his hip, digs in his pocket, removes his pepper spray and his extensible baton. Sits with them in his hands.

Bixby clenches and unclenches his fists.

'Boss,' says Howie.

Luther shoots her a look. 'Shut your mouth, Sergeant.'

Howie shuts her mouth. Sits there shaking, not knowing what to do.

Luther says, 'Help me, Steve. Help me catch this man. I promise we'll do the right thing by you. I promise.'

Bixby hugs the dog like a teddy bear. Kisses its muscular neck.

Then he says, 'A man came to me. A while ago. Two years? Three, maybe. He wanted a baby.'

'What was this man's name?'

'Henry.'

'Henry?'

'Grady, I think. I don't think it was his real name.'

Howie writes it down.

Luther says, 'Can you describe him? What did he look like? Black? White? Fat, thin?'

'White. Not big, not small. Very fit.'

219

'Fit how? Muscular, like a bodybuilder?'

'Like a runner. Like a marathon-runner-type build.'

'Hair colour?'

'Dark.'

'Long hair? Short hair?'

'Short and very neat. In a parting. He used Brylcreem.'

'How'd you know?'

'The smell. It reminded me of my granddad.'

'Accent?'

'Local. London.'

'Do you know where he lived?'

'No.'

'What kind of car did he drive?'

'I don't know.'

'Phone number?'

'He used different numbers. He seemed quite savvy.'

'Like you.'

'Like me.'

'How'd he dress?'

'Smart dress. Always suit and tie. Overcoat. One of those ones where the collar's made of a different cloth, like velvet.'

'And what's he like? His demeanour. Was he outgoing? Withdrawn? Friendly? Aggressive? What?'

'I don't know. He was just a bloke. You'd pass him in the street.'

'Okay,' Luther says. 'He wanted a baby. What did he want with it?'

'He didn't say. But he definitely wasn't a paedophile.'

'That's twice you've said that. What makes you so sure?'

'You ever walk into a strange pub, in a strange town, know someone you've never seen before is a policeman?'

'Point taken. But if he's not a paedophile, if he's not part of your network, how does he know where to find you?'

'Via a friend.'

'What friend?'

'A man called Finian Ward.'

'And where does Finian Ward live?'

'He doesn't. Liver cancer. Last Christmas.'

Luther checks his frustration. 'Did Finian Ward tell you how he and Henry knew each other?'

'No. But I trusted Finian. He was a good man.'

'And a paedophile.'

'By inclination. Not action. He was a very gentle man.'

'So Henry Grady comes to you, via Finian Ward. Says he wants a baby. But he's not a paedophile. So the baby's for his wife, maybe?'

'I thought it must be. Until . . . '

'Until what?'

Bixby can't meet his eye.

'Steve, until what?'

'Well,' Bixby says. 'I told him that babies aren't easy to get. They're always *with* somebody. Once they're two or three years old, there'll always be a moment when they're unprotected. But not babies. It's just not happening. But he knew all this.'

'How do you know that?'

'I was actually trying to put him off the idea, for his own sake — and for the baby's. I said the only possible way to get what he wanted, if he really couldn't adopt, was to buy a baby. There's always women willing to sell.'

Luther's leg jiggles. 'Is that what you did?'

'Yes. I told him about a man called Sava. Do you know him?'

'We've met, yeah. So then what?'

'He came back to me. Said he didn't want a junkie's baby or a hooker's baby or a foreign baby.'

'Why not?'

'He said you wouldn't buy a dog without knowing its pedigree. He wanted a pedigree baby.'

'What does that mean?'

'Good parents,' Bixby says. 'Good looking. Clever. Rich. Happy.'

'Happy. He said 'happy'. He actually used that word?'

Bixby nods. 'I told him it was a no-go. That kind of person, they never take their eyes off a baby. I told him, no way. It's just not going to happen.'

'And what did he say to that?'

'He said, there's always a way to make things happen.'

'And what was that way? What was the way to make it happen?'

'He told me he needed a woman,' Bixby says.

'To what?'

'Make him look harmless. Because people trust women.'

Luther thinks about the IVF group. About the strange couple who paid too much attention to the Lamberts. He knows this is the right man, the man calling himself Henry Grady. He can taste copper in his mouth, the taste of blood and anxiety. His heart is thin and fast.

'And that's what you did? You put Henry Grady in contact with a woman?'

'Yes.'

'What woman?'

'Sweet Jane Carr.'

'And where do I find Sweet Jane Carr?'

'In Holloway prison.'

'Since when?'

'Since about six weeks. She's on remand.'

'For what?'

'Sexual abuse of a minor,' Bixby says. 'She abused local kids on webcam. Pay per view.'

★　★　★

Luther leaves the flat on shaky legs, Howie at his heel.

He says, 'You okay?'

'I'm good,' she says, 'I'm fine.'

'But?'

'Boss, you just assaulted a witness. And intimidated another.'

'Extenuating circumstances.'

'I'm not sure the law recognizes that.'

'It does when you're dealing with paedophiles.'

He disappears into the dank stairwell, into the shadows.

Howie lingers.

She's there long enough to see Luther emerge from the building and walk towards the car.

She digs out her phone and asks in a shaky voice to speak to DSU Rose Teller.

'It's urgent,' she says.

★ ★ ★

Luther steps into the evening.

He knows Howie's troubled by what just happened. But he'll explain on the way to Holloway prison. He'll apologize, if that's what it takes.

He reaches the car. No keys in his pocket.

He turns to see DS Howie on the concrete walkway, just a shadow in the misty gloom. She's on the phone. She probably doesn't know it, but she's pacing.

The pacing is the tell.

Luther knows he's in trouble.

He ducks into the deeper shadows of the estate and hurries away.

In five minutes he's on Lavender Hill Road.

Three minutes after that he's in a taxi, en route to Holloway prison.

★ ★ ★

Caitlin doesn't know the bar, Café Piccolo. She's never been here before. It's got an untrendy, Italian vibe; less retro than cheesy. It's full of the early evening, after-office crowd.

She sits at a corner booth and works her way

224

through a bottle of wine. By the third glass, she's thinking about calling Carol, dragging her out and having a laugh. But she knows that if she actually sets eyes on Carol, she'll break down. And she won't be able to tell Carol why. And that won't be good.

She puts her phone away.

She considers popping upstairs, buying a packet of Silk Cut, sitting on a bench and smoking them all. She decides against it. It's cold outside and warm in here, even a little humid.

The waiter is giving her inquisitive looks when the first tosspot hits on her, asks if she's waiting for someone, or just had a bad day.

It sounds like there's going to be a punchline but there isn't. He's just testing the water, trying to establish if she's been stood up, if she's some kind of psycho bitch.

She gives him a hard look and he fucks off back to his mates.

Caitlin seethes as she drinks, then makes an effort to feel a Samaritan's compassion. She glances over and gives him a rueful half-wave. It's supposed to say 'sorry', but it doesn't come across like that; it comes across as a victory wave.

Caitlin burns with embarrassment and takes a sip of wine. She can feel it heavy in her stomach now, sloshing around.

She thinks about the Daltons, who have a daughter who is eleven years old.

She shoves that to the back of her mind.

She scrolls through her contacts, knowing

she's about to make a cardinal error. But she has to do something. She has to talk to somebody. So she calls Gavin.

He says, 'Hey, Cate. What's up?'

She hates the way he says it. Already, she regrets making the call. But what else is she supposed to do?

She says, 'Hey, Gav.'

'So,' says Gav.

'So,' she says. 'How've you been?'

'Pretty mental. Work and whatever. You?'

'Pretty mental.'

'Right,' says Gavin. 'So . . . '

'So I'm in this bar,' she says, 'a Trattoria.'

She enunciates fastidiously, as if the word 'Trattoria' was some kind of private joke between them. It's not.

'Right,' he says.

'And I'm a bit tipsy,' she says, 'a little bit woo-hoo, and I thought I'd ring and say hello. So hello!'

'Right,' he says. 'It's just . . . '

She doesn't want to hear what comes next because it involves Gav feeling bad for her; he's got his mates round, or some girl, or both. Gav's having a laugh, because Gav loves having a laugh.

She wants to say something bitchy and cutting, but she honestly can't think of anything. So she just sits there with her Greek-goddess hair piled on her head and the iPhone in her hand and she wants to share with him the enormity of the secret to which she is privy. The things that might be going on right now, right this second, to a family called the Daltons, who have an eleven-year-old girl.

She's got enough control to say, 'Cheers!' and hang up, leaving him genially baffled and secretly happy about the nervous breakdown she seems to be enduring in the wake of their breakup.

She drains her glass and gets the bill. Can't remember her PIN. She has to ask the waiter to hold on a moment, it'll come to her. In the end it does. She leaves a stupidly big tip, scrawls a signature, drops her purse in her bag, puts on her coat and staggers out.

She walks to the bus stop and waits, stamping her feet and shivering. It's really, really fucking cold.

She doesn't mind because it should sober her up. But all it does is make her want to pee.

She digs out her phone again. She thinks about calling Matt, back at the Samaritans office. But she already knows everything he's going to say.

So she puts the phone back in her pocket and waits for the bus.

She watches cars and taxis and minicabs.

A bus coughs and rumbles past on the other side of the road, a long bright bubble full of people.

A car stops at the lights. An ordinary car. There's a man at the wheel and his wife is next to him. They're chatting about whatever. In the back seat are two kids, a girl who must be about five, and a sleeping baby in a car seat.

Caitlin is close enough to take a single step

forward, gently rap on the window and say, *Don't go home, it's not safe.*

But these aren't the Daltons. They can't be. London is too big and too abundant.

But even in a city this teeming and this ravenous, lives cross and touch one another. Caitlin imagines reaching out her hand, rapping on the safety glass, saving these people.

The woman, the wife, can feel Caitlin staring. She turns her head and looks Caitlin in the eye with an unbroken lioness challenge — the face of a woman whose young children are asleep in the back of the car, and who would kill for them in an instant.

Caitlin wells up. She smiles.

The woman gives her an odd look, softer round the eyes. Then the lights change and the car pulls away and is gone, sucked round the veins of London, and Caitlin knows she will never see those people again.

She thinks about Megan, the friend who committed suicide. And she thinks about her moron of an ex. She thinks about her mum and her dad and her sister and her nieces and her nephews.

She thinks about her grandparents, the good smell of them and their infinite belief in the unqualified wonder of her.

Caitlin walks to a phone box.

She inserts a two pound coin.

She uses her iPhone to access the telephone directory. Then dials the first Dalton in the London directory.

The phone is answered on the ninth ring. A

228

foggy voice, the voice of a family man woken from sleep. 'Hello?'

'Hello,' says Caitlin. 'This is going to sound really weird, and I'm sorry if I'm wrong. I'm really sorry. I hope I'm wrong. But I think somebody might be planning to hurt you and your family.'

There are one hundred and sixty Daltons in the London phone book.

Caitlin calls them all.

18

Luther hates prisons. Hates Holloway in particular. It feels like a badly designed hospital.

He waits in the half-lit, after-hours visiting hall, as two wardens lead Sweet Jane Carr into the room.

She's so pretty it's almost obscene. She makes him think of Victorian erotica. But her frame is disproportionately gross.

He tries not to stare as she sits and crosses great ham forearms under massive breasts, regards him through lovely eyes.

She says, 'So what do you want?'

She's got a creepy, teeny-tiny voice. Like Marilyn Monroe on helium. She makes him think of the ghosts of little girls.

'I want your help,' he says. He sets his hands flat on the table, as if anchoring himself.

'To do what?' She purses rosebud lips, winsome and amused. He glimpses the worm-eaten thing inside her.

'A man you know,' Luther says. 'A friend of yours. Henry Grady.' He pauses, waits to see if that name gets a reaction. It doesn't. Sweet Jane's eyes twinkle. She smiles like a porcelain doll.

'He killed an entire family,' Luther says. 'I'm scared he's going to do it again.'

'Well,' she says. 'I can definitely tell you all about him, if you like.'

'I need you to do that. Please.'

She tilts her head to one side, juts out her lower lip. 'I hate it in here.'

'I bet you do.'

'It's full of dykes who want to go down on me. Screws leering through the peepholes at night. They don't call them *screws* for nothing. You can hear them wanking off. There's dried spunk on my door in the morning. You can flake it off with a fingernail. All the bitches in here are fucking jealous. They nick your stuff, they threaten you, they get punches in when nobody's watching.'

'Well, I'm sorry you're not enjoying it.'

The petulant pout turns into a flirtatious grin, tugs at the corners of her mouth.

He says, 'Listen. I don't have time for all this. I'm on a clock. I wouldn't have come to see you if I wasn't desperate. So what do you want?'

'Internet privileges.'

'That's not going to happen. Not for the kind of offence you're in here for.'

'It can be supervised. I just want to get to my message boards. I like cats. And pottery.'

'Nope.'

Her smile widens, shows ivory-yellow teeth. He knows that if he ever sleeps again, his dreams will be infested by spectres of this woman.

He wonders how many children see her in their dreams, then tucks the thought back inside himself, like a prolapse.

Then he glances meaningfully at his hand, flat on the table before him.

He waits until she's followed the line of his

231

gaze, then raises his thumb. He reveals a baggie of cocaine.

'You'll never let me have that,' says Sweet Jane Carr.

Warders watch from the far corner.

'You never will,' she says.

'Well,' says Luther. 'I'm a desperate man.'

He slips the bag to her. She takes it with a swift, practised movement.

'There's more to come,' he says.

'What do you want?'

'Henry Grady,' he says. 'Where did he live?'

'I don't know.'

'Where did you meet?'

'He always came to my place.'

'How did he contact you?'

'By text.'

'Never by email?'

'He didn't do emails.'

'What about his car? What kind of car did he drive?'

'A normal car. Like a Ford Focus or something.'

'What colour?'

'Dark.'

'Blue? Black?'

She shrugs.

'Old? New?'

'Oldish.'

'Inside, was it tidy or messy?'

'It was like new. It smelled nice.'

'Can you remember the registration?'

'Of course I can't, silly. What do I look like?'

He smiles. Tempted to answer.

'Tell me about what you did together.'

'Well, first of all, I had to pretend to be a social worker,' she says, widening her eyes. 'We'd knock on a door, go in like Mulder and Scully.'

'Go in where?'

'Houses with new babies.'

'How did he choose the houses?'

'I don't know. But he said he'd done it before, loads of times in the nineties. But never in such posh houses.'

'Can you remember the areas?'

'Off-hand, no.'

'And what did you do, once you were in these houses?'

'Ask to see the baby. Say there's been a complaint. Scare the shit out of them.'

'And what was the intent?'

'To get a baby out of the house.'

'And it never worked?'

'No. Nobody ever let us in. The paperwork wasn't good enough. They'd want to see ID, all the rest of it.'

'How many times did you try this?'

'Six or seven times.'

'Over how long?'

'Not long. Two weeks. He got more and more annoyed.'

'Annoyed?'

'He's a very angry man.'

'What makes you say that?'

'Because he was. He hated everyone. Dykes. Queers. Darkies. Pakis. Americans. Homeless. Paedos. He hated paedos the most.'

Luther's heart stops for a moment. 'What does

233

that mean, he hated paedos?'

'He said anyone who hurt a kiddie should be strung up for it. But first they should have their balls cut off in public.'

'What did you say to that?'

'That I sucked my first cock when I was three and it was yum yum in my tum tum.'

Luther looks down at his hands. He knows this woman's madness has seeped into him like the stink of cadaverine. It's impossible to wash off. You can wash and wash and wash. You have to wait until it fades away.

'You told him this?' he says.

'Oh, yeah. I hate it when people get on their high horse about paedos. It's all hype. Kids love it.'

He grips the edge of the table. Counts down from five. 'How did Henry react, when you told him this?'

'He got angry.'

'How angry?'

'He went absolutely tonto on me. Ranting and raving, his hair all sticking up. He reminded me of Hitler. He says no kid can enjoy it, it's not physically possible, they're too young to understand. And I said: *If they're too young to understand, what's the big deal?*'

'And what did he say to that?'

'That paedos come from defective genes. That they should be banned from breeding.'

'He say that about anyone else?'

'Everyone else. Murderers. Rapists. Jews. Arabs. Blacks.'

'They should all be — '

234

'Bred out.'

'That's what he said, is it? Those are his words. *Bred out*.'

She nods, enjoying herself. 'For the good of the human race.'

'Backtrack a bit,' he says. 'This argument. Where did it take place?'

'In the front seat of his car.'

'Exactly how angry did he get? Angry enough to hit you?'

'No.'

'Did you feel in any danger?'

She gives him a faint, patronizing smile. 'A man attacks you,' she says, 'you go for his eyes and his bollocks. I don't care how strong he is. Eyes and balls. They're a man's weakness. In every way.' She squeezes her breasts, does the Marilyn pout.

'Why were you in the car?'

'Because we were on the way to this self-help group. The infertile couples thing.'

'Okay,' says Luther. 'When did he take you there?'

'This is like a year after the social workers idea. He said that wasn't going to work. He couldn't get the kind of baby he wanted that way. He was really pissed off.'

'What did he mean, 'the kind of baby'?'

'He wanted a good one.'

'A good one?'

She smiles and nods, as delighted as Luther is horrified.

'So he took you to an infertility support group?'

'Yes.'

'And that didn't seem weird to you?'

'Not really. He had his eye on this one couple — '

'The Lamberts?'

'That's them. He said they were going to the support group even though she was pregnant. He was really excited. He said it was the best way to get to know them.'

'Backtrack again. 'He had his eye on this one couple'. What does that mean?'

'It means, he had like a shortlist of people he wanted to take a baby from. A newborn baby.'

'What shortlist?'

'I don't know.'

'How many people were on it?'

'I don't know. I wasn't interested. I didn't ask. But I do know the Lamberts were his favourites. He like, loved them.'

'He loved them? He was in love with Sarah Lambert? With Tom Lambert?'

'With them. Together. He said they were perfect. He showed me a tape of them fucking. I think it was them. It was difficult to see in the dark. But he said it was them.'

Luther has a feeling in his gut. 'He had a tape of the Lamberts . . . being intimate.'

She nods, delighted.

'Taken without their knowledge?'

'Lots of them. Yes. Tapes of her on the loo, tapes of him shaving. Tapes of them watching TV. Tapes of them screwing.'

Luther's hand is shaking. He sets down the pen.

'He had lots of tapes,' Sweet Jane says. 'Lots of families.'

'What families?'

'Fucked if I know. He just wanted to show them rutting each other. He thought if I saw normal people having normal sex the way normal people do, he'd make me normal.'

'Is that the word he used? 'Normal'?'

'It was his favourite word. Everyone's got their thing, right? Everyone's got something that turns them on. His was being normal. He just wanted to be normal.'

'How many couples did he show you?'

'I don't know. Ten? Twelve? It did nothing for me. Except this one couple . . . the wife was a tiny little thing. Shaved snatch. No tits to speak of. Nipples like threepenny coins. She was a bit of yum.'

'And these weren't films downloaded from the internet?'

'No. He'd taken them himself.'

'Without the couples' knowledge.'

'Apparently.'

'How did he get these films?'

'His son helped him.'

'His what?'

'Son.'

'What son? You didn't mention a son.'

'I think I just did.'

'How old is the son now?'

'I don't know. Twenty?'

'Did you meet the son?'

'Once or twice. Henry would drop him off while we were on the way to the hospital.'

'Drop him off where?'

'Nowhere in particular. Just places.'

'What's the son's name?'

'Patrick.'

'What does Patrick look like?'

'I don't know. Normal.'

The amused, pewter light in her eyes is dimming. She's getting bored. He knows he's coming to the end of it now.

'And after these meetings of the IVF group,' he says, 'he'd just sit and — what? Just watch Tom and Sarah Lambert. What happened then?'

'He tried to make friends with them.'

'Did he succeed?'

'Did he fuck. They thought he was creepy.'

'Why do you say that?'

'Because he was. He was all creepy and hand-wringy like a little toad. He made her flesh crawl. I think the man wanted to fuck me, though. He had that look. He couldn't stop looking at me.'

Luther can't stop looking at her either.

* * *

Ten minutes later, Sweet Jane Carr is removed to her cell.

Luther signs out and is led through the echoing maze, bleak with night. He steps outside, into the glow of prison lights. Drizzle dances in their gaunt radiance.

Outside the gates, two police cars are waiting.

Rose Teller is there. Arms crossed, head bowed.

He strides up to her.

'He called himself Henry Grady,' he says, too quickly for her to get a word in. 'I've got a good description. He's got a son, Patrick. And he's got some kind of database, a list of people he's watching — the way he watched the Lamberts. For whatever reason the Lamberts were his favourites. But there are more. And he's not a paedophile. He's a family man — '

She crosses her arms and shifts her weight. She's wearing an impatient, scowling expression.

'He wants to be normal,' Luther says. 'He thinks of himself as an outsider; he's always been an outsider. He didn't grow up in a conventional household. That could mean anything — a cult. Hippies. But most likely it means he was adopted. Adoption can have a negative effect on some kids; even a really good adoption. Henry never felt like he belonged. And now he's trying to make a family around him. That's why he gets so angry. Any dad would, if someone accused him of being a paedophile. He's — '

'All right,' she says. 'Stop now.'

The words are jammed behind his mouth, crammed up behind his eyes.

'We need to look for a man called Finian Ward,' he says. 'And any bogus social-worker activity in Bristol during the mid-nineties. I think that's how he knew to target Adrian York. He'd pose as a social worker and — '

'Stop,' says Teller.

He stops. His hands drop to his sides.

She says, 'Go home.'

'What do you mean? He's out there. Tonight.

Right now. And I'm getting close to him.'

'Hundreds of good coppers are after him. We'll feed everything you've given us into the pool.'

'Boss, you can't do this to me. I asked to come off the case. You made me stay on. And now here we are. I can smell him. I've got his stink.'

'And to get here, you assaulted one witness and threatened another.'

He grits his teeth, thinks of Howie and the phone call from the dank concrete balcony. 'Exigent circumstances,' he says.

'That's not a defence. Not in law. Not to me.'

'Boss,' he says. 'There's a family out there tonight. He's probably got keys to their house. He's going to let himself in and do what he wants to them.' He shows her his watch, the ticking second hand. 'Now,' he says. 'Tonight. You know what that means. You saw what he left of the Lamberts.'

'And you haven't slept for three days. It's showing.'

'What do you mean?'

'You can't keep still. You're pacing.'

'I'm *frustrated*.'

'You're wired.'

She takes his elbow, leads him away.

'I'm pretty sure Sava won't file a report,' she says. 'A bloke like that sees a bit of harassment as cost of business. And nobody will believe a word Bixby said.'

'So what's the problem?'

'The problem is, you did it.'

He exhales, helpless and trapped. He holds

out his hands as if petitioning the moon. 'Boss, I'm *fine*.'

'You got a pretty decent result from Jane Carr,' Teller says. 'How'd you pull that off? Don't say you flirted with her. Because I tell you, mate, you're not her type.' She skewers him on her bright raptorial gaze. 'What if we ask the screws to toss her cell? They going to find anything?'

He shoves his hands in his pockets, wanders in a baffled circle.

'I can't go home with all this happening,' he says. 'I can't.'

'That's not your decision.'

'Seriously,' he says. 'Make up your mind. I'm on or I'm off.'

'Go home, John.'

He pinches the bridge of his nose. 'All right,' he says. 'All right, I'll go home and I'll get my head down. But do me a favour?'

'Depends.'

'Anything happens, you get a good sniff, give me a call.'

'Done.'

He scuffs his feet. Scowls. 'I'm honestly fine,' he says.

But he accepts it, and heads home.

★ ★ ★

There is no single register of prank calls made in London during any twenty-four-hour period.

But tonight there are many more such calls than usual.

241

London-wide, mischievous teenage boys, hate-filled ex-lovers, racists, stoned students and the mentally ill call many hundreds of different families, warning them that Pete Black is coming for them.

Hundreds of people are terrorized. Several dozen of them call 999. They include a number of families who share the surname Dalton.

All calls are logged, but are subject to triage.

Nobody thinks the man who calls himself 'Pete Black' will call ahead to warn his targets he's on his way.

19

Luther's home shortly after 8.40 p.m. Zoe's not back yet.

He checks his mobile for messages before letting himself through the red door and into the dark hallway. Eleven missed calls. Three voicemails from Zoe, increasingly worried and exasperated. She gave up calling several hours ago.

He wonders where she is.

He turns off the phone, pockets it and steps further into the house, hangs his coat on the banister.

He doesn't know what to do.

He trudges through to the kitchen and plugs the phone in to charge.

He goes upstairs to the bathroom. He cleans his teeth and washes his face. He looks at himself in the mirror, beaded with water, then goes downstairs and turns on the TV. He cycles through the channels three times, then turns it off.

He walks around the house turning lights on. Then he goes back to the kitchen, checks his phone, clears away Zoe's breakfast things, puts the dishwasher on.

He opens the fridge and looks at their food, their bottled sauces, their fruit and milk and yogurt, displayed under surgically bright light. He stands in the cool breath long enough for the fridge to start beeping at him.

There's a carton of milk in there, bought on Monday when the Lambert baby was still in her mother's womb. And now the child lies with her parents on a slab. Their eyes are low and sly, the artfulness of the dead, as if they know something you don't, something you'll find out soon enough.

But the milk is still good enough to drink; he could make a cup of tea with it. He looks at the milk while the fridge beeps and he doesn't hear the keys in the latch or the door open or Zoe set her bags down in the hallway. He doesn't hear her walk down the hall and linger in the kitchen doorway.

She says, 'You're home.'

He ignores the redundancy. It's just one of those things people say to one another. Most words people say to each other don't mean what they seem to. Spoken words carry their real meaning like rats carry infected fleas.

'I called about a hundred times,' she says. 'Your phone was off.'

'If you leave your phone on, all it does is ring.'

The fridge is still beeping. He shuts the door. He thinks that if he could explain about the milk, then everything will be all right.

He says, 'Did you see the news?'

Her lip trembles with fury. 'Of course I saw the news. I've done nothing but talk about the fucking news all day. My mother called to talk about the news, and to ask if you were all right. The entire world's talking about the news. The only person who hasn't talked to me about the fucking news is you.'

He's rocked by her ferocity. He swallows it and says, 'Do you want a drink?'

'No.'

Nor does Luther. He puts the kettle on.

She says, 'There's nice stuff in the tin.'

She means the tall tin of loose-leaf black tea; it's the kind of thing she brings home from the farmer's market.

She'll take great pleasure in showing him these things, lifting them from shopping bags item by item. They linger in the kitchen — him drinking proper tea, Zoe drinking something herbal — and she talks him through the speciality bread, the organic meat, the spices and the wines and the organic vegetables, the rank boutique cheeses. She passes them to him for inspection. He comments on the leanness of the beef, the pleasing density of the bacon, the weight of the organic eggs, the tincture of the wine. He doesn't have much of a palate, food is food, but he loves those Saturday afternoons in the summer and autumn, sitting here in the kitchen with his wife.

Later, if it's a really good day he'll sit reading while she cooks. She's not a chatty chef; she likes to concentrate, empty her mind. She's prepared and methodical, first laying out the ingredients strictly in accordance with the recipe.

Only when she knows she's got everything she needs to hand does she begin to improvise. It's from this improvisation that she takes real pleasure.

She doesn't know it, but she talks to herself while she's cooking, rehearsing work conversations through half-opened lips, observations related to the food, things to do with her working week. Working it all through.

He likes to hunch over his book, only pretending to read, listening. He loves her fiercely and acutely in those moments, running through her private thoughts and imaginary conflicts.

Later, she sips wine and flicks through the Saturday newspapers as he washes up. He doesn't mind washing up. She's told him more than once that washing up is in his nature.

Now the water in the kettle seethes and Zoe is looking at him with ice in her eyes. He's worn out. A muscle in his upper arm twitches. He says, 'I should have called.'

'Yes, you should have called.'

'I was — '

'Busy?'

Yes, he wants to say. I was *busy*. But he doesn't. He says, 'I'm sorry.'

She takes off her coat, finally. Hangs it over the back of a kitchen chair. Then she embraces him, puts her head onto his neck so he can smell her hair and her skin; even that she's smoked a crafty cigarette today, probably guilt-ridden and scared on his behalf, pacing the forlorn smoking area outside Ford and Vargas. Calling him names under her breath, hating him because she was scared for him. The smell of that cigarette fills him with tenderness and regret.

'I should have called,' he says. 'I should have.

But I was caught up. It was pretty bad.'

'Because it was a baby?'

Their eyes lock. 'Babies are never easy.'

She squeezes past him, opens the fridge, takes out the wine.

'I thought you didn't want a drink.'

'I changed my mind. I can do that. I can change my mind.'

She pours herself a glass.

He waits. Then he says, 'What does that mean?'

'Nothing.'

'Nothing means nothing.'

'Well, that did. That meant nothing.'

Acting on autopilot, she passes him the bottle with the cork half jammed back in the neck. He puts the bottle back in the fridge and slings the heavy door shut.

She gulps wine, then says, 'We need to have a talk.'

'We're talking now.'

'Not about this. About me and you.'

'What about me and you?'

'I think you know. In your heart, you have to know.'

'Know *what*?'

'John, seriously. Do you have any idea how much I hate this?'

'Hate what, Zoe? I don't know what we're saying here.'

'This marriage,' she says.

His legs go weak.

He has to sit.

'You mean being married to me.'

'No. I mean . . . me and you together.'

'I don't understand. I don't know what you're saying.'

'You do know what I'm saying. I've been saying it for years now. I've been saying it louder and louder.'

'You're really going to do this? Today?'

'Seriously, John, when would you like me to say it?'

'I don't know. When the time's better.'

'And when's that? Because I tell you, I've been trying. I've been trying and trying. And you just never listen. You turn your back on me, again and again.'

'If this is about the leave of absence — '

'Of course it's not about the leave of sodding absence.'

'I told you, I swear to God, I absolutely swear to God, I put in the request. Christ, I tried to get myself *fired* today.'

'You don't understand,' she says. 'You're not listening. You never do. You think you do, but you don't.'

'Okay,' he says. 'I'm listening.'

'The leave of absence wasn't a request,' she says. 'It was an ultimatum.'

'I don't get you. I don't understand.'

She laughs again, bitterly. 'To see if you'd do what you promised, just once. And you couldn't do it. You said you would, time and time again. But you never did. And finally, I decided: I'll ask once more. And if he lies to me one more time, I'll know that he always will. He'll keep telling me what I want to hear, day after day, but they're just words.'

He blinks in hurt. She pities him. She says, 'Whatever you're going to say, don't say it. Because it'll be a lie.'

She waits for him to answer. He massages his forehead with the heel of his hand. Takes a breath.

He says, 'I know.'

She turns to him. 'About what?'

'The baby.'

'What baby?'

'Our baby.'

Luther gets up and goes to the fridge. He opens the ice tray, removes an ice cube. He rubs it over his forehead. Cold water drips down his shirt.

He shuts the fridge door. He's shivering, trembling from his feet to his fingertips. He can hear the tremor in his voice. He hates it.

'I found this little plastic cap,' he says. 'Behind the bin in the bathroom. I didn't know what it was. I thought it was for a thermometer. But it wasn't. And it worried me. It nagged at me, the way things do. At the time, I didn't even know why. I should've just thrown it away. But it was bugging me. I carried it around in my pocket for like a week. And then for some reason, it clicked. I knew what it was. So I went to the chemist. Bought the three most popular home pregnancy testing kits. Sure enough. You bought the market leader. Very wise.'

She drains her wine. Pours another.

He says, 'Was it mine?'

'Of course it was yours.' Clumsy with nerves, she knocks over the glass. They don't speak while she gets a roll of kitchen paper and tears off a few sheets. 'Christ, John. Why didn't you *say* anything?'

'I was waiting for you to tell me.'

She bites her lip, mops up the wine.

She drops the wine-soaked Kleenex in the pedal bin and leans her back against the worktop. She pulls back her hair, but can't find anything to tie it with.

'Shit,' she says.

Luther's in a kitchen chair, his elbows on his knees. He's looking away from her at the interlocking geometric pattern of light and shadow on the kitchen floor; black, white, ten shades of grey. 'So what happened?'

'Nothing. I lost it.'

'Why didn't you tell me?'

'Why do you think? You were busy.'

He winces at her unexpected cruelty.

'Look, there's nothing to tell,' she says. 'I was pregnant, then I started to bleed and then I wasn't pregnant. I spent the afternoon in hospital. You didn't come home that night.'

'I thought you'd had a termination.'

'Why would you think that?'

'Because you were pregnant and then you weren't. And you didn't tell me.'

'You didn't give me the chance.'

'You never wanted them. Kids.'

'Neither did you.' She trails off. 'Oh Jesus,' she says. 'The bear.'

She's talking about the big, plush teddy bear

she found sitting at the bottom of Luther's wardrobe.

'You told me that was for Rose's granddaughter.'

'What am I supposed to say?' he says. 'It's for the baby you secretly had aborted?'

'What did you do with it?'

'I didn't know what to do with it. I took it to Oxfam.'

She stands there.

He sits. Both of them look at the interlocking shadows on the floor.

'God,' she says. 'What a mess.'

Luther laughs an empty laugh.

Zoe reaches for her coat.

He says, 'Where are you going?'

'I don't know. Out.'

'Are you coming home?'

'I think it's best if I don't.'

'So where will you sleep?'

'At my mum's, probably.'

There's a tiny flex, a comma at one corner of her mouth, and he thinks she's lying. But he doesn't trust his judgement; he's angry and tired and bereft. He may be seeing lies where there are none. And if he goes down that road now, then however bad it might be right now, it'll only get worse.

He watches her put her coat on and smells cigarettes and knows she's not going to her mum's or to her sister's or to her friend's or to anywhere else he knows.

More than anything, what he wants is for Zoe to stay here, in this house, the house with the red

251

door, the house with both their names on the title deeds, John and Zoe Luther.

How proud they'd been, the day they moved in. Their first real house, too big for just the two of them. The area was a bit rough, but it was up and coming and anyway who cared? Luther used to fantasize about being an old man, dying in the room upstairs; it would be a library by then, with leather armchairs. And he'd be the one to go first; she'd come in one morning with a cup of tea in a china cup and a few biscuits on a plate and he'd be dead in his leather armchair with a book in his lap, a good book, much loved and well read.

And now she's belting her coat, waiting for him to say something.

He says, 'There's no need for you to go anywhere.'

'If I stay, we'll fight.'

'Look,' he says, and he wonders if she can hear the desperation in his voice. 'Look,' he says again. 'I'm not going to relax tonight. With all this, waiting for the phone to ring. I'm going to go mad if I hang around the house. So you stay here, okay? You stay here and I'll go.'

He reads a flare of disappointment in her eyes. And there's a dizzying lurch inside him to think that even now, at the teetering edge of their marriage, he's disappointing her.

She stands with her coat buttoned and belted. And because of that, because she's ready to walk out the door, he says it again, 'I'll go.'

She nods slowly, once. 'Okay.'

He goes to the kitchen door. Hesitates. 'Do

you want me to call you? Let you know how it goes?'

She doesn't answer. When he turns to ask again, she's crying.

He doesn't understand. He doesn't know how to say the right thing.

He says, 'Lock up properly. Lock the doors and windows.'

He steps outside. He shuts the kitchen door and walks away and is lost.

He thinks about dropping round to see Reed. But if he does, he might have to talk about it. And he doesn't want to talk about it.

But he's got to do something, he's got to go somewhere. So he stops off to buy a bag of chips and goes to see Bill Tanner.

He's holding the chips in soggy paper, smelling faintly of vinegar, when Bill opens the door and gives him a big, bright denture smile.

Luther knows something's wrong.

He walks in, automatically ducks his head.

They eat chips out of the paper on the Formica table. Bill slathers his chips in brown sauce from a glass bottle. There are snotty clogs of sauce round the thread of the screw top.

Bill says, 'I saw you on the telly.'

'Oh yeah,' says Luther. 'Did I look fat? The camera adds ten pounds, apparently.'

'Are you all right, son?'

Luther considers telling the old man how not all right he is. Instead, he says, 'You got kids, Bill?'

'Four. Although they're not kids no more.'

'Grandkids?'

'Great-grandkids, mate. Hundreds of the little sods. Like tadpoles.'

Luther chuckles. 'Where are they?'

'Who knows? When you get so old even your kids are in homes, you realize there's nobody in the world who gives a tinker's cuss if you live or die. So there you go. Rule number one: don't get old.'

'There's not much hope of that.'

'Ah. We all think that.'

'I could find them for you,' says Luther. 'Your grandkids. Let them know what's been going on.'

'My eldest grandson's in Australia,' Bill says. 'Went out as a plumber, back in the early nineties. They were crying out for tradesmen back then. He asked me along: *Come and live with us, Granddad.* But his missus didn't want me there. You can tell.'

'And the others?'

'I couldn't even give you their addresses.'

'Eat your chips,' Luther says. 'They'll put hair on your chest.'

Bill looks down at his chest. His shoulders shake.

Luther says, 'Bill? Are you okay, mate?'

The old man just clenches and unclenches his crippled fists.

Luther goes to the sink to wash the chip grease from his fingers, dries his hands on an old tea towel, a souvenir of a long-ago day trip to Blackpool. Then he kneels at the old man's side, pats his back. 'Hey,' he says. 'Hey. Hey.'

When the crying is over, Luther says, 'Can I make you a cup of tea?'

Bill sniffs, wipes his nose on his hand. 'There's whisky in the cupboard.'

Luther brings down the half bottle of whisky and pours a measure into a cloudy glass. 'So what happened?'

Bill's face is white-whiskered. He looks played-out. 'I should never have called your lot,' he says. 'They mean well. But it's calling the law that got me into this.'

Luther gathers up the remains of the fish and chips, shoves them into a carrier bag.

He twists and ties the handles of the carrier bag and places it in the doorway, ready to dump in a wheelie bin.

The old man sniffs.

Luther stares at the carrier bag. He's so tired, he can't seem to complete a thought.

Then it occurs to him.

He says, 'Bill — where's the dog?'

20

At 8.47 p.m., Stephanie Dalton picks up her elder son, Dan, from an evening drama class off the Chiswick High Road.

Dan's fifteen and wants to be an actor.

Steph and Marcus would like for him to be anything but, but what kind of career should they actually be hoping for these days? It's not like being a bank manager is any safer.

Steph grew up wanting to teach but fell into modelling at twenty-one, enjoyed a moderately successful career (catalogues, mostly) made some money, got tired of it all, then left and had the kids. Then Dan and Mia grew up a bit and Steph became bored hanging round the house all day.

She started a domestic cleaning company, called it Zita after the patron saint of cleaning — and of people who lost their keys, apparently. Although she didn't mention that bit on the website.

After Zita took off, she started a company called Handywoman, supplying women-only handyman services to women-only clients and the elderly. Handywoman had a rockier start than Zita, but it's grown into a franchise. All over the country, mothers and daughters, best friends, young mothers, drive around in little white Citroën vans, fixing taps and dry walls and power points. Steph's proud of that.

The downturn has hit them pretty hard, but they're riding it out. Things will turn round.

And Dan wants to be an actor. He's already got the looks, in a still-growing, lanky way. He's got the floppy fringe for it, and a certain way of wearing a shirt. And since he's been taking the lessons there's a new confidence in his voice, in his walk. She doesn't know if it's real or if it's an act. But she supposes that's the point.

Dan emerges from the shabby doorway and she flashes her headlights. He waves, huddled in his coat, and jogs across the road.

She reaches over to pop the passenger door. Dan slides in, bringing the night's cold and wet with him. Sits with his Crumpler messenger bag on his lap.

Steph sees the look on his face. He's not that good an actor, not yet.

She says, 'So what's wrong?'

'Nothing.'

She wants to reach out and brush the floppy fringe from his eyes. But she knows it'll embarrass him. 'Well, it's not nothing,' she says, 'I can see it's not nothing.'

'It's just, we've got these agents coming round,' he says. 'Like actual *agents?* We get to, like, quiz them about the business.'

The business, she thinks, simultaneously cringing and burning with love.

'And then after that,' he says, 'or before, or something. We're putting on this, like, *performance?* Like the best in the class. And I got chosen to play Rosenkrantz?'

'Oh my God,' she says. 'That's amazing!'

He beams at her. He looks pure and beautiful — somewhere in the sunlit grasslands between child and adult.

'Don't call Dad,' he says, 'I want to tell him when we get home.'

She pats his knee. 'Tell him yourself. He'll be so proud. He'll burst!'

Dan hugs his messenger bag.

'What should we have for tea?' Steph says, pulling away. 'Your choice. We're celebrating.'

'Don't jinx it,' he says.

'I'm not jinxing it. We're just celebrating this bit. Some good news. Everybody likes good news.'

'What about KFC?'

'We had KFC on your birthday.'

'Yeah, ages ago.'

'Six weeks.'

'Yeah. Ages.'

* * *

Not far behind them, Henry and Patrick watch from a stolen Toyota Corolla.

They watch Steph pull away, indicate, turn onto Chiswick High Street.

'Hurry up,' Henry says. 'You'll lose them.'

'We know where they live,' says Patrick. 'We've got a key. We can't lose them.'

'That's not the point. I like the hunt.'

Patrick indicates, pulls away.

Henry says, 'The kid. The one with the floppy hair. What's his name again?'

'Daniel,' says Patrick. 'Wants to be an actor.'

'That's right,' says Henry. He sometimes gets them mixed up — all the second-players on the watch list. He says, 'I'm going to cut his fucking head off. That'll make him famous.'

He grins at Patrick, sidelong and ravenous.

Patrick's arms flash with goosebumps. Its proper name is horripilation. Patrick knows that because he once looked it up in an old dictionary. The dictionary lay in what had once been Elaine's bedroom, but was now Henry's. It was next to the Bible, both of them water-stained and damp-smelling. They were inscribed inside with long-faded blue ink, given as a spelling prize when Elaine was a young girl.

So he knows that's what Henry gives him at times like this: horripilation.

And that's what looking in the dictionary gave him, too.

He thought of it, passing through time, sitting in the room already old the day Henry was born, older still the day Patrick was born. Sitting in the room through all those years and all those hands.

Only Patrick, the killer's son, used it to look up the proper word for gooseflesh before throwing the book into the garbage. The book's owner, once a clever child, lay beneath a compost heap in the garden, a half-rotted old lady.

★ ★ ★

Marcus Dalton is an architect, currently thanking God he didn't take the decision to strike out by himself when he was thirty-five.

He's kept the reasonably boring but reasonably safe job with a large firm based in Covent Garden.

Right now he's at home, playing on the Wii with Mia. She's eleven and she's kicking his ass at Super Mario Cart.

Marcus delights in getting his ass kicked. It makes him proud of her.

He's seen competitive parents at the sidelines of primary school football matches wrapped in parkas and scarves and muddy wellingtons; grown men and women with craziness in their eyes for loss of possession or an uncalled foul during a game played by eight-year-olds.

Marcus hates that, and hates them, and hates himself for not enjoying his kids' sporting activities. He'd rather spend time with them in less active ways. Being beaten on the Wii excuses him from congratulating or commiserating from the edge of a divoty soccer field where he sorely does not want to be.

In the kitchen, Gabriella the Gorgeous is making popcorn. Gabriella's tiny, Italian American, ravishing. In the early days, the nickname took some of the heat from her swanning round the house in micro-shorts and crop tops.

But Gabriella's part of the family now. Any incipient lust Marcus might passingly have felt has long since dissipated, exorcized by damp towels left on bathroom floors, Gabriella playing twee lo-fi rock at ear-bleeding volume, Gabriella never putting the milk back in the sodding fridge.

She comes in carrying a big Pyrex bowl of hot microwave popcorn, plonks it down on the sofa next to her.

She says, 'We had another phone call tonight.'

Marcus concentrates on the screen. On the second lap of Coconut Mall he keeps driving his avatar the wrong way up the escalator. 'Not him again?'

'I don't know. I guess. It was a girl this time though.'

'What did she say?'

'Kind of threat-type things.'

'What kind of threat-type things?'

'I don't really know. She sounded drunk or something. I think she was maybe crying.'

Mia says, 'Was it your boyfriend again?'

'Yes,' says Gabriella.

'He's crazy,' Mia says.

'He is.'

'Crazy in lurve,' says Mia.

Marcus bites down on his irritation. He gives Gabriella a look: *Let's talk about this later.*

Mia says, 'What time's Mum coming home?'

'She's on her way,' Marcus tells her. 'She's bringing KFC.'

'Yuck.'

'Daniel chose.'

'Daniel always chooses.'

She sticks out her tongue and makes a gagging noise. Marcus gently cuffs the back of her head and says, 'Behave.'

'I am behaving. I just don't want KFC. It's all greasy and there's all these *veins*. I want to be a vegetarian.'

'We could go and cook you an omelette?'

'Let's finish this level,' Mia says.

'Fine. What do you want in your omelette?'

'Just cheese.'

'There's some nice bacon.'

'Meh. Just cheese.'

'Salad?'

'Have we got them little tomatoes?'

'*Those* little tomatoes. I think so.'

'Then I'll have some salad. Did I tell you I like beetroot?'

'Since when?'

'I had some at Fiona's house. It was really nice. Not slimy. Have we got any?'

'I don't think so.'

'Can we get some next time we go to the shops?'

'Absolutely.'

They finish the level. Mia wins. Her Mii is called *Giant Wonder Mia*.

Gabriella asks if they want help in the kitchen. Marcus tells her no; this is a little bit of father-daughter time.

Marcus and Mia step into the kitchen together. She's still young enough to hold his hand as they go.

The kitchen is big and bright. The windows are black mirrors. They spend a lot of time in here.

Mia takes some eggs from the box, cracks them into a Pyrex dish. Marcus goes hunting for the frying pan. He doesn't find it in the drawer. It's in the dishwasher, residually warm from this morning's cycle.

He spritzes it with sunflower oil, puts it on the hob.

Mia grabs a fork and mixes the eggs. The trick is to fold them, not beat them. She sprinkles in a little salt, a good dash of pepper. She likes pepper.

She hears the key in the lock. The front door opens. It's a sound as familiar to her as the sound of her own heartbeat; Mia was born in this house, in a birthing pool in the dining room.

She's never lived anywhere else. It's a big house, a bit messy. But she loves it and never wants to leave. She's eleven years old, and home is heaven.

Gabriella shovels popcorn into her mouth and watches an episode of *The Biggest Loser* recorded on Sky Plus.

Gabriella never puts on weight; it doesn't matter what she eats. Partly because of this, *The Biggest Loser* is one of her favourite shows. She enjoys watching it while snacking on popcorn or ice cream or, once, a six-pack of doughnuts. The crystals of sugar at the edge of her lips, her fingers sticky with it, while shame-faced, dirigible-sized husbands, wives and daughters took to the scales like prisoners about to be executed.

But Steph disapproves of *The Biggest Loser*. Steph disapproves of all reality shows. She doesn't mind if Gabriella watches them, as long as the kids aren't around.

Gabriella thinks this is bullshit, but she doesn't have Sky Plus in her room — despite the dropping of some fairly heavy hints on deaf ears.

Steph takes a detour to the KFC drive-through, tries to pay with an expired debit card: she forgot to replace it with the new one that arrived about three weeks ago. So has to hunt round her receipt-stuffed purse to find cash.

They drive the rest of the way in silence, Dan's shoulders tense with the scale of his mortification, the greasy bucket in its plastic carrier bag balanced on his narrow lap.

Steph doesn't notice the car driving two or three places behind them.

She's experienced moments of urban terror: she's been burgled more than once — most recently less than a year ago. (She thought for a while that her house keys had been stolen. In fact, they turned up on her kitchen table as if placed there by a poltergeist.)

And she's had a few dodgy phone calls. The most recent sequence of them, she was relieved and strangely chagrined to learn, were from a lovelorn kid called Will who nursed a obsessional crush on Gabriella the Gorgeous.

Steph was distressed, and slightly vexed by young Will's lovelorn want of imagination. But a few difficult phone calls — first to the boy himself, and several to the police — soon put things right.

She's passed him on the high street several times since then. He says *hello* and drops his eyes and moves on. Steph feels sorry for him now, sorry for the embarrassment his uncontrolled love caused him. Letting teenagers fall in love is like letting them drive sports cars. There's far too much power in the engine.

She parks across the road, relieved to see the house, the lights on. She regrets her spontaneous offer of fried chicken because it smells and because it's terrible for you and because she loves the chips, dusted with salt and dipped in glutinous, just-warm-enough chicken gravy. And she knows she'll overcompensate tomorrow, have a tiny breakfast, a salad for lunch. And then, around 3.30, she'll get cranky and overcompensate again with a fat slice of carrot cake. She'll be revisited by guilt and she'll eat nothing for dinner except perhaps some noodles. She'll go to bed with a headache.

She slots the key in the lock, and turns it. She opens the door a crack.

She turns her head, to hurry Dan along. Even in the rain, he's dawdling. 'Hurry up,' she says, 'it's getting cold.'

Two men are walking just behind Dan's shoulder.

Steph doesn't know them. But at once, she knows them completely. One of them is young and handsome and scared. The other is compact and strutting, with hair in a neat parting.

Nazi hair, she thinks. That's what they called kids with hair like that when she was at school.

Both men are wearing backpacks.

Dan turns to follow her appalled gaze. The smaller man swings something. It's an aluminium baseball bat. He swings it low and vicious, at her son's knee.

Dan has long, skinny legs and big feet

— Steph's legs. Sometimes at night they still hurt with the growing.

Steph hears bone crack and thinks of ice cubes in glasses.

She draws in her breath but before she can scream the younger of the men rushes forward and shoves the hot, greasy bucket of chicken into her face.

She chokes and panics, stifled by a gorge of fried skin and flesh and hot fat.

The young man punches her in the stomach. Steph falls, gagging, to the ground. The young man starts kicking her.

Patrick turns from the woman and goes to the kid, Dan. He's howling about his broken leg like a fucking baby. Patrick glances nervously left and right. But no lights come on. Nobody comes to their window. Nobody shouts. Nobody interferes.

Nobody ever does.

Patrick hits the boy with a homemade cosh, a hiking sock filled with AA batteries. It wrecks the teeth in the kid's head. The kid coughs and cries and spits fragments of tooth all over the concrete path.

The kid grabs at his mouth and makes a weird muffled noise, like somebody trying to say something urgent through a thin partition wall.

Henry drags the woman into the house by her hair. He gets chicken all over his fingers.

Marcus sets down the omelette pan and says to his daughter, 'Stay here.'

She stares at him with wide eyes as he hurries away. She listens to the omelette burning on the stove. She can't believe her dad — so orderly, so safety-conscious — has forgotten it. And this thought makes her feel weak and afraid and very small. In its way it's worse than the horrible noises — the bangs and the crashes and most of all the terrible, terrible screams — that are coming from the other side of the house.

Mia needs to feel big. So she walks to the cooker and turns it off. Then she moves the pan off the hob.

She puts the hot pan into the damp sink. It sizzles, shockingly, like a serpent. She recoils from it.

A man in dark clothes drags Steph through the open door. Steph's face is smeared in some kind of matter.

Gabriella thinks at first that it must be vomit, that Steph's eaten her KFC and it's made her unwell and this man must have brought her home.

But only for a moment.

The man sees Gabriella and grins a wolf's grin, chop-licking, ear to ear. He kicks Steph in the ribs, then steps forward, raising a baseball bat.

Gabriella steps away. She stumbles over a shoe, one of Mia's Converse.

The man swings a bat. It connects with the side of Gabriella's head. She hears it. She falls.

The man stamps on her stomach three times, like he's putting out a camp fire.

Marcus runs into the hallway.

Steph lies with her eyes open. She's making strange movements with her right hand.

Dan is fighting with a young man in the front garden. The young man is hitting him again and again in the face.

Marcus makes a move to intervene, then notices the man in the living room. He's stamping on Gabriella's belly. He's only a door away from the kitchen.

Marcus calls out, '*Mia, run!*'

Then he races into the living room and punches the man in the back of the head.

He grabs the man's shoulders and throws him into the wall.

The man drops his baseball bat.

Gabriella drags herself to the far side of the room. She's making a sound. Marcus hopes he never hears a sound like it again.

He casts around, looking for something to kill the man with. That's his only thought.

His eyes settle on the TV power lead. He steps forward, meaning to grab it.

The younger man steps into the living room and stabs Marcus in the back with a hunting knife.

Mia stands frozen. She can feel the heat of the cooker on the back of her neck.

Because she's eleven years old, her life so far has been full of horror: the horror of lying in bed at night and worrying about Mum and Dad dying in a plane crash or getting divorced.

The horror of the wardrobe door. And the thing under the bed. And worst of all, the teddy bear Grandma bought her for her fourth birthday. It's perched on the edge of Mia's bed and glares at her through glassy, malevolent eyes.

268

When Mum and Dad have gone to bed Mia covers Bad Bear with a fleecy blanket, making him just a vague lumpy shape. It freaks her out to think of his amber eyes blazing in rage. But it's better than having him glower at you all night. (She'd wet the bed a few times, and made up some stories about drinking too much water before going to sleep. But really, it was Bad Bear.)

One day, Mia told her the au pair (in those days, a Spanish girl called Camilla) that she was too big for bears now. Perhaps it was time for a Poor Child to have him (the world, she knew at five years old, was full of Poor Children).

Camilla was touched by this gesture. And so was Steph. So Steph and Mia sat in Mia's room, on the edge of the bed, holding hands.

Steph said, 'Camilla told me you're too grown up for Cuddle Bear.' (Cuddle Bear was what Mia's mum and dad thought Bad Bear was called.)

Mia nodded and bit her lower lip. She could feel her eyes welling, because she was sure Mum was going to say no, that Bad Bear was a gift from Grandma, who had now passed.

Steph misread her daughter's welling eyes. She stroked her brow and her soft hair with a firm palm. 'Where would you like Cuddle Bear to go?'

Mia shrugged: *I dunno*.

'Well,' said Steph. 'I know they always want toys at the children's hospital.'

Mia endured a little shiver of terror at that thought: at how Bad Bear would delight in all those beds, all those sleeping children! But (and she feels a throb of guilt about this, even six years and half a life later) she nodded and said yes. And that was that. Bad Bear went to hospital.

No fear since has been anywhere near as bad.

Except for now. She stands in the kitchen and terrifying noises come from the hallway. The noise of men shouting and things falling over and what sounds like a horrible laugh, a screeching hysterical laugh. But it's not a laugh.

Mia pisses herself. The warmth runs down her legs and over her bare feet and pools on the tiles.

Dad calls out for the second time, '*Mia, run!*'

Mia remains frozen for a moment. Then something snaps inside her and she runs.

After stabbing Marcus, Patrick hurries to the front garden to drag Daniel inside.

Daniel's semi-conscious. Patrick dumps him near his mother.

He sees that look, the look that Henry told him about.

Henry was right. It looks like adoration.

Patrick hates Daniel for it. He stamps on Daniel's shattered knee.

After Patrick has incapacitated the husband, Henry turns to the au pair.

Although under normal circumstances he'd like to fuck her, Henry's not interested in her tonight. She's more of a pet than part of the family.

So he drags her by the hair to the middle of the room and cuts her throat in front of Marcus. There's a satisfying jet of arterial blood.

She twitches comically and Henry laughs. He catches Marcus's eye, the way two strange men will catch each other's eye on the seafront when a pretty girl walks past.

Marcus jellyfishes on the floor. He's muttering something about God.

Henry laughs, enjoying himself. He slips on the old brass knuckles and punches Marcus in the face — *woom woom woom*.

Marcus's nose explodes across his face. Henry thinks he's dead. But he's not.

'Pleath,' Marcus says, through his shattered mouth. 'Pleath. Pleath. Pleath.'

Henry loves that.

'Pleath what?' he says.

But then he remembers why he came here.

He says, 'Patrick?'

Patrick steps into the room. He's treading blood everywhere.

He's hangdog and surly, slope-shouldered.

Henry finds him disgusting, physically repulsive. He'd like to smash his stupid fucking sulky face in with the brass knuckles, *woom woom woom*, and that would be that. He'd leave him here, face smashed, brains plopping into his lap like Play-Doh.

Henry says, 'Where's the little girl?'

'Who? Mia?'

'Yes,' says Henry, with exaggerated patience. 'Mia.'

'I thought you had her.'

'Does it look like I've got her?'

Patrick doesn't answer.

'So go and get her,' Henry says.

'What about the mother and son?'

Henry shrugs off his backpack, unzips it, takes out the new hatchet. 'I'll sort them out.'

Patrick sets off to find Mia. He steps over the au pair — her foot is still doing a farcical little twitch, as if she's pretending to be asleep but unable to resist dancing to a favourite song heard on a distant radio.

For some reason this makes Patrick sad. That twitching foot, a single brown freckle on the sole.

Patrick heads to the kitchen. It's a big house with a big kitchen, but he knows his way around. He's been in here before.

Somebody's been making an omelette; there's a jug smeared with egg, a fork still sticking out of it. There's the black pan, a serious cook's pan, cooling and greasy in the butler sink.

Patrick's senses are heightened. He can feel heat radiating from the stove.

Nobody's in here.

He looks down. There's a puddle of piss on the floor.

The cupboard under the sink is open.

Patrick kneels. He opens the cupboard door. Sees cleaning equipment. Sponges. A roll of bin bags.

No Mia.

He opens the next cupboard. And the next.

He opens the pantry.

No Mia.

He clambers onto the kitchen bench, looks in the high kitchen cupboards. That would be a good place to hide. That's where Patrick would think about hiding if he were Mia's age. (Except

Patrick hadn't hidden at all, had he?)

Mia's not in the kitchen.

He pads down the hallway. He checks the cupboard under the stairs. A Dyson, a cobwebby Swiffer floor mop, a whole bunch of crap. He shines his little torch into the spidery corner.

No Mia.

He stands at the bottom of the stairs and shines his torch up and into the darkness.

If he were Mia, would he hide up there?

In the darkness? With Henry downstairs?

No.

Patrick heads to the garden.

Mia didn't want to go upstairs. It was dark. She knew she'd be trapped. So she sneaked out, into the garden.

It's a pretty big garden, high-walled on three sides. The walls are too high for her to climb.

An old potting shed abuts the back of the house. A long time ago, it was an outside lavatory or something. It's spidery and horrible. The old bricks are crumbly at the corners.

Mia's barefoot. She straddles the corner of the outhouse, digs her fingertips and toes into the crumbling mortar between the bricks. She tests it for depth, then lifts herself. Her fingers tremble with the strain.

Her feet scrabble. She rips a toenail. But Dad calls her a monkey because she's good at climbing.

She's halfway up the wall of the outhouse when a man walks into the kitchen.

Mia freezes on the wall like a gecko.

The only moving thing is her heart. It feels

conspicuous, a sick, wet, *whim! wham!* in her thin chest.

She watches the man, who has a strangely gentle and worried face, like a boy soldier. Then he opens a cupboard and looks inside. He sweeps all the stuff inside across the floor.

Mia knows the man is looking for her. It's difficult not to watch, the way it's difficult not to watch scary movies sometimes, because sometimes looking away is worse.

The man peers through the window. She watches his eyes scan the garden.

His eyes sweep over her.

She realizes that the kitchen light is on, which is why the kitchen looks as bright as a fish tank. The man is probably staring at his own reflection.

But that's difficult to accept. So when the man turns and storms out of the kitchen, she thinks it's a trap. She stays there, clinging to the wall, too scared to move.

He's gone for a long time.

Mia begins to climb again.

She grazes her fingers and her toes, and once her leg slips; she barks her shin to the knee. But she makes it. She heaves and struggles and pulls herself onto the roof of the old outhouse.

Then the young man comes back to the kitchen. He opens the door and steps into the garden.

Mia freezes on the roof of the outhouse. She squats there like a cat. She is higher than the man's head. If he doesn't look up, it's possible that he won't see her.

274

He pokes around the garden, probing the corners with the beam of a torch. When he turns in her direction, she sees that his face is different: it's scrunched up as if he's been crying. There's black stuff all over one side of his face, in the vague shape of a human hand. Except Mia knows it's not really black stuff, it's red stuff.

She gasps — and the man looks up.

He and Mia stare at one another, perfectly still.

Then Mia scrambles over the remaining few feet of wall between her and next-door's garden. She drops to the other side of the wall.

Her ankle twists and it hurts. She should be screaming, but she doesn't even think about screaming. She just sprints, hardly registers the damaged ankle.

She doesn't look back until she's crossed the wide garden, waded into the rose bushes where thorns scratch her.

There he is, scrambling onto the garden wall. He jumps down, a lot better than she had. He doesn't look like he's hurt his ankle at *all*.

He lowers into a crouch and scampers towards her.

Mia tries to climb but there's nothing to grab; the ivy the Robertsons used to cultivate before they moved away is too tangled and loose, it just spools away in her hands. She gets tangled and panicky. She risks one more look, just one more look over her shoulder.

There he is, the sad-faced young man with the red handprint over his face. He's just looking at her.

She doesn't know how long he's been there.

She's scared to see the young man is scared, too, because that means there's something even *worse* in her house — and whatever it is, it's in there with her parents. Mia wants to cry. Her knees are knocking together.

The man is breathing funny. He looks away, at the empty house the Robertsons used to live in, which is now for sale.

He says, 'Come on.'

'No,' says Mia, although her voice is small.

The man says, 'Listen. We don't have time. We don't. My dad's in that house and he's sent me out to get you.'

Mia begins to cry. She says, 'What does he want?'

'To make you his little girl.'

'I don't want to be his little girl.'

'Then come with me.'

'Who are you?'

'Patrick.' He thrusts out his hand. 'This way.'

When Mia doesn't take the hand, he simply strides to the kitchen door of the empty house and tries it. It's locked of course. So he takes off his hoodie and wraps it round his fist.

He puts his fist through the window, brushes loose glass from the frame. Then he wriggles like a worm through the broken window. He appears at the kitchen door and opens it. And still, Mia doesn't scream.

She thinks she shouldn't go with this man, but she hurries on bare feet to the Robertsons' kitchen door. She and the man hurry through the monstrous, echoing darkness of the empty house. The ghosts of all the families who lived here before watch from the black corners.

They come to the front door. Patrick opens it. They sneak out, back into the cold night.

And then they're running.

* * *

Henry finishes smearing the word on the wall. He calls out, 'Patrick?'

There's no answer.

Then he hears a noise.

It's a pane of glass shattering. And Henry knows. Just like that.

He looks at the mess in the room. The mess on his clothes and in his hair.

He jogs to the kitchen. The door is open. No glass is broken.

He thinks of the empty house next door.

He returns to the living room and hurries to pack. It takes too long. His things are wet and his hands are busy with rage.

Then he slings on the backpack and rushes out the front door.

He sprints for the car.

* * *

They run silently. Patrick has told her to be quiet as a mouse, not to make a noise, because if they do, his dad will know where they are.

Patrick is faster than Mia, whose feet are bare and tender on the hard pavement.

Now he turns, hopping up and down on the spot.

Hurry up! Come on! Please!

She tries. But there's a green bottle of lager in the gutter and Mia steps on a shard of glass.

She doesn't make much of a noise, and Patrick is proud of her.

But these are quiet streets.

★   ★   ★

Henry hears a child cry out.

A girl.

He runs faster. He pumps his arms. In his hand is a carpet knife.

★   ★   ★

Patrick runs to Mia. His tears have thinned the blood on the side of his face.

'I know it hurts,' he whispers. 'I know it does. But please.'

She limps to him, fast as she can.

Patrick kneels. He and Mia are face-to-face. 'Please let me carry you.'

She hesitates, balancing on one foot. But when she sees the way his eyes glance fearfully over her shoulder, she says, 'Okay.'

Patrick scoops Mia into his arms, the cold skin and warm core of her. She's all rods and knobs, heavier than she looks.

He runs.

The car isn't far.

* * *

Henry turns a corner at speed and sees them.

There's Patrick, hobbling along with the girl in his arms.

Her foot is blood black.

Henry laughs, but it doesn't sound like a laugh.

He runs faster still.

* * *

Patrick reaches the car and sets Mia down.

'Wait just for one minute. Watch the road for me.'

She leans against the car, watching the long straight avenue.

Patrick searches in his pockets for the keys. His hand is shaking.

* * *

Mia whimpers, deep in the back of her throat.

'What?' Patrick says. He's trying to get the key into the lock.

'He's coming.'

Patrick looks up to see Henry sprinting down the road. Lunatic, blood smeared. He's got a carpet knife in his hand.

Patrick knows he won't get the car started in time.

'Mia,' he says. 'Run now. Scream. Make as much noise as you can.'

Mia sees the look in his eyes. Then she bolts.

As she runs, she screams.

What she screams, again and again, is *Please*.

Patrick waits, keys in hand, as Henry descends upon him.

He isn't scared.

He's thinking of his bike. A BMX.

Henry doesn't slow. He just keeps coming and coming.

Patrick braces himself.

Henry punches his shoulder into Patrick's solar plexus. Patrick smashes into the bonnet of the car.

Henry grabs his throat, stretches him out. Rips and lacerates with the carpet knife.

As Patrick slips from the bonnet of the car, Henry runs in pursuit of the screaming child, knife in hand.

She's only little. She won't have gone far.

And Henry is very, very fast.

21

Luther drives to Highbury Fields and parks across the square. He knits his hands on the steering wheel and watches Crouch's red Jaguar.

He waits for a long time. He doesn't know how long. His mind is blank with hate.

Then he grabs the pickaxe handle from the front passenger footwell and gets out of the Volvo.

He marches across the park and smashes the driver's side window of the Jaguar.

The car begins to beep and shriek in panic.

From his pocket, Luther takes a brand new can of lighter fluid. He squirts it through the car's broken window, over the dashboard and the leather upholstery.

A car's interior contains the parts that are easiest to ignite: carpets, seating foam, soft plastic. And a fire in a car's interior spreads quickly.

He watches the car blaze. He's not scared of an explosion; petrol tanks are made of thick metal. It's unlikely the car will explode with concussive force. And if it does, then so be it. He'd welcome it.

He stands upwind, but the smoke still makes his eyes water.

He waits and waits. Flames singe his eyebrows.

He hears distant sirens.

And then Crouch emerges from his house. He's sockless in slip-on shoes, shock-headed, hurriedly dressed.

He approaches Luther with a strange, crazed expression.

Luther waits.

Crouch's hands and voice are shaking. He says, 'And who the fuck are you?'

Luther grabs Crouch's wrist, twists it, wrenches it between his shoulder blades. He frog-marches Crouch towards the burning car.

'If I break your neck and throw you into this car,' he says, 'by the time an ambulance gets here, you'll be a pool of melted fat.'

Crouch weeps.

Luther can feel the heat charring his tweed coat, drying his eyes.

'Stay away from the old man,' he says.

Then he drops Crouch to the pavement and strides away, across the park.

The sirens are closer. He knows they're for him. He doesn't care.

He returns to the Volvo. He sits and waits.

He watches fire-fighters extinguish the merrily burning car.

Crouch is still there. A woman Luther takes to be a hooker hangs around in the background.

Police take statements. One of them is a careworn, older detective in a rumpled suit and an overcoat.

Luther can't be sure, not from this distance, but he thinks it's Martin Schenk. Schenk works out of Complaints.

If he's right, it means Crouch has reported him as a police officer.

Luther doesn't care. He sits with hands on the steering wheel, fighting the urge to get out and stride over there, badge the officers and the fire-fighters out of the way, shove Crouch in the sternum, grab his neck and squeeze.

He's still thinking about it when the call comes in.

It's Teller. It's after 2 a.m. so he pretty much knows.

He picks up the phone.

'Sorry to wake you.'

'Don't worry,' he says. 'I was up.'

There's a pause. Teller wanting to say something. He helps her out. 'Where?'

'Chiswick.'

'How many?'

'Four at the scene. Mother. Father. Son. Au pair. The daughter's missing.'

He sits back and watches the fire-fighters douse the burning Jaguar with retardant foam. He enjoys the blackened skeleton of it, the melted plastic. 'How old's the daughter?'

'Eleven. Name's Mia. Mia Dalton.'

He wonders how bad it is. He says, 'Send me the address. I'll be there as quick as I can'

'Before you do that,' she says, 'there's something else.'

'What else?'

'We think we got one of them. The son.'

There's a long moment, like waiting for a second hand to tick. He says, 'What?'

'Multiple wounds,' she says. 'Two hundred metres from the scene. Witness heard an altercation; two men seemed to be fighting over a little girl. The little girl was bleeding.'

He grips the steering wheel harder, to stop himself floating away. 'This witness,' he says. 'He

283

didn't think to go out and help?'

' 'He' was a she. Sixty-five years old.'

'But not everyone who heard it was a sixty-five-year-old woman living alone, were they?'

'No.'

'The son?'

'Alive. On his way to operating theatre as we speak.'

'Will he live?'

'I don't have the latest. It's a bit tonto round here. The jury's out, apparently.'

'So there's no way I can interview him?'

'Not right now.'

'No ID?'

'Nothing on him. Wallet, cash, pre-paid credit card.'

'Pre-paid where?'

'We're looking into that.'

'It won't be traceable,' he says. 'They're too careful for that. You buy one of these cards for cash somewhere. Even better, you slip some hoodie a few quid to go in and buy one for you. You running his DNA?'

'It's being expedited.'

He unwinds the window, slips the magnetic bubble light on the roof. He sets the satnav and turns onto Fieldway Crescent, unseen by everyone.

Except possibly Schenk, who turns in his direction, puts a hand to his brow as if shielding it from the sun and squints across the darkness of the park.

When there's enough distance between Luther and Schenk, he puts the misery lights and the sirens on. He follows their lament all the way to Chiswick.

★ ★ ★

He's the last clown to arrive at the circus. He badges the log officer, ducks under the tape and into harsh lights that throw the night into sudden flat, high definition.

No one looks like they've slept for a week.

Teller says nothing. Just nods.

Luther digs his hands into his pockets. He thinks of his wife, wonders what she's doing.

He steps over the threshold and into the hallway.

He smells it.

SOCO are in here, men and women in jumpsuits, breathing masks, blue bootees. They've got cameras and rulers and tape.

Before Luther sees the remains, he sees the upturned furniture, the blood on the walls. The word.

He looks at it. He looks at the word on the wall, blood smeared on there with a human hand, thick as oil paint.

Luther looks at Teller. He sees pity in her eyes and the pity scares him because it's a reaction to the look on his face.

When he stumbles from the house, he knows that everybody is looking at him, casting sidelong glances.

Outside, the air's not cold enough. He wants to dive into icy water. He wants to hold his breath until it hurts.

Teller takes his elbow, gestures with her head.

They walk into that liminal time when night is passing into day.

She says, 'Do you want off?'

'Yes,' he says. 'I want off.'

'Then you're off.' She lets him think about it for a moment, then goes on. 'But you should know, if you come off the case, then that's it, that's who you are. It doesn't matter what you did before or what you do in the future. In their minds, you'll be the copper who let this happen and walked away. I know that's not fair. And I know it's not true. But this bastard said he'd do this if you didn't apologize to him. And although that could never happen, that's not the story the media's going to tell. The story is you and him. We *made* it you and him. It's our fault. And if you back off now — which I would if I were you, God help me — but if you do, this is who you become. The man who let what happened in there, happen.'

There are choppers in the sky. Their searchlights sweep the streets.

'It's not . . . ' he says, after a long pause. She doesn't hear him; his voice has gone. He coughs

286

into his fist to clear his throat, starts again. 'It's not unusual for a man like this to humiliate his victims post mortem. We've all seen it. He'll leave a woman with her legs spread, something inserted into her vagina. He'll mutilate her breasts and her face. He'll dump a hooker by a 'no dumping' sign. But I've never seen anything like this.'

Pete Black has removed the victim's heads and swapped them around.

The son's head grinning from the mother's body.

The au pair has been posed in the armchair with her own head in her lap.

'Like someone playing with toys,' he says. 'Like a fucked-up, petulant toddler ripping his sister's dolls to pieces. Putting Barbie's head on the teddy bear. The teddy's bear's head on the baby doll.'

He shudders in his coat. He wonders if he smells of smoke. Supposes he must. He scuffs his feet. 'Who're the victims?'

'Stephanie Dalton, Marcus Dalton, Daniel Dalton. Gabriella Magnoli. As far as we can tell, they're pretty much perfect. Mrs Dalton's a businesswoman. Used to be a model. He's an architect, wins awards, teaches, mentors. Students love him, apparently. The son's good-looking, wants to be an actor. The daughter — '

'What about her?' Luther says.

'What am I supposed to say?' Teller barks, forgetting herself. She has a daughter not much older than the missing girl. 'She's eleven. What else is there to say?'

'That's the point, isn't it?' Luther says. 'They're perfect. He watches them. He's jealous. He's resentful. He covets what they've got. Happiness. Family. Normality.'

Luther's finding energy now. Warmth in his blood. He says, 'Pete Black's son. Patrick. How old is he?'

'Twenty? Twenty-one?'

'Fingerprints on record?'

'Nope.'

Luther's smiling. He paces. He rubs the crown of his head.

Teller says, 'What?'

'I don't know.'

'Yes you do.'

Luther's laughing now. If he stopped for a moment, he'd see the look on Teller's face. But he's swaggering in carnivorous delight, clapping his hands.

'John,' says Teller.

He rubs his head, walks in a circle. 'Boss,' he says. 'I need to do something.'

'So go on then,' she says. 'What?'

'I can't tell you.'

He waits it out. You don't rush her.

'On a theoretical scale of one to ten,' she says, 'how much do I not want to know about this?'

'Twenty.' He steps in before she can protest. 'If I went through proper channels, waited for you to cross the Ts and give me the official nod, it would take weeks. And I need to do it now. As in this morning. And if it turns out I'm wrong, which I'm not — '

'But if you are?'

'If it turns out I'm wrong, there'll be hell to pay. You'll have to sack me. There'll be an outcry.'

There's a second, longer wait. At the end of it, she says, 'Is it going to help us find that little girl?'

'Yes.'

'Okay. Then sod off and do it.'

He nods. 'Where's Howie?'

'At the factory,' says Teller. 'Be gentle with her.'

As Luther walks away, Teller's phone rings. She checks it.

DSU Schenk.

She kills the call, pockets the phone. Doesn't want to know.

★　★　★

For a long time, Mia thinks she's dead because there is darkness and silence and because she can't breathe.

But she's not dead. She's in the boot of a car. She's got stuff over her mouth. She can't move her hands or feet.

She knows her mum and dad are dead, though, because the man told her that. Before stopping to transfer her to the boot, he just shoved her in the passenger well of the car and kept her head pressed down with the flat of his hand as he drove.

She was whimpering for her mum. She was scared and cold and she hurt all over and there was a feeling in her stomach.

289

Shut up about your mum and cunting dad, he said and she hated his voice.

She knows he's dangerous, like the stray dog that followed them when they were on holiday in Greece that one time.

It was walking at a funny angle and it had a weird look. Her dad was spooked by it. He lifted Mia and put her into her mum's arms — she'd been little then. Her dad and brother stooped at the roadside and gathered up armloads of little stones and threw them at the dog until it went away.

This man is the same as that dog. He has the same flecks of saliva round his lips, the same idiot rage in his eyes.

Mia remembers the Stranger Danger classes she took at school, that time the police lady came in to speak to them.

Know your name, address, and phone number. Avoid walking anywhere alone. If a stranger approaches you, you do not have to speak to him. Never approach a stranger in a motor vehicle. Just keep walking.

If a stranger grabs you, do everything you can to stop him or her from pulling you away or dragging you into his or her car. Drop to the ground, kick, hit, bite, scream. If someone is dragging you away, scream, 'This is not my dad,' or 'This is not my mum.'

None of that had been any good. Mia had screamed and screamed and nobody had come.

But Mia knows why. He's not a stranger. He's the mad dog in Greece. He's the thing that sometimes lived in her wardrobe, that peeked through the crack in the door when the lights were out, and Daniel was snoring in his feet-stinking room and Mum and Dad were cuddled up in their big bed. He's not a stranger, how can he be? She's known him all her life.

Mia prays. She tries to say something sensible, to ask God for something specific; Dad had talked to her about the way God answers prayers. He gave you what you *needed*, Dad said, which was not necessarily the same as what you wanted. You might pray for a mountain bike but that might not be what God wanted you to have. Or you might pray for Melissa James to fall over and break her ankle on her stupid inline skates, but God might not want you to have that either.

Mia can't believe that God wants this for her.

But on the other hand, she heard her dad screaming tonight and although she's never heard anyone die before, she knows that's what it was. Her strong and handsome dad dying in terror and helplessness and pain. And she's pretty sure God can't have wanted that, either. But it happened.

So she needs to pray, but she's confused and all that will come is *Please God please God please God please.*

It goes round and round her head like a train.

She lies curled up in the dark, smelling the car's wet carpet.

★ ★ ★

Under yellowish light, the Serious Crime Unit is brim-full of uniformed and plain-clothed personnel.

Men and women in shirtsleeves, smelling sour; people who should be home but aren't.

They watch Luther pass. He feels their eyes.

He stops at Howie's desk. She's hunched, red-faced. Pretending not to have seen him, praying that he'll walk on by.

He waits until she turns her head and pulls a worried face. She says, 'Boss . . . '

'I don't care about last night,' Luther says. 'You did the right thing. All I care about is, are you ready to work with me now? Right now. Or do I need to pull in someone else?'

'No,' she says. 'Don't do that.'

'Good.'

He marches to his cramped little office, full of Benny's energy drinks and sandwich containers.

Howie follows, shuts the door behind her.

'Seriously,' she says.

'We don't need to talk about it.'

'I feel terrible. I didn't know what to do.'

'You did the right thing,' he says again. 'Let's leave it.'

'But if I hadn't . . . '

'What?'

'Would you have found him? I mean, before . . . '

'Before he did this? Tonight?'

'Yes.'

He locks eyes with her. For a cruel moment he considers saying *yes*. Letting her live with it.

He sits. 'No,' he says. 'I don't think so. I was

292

trying. I was really trying, but I don't think I could've done that.'

She nods. She doesn't know if he's telling the truth.

Neither does Luther.

'Look,' he says. 'I got tunnel vision. I lost my sense of perspective. You're right: I needed someone to stop me. You did me a favour. And it took courage.'

He thinks about telling Howie about Irene, an old woman, now long-dead, found mummified in her chair. His callow shame for not stepping up and confronting his superiors for the jokes they told. The lack of respect.

He doesn't tell her. He just says, 'I admire what you did.'

There is a long, good moment.

'So,' Howie says, 'what are we looking for?'

'I need a current address.'

'Whose address?'

Luther tells her.

Howie doesn't look at him. Doesn't register the name. Just logs on, enters her password, accesses the database. A universe of enormity. Faces stored as binary data. Faces that grin in school photographs, wedding photographs, faces that grin from newsprint and news broadcasts.

She double-checks the spelling and hits *Return*.

And there she is.

And now Howie understands. She turns to Luther. There's an expression on her face that Luther has seen before. There's a kind of admiration in it. But there's a kind of pity too.

Luther says, 'What do you think?'

She nods.

'Print me this stuff off,' Luther says. 'And get me a picture of Mia.'

Howie is staring into the middle distance. She says, 'Holy shit.'

Luther hesitates in the doorway. He wants to say something wise, something about the human spirit. But there's nothing to say and there are no lessons to be learned.

'You need to hurry up,' he says, and leaves her to it.

* * *

Henry drives through the electric gates and parks the car. He gets out and opens the boot.

Mia's curled up inside.

She's shocked and compliant.

She looks up at him. He thinks of the tired look in a bait dog's eyes, the surrender, and knows he won't need the ketamine.

But he keeps it to hand anyway, in case it's a trick. Henry's been tricked before. Henry has learned his lessons the hard way.

He unties her and hands her the choke collar. 'Be a good girl and put this on.'

She slips the chain over her head.

Henry gives it a gentle but sharp tug, just to show he can. Then he smiles to pretend he's only playing.

Mia's legs are stiff and everything about her hurts, and there's a swimmy feeling as if none of this is really happening. She climbs out of the

294

boot of the car and into the garden.

It doesn't seem possible that she can be here in the first glimmers of daylight and she can be standing in a huge garden, one of the biggest gardens she's ever seen, with a man all covered in dried blood. He's got blood in his hair and it's dried like thin black mud all over his face. He's got a black crust of blood inside the whorls of his ears and under his nails.

When she really looks at the house she sees that it's very large but unmaintained. It doesn't look like a rich man's house. It looks like a haunted house. Or a witch's house.

'Shhhh,' says the man.

Mia nods submission. She knows that if she makes a noise, he'll pull on the chain and she won't be able to breathe.

She walks alongside the man, at his heel, towards the house.

He says, 'Do you like dogs?'

Mia nods.

'Good,' the man says. 'We've got lots of dogs.'

He leads her into the house. Inside, it's old-fashioned. Wood panelling and hunting pictures on the walls. The glass in the frames is so smeared and dusty you can hardly see the pictures. It smells funny, like the windows have been kept shut for a hundred years and nobody has ever washed the sheets.

The man leads her to a door under the stairs. He makes her stand to one side. Then he pulls back some heavy iron bolts that keep the door locked. He leans into what Mia takes to be a cupboard and pulls on a light cord. A bare bulb comes on, dusty on top. The dust starts to smell as the bulb gets hotter.

'Down we go,' he says.

Mia is uncertain. But the man jerks the chain and she steps through the door. It's not a cupboard. There are stairs leading down.

It's all concrete down here, and the sound is echoey.

Then there's a corridor with cupboards lining it, with mops and buckets in the cupboards, except all the mops are old and their grey heads have dried and gone stiff. The mop buckets are dented metal. They smell like hospital disinfectant, a clean smell that's also a dirty smell.

At the end of the corridor is a door.

The door has iron bolts on it, and a big, heavy padlock. The man hangs the loop of the dog lead over a big hook set high in the wall. Mia has to stand on tiptoes and it gets hard to breathe. He struggles to unlock the padlock and pull back the rusty bolts.

The door opens onto a little room. It's the kind of room where if you were on holiday in a house like this with your friends and your brother, you'd dare each other to go inside.

It's not that much smaller than her bedroom at home, but it feels much smaller because there are no windows. There are spiderwebs every-where, and in the spiderwebs are tiny, dry black beetle husks. There's only one bulb and it's a kind of sickly yellow that makes the room seem darker not lighter.

The man unhooks her and says, 'In you go.'

She tells him she can't, so he pulls on the choke chain until the world goes red. Then he gently shoves her inside.

There is a low bed with a damp grey blanket and a thin pillow like Mia had to sleep on once on holiday in France, except this pillow doesn't have a pillow-case and it's got big yellow circles on it, stains that remind her of skin disease.

'Sit down,' says the man.

She sits on the edge of the horrible bed. It makes her skin crawl along her bones like a caterpillar on a tree. She glances into a corner and in the corner there's a little bookshelf and on the bookshelf are some books.

They're children's books: *The House at Pooh Corner*, *The Secret Garden*, *The Tiger Who Came to Tea*. The books are very old and dog-eared and some of the pages have come loose from the binding. Seeing them makes terror mushroom inside her. She glances at the open door and makes a move and the man slaps her in the face.

She sits on the edge of the bed. She can't speak.

The man kneels down. He puts his face very close to hers. She can smell his breath. He says, 'Are you hungry?'

She shakes her head.

'Thirsty?'

She nods.

'I'll get you some water in a minute. Okay?'

She nods.

'Now. I know that right now you're scared.

297

Last night was very upsetting for all of us, wasn't it?'

She doesn't know what to say. She says, 'That's all right.'

'Good girl,' he says. 'I know this isn't the nicest bedroom in the world, but you'll soon get used to it.'

Mia swallows. Her throat is dry and shaky. She says, 'What do you mean?'

'Well. This is your home now.'

'I don't want it to be my home.'

'I know you feel like that now,' says the man. 'And you'll keep feeling like that for a little while. But soon it'll change, and it'll get so you like it here. And once you've grown to like it a little bit, I'll let you come upstairs, watch some TV. Do you like TV?'

'Yes,' says Mia.

'Good,' says the man. Then he gives her a look like he loves her and he's glad she's home. It makes her wet herself again. The dark pool spreads all over the blanket.

'Don't worry about that,' says the man. 'It'll dry.'

He shuts the door and Mia hears the screeching slide of the bolt.

She sits in silence, clasping the edge of the bed. She's too scared to move. She can't even think. When she turns her head she sees the bookshelf in the corner and its meaning wells up inside her until the thought is too big for her head.

An hour later, or five minutes, he comes back. She hears the door under the stairs opening, his

298

footsteps on the concrete steps. Then the frightful shriek of the rusty bolt and the hinge and he stands in the doorway.

In one hand he's got a bucket.

He passes it to her. He says, 'This is for you to do your business in. But if you look extra closely, there's a present inside.'

She stares into the blue plastic bucket. Inside it is a tiny rabbit. It's trembling. She reaches in to lift it out. It turns in the bucket and bites her finger.

She withdraws sharply. She considers the baby rabbit, cowering and terrified in its circular blue prison.

'Just leave him in there for a bit,' says the man. 'Then tip over the bucket. Let him have a sniff round and get used to the place. Once he's done that, you can be best friends. Would you like that?'

She gives the man a nod because she's too scared not to.

'Smile,' says the man. 'I just got you a present.'

She smiles.

'That's good,' says the man. 'What are you going to call it?'

'I don't know.'

'It's got to have a name,' says the man.

Mia can't think of any names. She can't think of any words at all. But she wants to please the man. She glances in desperation at the bookshelf.

'Peter,' she says.

'Excellent,' says the man. Then he says, 'Well, you and Peter have had a long night. Why don't you take forty winks?'

'Okay.'

'If you need to do a wee or a poo,' he says, 'do it in that bucket, okay?'

'Okay.'

'I'll get you a proper toilet tomorrow. Ones like they have in caravans. That'll be nice.'

'Yes,' she says.

'Good,' says the man. 'Goodnight, then.'

'Goodnight.'

The man hesitates in the doorway, seems to chew something over. Then he says, 'Do you like babies?'

'Yes,' says Mia.

'Do you want lots of babies, when you've grown up?'

'Yes,' says Mia.

'Good,' says the man.

He closes and bolts the door and walks upstairs and closes and bolts that door, too.

And in here it stinks of mouldy blankets and damp air and those old books, the smell of age and decay in them. Mia knows she will never open those books, not even if she's so bored she wants to die, because she knows that many children have leafed through those books in the before time. There may be drawings in there in another childish hand and if there are she couldn't bear it.

Mia sits on the bed, looking down at the rabbit. Its nose is twitching, super-alert to its surroundings.

Gently, Mia tips the bucket onto its side. Then she inches back on the bed and puts her back to

300

the cold wall and tries not to move or breathe and just concentrates on the rabbit.

After a long, long time the bucket moves slightly on the cold floor. She can see the rabbit's nose, twitching away at the edge.

Then the rabbit pokes out its head and looks around. Its eyes are liquid brown.

The rabbit bolts from the bucket so quickly Mia gives out a little scream and jumps.

The rabbit bolts under the bed into the corner. It huddles there, terror-stricken.

Mia knows not to disturb it. She knows to give it time. She begins, patiently, to pick the scab on her knee. She sings herself a song. It's a happy song that makes her think of happy times. But thinking of happy times is like being kicked in the tummy. She doesn't know what to do.

Mia shuts down. She curls into a ball on the bed. She puts her thumb in her mouth.

Sucking it, she falls asleep.

22

Zoe's propped up in bed, feeling jetlagged and half real. She's been awake all night, trying not to think of it.

She gives up, reaches for her laptop. Navigates to a news website.

Suspected kidnapper of Mia Dalton, she hears. *Murder of Dalton family. Second home invasion in two days. No comment on suspected link to the killer of Sarah and Tom Lambert and the kidnapping of baby Emma Lambert. London stunned. DCI John Luther.*

And there's John. Tiny on the laptop screen. Stomping away from a drizzly crime scene, a big man with a big walk, buttoning his coat.

Zoe's phone is charging at the wall. She grabs it and calls John.

'DCI Luther,' he says.

'John,' she says. 'It's me.'

There's a pause. He ends it by saying, 'Not now.' He hangs up.

John has been many things before: distracted, evasive, depressed, wild. But he's never been dismissive.

He always says how remarkable he finds it, that people are more polite to strangers than to the people they love. He strives to be courteous to her, takes pride in it, and she loves that about him.

Loved that about him.

That's when Zoe knows they really are done. When John slips into the past tense.

★ ★ ★

Luther steps out of the station and hurries across the street. Howie's leaning against his car, arms crossed, waiting in the rain.

She passes him a buff envelope.

He opens it. Rain splats on the paper.

He scans the document, then looks up. 'I've never even been to Swindon. How far is it?'

'Sixty-odd miles. I'll drive.'

Before getting in, he hesitates.

He says, 'Isobel, are you sure you're okay about this?'

She can't meet his eyes. 'I am if you're sure you're right.'

'I'm right.'

'Then I'm sure. Hop in.'

He holds up a finger.

'One call,' he says.

Howie gets in the car and starts the engine.

She feels sick.

Luther calls Ian Reed.

Reed says, 'What's up?'

He's bleary. He's been asleep. For a moment, Luther is disoriented by this thought. He realizes that, separated for just a few days, he and Reed have somehow slipped into different worlds.

Reed says, 'So how's it going?'

'Complicated. How's the neck?'

'Better.'

'Better enough to get you into work?'

'Do I need to?'

'Mate,' says Luther. 'I really need you. I'm doing some bobbing and weaving here.'

'Let me get dressed. I'll see you at the factory.'

Luther thanks him, then hangs up and gets in the car.

He and DS Howie head to Swindon.

★ ★ ★

Reed removes the soft neck brace and calls Teller to let her know he's coming in.

She's too busy to thank him; she just briskly and efficiently briefs him. He drinks a mug of instant coffee and knots his tie.

He tells her he'll be at work within the hour, then goes to get his jacket.

He's necking painkillers with water when the intercom buzzes, sudden and fretful.

Reed opens the door on a dishevelled, spectacled middle-aged man. He's affecting the bewildered air of a curate out hunting for fossils. Reed's never met him, but he recognizes Detective Superintendent Martin Schenk at once.

Schenk removes his slightly absurd beanie. A few strands of hair stand electrified. He gives Reed a shy grin. 'DCI Reed?'

'You got me, Guv.'

'You're looking very well, considering.'

'I'm doing okay. Keen to get back on the job.'

'Quite so, quite so.' Schenk twists the beanie in his hands, as if anxious. Schenk is not anxious. 'A very busy night,' he says. 'For your colleagues.'

'So I hear,' Reed says. 'That's why I'm up. All hands on deck.'

'One of the perpetrators of this enormity,' Schenk says, 'is in the ICU, as I understand it.'

'Apparently. The son.'

'Under armed guard.' Schenk shakes his head, as if to lament the state of the world. 'So you're pitching in?'

'I can walk,' Reed says. 'I can still pick up a phone. I'll leave the actual running round to someone else.'

Schenk nods in admiration. The admiration is real. He says, 'Would you mind if we had a chat first?'

'Not in principle,' says Reed. 'In practice, Guv, it's not the best time.'

'Absolutely. Which is presumably why I'm having such trouble getting through to Detective Superintendent Teller. If I was a more paranoid man, I'd think she was avoiding me.'

'Well, she's pretty hectic.'

'Absolutely. It's just — we do have one or two things to clear up.'

'I told you,' Reed says. 'I don't know who assaulted me. It was — '

'All over very quickly. Absolutely. You've already been over that. Absolutely.'

'Then what?'

'Are you familiar with a chap called Julian Crouch?'

'I know of him, yeah. Heard of him. He's a

305

dirty fucker. Pardon my French.'

'Oh, I've been a copper since dinosaurs roamed the earth,' Schenk says. 'There's not much language I haven't heard. I was nicking people like Julian Crouch when it was all 'blags', 'far-out' and 'nostrils'.'

Nostrils is seventies slang for a sawn-off shotgun. Reed appreciates the reference, and likes Schenk for it.

Reed is scared of liking Schenk.

'So what about him?' Reed says. 'Julian Crouch. What's he got to say for himself?'

'That you've been harassing him.'

'When?'

'Tonight.'

'As alibis go I've got a pretty good one.'

'Well, he did suggest it may not have been you *personally*.'

'Then who did I send? My dad?'

Schenk smiles, sadly. 'Somebody torched Mr Crouch's car this morning.'

'Somebody what?'

'Torched his car. A Jaguar. Vintage.'

Reed laughs. Knows he shouldn't, but can't help it. 'When?'

'Four or five hours ago?'

The mood must be contagious, because Schenk gives him a smile so broad and open it's almost beautiful.

'Look,' says Reed, sobering. 'The man's a dirtbox. He's made more enemies than you and me put together. It could be anyone. Besides which, I'm a copper. I don't go round torching people's cars.'

'The, um, chap who actually torched the car — '

'Did Crouch get a look at him?'

'Oh yes. Didn't I mention?'

'No. You left out that bit.'

'I'm sorry,' Schenk says. 'I'm jumbled up. When I get a call that early in the morning, I'm all at sixes and sevens until I've had a decent breakfast. And all the proper cafés are closing. Have you noticed that? You want a full English, but these days it's all *low GI* this and *good cholesterol* that. It hardly counts as breakfast at all. A copper needs a decent fry-up. Although don't mention that to my wife.'

'So anyway,' says Reed.

'Yes,' says Schenk. 'Sorry.' He digs out his notebook, licks the end of a pencil stub. 'Well, I won't use the racial terms employed by Mr Crouch, but he describes a very tall black man — *six foot fucking seven* is, I believe, the term he used. Wearing a long coat. Possibly tweed.'

'And . . . ' says Reed.

'Well,' says Schenk, putting the notebook away, maintaining the charade that it wasn't a prop. 'I know you and a DCI John Luther are very close. And this description, forgive me if I'm wrong, but does it evoke DCI Luther to you the way it does to me?'

'I don't know about that,' Reed says.

'But it doesn't exactly rule him out, does it?'

'This wasn't John.'

'How do you know?'

'Because after a week like John's had, the last

thing he's got time to do is go round setting fire to people's cars.'

'Not even to avenge a grave insult to an old friend?'

Reed is quiet now. Knowing better than to speak.

'Coppers talk,' says Schenk. 'It's common currency you were beaten up by Crouch's thugs.'

'Gossip isn't the same thing as evidence. I don't know who beat me up. And John wouldn't go off piste based on chitchat.'

'And you're sure of that?'

'He loves his job,' Reed says, 'he wouldn't jeopardize it over something like this. It's not in him.'

'But as you say, he's had a traumatic time. On a day like that, who'd blame a man for going a little over the edge?'

'All you've got to do,' Reed says, 'is speak to his wife. I'm sure she'll tell you where he was.'

'I intend to. Zoe is it?'

'Yeah,' says Reed. 'Zoe.'

'And how are Zoe and John?'

'What do you mean?'

'Well. Marriage to a copper — it can be difficult. We all know that.'

'Tell me about it,' Reed says.

Schenk gives him a meek, humorous look that suggests he'd like to if only he wasn't here, doing this.

'Well anyway,' Schenk says. 'I'm sure it's nothing.'

He means exactly the opposite.

Reed looks at him. Bright blue eyes in pale

skin. 'I don't mean to be rude,' he says, indicating the door.

'Goodness gracious,' Schenk says. 'What am I thinking? Can I give you a lift? Do my bit?'

'Thanks, but I'll be fine.'

'With the whiplash?'

'Honestly, I'm good. Codeine. Swear by it.'

'Then at least let me walk you to your car.'

He walks him all the way and stands at the kerb as Reed pulls into the traffic.

★   ★   ★

Christine James is woken by strident hammering at the front door. At first, she thinks it's next door having another barney. She turns over, bundles the duvet round her head, ignores it.

But there it is again. Like someone's hitting the door with a sledgehammer. Then a voice.

'Christine? Christine James?'

Blinking, Christine pulls the duvet to her throat and bellows: 'Who is it?'

'Detective Chief Inspector John Luther, from the Serious Crime Unit in London. I need to speak to you urgently.'

'What about?'

'Please open the door.'

Christine gets out of bed. She considers going downstairs. Instead, she opens the curtains.

She sees a pretty red-headed young woman leaning with her arms crossed against the bonnet of an old Volvo.

Christine has spent enough time with the police — family liaison officers, detectives, press officers, all the rest of it.

She knows them at once.

She opens the window, pokes her head out and cranes down to look. A big, black police officer is standing at the door, looking up at her.

The street is quiet. It's a nice street. She's got some nice neighbours. She's got an okay life, a decent job at WHSmith's head office. She's come a long way.

She's got that feeling, deep in her gut.

It's like every other big event in your life: your first day at school, your first kiss, losing your cherry, your first day at your first job, getting married. All those days you anticipate, rehearsing in your imagination, going over them again and again and again. But when the day comes, it's never like you expected it to be.

For years, Christine was counselled by a woman from the Elise Fox Foundation. *Closure may never come, the woman told her, you have to prepare yourself for that. And if it does come, it may not be what you were hoping for. You have to prepare yourself for that, too.*

Christine had cried at that point, because the woman was kind, and had been through something.

But the woman knew Christine would fantasize about this day anyway. It was just one of the things you did, one of the ways you get through the not knowing.

Christine knows this is the day.

It's six o'clock in the morning and she's leaning out the bedroom window and a tall policeman's craning his head to look up at her, saying in a low, deep voice, a nice voice, 'Ms James. It's very important.'

'I'll be down in a minute,' says Christine. 'Just let me put some clothes on.'

Ten minutes later, she's in the back of a police car, hammering under lights and sirens towards London.

The red-headed young woman drives faster than Christine has ever been driven before. For a while it gives her motion sickness.

Then she realizes it's not motion sickness. It's just the old familiar nausea, an enemy so old it's almost a friend.

★ ★ ★

Reed drives for half a mile through growing traffic before he feels safe enough to call Luther.

'Wotcher,' Luther shouts down the line.

Reed can hear the siren's lament. He says, 'Where are you?'

'Just inside the M25.'

'Doing what?'

'Witness transport.'

'Can you talk now?'

'About what?'

'Someone torched Julian Crouch's car last night,' Reed says. 'Big black geezer. Tweed coat.'

'That's a shame,' Luther shouts. 'I'm not much of a car person, but that thing was nice. That was a nice car.'

'So,' says Reed. 'I've had Complaints round.'

'Already?'

'Yeah.'

'Who's on the case?'

'Martin Schenk. You know him?'

'I know his work.'

'So do I. He's not the kind of dog you want sniffing your arse.'

'He's not, is he? Shit.'

Reed imagines Luther scratching his head and thinking this through as outer London flashes past, the car hammering it under blues and twos.

'So,' says Reed. 'The minute Schenk sets eyes on any copper who matches the description Crouch gave, that copper's in deep shit.'

'Even if he's busy?'

'If they think he's going round torching vintage Jags, it doesn't matter how busy he is.'

'But if they pull in the wrong copper,' Luther says, 'that wouldn't be good for Mia Dalton.'

'How are you looking on that?'

'I'm close. I can do it.'

'Okay,' says Reed. 'So Crouch needs to change his mind about what he saw.'

'He does,' says Luther. 'Can you take care of that?'

'I can give it a try.'

'Excellent. So where's Schenk right now?'

'That's the thing. He's on his way to speak to Zoe.'

'Shit.'

'Yeah,' says Reed. Then he says, 'I'll tell you what, whoever torched Crouch's car, I don't think he was thinking straight.'

'I don't think he was,' Luther says. 'I think he was probably having a bad day.'

'I think he probably was.'

'Can you text me Schenk's number?'

'On its way.'

Reed hangs up, begins to thumb out a text as he drives.

★   ★   ★

Luther hangs up. He turns to Howie. 'I need you to pull over.'

She gives him a look: *You're joking.*

'It's important,' he says. 'I'll be two minutes.'

Howie pulls over to the hard shoulder.

Christine James sits in the back, looking wide-eyed and lost.

Howie shoots her a reassuring glance.

Then Luther turns in his seat to face her. He says, 'Would you mind if I borrowed your phone? I won't be long.'

Christine blinks at him. As if this morning could get any stranger. Then she rifles in her handbag and passes Luther a battered pink clamshell Motorola.

Luther paces the hard shoulder in the morning rain. He uses his own phone to call Schenk's number.

Schenk is quick to answer, barking his name by way of salutation: 'Schenk.'

Luther can hear he's at the wheel, on the hands-free.

'Hi,' Luther says. 'DCI Luther here. I was asked to give you a call?'

'DCI Luther! Thanks for getting back to me so quickly.'

'Not a problem. How can I help?'

'Well, it's silly really.'

Luther makes himself ride that out without answering. He waits for two or three seconds, watching the motorway traffic, then says, 'So what can I do to help?'

'Silly as it is, this is obviously a matter I'd prefer to discuss face-to-face.'

'So let's do that. Where are you now?'

'En route to Peckham.'

'Then you could take a detour? I'm near the station. Can you make it over here?'

'Well,' says Schenk. 'I could, yes. But I do have this one call to make.'

'I can't promise to be around later,' Luther says. 'We're having a funny old day.'

'Quite. Well, if you could make yourself available at Hobb Lane, I'd certainly appreciate it.'

'I'll try, I'll definitely try.'

'Then I'll see you as soon as I can.'

Luther hangs up. He swears, rubs his head, paces. Then he calls home. 'Zoe? It's me.'

Zoe sounds weary. The mild sense of dislocation that follows a sleepless night.

'John, listen. I don't want to argue.'

'Nor do I,' he says. 'Forget about last night.'

'How can I?'

'That's not what I mean. I just mean, this isn't about last night. Listen, I haven't got time to talk. Not properly. So I'm going to be quick, okay?'

'Go on.' Less weary now. A warning edge of chipped flint.

314

'I need to ask you a favour,' he says. 'Not a nice favour.'

'What favour?'

'First, I've got to tell you, I'm not asking lightly. I'm asking it for the little girl, Mia Dalton. You've seen her on the news. You must have. This is about her. About getting her back.'

'What are you asking me to do?'

'Lie for me.'

'Lie to who?'

'To a policeman.'

He tells her what he needs. And at the end of it, she sighs. He can picture her, barefoot in pyjamas, tugging at her hair.

'Fuck you, John,' she says. 'I mean seriously. Fuck you, for asking me to do this.'

'I know. But will you do it?'

'Do I have a choice?'

He thanks her and hangs up. Then he makes one last call, using Ms James's pink phone.

'Boss?'

'What?' says Teller.

'How's the patient?'

'In the ICU.'

'Conscious?'

'No.'

'Okay, listen. I need you to do me a favour.'

'What now?'

'In about two minutes, I need you to call me.'

'Why am I doing that?'

'So there's a record.'

'And what are we saying during this imaginary conversation?'

'You're ordering me from the station to the

hospital as a matter of urgency.'

'And — real world now — why would you ask me to do that?'

'Because I've got Complaints sniffing round my ass.'

'Jesus Christ,' she says. 'Today?'

'Today.'

'I've had Martin Schenk badgering me,' she says. 'Leaving messages. So now I know why. What did you do?'

'Nothing. But if you don't help me out here, Schenk will make sure I'm pulled off this thing. I can't let him do that. I need to find Mia Dalton. Now. Today.'

'If you're asking me for an alibi,' she says, 'it won't hold water. As soon as Complaints look into it, it'll fall to pieces. There's a factory full of coppers who'll testify you weren't there at the time the call was made. Then we'll both be in it.'

'I know that. It just needs to stand for a few hours.'

'Why?'

'Because the allegation's going to be withdrawn.'

'Okay, stop there,' she says. 'Don't tell me any more. Don't hint. Don't imply. Shut up.'

'Okay. But call me, yeah? In two minutes?'

She agrees with a grunt. Then says, 'Whose phone are you calling from?'

'Don't ask.'

'John, am I going to get sacked over this?'

'Nope.'

He hangs up and hurries back to the car, hunched and jogging in the rain. He gives the

316

Motorola back to Ms James, thanks her.

Howie pulls away. Tyres hiss wet, aquaplane. Sirens wail.

Howie doesn't look at Luther. Doesn't ask.

A minute later, Luther's phone rings.

He checks the number: DSU Teller.

He says, 'Morning, Boss. We're on our way. How's the patient?'

23

Zoe answers the door to a middle-aged, dishevelled man in an overcoat. Thinning hair plastered to his scalp, a look of slightly nonplussed benevolence. 'Mrs Luther?'

'Mr Schenk?'

'Martin, please. May I?'

'Of course,' she says, standing aside. 'John told me you'd call.'

Schenk pauses only for half a second. 'He did?'

Zoe feels a surge of embarrassment. 'He just called,' she says. 'You told him you were in the area. I suppose he — '

'Put two and two together.'

She smiles and nods.

'Well,' Schenk says. 'That's his job. Talking of which, how are they on the missing girl? Little Mia Dalton. Do you know?'

'Apparently they're on the edge of some breakthrough. I don't know what.'

'Well, please God you're right.' He glances sheepishly over her shoulder, into the house. 'I wonder if I might? Just for a moment.'

She says, 'Oh, gosh. Please. I'm sorry.'

Schenk follows her through to the kitchen on sopping wet feet. Zoe wants to help him.

'You're very kind,' he says, at her shoulder. 'I've been up half the night. And your house is very warm.'

'I feel the cold,' she says. 'Always did. I think I was built for warmer climes.'

'As was I. Warm climes and red wines.'

She smiles at that because he doesn't look like a red-wine drinker. He looks like a Guinness and whisky man.

She takes his coat — faint dog smell in the tweed — she bets he keeps terriers. He sits on a stool at the breakfast bar while she pours them each a coffee.

John had told her to have a hot drink prepared. It'll get Schenk out the house more quickly.

'It's a terrible business,' Schenk says. 'This poor child.'

'Horrible. Are you involved with it at all?'

'Goodness me, no. Thanks be to God.' He takes the coffee from her hand, thanks her. 'A lot of coppers are taking it very badly.'

'You know how it is with coppers and kids.'

'Oh, yes. But there's more to it than that. Did John tell you?'

'Tell me what?'

'Well, it was . . . a very upsetting crime scene. Police officers see a great deal. But sometimes, well . . . Many people who saw what John saw last night will be very upset. He really didn't tell you?'

'He doesn't tell me anything. He thinks it's disrespectful to the dead.'

'That's very admirable.'

'Well, he's a very admirable man.'

'So I hear. Many fine officers speak highly of him.'

319

'He's dedicated. He works hard.'

She clasps her hands in her lap, fights the urge to tear a kitchen towel to shreds, to pick imaginary lint from her lapel.

'The man, or men, who slaughtered this family,' Schenk says. 'And who then took that poor little girl. They left a message in the victims' blood. On the wall. The word *Pigs*. Seeing something like that, it can be difficult to walk away from. It's likely John will need to take a break after this.'

She laughs out loud before she can stop herself.

'I'm sorry,' Schenk says. 'Did I go touching a raw nerve?'

'Not at all,' she says. 'It's just — well, I've been trying to make John take a break since God was a boy.'

'And he won't?'

'He says he can't relax.'

'Ah,' says Schenk. 'I was a murder detective, for my sins. So I know what it's like. My Avril, I put her through some dark years. All the worrying, it's very difficult. Although mind you, I sympathize with John, too — wanting to tell you everything, just so you understand. But then again, wanting to shield you from it.'

'How long were you a murder detective?'

'Most of my career. Until I got stabbed.' He brushes her reaction away with a dismissive wave. 'Oh, it was nothing in the grand scheme of things. A little pneumothorax. A day or two in hospital. Then home to a very frosty Mrs Schenk.' He chuckles fondly at the memory. 'I

320

told her, okay I'll make the move. But you should know they call Complaints the *Rat Squad*. I won't be liked.'

'What did she say to that?'

'*I like you enough to make up for the rest of them.*'

'That's very sweet.'

'She's a very sweet woman. You'd like her.'

'How long have you been married?'

'Since before God was a boy.' He blushes, then shows her his wedding ring. Plain gold band. 'Childhood sweethearts.'

'Oh,' Zoe laughs, 'that's something I know all about. Well, practically.'

'So I hear! You and DCI Luther — '

'Met at university, yes. How do you know that?'

'Because, sadly — and I do mean sadly — I've been asking some questions about your husband. I'm very worried about him.'

You and me both, she thinks.

She says, 'In what way?'

'Well, as I say. The psychological pressures. It causes a lot of problems. Mental health issues. Marital issues.'

'His mental health is fine.'

'Well, that's good to know. And, if I may, your marriage . . . '

She looks him in the eye and knows how dangerous it would be to lie. 'The marriage is pretty bad,' she says.

'I see. I'm very sorry.'

'We'll get through it.'

'Well, I certainly hope you do. So I wonder,

during what's obviously been a period of increased stress, has DCI Luther been, say, drinking more than usual?'

'He doesn't drink. Never really had a taste for it. He'll have a beer at the weekend sometimes.'

'Well, that's something. That's certainly something. Now, Mrs Luther — '

'Zoe, please.'

'Thank you. You've already been more than generous, inviting me into your home, knowing the kind of thing I came to ask. So it pains me to embarrass myself by asking this question . . . '

'Not at all,' she says. Her foot is tapping. She makes it stop. 'Ask away. It's your job.'

'Could you tell me about John's movements last night?'

'Well, Rose sent him home.'

'And he got home when?'

'About eleven, eleven thirty?'

'And what did he do, when he got home?'

'He lay on the bed and fell asleep. Didn't even take his shoes off. Then, what seems about five minutes later, the phone goes. It's Rose. Detective Chief Superintendent Teller. She wants him at some crime scene, the one you're talking about I suppose. So up he gets, and drags himself out. He hasn't told me the details, but I do understand things were . . . emotional last night.'

'And in between arriving home at eleven thirty, and going out again about . . . '

'I was pretty much asleep. Two forty-five, was it? Something like that.'

'Otherwise, he was with you?'

322

'He was. Yes.'

He looks at her for a long time with those glinting eyes in that soft face, beautifully shaved. Gives her a sad smile, a brave smile that the world should be this way for them both. 'Well, I'm glad to hear that.'

She nods. Can't speak.

After a moment, Schenk checks his watch and says, 'Well, goodness me. I must get going. I have an appointment with your husband.'

He grabs his damp coat, slips it on.

Zoe says, 'What did he do?'

'Who?'

'The person,' she says. 'Whatever John's being blamed for.'

'There's a man named Crouch,' Schenk says. 'A very nasty piece of work. There's a rumour, although I should stress it's only a rumour, that associates of Crouch had DCI Ian Reed assaulted. Do you know DCI Reed?'

'He's a family friend. I know him well.'

'Of course. Well, very late last night someone torched Mr Crouch's car. A vintage Jaguar. Mr Crouch gave a description of the offender. His description closely matches DCI Luther.'

'I see.'

'But of course,' says Schenk, 'it wasn't him. Because he was tucked up in bed at the time, with you.'

She smiles.

'I'll let myself out,' says Schenk. 'You stay in this nice kitchen. Out of the wet. It's dreadful out there, really.'

She watches the space where Schenk had been

standing until she hears the front door open, linger, close. And Schenk is gone.

She stays in the kitchen. After a minute, her hands start to shake. Then her legs. She sits. Tugging at her hair.

★ ★ ★

Reed's known Bill Winingham since he was a woodentop. Winingham's Glaswegian, in his sixties now — still tough and wiry. Severe white crew cut, haggard face. A fisherman's sweater frayed at the sleeves.

He's a decent man, old school. He's a fence and Reed's long-term confidential informant. They've got the kind of relationship good police work is based on. Over fifteen years, it's developed into a kind of friendship.

They meet at a coffee bar in Shoreditch. Exposed brick walls, stainless-steel espresso machines, vintage Formica tables and chairs.

They take a corner table and small-talk for a while. Winingham subtly makes it plain that he knows nothing about Pete Black. Reed brushes off the intimation with a flick of the wrist, batting away a mosquito. Then he says, 'So anyway. I need a favour.'

'What kind of favour?'

'You know the kind of favour I usually ask you? Legal and above board and all that?'

'Aye.'

'Well, this isn't that kind of favour.'

Neither man alters his bearing, his tone of voice. They've been at this game far too long.

Winingham says, 'So what's the problem?'

'A friend of mine tried to help me, and ended up getting in trouble for it. Now I'm trying to help him out of some deep shit.'

Winingham adds sugar to his coffee. Stirs. 'What are you asking me?'

'I need some weight. And a rental. A really dirty one.'

He means a rental firearm. There are people who hire out illegal firearms. Many of the weapons have been used in a number of crimes by a number of different people.

Winingham exhales, long and slow. Not playing it for drama, just letting Reed know the scale of the ask.

He picks at the half-stale Danish on a plate before him. 'That's a bit heavy for me.'

Reed leans close, takes Winingham's elbow. 'You saw this little girl,' he says. 'The girl in the news? Got taken last night?'

'I heard, aye.'

'This could help her, mate.'

'What are you doing? Are you fitting someone up?'

'You know better than to ask that. Come on.'

Winingham licks a fleck of pastry from his fingertip. 'I don't know, Ian. I don't know. It's heavy. It's not my kind of business.'

'I wouldn't ask if it wasn't important.'

'I know, I know. But still.'

Reed sits back.

Winingham is slow to move, slow to speak. Qualities learned from long experience.

Reed pushes back his chair and leaps to his

feet, strides to the counter. He orders two more coffees and a bottle of water. He opens the water as he returns to the table. He sits. He taps his foot and sips the water. It's so cold it hurts his teeth.

Finally, Winingham says, 'Okay. I can arrange that. But it won't be cheap. And we'll be dealing with some fairly serious people.'

'I'm good for the money.'

'No, Ian. No, it doesn't work like that. I pay them. You pay me.'

Their eyes meet.

Reed screws the top back on his bottle, puts the bottle on the table.

'What are we saying here?'

'I've come across an opportunity,' Winingham says.

'No — '

'Hear me out, son.'

Reed gestures. Sorry. Go ahead.

'There's a fine-art dealer,' Winingham says. 'A bloke by the name of Carrodus. Bent as a pin. He came to me, a few days ago. He's looking to free up some capital. Make it portable.'

'How?'

'Uncut diamonds.'

Reed nods. Waits.

'The reason he wants the stones,' Winingham explains, 'is because not all those paintings he sold were kosher. There's a few Russian oligarchs with nicely done fakes on their walls. And now this bloke Carrodus, he's in love. He's got a very beautiful young wife. French. And he wants to clear off, out of it.

Start a new life. And who can blame him, eh?'

'I don't get the favour.'

'I source the diamonds for Carrodus,' Winingham says. 'I take my ten per cent.' He sips coffee. 'And then my nephew robs him.'

Reed doesn't answer. He plays with a tube of sugar. 'This doesn't sound like you.'

'Oh, nobody gets hurt,' Winingham says. 'My nephew couldn't hurt a fly. He's an economist, for fuck's sake. It's just a big score. A once in a lifetime thing.'

'How big a score we talking?'

'Top end, eight million.'

Reed looks at him.

'That's at the top end, mind. It could dip to six.'

'Six million, low end? And nobody gets hurt?'

'Nope. And because we're robbing a thief of stolen goods, nobody need ever know. Least of all your lot. It's a sweet thing. It's the kind of score you wait an entire life for.'

'So who does the job?'

'No local faces. Nobody known. We're going to use a friend of my nephew's. American geezer. He flies in, takes a look at the Houses of Parliament and Tower Bridge, takes some photos, does the job and fucks off back to Arizona or wherever.'

Reed rearranges grains of sugar on the surface of the table. 'What do I do?'

'Just keep your ear to the ground,' Winingham says. 'Make sure Carrodus hasn't gone mouthing it about to the wrong people. And keep the police away.'

'And seriously, nobody gets hurt?'

'Not a chance. You need to see my nephew.'

Reed's heart is a bird in his chest. 'I'd need more than this favour. I'd need a proper cut.'

'You'll get a cut. Two hundred thousand. A rental, no questions asked. Some weight.'

Winingham sits there, patiently. Lets him think it through.

In the end, Reed licks his dry lips and offers his hand across the table.

★   ★   ★

Uniformed coppers clear a path through the mobbed press. Howie parks close to the main hospital entrance.

She gets out, opens the rear doors and leads a confused, blank-faced Christine James through the automatic doors, across the foyer, to the lifts and upstairs.

Outside the Intensive Care Unit, she introduces Ms James to the family liaison officer, Cathy Hibbs.

Hibbs leads Ms James into a private room, asks if she'd like a hot drink.

Ms James doesn't seem to know. She's bewildered. She's got the innocent, blinking expression of an early onset Alzheimer's case.

She doesn't say a word, except to thank Hibbs for the cup of hospital coffee.

In the foyer, Luther and Howie find a quiet corner away from the assembled media.

Luther says, 'I need you to stay here and keep me updated.'

'Absolutely. Where will you be?'

'I'll be around. I've just got a few things to sort out.'

'Boss . . . ' she says.

Luther says, 'I'll be as quick as I can.'

He means it. Howie can see the anxiety in his eyes; the intense need to do something she doesn't want to know about, and to do it quickly.

She doesn't ask. She's learned that much.

She watches him stride away.

24

Barry Tonga's wife, Huihana, runs Frangipani, a small florist in Hackney.

Grey winter light filters through the picture window, deepens the shade of the green foliage; seems to brighten the lilies, roses, tulips, chrysanthemums.

Huihana looks up from behind the counter when Reed and Luther enter. Luther badges her and shushes her.

The flagstones are damp beneath his feet.

Huihana steps away.

Luther and Reed find Barry Tonga out back, listening to an iPod as he prepares a large wedding bouquet. On the table before him are laid out garden string, adhesive floristry tape, ivory roses, eucalyptus stems, beaded wires and wide organza ribbon. He's got a pair of secateurs in his hand.

He looks at them. He takes out one of his ear buds, lets it dangle. Luther can hear a hissy sibilance that he half recognizes. He thinks it might be Fleetwood Mac, although that doesn't seem right.

'Wotcher,' says Reed.

Tonga nods. 'How's it going?'

Reed rotates his head on his neck. 'Better, Barry. Yeah. How are you?'

'All right, ta.'

'Good,' says Reed. 'Good, good, good.'

Luther steps up. Tonga stands a head taller than him.

'We're in a rush,' Luther says. 'So do me a favour, put down the bouquet and come with us.'

'Why?' says Tonga. 'Where we going?'

'To the woods. We're going to beat you shitless, shoot you in the head and throw you in the river.' He shows his teeth; you wouldn't call it a smile. 'Only joking.'

Barry Tonga stands there with the secateurs, towering over them.

His eyes flit from Reed to Luther. Luther can still hear the tinny drumbeat emerging from the dangling ear bud.

★   ★   ★

They cuff Tonga and drive him to the corner of Meriam Avenue. Reed points out a low-rise, redbrick building. Ex-local authority. Tonga's flat.

Three police cars are parked outside it.

Tonga says, 'That's my flat.'

'I know,' says Reed. 'I've just been in there.'

'What do you mean? What's going on? Why's Billy Filth all over it?'

'What's going on is this,' says Reed. 'You gave me a kicking and now life as you know it is coming to an end.'

'What's that supposed to mean?'

'It means, we got you away from your wife's shop about five minutes before a swarm of coppers descended on it, looking for you.'

'This is bullshit, man. What did I do?'

'Besides assaulting a police officer?'

'I didn't assault any police officer.'

Reed laughs, then turns in his seat, stuns Tonga with his sudden, shocking malevolence. 'Giving me a kicking's all in the game, Barry. But you intimidated an old man, you cowardly fucker. Look at the size of you. You should be ashamed. You killed his little dog.'

Tonga holds Reed's gaze, but not for long. He looks at his lap and shifts a bit in his seat. He mutters something about the dog.

'What?' says Reed. 'You're embarrassed by that, are you?'

'I want my lawyer.'

'He wants his lawyer,' Reed says.

Reed and Luther laugh.

'You're not under arrest,' Luther says. 'This is a kidnap.'

'What do you mean? You're Filthy Bill, right? I saw the badges and that.'

Reed points to the police vehicles outside Tonga's door. 'What we did,' he says. 'We called in an anonymous tip to someone who'd take it very seriously indeed.'

'What kind of tip?'

'That there was a dirty gun on the premises.'

'There's no gun,' says Barry Tonga. 'Not in my house.'

'Oh, I think you'll find there is,' says Reed. 'One that's been used in a number of previous crimes. Including two shootings.'

He enjoys the sweat on Tonga's brow.

'As well as the gun,' Reed says, 'they'll find a

few ounces of heroin. Enough for intent to supply. Send you down for a long time. Long enough for your wife to find someone else who's good with organza.'

'This is shit, man,' Tonga says. 'It's shit. This is police corruption. This is wrong.'

'Totally,' says Luther.

Tonga sits back. The car lurches on its springs. He looks at them from under his brow.

'So what do you want?'

'To tell our bosses that you've been working for us. Off the books.'

'As what?'

'A grass.'

'I'm not a grass.'

'No. But you'll pretend to be.'

'And if I do that, what then?'

'We protect you,' Luther says.

'What does that mean, though, protect me? Protect me from what?'

'From us.'

'How?'

'You admit to harassing the old man,' Reed says. 'You say you were acting on Julian Crouch's instruction.'

Tonga watches as two Scenes of Crime Officers emerge from his flat. One of them passes an evidence bag to a uniformed sergeant.

'Okay, I can do that,' he says. 'I don't have a problem with that. Crouch is a prick. But the gun. A gun's a big deal. You can't magic a gun away.'

'Well, there's the beauty of it,' Luther says. 'You say Crouch supplied the gun. You'd never seen it before yesterday.'

'Yeah, but why would he do that?'

'Because he wanted you to get rid of the old man.'

'Get rid? As in, kill him?'

Luther nods.

'The old geezer?'

Luther nods.

'Crouch?'

Luther nods.

'He hasn't got the bottle. The man's a pantywaist.'

'Doesn't matter.'

'And you're seriously doing this for him? For that old geezer?'

'Yep,' says Reed.

'Planting guns, planting drugs, perjuring a witness?'

'Yep,' says Reed.

'Fair play to you,' says Barry Tonga. 'I can respect that.'

'That's nice,' says Luther. 'Hurry up. Yes or no.'

'You can't get away with shit like this, though. It can't be done.'

Luther cries out in fury and slams his hand onto the dashboard.

The glovebox pops open, spills out old papers and crushed wax cups.

Tonga cringes.

Luther starts the engine.

'Wait!' says Tonga. 'Where are you going?'

'Over there,' Reed says, pointing to the police outside Tonga's flat.

'What? Why?'

'To hand you over, Barry. You're a wanted man. And we're in a rush. We can't hang around all day, waiting for you to make up your mind.'

'Whoa,' says Tonga. 'Slow down.'

Luther doesn't kill the engine, but he doesn't pull away either. He says, 'What? I haven't got time to piss about.'

'If I help,' Tonga says, 'that's it? No comebacks.'

'No comebacks,' Reed says.

'What about Kidman?'

'Will you testify against him?'

'To what?'

'Conspiracy.'

'Shit, yeah. The man's a dick. There was no need to hurt the little dog. My nanna had a dog like that.'

'Mine too,' Luther says. 'So where are we? Yes or no?'

'Yes,' says Tonga.

★ ★ ★

Henry marches round the house, closing curtains and locking doors.

He knows that, soon enough, he and Mia will have to decamp, find a new house and begin again. That'll mean leaving London, maybe even the country.

But to do that, Henry's going to need to make some money. There's less than five hundred pounds in the strongbox, and less than a hundred in the ancient bank account he maintains in the name of Henry Jones.

But more than anything, for the next week or two it means gritting his teeth, holding his nerve and staying put.

Henry's got diarrhoea. He paces the floor. He keeps vomiting into the kitchen sink.

But he's done this kind of thing enough before to know the house is safe; it's a safe place. There's nothing to lead anyone back here. Not now he's killed Patrick.

You never get used to it, not really. You never relax. But Henry doesn't mind it, living on his nerves like this. It makes him feel alive.

He knows he'll miss Patrick. He wonders if he should have exerted more parental discipline in the early days. Perhaps that would have intensified the emotional imprinting.

But that's exactly the problem with adopted children — ultimately, you don't know what you're getting.

That's why far more children are murdered by step-parents than birth parents. And *step-parents* obviously means *step-fathers*. (To be fair, step-mothers often exact their own toll — less murderous, perhaps, but no less barbarous.)

All Henry ever wanted was to be a good dad. It would've been easier if he'd been able to have his own kids, but he gave up trying for that years ago.

Nothing was wrong with him. Not physically. He just got so fucking *tense*. While a woman lay next to him, keening and moaning like a dog in pain, his cock would shrink to an inch of inert gristle, like connective tissue in a pork chop.

She'd kiss it, tug it, do whatever else she thought might work. But nothing did.

The second she left the room, however, or the minute Henry crouched outside her window or crept round her house without her knowing it, *boom!* there it was, rising first like a daffodil then an iron rod. She was a perfect idea. No matter her cellulite arse, her saggy tits.

Of course, Henry quickly realized it was all about who was boss. So his first attempt at starting a family was with Joanne.

He could fuck Joanne, all right. She knew who was boss. He could fuck her for hours, until his cock was red raw. He kept her chained in the basement in the old house, the one in the West Country.

But pretty soon, despite keeping her fit and well and despite her whimpering protestations of undying love, it became clear that Joanne would never conceive a child.

For a while, Joanne cohabited with Lindsay — same basement, same house.

Henry ate lots of vitamins and protein, stuff that was good for sperm production. But neither woman would quicken. They were both hookers, so probably there was something wrong with their wombs. It was all the abortions, all that scraping out of their insides.

And it turned out, there was an optimum time they could be kept in the basement. He moved sunlamps down there, gave them a decent diet, lots of greens and red berries. But that didn't stop them becoming depressed and listless.

That was when he bought his first dogs. The

dogs ate Joanne and Lindsay.

By the time Oona moved in (she was chosen for her hips, as much as her availability, stumbling back alone from Reeves nightclub after a row with her boyfriend) Henry had become pretty half-hearted about it all.

He took Oona to the basement, but she never learned to love it the way Joanna had, submitting to intercourse with a stoic silence that Henry found off-putting.

Her heart really wasn't in it.

Around then, Henry decided to change tactics. And those tactics had worked pretty well, all things considered.

Patrick had grown into a good lad until he began to show that sullen, defiant streak. It had come in late — so late that, for a while, Henry believed they might have escaped that stage altogether. But in the end, breeding will out.

Briefly, Henry had considered giving up and just buying an orphan from Eastern Europe. But there was still that question of breeding, of what you get in the package. *Caveat emptor.*

Which had been the point of Baby Emma. Her breeding was perfect. The Lamberts were perfect. But that fiasco had nearly left everyone in London thinking he was a child killer or a pervert.

So now Henry's arrived at a place that, in a perfect world, he'd have chosen to avoid.

By the time Mia becomes ready to breed she'll love him as a father, which makes what Henry's planning a creepy kind of incest.

That makes Henry uncomfortable, but it makes him excited too. He won't touch Mia that way until she wants him to. But the thought of it, the extra level of transgression, is stimulating. It'll be exciting. Father and daughter, lovers, parents.

As these thoughts run through Henry's head he's obliged several times to masturbate into a cotton handkerchief.

This has more to do with survival than pleasure. Henry knows that sexual desire muddies logical thought. Being sexually aroused is like being chained to a madman.

So he sits with his fly unzipped and the sodden handkerchief clasped like a flower-head in one hand. He strokes his belly and watches the blank TV and makes plans.

He imagines that from downstairs he can hear sobbing, but he knows he can't. He and Patrick tested the basement enough times, with tape recorders and sound meters. You think you can hear crying in an empty house, but you play back the tape and all you get is silence.

The sobbing is just Henry's imagination. There's just him and the blank TV, the feel of his taut belly under the palm of his hand. He turns on the TV, flicks from channel to channel. Keeps the volume down. Enjoys the pictures.

The house in Chiswick. Pasty-faced police. Eager onlookers. The tape, the lights, the rain. Earnest reporters.

A hospital. A gaggle of police.

And passing through it, a face he recognizes.

A woman. Much older than the last time he

saw her. Her face taut and exhausted, pale under the rain lights.

Police lead her through the automatic sliding doors of the London hospital.

Henry's penis shrinks. His balls retreat into his body.

He has a feeling of lightness, like he's leaving his body.

★　★　★

Julian wanders in a slight daze up and down the congested, confusing Chapel Market; past the fruit and veg stalls, the fishmongers, the cheap clothes, the transistor radios, multi-packs of batteries. There's even a computer-repair stall, which would strike Julian as quirkily interesting, if he wasn't so fretful.

Half an hour ago, Barry Tonga called to say they had to meet urgently. Soon as possible. Somewhere public. He mustn't tell anyone. Least of all Lee Kidman.

Tonga wouldn't say why.

That's got to be bad, doesn't it?

So he squeezes up and down the congested road, past the smell of fish, then the whiff of banana, trying to get a glimpse of Tonga's huge frame somewhere in the tides of people.

But it's not Barry Tonga he sees. It's Reed and Luther.

Julian briefly considers running away, but what would be the point? They'd chase him and arrest him and use it as an excuse to give him a quiet beating.

340

If he doesn't run, what can they do with all these people around?

'Wotcher,' says Luther.

'Hello, you car-burning fucking psychopath,' says Julian.

Luther laughs, twitchy and wired.

Luther and Reed hustle Julian into Manze's pie and mash shop: wooden benches, tiled walls, marble counters.

They order three large mince beef and onion. The waitress scoops the mash onto the plates with a spatula, spreads green liquor down the middle.

They collect their cutlery and find a quiet, high-backed booth. Luther sees that Julian sits nearest the wall, then squashes himself in beside him.

He frowns, beetle-browed and distracted. He fidgets with salt and pepper shakers. Radiates an urgent desire to be elsewhere.

Reed is very liberal with the chilli vinegar. Then he tucks into his pie with gusto.

He looks at Luther. 'You not eating?'

Luther shrugs, distracted and fretful.

Crushed against the wall, Julian looks at them both in terror.

Luther says, 'Sorry to rush you, Julian. But we haven't got much time.'

'I can imagine,' says Julian. 'London must be absolutely full of cars you haven't set fire to yet.'

Luther swivels his face. Gives Julian a monumental, brutal stare.

Julian wants to piss. He looks longingly at a passing customer, a builder with a newspaper

341

tucked under his arm. But the builder walks past, oblivious, texting.

'So,' Luther says, 'you've got friends in the police, yeah?'

'My lawyer does. Why?'

'I just wondered why Complaints were so quick off the mark. I've got a bloke sniffing round me. Martin Schenk.'

'Yeah, I met him. Are we being recorded?'

'No,' says Luther. 'No, this is off the record.'

'Are you going to hit me?'

'What, in here? Do I look stupid?'

'You did set fire to my car.'

'Good point. The thing is, though, Julian, we do need to have a chat.'

'I don't see what about.'

Reed grins through a mouthful of pie.

'We know you're in trouble,' Luther says. 'Financially.'

'You don't know the half of it.'

'I bet. And do you know what else I bet?'

'No,' says Julian Crouch. 'What else do you bet?'

'I bet you're not the complete prick you appear to be. Intimidating old men. War heroes. I bet you're actually pretty ashamed of yourself. Deep down.'

Crouch says nothing, all huddled against the wall while Reed tucks into his lunch and Luther scowls, fidgeting with the salt and pepper like he can't wait to get away, be somewhere else.

'Trouble is,' Luther says, 'everyone knows you're in deep financial shit. Deep enough to really, really want that old man out of your way.'

'So?'

'So there's a very short list of motivations for murder,' Luther says. 'Sex and money being the two odds-on favourites. You've got a nasty divorce going on. There's your sex. And as for your business portfolio — well. There's your money. What a mess you're in, eh? What a mess.'

Julian frowns, juts out his lower lip. He mentally rewinds. Then he says, 'What do you mean, motivations for murder?'

'I mean,' says Luther. 'You're about to be indicted.'

'For what?'

'Conspiracy to murder.'

Julian makes to stand. Luther says, 'Calm down. And sit down.'

Julian sits down.

'We found the gun,' Luther says.

'What gun? What do you mean?'

'Oh, I think you know what gun.'

'No, I don't know what gun. What gun? I don't have a gun. Do I look like I've got a gun?'

'Thing about this gun,' Luther says. 'They found it in Barry Tonga's flat. Do you know Barry Tonga?'

'I don't think I do, no. Barry who?'

Luther gives him a bright, predacious grin. 'That's the spirit. If in doubt, lie.'

Julian changes tack. 'What about Tonga? What's he got to do with this?'

'Well. Between me, you and the gatepost, Barry works for us. He's what you'd call a confidential informant. Has been for years. And he's going to testify that you paid him five grand to stage a burglary at the old man's house. And shoot him dead.'

'But that's not true. That's fucking outrageous. It's not true. He can't say that.'

'He's saying it.'

'How can he say that if it's not true?'

'We found the gun.'

'What gun? There isn't a gun. What gun?'

'The gun you gave him,' Reed says. 'The gun that ballistics will discover has been used in any number of other crimes. Including a shooting.'

'Two shootings,' Luther says.

'Sorry,' says Reed. 'Absolutely right. Two shootings.'

Julian gapes at them.

'You can't do this,' he says. 'You can't.'

Silence.

'Shit,' says Julian. 'So what am I going to do?'

'Go to prison.'

'I can't go to prison. I've got a phobia.'

'That's a new one,' says Reed.

'It's true. It's got a name. It's a syndrome.'

'I bet it is.'

'Well anyway,' says Luther. 'That's really why we're here. To give you some advice.'

'I don't get you. What's happening? I don't know what the fuck you're talking about. You're talking in riddles.'

'Just calm down and listen,' Luther says. 'And speak a bit more quietly.'

Julian calms down and listens. He speaks a bit more quietly.

Luther says, 'You're finished here, Julian. You

know that. You've been finished for a long time. You must be tired of it all. All this shit you're pulling, just to keep afloat. Creditors, ex-wives, mortgages, bank loans, sitting tenants. It must be a nightmare for you. If I were you,' Luther says, 'do you know what I'd do?'

'No.'

'I'd call my accountant. Then I'd go to Heathrow and buy a ticket. And I'd do it really, really soon.'

Julian blinks at him. He says, 'You're asking me to leave my home.'

'That's right,' Luther says.

'And all this is for the old man in that house?'

Luther doesn't answer. He unscrews the maroon lid from the malt vinegar. Then he screws it back on again.

Julian says, 'Or is it because without me, there won't be any charges against you?'

Luther grins. Then his phone vibrates in his pocket. He checks it out.

It's a text from Howie: Patrick's conscious.

Luther reads the text, pockets the phone.

He says, 'We've got Tonga in hiding for thirty-six hours. That's enough time for you to pack your bags and get away. After that, we bring him in, he makes his statement — and you're in big trouble.'

Luther squeezes out of the booth, wipes his mouth with a paper napkin, dumps the napkin on the table and leaves.

Reed lingers a few moments, to finish his pie. Then he claps Julian on the shoulder, says, 'Happy travels, dickhead,' and follows.

345

Henry hurries to the garage.

Passing the dogs, he can feel their flat amber gaze. They're waiting for him to chuck in a rabbit or a cat.

But Henry ignores them for the moment and jogs instead to the tall metal locker at the far end of the garage. He opens it with a small key and runs a quick inventory: Dexamethazone, Talivin, codeine, procain penicillin, testosterone, ketamine.

There are catheters, needles, syringes, gauze, hydrogen peroxide, Betadine, suture needles, staple gun and staple remover, surgical scissors, forceps.

In the far, cobwebby corner stands a rusty oxygen cylinder. Still good.

In the attic, he knows, is a large, empty weapons case. In the cupboard under the sink is a multipack of duct tape.

You can't have enough duct tape.

The inventory relaxes him. He counts again, and again. When he's tallied three times, he knows what to do.

As he prepares the first syringe of amphetamines, he apologizes to the dogs.

25

Reed hails a cab. He's at the factory in about twenty minutes.

He walks in to find Benny Deadhead has colonized his desk.

'Sorry,' says Benny.

'That's all right,' says Reed. He hangs his wet coat over the back of Luther's chair and logs in.

Benny says, 'How's the neck?'

Reed waggles his head around to show how much better it is.

★ ★ ★

Luther nods to the uniforms guarding the door and, ducking his head, steps quietly into Patrick's hospital room. He's carrying a slim buff folder.

The room is an artificial, greenish twilight. The kid's hooked up to a ventilator, a heart monitor.

Howie's in here, dozing on a moulded plastic chair, head nodding to her chest.

She jumps, looks up, sees Luther. Collects herself.

Luther says, 'He spoken yet?'

'No.'

Luther shakes his head, like it wasn't a question worth asking. He steps closer to the bed, to the bandaged kid, the morphine drip.

The kid opens his eyes. Knows Luther is there.

Luther pulls up a chair and puts his face close to the kid's.

'You probably expect me to feel compassion for you,' he says. 'And I do. I think it's grim, what your dad did to you. But anyone who ever killed anyone was a baby once, so in the end the things you did, that's down to you. But you can help us. You can help us put that right.'

The kid turns his head on the pillow. Away from Luther.

'I know you love him,' Luther says. 'I know you don't want to hurt him. You can't help it; it's what happens to us. Love can be a kind of survival mechanism. Sometimes we love the people we need *because* we need them. Like dogs. But at the same time, it doesn't mean you liked doing what you did together, these terrible things. Because you didn't. Do you know how I know that?'

The kid stares him down. One of his eyes is swollen shut.

'I know you dialled 999,' Luther says. 'The night he killed the Lamberts and took their baby. I know you tried to get him caught.'

The kid looks away, blinks at the ceiling.

'And it wasn't just the 999 calls, was it? Because last night, someone rang round all the families in London by the name of Dalton. Warning them. Or trying to. Why would someone do that, d'you think?'

Luther reaches into the folder, brings out a photograph of Mia Dalton. She's smiling, on a beach somewhere. 'Now he's taken Mia. But you know that, right? You know exactly what he's planning to do — because you tried to help Mia get away from him.'

He sits back, crosses his arms, the picture of Mia held like a playing card he's about to throw in.

'A lot of people,' he says, 'I mean a *lot* of people, think you were trying to take her for yourself; that you wanted to do things with her. In private. If you know what I mean. But I don't think that's true. I think you were trying to protect her. You didn't want her fucked up like you were fucked up.'

The kid makes weak fists. Muscles move in his skinny forearms. He glares at the ceiling with one eye.

Luther leans in closer. Sees the green light refracted through the meniscus of tears on the surface of the kid's eye.

'I could tell you all about her,' he says. 'I could tell you she likes ponies and Justin Bieber. But the thing is, I'd be wasting my time, wouldn't I? Because you and your dad know that already. You know everything about her.'

Nothing.

'Except he's not your dad,' says Luther. 'We have to remember that, don't we? That's the important thing. He's not really your dad.'

The kid closes his eyes.

'It's not admissible in court,' Luther says. 'But I've been following your heart on that monitor. The machine that goes ping.' He grins. 'Did you ever see that sketch? Probably not. Before your time. This is way back in the seventies, back when I was a little kid. But anyway, the machine that goes ping tells me when you're lying and when you're not — even when you're not talking. Because when I said he wasn't your dad, it spiked.'

The kid mumbles something, perhaps a denial. It's too low to hear.

Luther takes a long, calming breath. Then he leans in even closer, close enough to brush the kid's ear with his lips.

'The man who calls himself your dad,' he says. 'The man who calls himself Henry Grady. He kidnapped you on eighth of September 1995. You'd just turned six.'

The kid's lip quivers.

Luther slips another photograph from the folder. He holds it up. 'Do you recognize yourself?'

The kid screws his eyes shut. Refuses to look.

Luther stands. He holds the photograph close to the kid's eyes.

'This is you,' he says. 'Or it used to be.'

The kid makes fists so tight the flesh goes white. Livid purple in patches.

'The DNA will prove it,' Luther says, low and insistent. 'We know what he did to you, your dad. And we know you tried to stop him. Twice. And this is what you get for it. So why don't you help us? Why don't you help Mia?'

Still no answer.

Nothing except spikes and barbs on the heart monitor.

Luther meets Howie's eye.

Luther pads to the door. He opens it, puts his

350

head round the corner. Whispers, 'Okay. You can come in now.'

They wait a long time.

The kid's eyes are fixed on the door when Christine James, whose married name was York, shuffles into the room.

Her face is gaunt, full of lines and fine ridges. She's twisting the strap of her handbag between two hands. She's shaking so hard the family liaison officer is supporting her weight.

Luther looks away from Howie's accusing gaze.

Patrick begins to vibrate. He emits a low whine and looks away.

He's saying, 'Sorry, Mum. I'm sorry, Mum. I'm sorry, Mum.'

★ ★ ★

Adrian York got the bike for his birthday. It was a Saturday morning. Nearly lunchtime. He and Jamie Smart had been riding in the skateboard park; it was visible from the house. His mum was watching from the bedroom window.

Adrian wanted to go out alone, because he was a big boy.

Now Jamie Smart has gone home and Adrian sits on the kerb at the edge of the field, the bike propped against a lamp post. He can see the back garden. He's drinking a can of Fanta. He's feeling pretty good. He's six years old.

A van pulls up. The worried-looking driver gets out and jogs across the quiet road. He said, 'Mate — what's your name?'

'Adrian.'

'Adrian what?'

'Adrian York.'

'Right. I thought it must be you.'

'Why?' said Adrian York.

'I'm sorry, mate. There's been an accident. You'd better come with me.'

The man is breathing strangely. When Adrian hesitates, the man licks his lips and says, 'I've been sent to take you to your mum. You'd better get in.'

'I'd better not,' says Adrian York.

'Your mum might be dying,' says the man. 'You'd better hurry up.'

Adrian York looks at the window. He sees that his mum isn't there, where she's supposed to be, watching him. He wonders if the man is right.

He begins to cry.

'You'll get me in trouble if I go back without you,' says the man. 'The police sent me to get you. You'll get us both in really bad trouble.'

'What about my bike?' says Adrian York.

But the man doesn't answer. He just scoops Adrian York into his arms and carries him to the van.

One of its brake lights is shattered.

★ ★ ★

The family liaison officer, Luther and Howie linger in the corners like undertakers.

They give Christine James a few minutes with her child. It's a few minutes more than she can take.

She clutches Adrian's hand, squeezes it, presses it to her face. She weeps, wretched and unhinged. She calls on God. Oh God, she says. Oh God, oh my God, oh my God, oh my boy, my boy, my boy.

Adrian lies there. All he can say is 'Sorry, Mum. Sorry, sorry, sorry.'

★ ★ ★

At length, the family liaison officer leads a shuffling, dazed Christine James from the room, back into the hospital light.

Luther feels Howie's eyes on him.

He burns with shame.

Then he returns softly to Adrian's side.

'What's his name?' he says. 'What's his real name?'

After a long time, the kid whispers, 'Henry.'

'Henry what?'

'Clarke. Nicholl. Brennan.'

'But always Henry?'

The kid makes a gesture. It's almost a nod.

'But you must know,' Luther says. 'After all these years, you must know his real name.'

'Madsen.'

Henry Madsen.

Luther's hands itch to do something. He wants to grab a pencil, take out his notebook, write it down, circle it, underline it.

He bites the inside of his mouth. Makes himself wait.

'Adrian,' he says. 'Patrick. Where do you and Henry live?'

26

Henry Madsen lives in a large, rambling old property that stands on a quarter-acre of grounds, isolated from its neighbours by high hedges and a screen of trees. It overlooks Richmond Park.

The house is already on fire when the first responders arrive.

The blaze has picked up by the time the fire crew shows up, a few minutes later. They are closely followed by an Armed Response Unit and the EMTs.

A number of pit bull terriers run loose in the grounds. They attack the first responders, then the fire crew. This slows the operation.

The order is given to shoot the dogs.

By then, the fire has taken a firmer hold.

En route to Richmond Park, Luther calls Benny.

'Going back twenty-five years,' Benny tells him. 'We've got six Henry Madsens. Four we can dismiss outright: white-collar criminals. Traffic offences, that sort of thing.'

'No one on the sex offenders register?'

'Oh yes. Henry John Madsen. String of juvenile offences: burglary, vandalism, theft, assault, arson.'

'Arson?'

'Attempted murder of his adoptive parents.'

'What's the story?'

'He broke into their house and set fire to their beds.'

'That's our boy,' Luther says. 'What happened to him after that?'

'He does his time. Comes out at eighteen. Has some counselling. He re-offends at nineteen — GBH during a pub conversation about abortion. Apparently he's anti. He's remanded into psychiatric care. Comes out at twenty-one. After that he drops off the radar.'

'Which isn't to say he hasn't been busy. You got photographs?'

'Old ones.'

'How's he look?'

'Short hair. Very neat.'

'Parted?'

'On the left.'

'No glasses, no beards, no moustaches?'

'No.'

'Excellent. Let's get this prick's face all over the news.'

'Won't that make him panic?'

'It'll drive him to ground,' Luther says. 'Make him hole up somewhere. Stay in London.'

'Yeah, but where?'

'Well, mate. That's the question.'

★   ★   ★

Twenty minutes later, Luther reaches the scene. He's wearing a high-viz jacket over the parka he keeps in the trunk of the Volvo. He had to ditch the overcoat. It smelled of petrol and smoke.

He approaches Teller. Nods at the burning

355

building. 'How long to make this place safe?'

It can take days for a building to cool properly and structural damage to be assessed. Normally, it would be tomorrow at least before Luther was granted access to the house.

But Teller makes some phone calls. She shouts and wheedles and pleads. She claims exigent circumstances, the threat to Mia Dalton's life.

The fire-fighters are still darkening the glowing embers when Luther slips on a Cromwell 600 helmet and breathing apparatus, then walks past the corpses of the dogs, through the high spray of the dampening hoses and into the charred house.

The hallway is blackened with soot, ash, and smoke. The windows are blown out. Everything's wet. He hadn't expected so much water. It's still raining down on his head. Holes in the wall expose pink insulation material. The swollen ceiling threatens to collapse.

Upstairs, he finds a child's bedroom. A cot, a changing mat. Clothes on a rail: boys' and girls'. Many still display price tags. On the wall are hung burned prints of Pooh Bear. In the cot is an ancient, water-sodden teddy.

Luther looks at the teddy bear.

He checks out two adult bedrooms. Water-drenched beds, burned clothing. Everything doused in accelerant and set alight.

Downstairs, a torched library. Nazis. Eugenics. Dog-rearing. Biology. Burned portraits of prominent National Socialists. Speer and Hitler. Noble dogs.

All of it forensically useless.

The kitchen has been touched less by the fire. It's wet and badly smoke damaged, but one or two of the windows, although streaked black, haven't blown.

Luther looks in the pantry. Canned goods. He looks in the cupboards. Pots and pans. He looks in the tall cupboard nearest the kitchen door. A bottle sterilization kit.

Several bottles. All of them blackened now.

He opens the fridge. And there, essentially undamaged, are ranks and ranks of children's milk bottles.

He takes one of the bottles from the fridge. Shakes it. Puts it close to his face. But he's seeing it through a screen.

His heart is beating.

He searches the fridge. At the back, he finds a bar of chocolate, half eaten. Teeth prints.

A fire-fighter leads him through a reinforced door down to the basement. Luther feels the weight of the house above him. They edge along a dark, earth corridor, heavy with smoke. He concentrates on his breathing, worried he might panic down here.

They arrive at what might have been a vegetable storage room. Another reinforced door.

The fire-fighter opens it.

A bed. A bookcase.

Luther looks at the books. Water damaged. He knows he wouldn't like to touch them with an ungloved hand. He doesn't believe in ghosts, but it seems to him that objects soaked in human misery retain traces of it.

357

He leaves that terrible basement, his breath quick and loud in his ears. He goes upstairs and outside. The water from the dampening hoses is a mist over his head. There are slick patches of mud. A helicopter overhead.

Behind a rainbow in the mist stands Rose Teller. 'Anything?'

'He's gone. Mia's with him.'

'Well, thank God for small mercies.'

He grunts at that. Looks at the plumes of smoke that rise from the house, spread thinner and thinner against the pale dome of London sky.

'He'll need to leave London,' Luther says.

'You think the son can help us, tell us where he's likely to go?'

'Madsen didn't tell him anything.'

He frowns.

He looks at the dog corpses dotted like fungi all over the wet lawn.

He cups his mouth.

He wanders to the nearest dog corpse.

He kneels.

He has a flash of something — a memory of kneeling at the corpse of a dog, a yellow dog, a retriever in a strange hallway. And then the memory, if it was a memory, is gone.

This dog, a pit bull terrier, has been shot in the shoulder. Then one of the ARV mob has walked over and put a bullet through its head, an act of mercy.

The bullet has passed through the dog's skull and into the soil.

A chunk of the dog's upper lip on one side is

missing. But it's an old scar, long-healed. Her nose is mutilated.

Luther reaches out an index finger and draws it along her fur. She's still warm. He feels it through the latex gloves.

Her chest and flanks are heavily criss-crossed with old scars.

He pats the dog, fondly. He brushes against the nap of her fur. Feels the slight, pleasing resistance.

Then he walks across the garden to another dog: pale brown with a white flash. The bullet has blown away half its face. It's impossible to see any scarring there. But there are ropes of scar tissues on its back and ribs. Heavy damage to its hind legs.

The third dog has more Staffordshire than pit bull in it. Luther is sentimental about dogs, the way Reed is about old soldiers. Especially Staffies. Staffies have qualities that Luther admires. A Staffy will fight to the death to defend a child. It will bite down and it won't let go.

He trudges round to the back of the house, to the double garage. He enters. Finds cages full of panicking, white-eyed dogs. They leap at the wire. They bare their teeth. They roll insane and murderous eyes.

They do not bark.

Luther watches them. He's perversely tempted to slip a hand through the bars of the cage. Just to see what they'd do with it.

Then he turns and strides away.

Teller's waiting in the square of light at the

end of the garage. He walks past her.

He says, 'Let me know if anyone finds anything.'

★ ★ ★

He shoves through the crowds outside, through the people and the media.

He looks around and finds Howie. She's grabbing a coffee with an EMT crew and a couple of uniforms.

He leads her away by the elbow.

She says, 'What's up?'

'Isobel,' he says. 'I'm giving you a choice now.'

'I don't get you.'

'Madsen knows we're just behind him,' Luther says. 'It's going to get messy.'

'Messier than it already is?'

'Yes.'

'Boss, I don't get what you're asking.'

'Come with me,' he says, 'and there could be repercussions for you. Stay and there won't be. It's up to you. But if you come, we're in it together. Come what may. You with me?'

Howie hesitates. But only for a moment. She ditches her coffee and follows Luther to the car at a half-jog.

★ ★ ★

Henry drives her somewhere quiet: there are trees and no traffic sounds. He pulls over to the side of the road. There is the sound of tyres in wet leaves.

360

He presses Mia further down into the passenger footwell and leans over to open the glove box. He takes out a notepad and begins to scribble something. He writes faster than Mia can believe.

He writes, crosses out, writes again, more neatly.

When a lot of time has passed, he says, 'Sit up.'

Mia looks at him through her hair. She is shaking.

'Sit here,' he says. 'Next to me.'

She sits up, next to him.

He lays the notepad in her lap and flicks on the interior light. 'Can you read that? Can you read my writing?'

Mia nods.

'Good,' he says. 'Now. We're going to play a trick on someone. Is that okay?'

Mia nods.

'It's a kind of joke. What I'm going to make you say isn't true. But if you don't do as I say, I'm going to have to punish you, okay? I don't want to, but I will.'

Mia sniffs and nods.

'Excellent,' he says. 'Ready?'

She nods again.

He produces a mobile phone. Mia knows it's her dad's. It's her dad's iPhone and it's full of photographs of her and her brother and her mum. Her dad embarrasses her by showing them to everyone, all the time.

Henry dials a number from memory, then puts the phone to Mia's ear.

Mia hears the ringing phone down the line, then a nice voice is saying, 'Hello?'

Mia glances sideways at the man, who nods.

'My name is Mia Dalton,' says Mia, reading the note.

She has to hesitate before she reads the rest. Her voice catches in her throat and she looks fearfully at the man.

But he doesn't seem to mind.

The more scared she sounds, the more he seems to like it.

27

Howie pulls up close to Milton House. She kills the engine, glances at Luther. 'You okay there, Boss?'

'Yeah. Why?'

'You don't look right.'

'When we've got Mia Dalton back,' he says, 'I'll go to bed for a week.'

'I'll join you,' says Howie. Then she blushes from her sternum to her hairline. She's a redhead, so it shows. 'By which I don't mean — '

'I know what you mean,' Luther says. 'Wait here. Keep an eye on things.'

She watches him swagger towards the morose grey columns. She wonders if this display is in inverse proportion to his confidence; the shakier the man, the bigger the walk.

Luther passes a skeletal, rusting children's playground. No kids playing. A skinny dog trots in a delirious circle. Broken glass on the happy, cracked mosaic.

He chin-nods to a group of hoodies who loiter like crows on the stationary roundabout. Then he ducks his head and enters the permanent twilight of Milton House.

Luther takes the stairs three at a time. They stink.

He's breathless and ill-tempered when he bangs on Steve Bixby's door. 'Steve. DCI Luther. Open up.'

No answer.

He beats on the door. It jolts in its frame. Luther can feel the resistance of heavy-duty deadbolts and mortice locks.

He backs off a step, wipes his mouth with the back of his hand.

The door to the adjacent flat opens. A woman, a girl really, stares at him. Pasty face. Kappa.

It was on an estate just like this that Luther met his first thirty-year-old grandmother.

He nods at Bixby's door. 'He in?'

'You're waking the baby.'

'Do you know where he might have gone?'

'Do I look like Derren Brown?'

'How much do you know about him?' Luther says. 'The man who lives next door to you and your babies?'

That's enough for Bixby, who's listening on the other side of the door.

He calls out, 'All right!'

Luther waits while Bixby goes through the rigmarole of getting the door unlocked and opened.

He stands in the doorway, the dog at his heels. 'What now?'

Luther plants a hand on Bixby's sternum and shoves. Bixby pinwheels backwards. Falls on his bony arse.

Luther steps in. The air in the flat is rank with Bixby, dog and frying.

The dog backs away. It angles itself into the corner and lowers at him, daring him to make a move.

Luther turns.

The neighbour stands in the open doorway, mobile phone in hand. She's filming him.

'You can't do that,' she says. 'He's got human rights.'

Luther grabs her wrist, twists it, seizes the phone, pockets it, shoves her out of the flat and slams the door.

She presses her face to the window. Mashes her nose against it. Sees Bixby on the ground.

Luther pulls the curtains.

'*Oi! Give me my phone. Thieving cunt.*'

Luther lifts Bixby to his feet. Rams him into the jerry-built wall.

Dog ornaments topple to the dank carpet.

The old pit bull watches from the corner. Its shanks tremble. It's pissed itself.

Luther puts his face to Bixby's. 'You're a liar, Steve. You said you didn't know Henry Madsen very well. You cooked up some story about some fictional dead mate, Finian Ward, putting you in contact. But that was bullshit. Because you do, don't you? You know him.'

Bixby swallows. Glances at the window. The neighbour's still out there, banging on the glass, crying out obscenities and threats.

Luther squeezes Bixby's jaw. Turns his head until they're eye to eye. 'Which makes you an accessory after the fact.'

'To what?'

'To all the things he's done since we last spoke.'

'She's right,' says Bixby, nodding at the window. 'This is assault.'

Luther laughs. Then he slaps Bixby in the

chops. Once. Gently. 'Where is he?'

'I don't know.'

He slaps Bixby again. Not so gently. Bixby's eyes water.

'Where is he? Where's Henry?'

The dog advances and retreats. Makes snapping feints at Luther's legs. He turns to it. It runs away in a transport of panic.

Luther twists Bixby's ear. 'Where is he?'

'I don't. Fucking. Know.'

Luther weighs it up. Then he lets Bixby go.

He reaches out. Grabs the toothless dog.

It twists in his hands, trying to bite. It gums the fabric of his parka. It's still strong, all sinew and muscle. And it's heavy.

Luther closes one fist around its collar and one fist around its hind legs. The dog yelps and strains, tries to twist free.

Luther marches to the door. Struggles to open it.

He shoves the neighbour out of the way. Then he dangles the dog over the concrete balcony.

The neighbour stares at him. Her mouth is open.

Bixby hurries to the door.

The neighbour is shouting for Luther to let him go, that he's only a dog. That he didn't hurt no one.

Luther ignores her. He grins at Bixby.

'Where is he?'

★ ★ ★

An agitation passes among the hoodies in the playground. Howie follows it to source. She looks up.

From where she's sitting, it looks very much like DCI Luther is dangling a dog off a high balcony and threatening to drop it.

The gaggle of hoodies call out, make the hand gestures and half-dance moves that remind Howie of rap videos. Except the kids are white and the jeans hang low off their skinny arses. It just looks wrong.

'Hurry up,' Luther says. 'I can't hold it much longer.'

Bixby jiggles on the spot like he needs to piss. He wrings his hands. He says, 'Please.'

Drawn by the neighbour's protest, a small, inquisitive crowd is beginning to assemble on the concrete walkway.

'Police,' he says. 'This dog is dangerous. Until the animal control officers get here, I need you to clear this walkway.'

It's a lie. It'll look good on YouTube. The crowd doesn't believe him.

'Please,' says Bixby. 'Please.'

Someone says, 'Let the poor fucking animal go.'

Then they're all saying it.

Luther just dangles the dog over the edge and holds Bixby's gaze as the sullen, fractious crowd begins to swell, fed by communicating stairwells and walkways.

'Please clear the walkway until an Animal Control Unit arrives,' Luther says. 'Thank you.'

The dog is too terrified to struggle. It just gazes unhappily at the concrete far below.

'He's getting really heavy, Steve. My arms are hurting. My hands are shaking.'

'Please,' Bixby says.

'I can't hold him,' Luther says. 'I can feel my hands slipping.'

'All right,' says Bixby. 'All right. Come in. Just don't hurt him.'

Howie watches the group of kids condense like a storm front. Not a crowd. Not yet. But soon.

Already the mobile phones are out. Soon Luther will be up there on Facebook and YouTube, dangling a dog fifty feet in the air.

She can see he's shouting something. God knows what.

She rolls her eyes. Swears. Makes sure she's got her pepper spray, ASP, radio. Gets out of the car.

'All right,' she says, approaching the kids. 'All right. Break it up. Move along.'

They turn to her with pale grinning ratboy faces. Shove each other. Turn their phones on her.

She presents an air of weary detachment. Actually, she's terrified.

One of the kids says, 'What's your mate doing with that dog, Miss?'

Miss, as if she were a teacher.

Howie gets a few seconds' reprieve as his grinning mates roast him.

She looks up. Sees the crowd gathering on the balcony. Pressing closer and closer to Luther.

And the poor dog, dangling down like a bag of kitchen rubbish.

She gives up. Returns to her car, calls in backup. 'You might want to hurry,' she says. 'Officer in peril.'

Then she sits at the wheel. She watches and waits.

★ ★ ★

Luther pulls in the dog. His hands are numb. The dog wriggles into him. He holds it tight. It wants him to love it. He loves it.

He cuddles the dog, pats it. He can feel its heavy heartbeat. It licks his face.

He forces its tongue away from his skin. Hugs it to his chest. It nestles there, grateful and terrified. It's heavy, like an ingot of metal. Luther's arms are numb. His fingers hurt.

He follows Bixby into the flat. Sets down the dog.

It scampers into the kitchen. Luther deadbolts the door. Makes sure the curtains are closed.

There is a silence outside before someone bangs on the door and cries out in some kind of protest.

Bixby looks at it all in dismay, tugging at his throat.

Distantly, the sound of approaching sirens.

Outside, the crowd gets louder. Someone kicks the door again, harder this time.

Luther grabs Bixby's shoulder and hustles him into the kitchen. Sits him down.

The dog quivers by the fridge, regards him in abject terror.

Luther says, 'I haven't got much time.' He puts his back to the flimsy kitchen door and folds his arms. 'So hurry up.'

'All right,' Bixby says. 'He did come round.'

'When?'

'Not long ago.'

'A day? A week? *When?*'

'About an hour.'

'An *hour?* So what did he want?'

Bixby mumbles.

'I can't hear you.'

Bixby mumbles again, looks away.

'Steve,' says Luther.

Bixby's eyes flare with shame and fury. 'He said he had a girl to sell me. All right?'

'To *sell* you?'

'He wanted ten grand. I said, I haven't got ten grand. He said, okay seven grand. I said, I haven't got it.'

'Why does he want the money?'

'To get out of London.'

'And were you tempted? To buy her?'

'What do you want me to say? Yes? Do I look totally mad to you?'

'What did he say to you? Exactly. Exact words. What did he say?'

'That she's very pretty. And loving.'

'Loving. Jesus.'

'And she could be all mine.'

'Did you see her? Did you actually set eyes on her?'

'No!'

'But she was alive?'

'She'd have to be.'

'How well do you know him, Steve?'

'Not that well. I'd just see him at the fights. He was always there.'

'Dog fights?'

'Yeah.'

'And that's where he first approached you — at a dog fight.'

'Yeah.'

'He told you he wanted to buy a child.'

'Not straight away. Months later. But eventually, yeah.'

'So you were friends?'

'No. I just saw him at the fights.'

'And after a few months, you put him in contact with Vasile Sava. Then with Sweet Jane Carr.'

Bixby nods.

'What about since then?'

'Nothing really. I see him now and again at the fights. We say hello.'

'What's he doing at all these fights? Is he a punter, an owner, what?'

'He's a breeder. And he's a vet. He works mostly for a bloke called Gary Braddon.'

'So let me get this right. You're not friends.'

'No. He's always been pretty clear that he hates people like me. People with my problem.'

'So if he came to you, he must've been desperate, right?'

'I don't know. I suppose so.'

'Don't suppose. Tell me where else he can go to sell the girl?'

'I don't know. I honestly don't know. But even if there was someone, which I doubt, they'd be mad to get involved with him right now, wouldn't they? With him all over the telly. Nobody's that stupid.'

Luther calls Ian Reed.

'Ian,' he says. 'You need to pull in a bloke call Gary Braddon. Organizes dog fights. Put the strong arm on him. He's a dog lover, right? These are sentimental people. If you tell him a little girl's been kidnapped, he'll sing in a second. Use photographs of Mia.' He glances at Bixby. 'Pretty ones.'

He hangs up, waits for backup to arrive.

★   ★   ★

Howie passes through the crowd at the tail end of a riot squad. She's wearing a luminous police vest, baton in hand.

She watches from a distance as the riot squad pulls Bixby and Luther from the flat, which is being mobbed by irate residents.

A few bottles are thrown at a few shields. Half a dozen arrests are made. They'll be charged with affray and given community service sentences.

Luther and Bixby are marched out under protection. Bixby is bundled into the back of a van along with his dog.

Luther and Howie make their way to the Volvo. Get in. A bottle smashes against the rear windshield.

Howie says, 'And how often does this happen?'

Luther says, 'I've never actually started a riot before.'

As Howie reverses out, eggs explode against the bodywork, the windows. She ducks instinctively with each impact. And then they're on the road. Luther doesn't say anything to her. Just calls Benny Deadhead.

'Benny, mate. How're we doing on Madsen's adoptive parents?'

'Jan and Jeremy Madsen,' Benny says. 'She was a pharmacist. He was a vet.'

'Address?'

'Finchley,' Benny says. 'Same house they've lived in for forty years.'

28

Reed sits himself down in Luther's chair and calls the Status Dogs Unit. The call is taken by Sergeant Graham Cooke. Reed introduces himself, briefly outlines the situation.

Cooke says, 'Does this have anything to do with that little girl?'

'It may do, yeah.'

'Then let me sit down a minute. Close the door, get a pen.'

Reed waits. Then Cooke comes back to the phone and says, 'What do you need to know?'

'Let's start with, who is he?'

'Gary Braddon. Born Caerphilly, 1963. History of association with the far right.'

'And he likes dogs, does he?'

'Well, it depends what you mean by 'like'. He's got previous: keeping a dog for fighting, causing unnecessary suffering to a dog by failing to seek veterinary care for its wounds. Also convicted of possessing equipment associated with training dogs to fight. Five counts of illegally owning pit bull terrier-type dogs for the purposes of fighting.'

'Meaning what?'

'Meaning, he's not allowed to keep dogs. So he keeps them off site. We never established where.'

'Well, I think I might be able to help you out there. The name 'Henry Madsen' mean anything?'

'Not off the top of my head, no.'

'He's Braddon's vet. And corner man.'

'Braddon's vet goes by the name of Henry Mercer.'

'That'll be our boy.'

'Allegedly runs the best training yard in London, although we never tracked it down. He's a very secretive boy, Mr Mercer.'

'He is that,' Reed says. 'So is there money in this game? Because money's an issue right now.'

'There's plenty. Your dog wins three fights, it's a champion. Five, it's a grand champion — that's what they aim for. So they put the dogs through a training regime, get them down to an agreed fighting weight, just like a boxer. That means treadmill work, diet, stamina, running around. And steroids, so you can get them completely lean, no fat.'

'Do you think Henry could go to Braddon for money?'

'You think he's the man who kidnapped Baby Emma and that other little girl?'

'We're pretty sure, yeah.'

'Then not in a million years. Braddon's a right-wing nutcase. And he's a dog lover. Two inches to the right of Mussolini. That's a dangerous combination for a man who kidnaps children. Mercer, Madsen, whatever his name is, Braddon would cut his balls off and feed him to the dogs if he ever showed his face.'

'All right,' says Reed. 'So this is the problem we've got: our man's gone to ground somewhere in London. And you're right, he's very secretive. He's got no friends to speak of, and he's got no money. He needs somewhere to hole up.'

Cooke hesitates a moment then says, 'Braddon's dog fights tend to be held in any one of a number of vacant properties. Mercer, or Madsen, he'd have keys to them all.'

'You know the locations?'

'Absolutely.'

'Can you send us a complete list, soon as? And any other material you might have to hand that's going to help expedite a warrant to search.'

'Plenty of that,' says Cooke.

Reed says, 'What do you drink?'

'I don't mind a whisky.'

'There's a bottle on the way,' Reed says. 'We owe you one.'

Cooke asks Reed to give him a little time.

Fifteen minutes later he comes back with a list of five properties used by Gary Braddon as venues for holding dog fights.

* * *

Within the hour, Search Team One, with DS Justin Ripley acting as Police Search Adviser, arrives at the first address on the list.

It's an abandoned kitchen interiors shop in Lewisham.

They find cupboards have been removed and converted to make a dog-fighting pit, much like a boxing ring.

A comprehensive search proves the property to be unoccupied. Search Team One finds no indication that Mia Dalton or Henry Madsen have been present.

Search Team Two, headed by DS 'Scary' Mary Lally, stumbles upon an extemporized dog fight in progress behind a tyre-replacement garage in Deptford.

Watched by a dozen men, two pit bull terriers quietly maul each other in a pit fourteen feet square and three feet high.

Diagonal 'scratch lines' are drawn on opposite corners of the pits. These are the lines behind which the dogs must remain until the referee commands them to be released.

Four arrests are made. Two of the dogs will later be destroyed.

They find no evidence that Mia Dalton or Henry Madsen have been present.

29

Luther and Howie drive to Finchley.

On Royal Drive, they pass the site of the Colney Hatch Lunatic Asylum, now converted into high-end apartments. The Asylum used to be home to Aaron Kosminski. Luther's pretty much convinced that Kosminski was Jack the Ripper.

Jeremy and Jan Madsen live in a gabled, semi-detached Edwardian house in a Finchley cul-de-sac.

Jan Madsen comes to the door. She's an imposing presence: chiselled jaw, strong cheekbones. Greying pre-Raphaelite hair. She's seventy-two, a retired pharmacist. She gives Luther a regal once-over and says, 'Is it about my son?'

Luther nods. Tucks his badge into his pocket.

She invites them in. Brisk with anxiety.

The house is clean. In the living room are knick-knacks and family photographs, a TV that was top of the line when it was acquired, twenty-five years ago. Fruit in a blue and white ceramic bowl; the coral skeleton of recently eaten grapes. An old HP computer is plugged into the wall, screen black. Two credit cards on the table. A cup of milky tea on a coaster next to it. Evidence of cats, although no cats are to be seen.

Jan faces Luther and Howie, her son a spectre between them. 'Would you like a cup of tea?'

378

Howie smiles agreeably. 'No, thank you.'

'There's plenty in the pot.'

'Honestly. But thank you.'

'Coffee?'

'Thank you, we're good.'

'Water? Something to eat?'

Howie smiles. 'Really. We're fine.'

Jan invites them to sit.

Luther and Howie perch on the edge of a Laura Ashley sofa.

Jan sits in a matching armchair. Wrings her gardener's hands, knotty with arthritis.

Anxious people are compelled to fill silence. So Luther and Howie sit and wait.

'It's vile,' she says. 'The things he's done. It's vile. He wasn't brought up like that.'

'I can see that,' Luther says. 'You have a very lovely house. Have you lived here long?'

'Since 1965.' Said with pride and a touch of something like embarrassment.

'And is your husband — '

'Upstairs,' she says. 'I'm afraid he's not well. Fibromyalgia. And all this . . . '

Luther nods and, with a small gesture, directs Howie to go upstairs and check on the husband.

Howie half stands, addresses Jan Madsen. 'Do you mind?'

'Not at all. Second door on your right, top of the stairs.'

Howie thanks her, then leaves the room and heads upstairs, into the smell of Mr Sheen furniture polish.

She raps gently on the bedroom door. Hears a whispered, *Come in?*

Howie opens the door. Jeremy Madsen lies in bed. A tall, raw-boned man, balding and heavily liver-spotted. His wife's senior by perhaps a decade.

She takes in the room, the cluttered dressing table and the solemn wardrobes. Leather slippers arranged next to the bed.

Howie introduces herself, shows her badge, and whispers, 'I'm sorry to bother you.'

Jeremy sits up. He has a slight palsy. He squints through one eye. 'I'm sorry,' he whispers in return. 'Migraine. Very bad.'

'You've had a shock,' says Howie.

'I can answer your questions,' he whispers.

'I'm sure that won't be necessary. I'm sure your wife can give us everything we need. Please.'

Jeremy nods. The movement causes his face to twist in pain.

Howie says, 'Can I get you anything? Some water?'

'I'll be fine.' His liver-spotted hand shakes like a diabetic's. 'I just need to — if you wouldn't mind?'

'No, of course not'

Howie takes Jeremy's shoulder, bony through the soft pyjamas. She helps him lie back down.

She hovers at the edge of the bed as he turns into a foetal position.

Embarrassed, Howie slips from the room and heads downstairs.

In the living room, Luther leans forward, still perched on the edge of the floral sofa. 'Has Henry been in contact?'

Jan Madsen nods. 'He did call, yes.'

'When?'

'About an hour ago.'

'What did he say?'

'Nothing. There was just noise on the line.'

'Then how did you know it was him?'

'I'd been waiting.' She almost spits it. 'He always did come to us when he was in trouble.'

She plucks at her knee, can't meet Luther's eye.

'What did he want?'

'Money. What else?'

Howie enters the room and quietly sits.

'Henry called,' Luther says. 'An hour ago. Didn't speak.'

Howie immediately stands. 'I'll get a trace on the call.'

Luther reaches up, takes her arm. Shakes his head. 'He'll be long gone. I'll text through a request to trace.'

Howie hesitates, unsure, then rejoins him on the sofa. Their thighs are touching.

Luther raises his hip, digs out his phone. Begins awkwardly to thumb out a message. Frowning as he concentrates, he says, 'You're aware that Henry is a suspect in a very serious crime?'

Jan nods. Looks away. Toys with her bare wedding-ring finger. Luther looks at the pale band where the wedding ring had been, then at those swollen, arthritic knuckles.

'I have to ask,' he says. 'Why didn't you call the police when he rang?'

'To say what? My estranged son called, didn't

say anything and then hung up? I'd have been wasting your time.'

For a moment, Luther discontinues his meticulous, hunt-and-peck texting. 'Mrs Madsen. Nobody's blaming you for this.'

She nods, pretending to believe him. Tugs at her wedding-ring finger.

'Are you and Henry in contact?' Howie says. 'Generally speaking?'

'We haven't heard a peep in twenty years.'

Luther lowers his voice. 'We understand that Henry was adopted?'

Jan snorts at her lap; an expression of ancient, incalculable bitterness. 'Do you have children?'

'No,' Luther says.

'Well, we tried,' says Jan. 'Jeremy and I. We tried and tried. No IVF in those days. This is the early seventies.'

'And how old was Henry when you adopted him?'

'Two. Just turned two. He was a helpless little thing. You wouldn't treat a dog the way his mother treated him. The poor little thing, he'd been beaten, starved and God knows what. Locked him in a cupboard when her gentleman callers paid a visit. She hit him. Called him all sorts of things. Effing this, effing that.' That bitter laugh. 'God, we were so nervous. But people had told us, *You'll fall in love at first sight*, or *Once you see him it'll all just slot into place*. But walking into that room, seeing that little boy with his dirty knees and his hair all sticking up. I looked at him and my first thought was: *I don't like the look of you.*

'And I detested myself for it. Absolutely detested myself. I was riddled with guilt from the minute we got him home. After that, I think I was in denial.'

In the slightly hesitant use of the term, Luther hears years of anguish and self-recrimination.

'If you don't feel the kind of love you think you should be feeling,' she says, 'they pick up on it. They do. Children are so perceptive.'

'There's something called Adoptive Child Syndrome,' Luther tells her. 'About ten per cent of adopted children show some kind of behavioural disorder. It's nobody's fault.'

'We didn't have syndromes back then,' she says. 'In our day it was all about nurture. And the truth is, I didn't feel maternal towards him.' She's watching her hands. She begins to tug on them, knuckle by knuckle. 'I did feel *protective*,' she says. 'I couldn't bear the thought of anything bad happening to him. And I felt *sorry* for him. But I didn't love him. Not like that. Not for a long time. And by then, by the time I'd come to love him as my own child, as a mother's supposed to, well. It was too late.'

'How old was he when the trouble started?'

'Seven, I suppose. Jeremy and I went for an anniversary dinner. Just this little Bistro they used to have on the High Road. We left him with a babysitter for the first time. He set fire to his bed.'

Luther winces.

'And it just got worse from there. We tried everything. Psychiatrists. Psychologists. Whatever we thought might possibly work, we tried it.'

She coughs into her fist and sits back. Drained, to be reliving it all.

Luther says, 'Can I get you a glass of water?'

'If you wouldn't mind, thank you.'

Luther heads to the kitchen. On the way, he nods to Howie. Points to his phone.

Howie frowns: *What?*

Luther steps into the kitchen, texting. He finds the glasses in a high cupboard and draws off a glass of water.

On the window behind the sink is a small jar of petroleum jelly. The lid is loose.

Luther looks at it as he finishes the text. He addresses it to Rose Teller, Ian Reed, Benny Deadhead and Isobel Howie.

Then he carries the glass of water through to Jan Madsen.

She takes it, gratefully. Takes a sip. Sits holding it in her lap.

'Adopted kids,' Luther says, sitting. 'They sometimes get to wondering about their biological parents. Especially the birth mother.'

'Don't they just. God knows, Henry made an absolute Madonna of his. Concocted all these mad fantasies about her.'

'Such as?'

'Such as, he came from bad blood.'

'That's how he put it? Bad blood?'

'Bad blood. He was obsessed with the idea.'

'Where did it come from?'

'Jeremy's a vet. Retired now, obviously. But the only thing Henry ever showed any positive interest in was the animals. So we tried to get him involved. We bought him a little mongrel pup. Digby. We thought that might help.'

'Did it?'

She takes another sip of water. Her hand is shaking. She says, 'God knows. He had it for a few weeks. Then it ran away and never came home.'

Luther thinks he knows what happened to the dog. He thinks Jan Madsen probably knows, too.

He sends the text, then pockets his phone and says, 'What did you actually tell Henry about his birth mother?'

'That she was too young. That she loved him, but wanted to give him a better life than she could provide. But he wouldn't believe us. And he was right. The truth is, she was a prostitute. And mentally ill. She used to self-administer electric shocks to her own head. Using a car battery.'

'So you lied to him.'

'What choice did we have? Lie to him or tell the truth and break his heart? Which would you have chosen?'

Howie's phone vibrates with an incoming text. She reaches for it.

'Apparently it's not uncommon,' Jan says. 'Troubled adoptees try to provoke rejection. They're trying to make their adoptive parents prove their love by behaving more and more unacceptably. And that was Henry to a T. We completely lost control of him. There was animal cruelty. Shoplifting. More burglary. Sexual misconduct.'

Luther reaches for his notebook, flips it open. He pats down his pockets, looking for a pen.

'What kind of misconduct?'

'He exposed himself,' says Jan Madsen. 'To some very young girls.'

Howie checks her phone.

She sees the incoming text is from Luther's phone:

Henry Madsen is here.
Parents house
15 Cavalry Close. Finchley.
Madsen upstairs — father poss hostage
Mia Dalton upstairs? Possible hostage
Please assist ASAP.

Howie stares at the phone for six or seven long seconds. She reads the message half a dozen times.

Her eyes flick from the message to Luther and back again. Luther gives no indication.

He just sits there, scribbling a note as Jan talks.

★   ★   ★

Scary Mary Lally leads Search Team Two to a vacant residential property on a quiet street in Muswell Hill.

The house is in the early stages of renovation. There is a skip outside. The house is full of the previous resident's furniture. Gypsum board, plaster, paint cans and drop sheets.

In the garage in the rear of the property they find the deceased owner's car and boxes of personal effects.

While searching the garden, the dogs become agitated.

Lally follows the dog handler into the house, where the dogs become progressively more excited.

DS Lally calls DCI Reed.

'Mia's definitely been here,' she says. 'Her smell's all over the place. We found hair dye in the sink upstairs.'

'So he's dyed her hair? He's disguising her?'

'Looks like it, Guv.'

Reed thanks her. He says, 'Post somebody to keep an eye on the place. Make sure he doesn't come back.'

Reed is still on the phone to Lally when a text message arrives. It's from Luther.

Reed skims it, then stands so abruptly he kicks his chair over. His neck spasms. He grabs it. He says, 'Look, Mary. Something's come up. Keep looking and let me know.'

He hangs up the desk phone and turns to face Benny.

Benny is slowly looking up from his own phone.

'Holy shit,' Reed says.

Clutching his neck, he runs out the door and sprints across the bullpen. He bursts into Teller's office.

She's already putting on her coat.

'Right,' she says. 'Let's have it.' She strides away, on her radio.

Reed follows, thumbing out a hasty reply: sit tite! on our way.

* * *

Howie pockets her phone and waits for Luther's next move.

He glances over his notebook and says, 'So when was the last time you actually saw Henry?'

'When he came out of prison.'

'This is when he was, what? Twenty-one, twenty-two?'

'Yes. He came to see us.'

'And what did he say?'

'That he hated us. That he never wanted to see us again. And,' she looks Luther in the eye, 'that he was going to start his own family. A big family. Five sons. Five daughters. They were going to live on a farm. Raise animals. Pedigree animals. Rare breeds. He was going to love them all. The animals and the children. He was going to give them all the love in the world. But as far as he was concerned, Jeremy and I were dead.'

'And he hasn't been in contact since?'

She shakes her head, frowning. 'There are times the phone goes and nobody's there. And I wonder. And sometimes when I'm locking up at night, you forget to close the curtains. You glance outside and you do think — there's someone out there, in the darkness at the end of the garden. Do you think that may have been him?'

'No,' Luther lies. Then he rips the top sheet off his notebook and passes it to her.

Is he here?

She reads it. Her eyes well. She looks into Luther's eyes and nods.

Luther is very calm. He mouths the words: *Keep talking.* He passes her another note.

Young girl with him?

Jan shakes her head vigorously, gestures for his notepad.

NO! HE BURIED LITTLE GIRL

Luther mouths the word, *Buried?*

'He was a very troubled young man,' Luther says, passing her the notepad. 'None of this was your fault.'

Jan scribbles on the notepad.

Little girl on phone, not Henry.

She hands him the notepad.
Luther writes:

Mia?!!

Passes her the notepad. She reads it. Nods. Yes, Mia.

Then she writes:

Mia read out a message
Henry will bury her.
Enough air for 2 hours.
Henry will give us Mia . . . if we give him
money.

389

Her eyes go to the computer, and Luther understands. The Madsens were in the middle of transferring money to Henry's bank account when Luther and Howie showed up.

If we call police or Henry arrested

Jan writes,

Mia dies. No-one ever finds her.

Luther takes the note, scans it, passes it to Howie.

He stands, pockets his notebook.

Jan Madsen begins to cry.

'DS Howie,' Luther says, 'why don't you take Mrs Madsen into the garden for some fresh air? Mrs Madsen, I'm sorry this has been so difficult.'

Then he walks into the hallway.

He looks up the stairs.

He says, 'So did you hear all that, Henry?'

* * *

Multiple police units vector in on the address in Finchley. Among them are three Armed Response Vehicles. A Jankel armoured Guardian Tactical Intervention Vehicle, which is a large 4×4 with bullet-proof windscreen and blast-proof flooring. It contains eight CO19 Specialist Firearms Officers in dark blue Nomex fire-resistant overalls and Kevlar body armour, assault vests with stun grenades, tear-gas canisters, SF-10 respirator and C100 ceramic helmets.

The Air Support Unit dispatches India 97 and India 98 from Lippits Hill.

Reed sits in the back seat of a marked BMW area car, one of a convoy of four racing under blues and twos.

He flexes his jaw. Clenches and unclenches his fist. London goes past.

Nine million people.

★ ★ ★

Search Team One searches the basement of a condemned block of flats in Walthamstow.

They find signs of a blood-stained pit, the smell of shit and sweat and alcohol.

The electric lights crackle overhead.

There is no sign of Mia Dalton or Henry Madsen.

★ ★ ★

Luther stands on the stairs.

'I know you told your mum to get rid of us,' he says. 'And she did a good job. She tried really hard. She answered our questions very honestly. But she's not wearing her wedding ring, is she? It doesn't look to me like she's taken it off for forty years. And there's a jar of Vaseline in the kitchen, next to the tap, as if she'd just taken the ring off. It's a nice ring. I saw it in the photos. Probably worth a bob or two, eh?'

He waits out a long silence.

'So listen,' he says. 'I've called it in. We've got a load of coppers on their way. So it's all done. Either we get a very, very messy siege and you end up dead. Or you come with me.'

★ ★ ★

Howie takes Jan by the elbow. She leads her to the adjoining door and through the long, narrow kitchen.

Jan is shaking so badly she's finding it difficult to walk.

★ ★ ★

Luther pauses on the second stair. 'All right, Henry. I'm coming up.'

He produces his ASP extendable baton, keeps it collapsed in his fist.

He takes the stairs slowly, one by one.

There are fifteen steps.

★ ★ ★

Howie helps Jan past the cupboard units, the fridge, an old-fashioned larder, a chest freezer in the corner.

'That poor little girl,' Jan says. 'That poor little darling. What's going to happen?'

'We'll find her,' Howie says.

She reaches the kitchen door.

It's an old-fashioned door with a heavy mortice lock; the kind that requires a large metal key.

The door is locked.

Luther reaches the top of the stairs and edges along the landing.

He opens the first bedroom door. It's a sewing room.

He stands framed in darkness. Street lamps filter through pale curtains, give the room an orange glow.

There's no one here.

He turns to the master-bedroom door.

It's slightly ajar.

He steps inside.

Jeremy Madsen lies on the bed.

* * *

Howie tries the handle. Turns in frustration to Jan Madsen. 'Where's the key?'

She sees the look in Jan's eyes.

Panic.

Howie follows the line of Jan's gaze.

Jan is looking at the two old, black deadbolts fitted to the door — one at head-height, the other near the ground.

She wonders for a moment about their significance.

Then she notices that each deadbolt is in the open position, as if someone had been trying to leave by the back door.

But has failed because the door is locked and needs a key to open it.

And then Howie knows.

She turns, pushing Jan behind her, reaching

for her pepper spray as Henry Madsen steps out of the broom cupboard.

She sees his face for the first time, the twisted thing in his eyes and then she looks at the long screwdriver in his fist, yellow handle, ten-inch, flat-head —

Howie yells, 'Down on the ground! Down on the ground, now!'

As Madsen jams the screwdriver between her ribs, just under her breast, and twists it.

★   ★   ★

Luther hears Howie bellowing and Jan Madsen screaming and sees the animal terror in the eyes of Jeremy Madsen.

He turns and runs.

He's at the top of the stairs when Henry Madsen reaches the front door.

Madsen glances over his shoulder, sees Luther.

He mishandles the lock. His hands are wet with blood.

Luther vaults the stairs as Henry Madsen opens the door.

Luther throws out a hand, slams it shut.

Then he punches his shoulder into Henry Madsen.

Madsen slams into the solid wood door.

Luther takes Madsen by the lapels. Smashes him into the door, into the wall. Into the door again.

He looks up, holding a collapsed Madsen in his hands.

Jeremy Madsen stands at the top of the stairs, cadaverous with shock.

'Move,' Luther says. 'Back to your room.'

'My wife — '

'Move!' Luther screams, and Jeremy retreats like a spectre to his sickbed.

Henry Madsen grins, and with a movement of the tongue, produces a razor blade. He grips it in his front teeth and slashes at Luther.

Luther steps back.

Madsen runs for the kitchen.

Luther a moment behind him.

Madsen slips in blood that has pooled on the tiles. His legs go out from under him.

He scrambles to his feet.

Luther tackles him to the floor again.

Madsen slashes at him with the blade between his teeth.

Luther grabs Madsen's wrist, twists it, jams it up between his shoulders.

Madsen cries out. Drops the razor blade.

He lies face down.

Luther places his knee into Madsen's back. Then he stands, keeping Madsen's arm in a wristlock, and kicks him three times in the ribs.

He drags Madsen across the blood-smeared floor and cuffs him to the oven-door handle. It's an old oven. The handle is heavy, a little greasy underneath.

Madsen lies with legs askew.

Luther hurries to Jan Madsen. She's curled by the back door. A yellow-handled screwdriver protrudes from her eye socket.

Howie is alive. The screwdriver has opened a hole in her chest wall. Blood froths at the lips of the wound; it means her lung has collapsed. Soon she'll enter irreversible shock. She's dying.

Luther fumbles in his pocket, digs out his wallet. Removes a credit card. He rips open Howie's shirt. The bubbling wound on her pale flesh, dotted with moles, strikes him as obscene. He presses the card to the hole, the frothing blood.

He says, 'Isobel. Isobel, can you press here?'

He guides her hand. It's light in his grip. He waits until she's pressing down on the credit card.

Her face is the wrong colour.

He says, 'Keep it pressed down.' He runs to the kitchen drawers. Opens and shuts them.

Henry looks at him from the floor, an artful little grin on his face.

Luther wants to kick it.

In the lowest kitchen drawer, Luther comes across a roll of cling film.

He grabs it, runs to Howie. Kneels. He says, 'Come on. Sit. Just for a moment.'

He tries to help her into a sitting position. But she can't do it. She panics. She can't breathe. Her breath comes in ugly, sucking gasps.

Okay.

Luther lays her on the floor. Rips off a square of cling film. Presses that to the wound. Howie's next breath sucks it in a little, sealing the hole.

Luther wraps cling film round and round Howie's body. The cellophane is blood-smeared and slippy.

He kneels there, concentrating, telling her she's okay, she's okay, she's okay.

★   ★   ★

When Luther has done what he can for Howie, he returns to Madsen.

'Henry, where's Mia?'

Madsen gives him a defeated and bitter grin.

The life goes out of Luther.

He looks around, at the blood and the chaos. The agony of Howie's breathing. Jan Madsen, killed by her own child.

At this kitchen in which ten thousand marital meals were cooked, ten thousand cups of tea were brewed. An entire marriage, zeroing in on this evening. Converging like ship and iceberg.

Luther sits on the bloody floor, next to Henry. He leans his back on the kitchen drawers.

The approaching sirens grow frantic.

Luther says, 'You're not going to tell me, are you?'

Madsen shrugs.

Luther looks at the kitchen clock. It's above the door. It's been ticking there since Margaret Thatcher was prime minister, promising to bring hope where there had been despair.

It's 11.19 p.m.

'How long has she got?'

'Until about midnight.'

Luther laughs.

'So we arrest you. And you sit there in silence, loving every minute of it. The power it gives you, eh? The control. To know this little girl is dying somewhere in the dark. And you'll be surrounded by all these coppers who can't do a thing about it. That must be quite a buzz. For a man like you. To know how much better you are than everyone else.'

Madsen just sits there.

Luther's skull bursts open like an egg sac. Spiders crawl out.

He scuttles to Howie. He kisses her cheek.

He says, 'Hang on. They're nearly here. Can you hear them?'

She makes a noise. He's not sure if it's an answer or not.

He takes the car keys from her pocket and returns to Madsen. He uncuffs him.

He drags Madsen to his feet. Marches him to the door in an armlock.

Madsen struggles. 'Where are we going?'

The sirens are closer.

Luther has to hurry.

He marches Madsen down the pavement.

He opens the car door and shoves Madsen into the front passenger footwell.

As he does so, an ambulance arrives at the end of the street.

In a few seconds, they're going to see him.

As the ambulance pulls up, Luther gets in the Volvo and starts the engine.

In the rear-view mirror, he watches paramedics rush into the Madsen house.

Behind them, the first marked police vehicles pull up. Officers spill out.

Luther starts the engine and pulls away. He pulls out his radio. 'This is DCI Luther,' he says.

'I'm on foot, in pursuit of suspect believed to be Henry Madsen . . . '

When he's finished, Madsen blinks at him.

It's pleasing to see the first signs of real fear in his eyes.

He says, 'Where are we going?'

'Somewhere private.'

'What for?'

Luther drives.

He leaves the police lights far behind, flashing blue and silent in the darkness.

30

Teller and Reed arrive as Howie is being loaded into the back of the ambulance.

The body of Jan Madsen is still in the kitchen. Jeremy Madsen sits in the back seat of an area car, surveying the blue flashing street as if none of this were real.

Teller takes Reed's elbow and leads him away from the tape. 'Off the record,' she says.

Reed nods. His neck spasms. He grabs it, massages it. 'Off the record,' he says.

'Where the fuck did Luther go?'

'Rose, I don't know. I swear to God. I don't know.'

'Has he lost it?'

'Do you mean, is he going to do something stupid?'

'Yes. I mean, is he going to do something stupid?'

'It depends what you mean by stupid.'

She gets up close, into Reed's face. 'Now's not the time,' she says through her teeth. 'I've got an officer down, I'm up to my elbows in dead people. I've got a missing girl, a missing suspect and a missing officer. So my sense of humour is pretty frayed round the edges.'

Reed breaks the moment by reaching into his pocket. He pops the lid on a plastic container and dry-swallows a fistful of codeine.

'Fuck me,' says Teller. She runs hands through her hair.

Reed swallows and scowls. Codeine feels good, but doesn't taste it. He says, 'You honestly want my opinion?'

'Yes, Ian. I honestly do.'

'This is my opinion, Rose. It's not based on fact.'

'Go on.'

'Whatever he's doing, he's doing it for a reason.'

'I know that, for fuck's sake. But what's the reason?'

She dismisses him with a cold eye. He stalks off, hands in pockets.

Teller calls Zoe.

The phone rings for a long time before Zoe answers.

'Rose? What's wrong?'

'What I'm going to tell you,' Teller says, having to speak up above the noise, 'I shouldn't be telling you. Because we're in a shit situation here and if anyone gets wind of it — '

'Has this got anything to do with Schenk?'

'What about Schenk?'

'He came to see me this morning — '

'I'm going to stop you there, Zoe. Right there. There's stuff it's best I don't hear.'

'I'm sorry. I assumed that's why you called.'

Teller looks at Reed. He's standing, arms crossed, in the middle of the road, craning his neck to watch a helicopter searchlight sweeping streets and gardens.

'No,' Teller says. 'It's not that. Well, I don't

think so.' She kneads her brow. She hasn't showered or changed her clothes in forty-eight hours. 'For fuck's sake,' she says. 'Who knows, where John's concerned?'

Zoe waits on the line. Teller can picture her expression, and briefly detests her.

'Have you heard from him,' Teller says, 'in the last hour or two?'

'No. Why?'

'Is that actually true? I'm not Schenk, and this isn't some arsehole's toy car we're talking about. This is important.'

'Rose, I haven't heard from him. Why?'

'Because we've lost him.'

'What do you mean, you've lost him?'

'If this goes any further, Zoe, I mean any further at all, then we're absolutely fucked. Have you got that? He's fucked us, one and all.'

'Rose, it won't go any further. I won't say a thing.'

Teller recounts the events of the day. The Daltons. Mia Dalton. Patrick, who was Adrian York. York's mother. Henry Madsen and his dead dogs and his burning house and the terrible cell in the basement.

She tells Zoe about Madsen's adoptive parents. His mother slaughtered in the family kitchen. And about DS Howie, stabbed under the breast, fighting for her life in the back of an ambulance.

Zoe is at Mark's.

They're in the living room, cuddled up naked under a soft blanket. They've been watching a

DVD, sharing a bottle of wine and smoking a joint.

Now Mark sits with the DVD remote in hand, thumb hovering over the pause button as Zoe listens to Teller.

Her eyes widen and her hand goes slowly to her throat.

She looks fragile and lovely and for a moment Mark pities Luther for loving this woman and losing her.

Zoe says, 'I don't understand. What are you trying to tell me?'

'As far as I can see,' says Teller, shouting above the noise of her less cosy surroundings, 'we've got two options. Option one: little Mia's dead and John's quietly taken Henry Madsen away to kill him.'

She gives Zoe a moment to process this.

'What's option two?'

'We don't know what option two might be.'

When Zoe's able to speak, her voice is very small. She says, 'Rose, I haven't heard from him. I absolutely swear.'

'You'll have to speak up. It's noisy here.'

'*He hasn't called!*'

'All right,' Teller says. 'But not a word to anyone, okay? Because this could be really bad.'

'Not a word.'

'And if he does get in contact . . . '

'I'll call you. Straight away.'

'Straight away.'

'Absolutely. The moment. Rose?'

'Yeah?'

'Is he okay?'

'To be honest with you — no, I don't think he is.'

There's nothing more to say. Zoe mumbles thanks and hangs up.

She stares at the phone.

Mark doesn't ask. He just puts a warm arm around her bare shoulders. They huddle there, naked on the sofa, under a blanket that smells faintly of sex, in this good house with its air of weed and sharp green plants and books and leather.

★ ★ ★

Luther drives onto Colney Hatch Lane, turns at speed.

Madsen pounds at the windows, mouths to the other cars, people on the streets.

Luther speeds past. He turns onto Hampden Road, using two wheels, then Sydney Road.

By degrees, the streets become quieter. Luther does not slow down.

He turns onto Alexandra Road. It's silent, but for the clamouring engine of the old Volvo. The street is lined with 1930s redbrick flats, functional and neat.

Then the flats run out and the road reveals itself to be a cul-de-sac — except for a pathway which leads, via a primary-coloured fence, off the street to a park.

Luther stops the car with a skid. He and Madsen sit for a moment.

Luther says, 'Get out.'

'No.'

Luther laughs.

'You can't do this,' says Madsen.

Luther drags Madsen from the car. Madsen cries out. He screams and begs. His voice cracks. But Luther knows that nobody will come to Madsen's assistance, because Luther knows that nobody ever does.

He locks his elbow round Madsen's carotid artery and squeezes. In a few moments, Madsen's legs go weak, threaten to fold from under him.

Luther frog-marches him, dazed, into the park.

There is a stark, white hunter's moon. Across it, clouds blow, loose as cannon smoke.

He shoves Madsen past the playground, the red swings, the jaunty roundabout, into the darkness beyond; an urban wasteland whose borders are marked by feral birch and ash saplings.

Madsen's head is clearing. He draws in a lungful of air; ready to bawl for help. Luther throws him to the ground. Drags him along.

This area used to be a sewage works, then a rubbish tip. It's been derelict since 1963. Five years ago, Luther attended the scene of a murder here. A prostitute called Dawn Cadell.

He drags Henry through the pale, wild saplings onto a tussocked grassland colonized by invasive rhododendrons, buddleia, Japanese knotweed. He navigates the waist-high foliage by moonlight.

He hauls Madsen to his feet and shoves him

into the trees, a heavy young forest of oak and ash.

Under that whispering canopy, it's quiet. The moon's eye winks out. There's just the ragged sound of their exerted breathing, the night wind through invasive weeds. The faint ambient radiance of electric light pollution.

Human feet have created a system of paths through the trees. They're called desire paths.

Luther always liked that.

He marches Henry down the largest of them.

They pass into a clearing. The white moon shines bright on a thick, weedy meadow that's littered with the rusty corpses of cars. No wheels. No windows. No glass. A bone yard of Metros, Beetles, an upended post-office van, scattered like the husks of giant insects.

And nestling close to the treeline, half swamped with foxglove and lupin and briar, is the rotting corpse of a caravan.

Luther marches Henry to the caravan and shoves him inside.

It smells strongly of damp and decomposition.

Luther forces Henry to sit on the U-shaped bench surrounding the dining table, which is still bolted to the floor. The bench's vinyl is ripped, exposing the foam beneath. It crawls and ticks with invertebrates.

They sit in darkness and silence.

Madsen shudders, monkey-grinning.

When he's got his breath back, Luther says, 'So where is she, Henry?'

Madsen hugs himself for warmth. 'What time is it?'

'Eleven thirty-two. Where is she?'

'Kill me, you'll never know.'

'Well, that's true. But it doesn't end well for you either, does it?'

A long moment of silence.

'Half an hour,' Madsen says. 'Can you stand it?'

'No. Can you?'

Madsen laughs.

Luther sits back. Regards him through the rich, fungal darkness. Reek of leaf humus, rotten plywood. Rubber gone to rot.

Madsen leans forward. 'You can hurt me all you like,' he says. 'But you'll do life for it. And I won't tell you a fucking thing.' His quaking begins to subside as dominance and control pass back to him. 'Still,' he says. 'At least you'll know she died a virgin.'

They breathe the same fetid air.

Madsen breaks the silence. 'What time is it now?'

'Eleven thirty-eight.'

'Just over twenty minutes.'

Luther shudders with cold.

'If you wanted to kill me,' Madsen says, 'the place to do it was back at Mum's house. Who'd ever know if it was self-defence or not, eh? So here's what I think. I think you want little Mia back more than you want anything in the world.'

'Yes,' says Luther.

'So there's got to be a way out of this, hasn't there? There's got to be a way I get what I want and you get what you want.'

Rats creep in the cancerous frame of the

407

squalid caravan. Reptilian tails drag over blisters of rust.

'It's not going to happen,' Luther says, at length. 'If I let you go and you've lied, I've got nothing. And you're a liar, Henry. That's your problem. You're a liar.'

They sit.

Madsen says, 'How long?'

Luther looks at his watch. He doesn't answer.

He stands. He goes to the caravan door.

Madsen says, 'Where are you going?'

'To call my wife.'

Luther steps into the moonlight. Wet grass to his knees. Rosebay willowherb. Bits of pram extend from it, the arc of a corroded oil drum. Low-hanging trees, heavy with recent rainfall. The pale, oxidizing caravan with its corrupt human cargo.

He watches the beam of a distant helicopter as it probes the streets. Searching for him. Searching for Madsen.

He turns on his phone and calls Zoe.

Her phone rings and rings and rings.

He waits.

★　★　★

Zoe jumps when her phone rings.

She grabs it. It's John.

She looks at Mark before answering. He makes a gesture: *Do what you have to.*

So Zoe stands naked in the middle of Mark's living room, wrappéd in the blanket like a Roman statue.

Mark sits bollock-naked on the sofa, places a Moroccan cushion over his lap, rolls a calming joint.

In a better world, on a happier night, it would be funny.

Zoe takes the call. 'John?'

He hears her voice saying his name. Twenty years of love in it.

'Zoe,' he says. His voice is rendered a near murmur by the solitude and the darkness.

He says, 'I don't know what to do.'

'Where are you? Everyone's looking for you.'

He sees the helicopter searchlight poking the gardens, the allotments, the suburban sheds.

'I can't tell you.'

'We're frightened for you,' she says. 'Everyone's really scared. Come home.'

'I can't. I'm lost. I don't know where I am.' He wants more than anything in the world to be with her now; to have her naked and warm and in his arms. 'I need help,' he says. 'I need your help.'

'Whatever I can do,' she says. 'Whatever it is.'

'I've got him,' says Luther. 'The man who did this. All these terrible things. I've got him.'

'John, that's — '

'But the little girl he took. He buried her somewhere. Buried her alive. I don't know where she is. She's only got a few minutes left. She's terrified. Right now. She's in a box in the ground and she's terrified. She's dying. But he won't tell me where she is. He's enjoying it. The pain he's causing. The power he's got. He'd rather let her die.'

He waits for a reaction. But there's only silence on the line.

He says her name.

And still, that silence.

'I could hurt him,' he says at last. 'If I did that, I think I could find her.'

He can hear her sobbing now. Trying not to.

'But I'd have to really hurt him,' he says. 'I mean, really hurt him. So I need you to tell me what to do. What's the right thing to do? I need you to tell me. I need your help.'

Zoe is weeping. 'I don't know what to say,' she says. 'I don't know. I don't know what to say. I'm sorry. I don't know.'

'No,' says Luther. 'No, of course not.'

He hangs up. He turns off his phone.

He looks at the moon until his heart has slowed and his voice has regained some strength. Then he turns the phone on again and calls Ian Reed.

★ ★ ★

Henry doesn't hear the content of that first call. But he reads body language well.

He sees that Luther is resigned to something. His head weighing heavy on his chest.

Henry turns to the caravan window, tries to slide it open.

He can't.

It's rusted shut.

Then he runs a hungry finger around the

410

window seal. The rubber has hardened and cracked. It's brittle and crumbles to the touch.

Henry braces himself against the dining table. He presses the window with the palms of his hands.

He heaves and heaves.

The window frame squeals.

He doesn't care.

With a long screech, the window pops from its frame.

Henry squeezes through the gap. He jumps into the nettles and the brambles.

He picks a desire path and runs.

★   ★   ★

Luther listens to Henry battering his way out of the caravan.

He looks at his watch.

Finally, Reed answers. 'John, for fuck's sake. Where are you?'

'Have you found her?'

'We searched all five properties on the list. They'd been at one, briefly. By the time the search team got there, they'd moved on.'

'What kind of property?'

'House. They were converting it.'

'Where was it?'

'Muswell Hill.'

'How far from Madsen's parents'?'

'I don't know. Two miles? A bit less?'

'She's there.'

'John, she's not.'

'He was going to sell her to his parents. So he needed to keep her close. She's there.'

'We searched. We used dogs. There's nothing there.'

'You checked the garden?'

'Garden, outbuildings, garage. Everywhere.'

'Have you been there? You personally? Have you seen the house?'

'No.'

'So get there, Ian.'

'John, mate. Slow down.'

'She's there. She's somewhere at that house. He's buried her and she's there. You've got about ten minutes. She's suffocating.'

Reed wavers. Then says, 'On my way.'

'Good.'

'Where are you?'

'Following a lead. I'll call you.'

Luther hangs up.

He turns off his phone.

He can see Madsen, black on black, sinuous as an urban fox flitting through the trees.

He follows.

★   ★   ★

Henry races through the trees.

He's fast, and he's scared. His feet barely contact the wet compacted mud. The winter moon lights his way.

Every now and again he turns and sees the big man coming for him. Not hurrying.

The lane parallels a thin, muddy stream. But the bank is steep and dense with nettles and

412

briar on the far side. Impossible to cross.

So he keeps running, headlong.

At a long curve in the path, Henry reaches a thick bush of nettles and rhododendron. Behind it, garlanded with litter, spiked railings give onto a railway cutting.

Across the glinting black and silver river of railway line is an industrial park.

Henry wades through the nettles, tracing the line of the fence. He's looking for a weapon, or a way out. There's always a way out.

Twenty or thirty metres along, he finds a gap in the fence and slips through.

He slides down the embankment, then races across the railway lines.

He glances over his shoulder. And there's Luther. Squeezing himself through the gap in the fence, sliding down the embankment. Implacable.

Henry scrambles up the other side of the cutting. Arrives at a chain-link fence. He scales the fence, throws himself over the top bar. Drops onto tarmac.

It's littered with seeped-in patches of oil, fat circular pads of moss, broken glass.

He turns, fingers hooked in the links of the fence and, back-lit by orange distant sodium light, he squints into the darkness.

For a moment, he can't see Luther. Not until his eyes are dark-adapted.

And then he sees him.

Luther is running across the railway lines.

Henry turns, puffs out his chest, runs.

* * *

Luther scrambles up the embankment, using tufts of grass as handholds. At the top, he peers through the fence. Sees Madsen disappearing into the shabby industrial estate.

Luther climbs the fence, throws himself over the top, drops onto tarmac.

* * *

Henry doesn't know the way out.

The industrial park is deserted and seemingly infinite. Full of dark corners, discarded engine parts, broken glass. Dented oil drums lie dead on their sides.

Most of the buildings are in a state of dereliction, loading docks barricaded with sheet metal and plywood. Concrete access ramps thick with thistle and willowherb.

An old security light winks on, exposing Henry as starkly and perfectly as a helicopter searchlight.

He runs for the darkness, sprints down a wide desolate avenue, flanked by dead buildings.

The wind buffets the unsecured corner of a sheet of corrugated iron. It covers the entrance to a vast redbrick brewery, long since abandoned.

Purblind by the security light, Henry makes for it. He feels the rust on the iron like sugar on a tabletop, the crumbling sharp edges beneath his fingertips.

414

He pulls back the corner and slips into the immense damp blackness of the old loading bay.

★　★　★

Luther loses sight of Madsen. But then, round a corner, he sees a light blink on.

He glances sharply away, to preserve his night vision. Stands with eyes closed, a soft disc of moss beneath his foot. He counts to thirty.

As he's counting, he hears the shriek of metal on concrete.

When he opens his eyes, the security light has shut off.

He follows in Henry's footsteps, but ducks right where Henry had gone left. Skirts the fringes of the Worldwide Tyres warehouse, turns left and left again.

He doesn't activate the security light.

He turns the corner onto a wide avenue. On the other side is an old tower brewery.

He stands there for a long time, catching his breath. Watches clouds scud across the blank eye of the moon.

He waits.

Sees movement. The wind catching the loose corner of a sheet of corrugated iron.

Luther walks.

He reaches the corrugated iron, pulls it aside. It screams in pain.

He enters the loading dock.

The darkness smells of brick dust and mildew, a hundred years of brewing. The ammonia stink of pigeon shit.

In the corner, abandoned, he passes a spillage of ancient LPs. A teetering pile of magazines, swollen and fungal with age. *Pike Fishing.* Grinning 1970s men hold foot-long fish.

He hears a ringing echo. Metal on concrete.

It emanates from a far, dark corridor.

Luther is calm. He follows the echo.

★　★　★

Teller and Reed pull up to a tumbledown, 1920s semi in Muswell Hill.

The search team's still here, a full squad of emergency vehicles.

A uniformed constable stands posted at the gate. Teller leaps from the car and runs to her.

'Nothing?'

'No, Ma'am.'

'According to John, her oxygen ran out about two minutes ago.'

Reed is moments behind her. He hurries past. 'If John says she's here, she's here.'

He enters the house.

It smells of new plaster and old rising damp. It's full of police, arc lamps, exaggerated shadows. He passes through into the floodlit garden, finds Lally. She's wearing Gore-Tex and heavy boots.

He says, 'You went over it all again?'

She nods. 'Garden, basement, garage, outbuildings. There's nothing. No sign the ground was disturbed. He's lying, Guv.'

Reed checks his watch.

Lally says, 'How long has she got?'

416

Reed can't answer. He paces the floodlit garden, follows his own shadow. Thumbs out a text.

searched house again!! No sign. Are you SURE??

*   *   *

Luther strides across the concrete. Madsen a flitting shadow before him.

He texts as he walks.

LOOK AGAIN

*   *   *

Henry sprints down a ruined tiled corridor.

It ends in a metal stairwell leading to a steel walkway above.

It's go up, or go back.

And he can't go back.

He scans the dark corners for what predators may lurk there. He sees nothing. There's just the sound of dripping water, his own harsh breath.

Until.

A footstep.

Somewhere out there. In the shadows. Henry bolts up the ladder.

*   *   *

Reed runs outside, finds Teller examining the picture of Mia Dalton.

She looks up. Can't hide a flare of hope in her eyes.

'Nothing,' Reed says.

Teller grits her teeth and looks away.

Henry takes a retreating step. And another. Moving backwards as the echoing footsteps in the vastness of this terrible place grow closer and closer.

He scrambles up the second rusty ladder, runs along the raised iron walkway.

The walkway ends in a third ladder. It takes him to a fourth level. Then a fifth.

When he's high up, moonlight filters through dirty pitched-roof windows, revealing the iron walkway runs adjacent to a steel framework that once suspended the brewery's colossal fermenting tanks. Where the tanks once stood are now vast circular holes. The last of the holes is spanned by a very basic bridge.

The bridge leads to a steel door.

The steel door is the only way out.

Henry examines the bridge and the chasm it crosses. It swan-dives into a void.

He turns from it.

He won't cross that corroded bridge over that monstrous drop.

Breathing heavily, he casts round, seeking an alternative way out.

And hears that noise in the silence.

Luther, coming closer.

Henry waits.

Luther reaches the upper walkway. He advances on Henry.

Henry crosses the bridge, towards the door. The structure groans under his weight.

He's halfway across when something falls, a sheared bolt. It plunges, reverberating, into the void.

Henry ignores it.

He reaches the far side, the riveted steel door. It's locked.

He casts round on his hands and knees. He scrabbles in the clinker until his hand settles on a length of iron piping. It's heavy.

He heaves and strains, then rips the piping from the crumbling wall. He turns, gripping the pipe in two hands, meaning to batter at the door handle with it.

Then he sees Luther.

He's standing at the other side of the bridge, watching him.

Luther and Madsen stand at either end of the span, eyes locked.

Luther bares his teeth like a dog.

Henry raises the length of pipe. He's killed people with less.

They advance, slowly at first, advancing towards the centre of the bridge.

Luther snarls.

Henry raises the pipe, bellows in hatred and rage.

They run.

The bridge jolts under their weight. Then it gives way beneath Henry's feet.

Henry falls.

He drops the iron pipe. It tumbles end on end into nothing.

Henry grabs the pendulous edge of walkway with one hand.

He hangs there, scrabbling. He tries to climb.

But he can't. Shifting his weight makes the structure groan in complaint, threatening to collapse altogether.

Luther edges as close as he can to the rent in the floor. He braces himself.

'You're going to fall, Henry.'

Madsen tries to clamber up.

He can't.

The bridge jolts, gives way a few more centimetres.

Madsen is jarred. But hangs on.

There's a weird shriek and pop as support wires give way.

Luther leans over as far as he dares. 'Where is she? Where's Mia?'

Madsen's feet kick and flail, seeking a toehold that isn't there.

'In the living room! For God's sake, she's in the living room. There's a panel behind the plasterboard.'

Luther digs out his phone. 'Be exact.'

★ ★ ★

Reed's phone rings. It's Luther.

He snatches it up. 'John?'

'You said they were renovating the house?'

'Yeah, the place is a mess, mate.'

'He lied. She's not in the ground. She's behind the plasterboard in the living room. There's a panel.'

Reed swears, hangs up. Runs into the house, into the cluttered and bustling living room.

* * *

Luther waits.

Henry dangles. His hand is bloodless from gripping the greasy, powdery iron. He says, 'Please!'

Luther kneels.

'Thing is,' he says, 'what if you're lying? Because you've done that before, haven't you? You lied and lied and lied.'

'I'm not lying! Please!'

* * *

Reed races to the tiny, cluttered living room.

He's followed by Teller and six uniformed members of the search team.

Together, they heave aside an old walnut dresser. Doing so exposes a large, freshly plastered square of gypsum board.

Reed grabs a crowbar and levers at the wet edge of gypsum board.

The others join him. They hammer and rip at the plasterboard wall, rip it down section by section.

* * *

Luther watches Madsen struggle. He listens to him beg and plead.

He checks his watch.

12.04.

* * *

Behind the plasterboard, behind a layer of pink fibreglass wall insulation, they find an upright, coffin-sized container. It's been wrapped in mineral wool lagging, obtained from the hot water cylinder.

The coffin is attached to a small oxygen cylinder. The needle on the cylinder gauge reads *empty*.

Reed picks up his phone. The line still connected. 'John, I think she's here!'

Luther looks down into Madsen's eye. Speaks into the phone. 'Is she alive?'

★   ★   ★

The coffin is a large weapons case, made airtight with duct tape and sealed with six throw-latches.

Four officers, Reed included, heave it from the cavity inside the wall and lay it flat.

Reed digs out his thumb knife, cuts along the duct tape, then throws the latches one by one.

He lifts the lid of the case.

Inside is Mia Dalton. Eyes closed. Arms crossed over her chest. They've been taped, to stop her pounding and scratching at the walls of her casket. Seeing that brings it home.

Reed stands up and back.

Suddenly, he's frozen.

Teller steps up. She hauls Mia from the coffin; a skinny little dark-haired girl. She lays her out on the filthy floor. Puts an ear to her chest.

Shit.

She turns Mia's head, clears her airway. Then tilts back her head. Pinches her nose. Covers

Mia's mouth with hers, and gently forces air into her lungs.

Mia's chest rises.

⋆ ⋆ ⋆

Luther watches Madsen. There's silence, except for the reverberations of Madsen's begging.

⋆ ⋆ ⋆

Reed keeps the phone to his ear as Teller continues to administer CPR.

Down the line, he can hear echoing screaming.

He lowers the phone and watches Teller.

Until Mia Dalton takes in a great *whoop* of air and sits up — blinking, bewildered, terror-stricken.

Teller cries out and embraces the child. 'Oh, good girl,' she says. 'Good girl. Good girl.'

Reed's legs go weak. He braces himself against the wall, lifts the phone. 'We've got her!'

'Good,' says Luther.

Reed listens to the screams.

Please. Please. I'm falling. I'm going to fall.

He thinks for a moment. Then he hangs up, pockets his phone.

He steps aside to make way for the incoming paramedics.

Teller is hugging Mia tight. Rocking her, calling her a good girl, a good girl.

The paramedics have to ask three times before she'll let Mia go.

★ ★ ★

Luther stares at Madsen, hanging pendent.

'Please,' says Madsen. 'I can't hold on.'

Luther considers it. 'Tell me about the others, Henry.'

'PLEASE,' says Madsen.

'How many more were there?'

'None!'

'HOW MANY MORE? There was Adrian, wasn't there? There was baby Emma. I dug her out of the ground myself. But I was too late. SO HOW MANY MORE?'

No answer comes.

But Madsen's terror slips away. Control passes to him.

He stares up at Luther. In agony. And in defiance.

Luther surges with hate. It rises from in his feet. It spreads in his chest and shoulders like wings unfurling.

He reaches out a foot.

He hesitates.

He meets Madsen's eyes.

Then he places his foot on Madsen's fingers.

Madsen screams.

Luther presses down. He brings all his weight to bear.

And then he steps back.

Madsen's hand slips.

There's an insane flurry as he scrabbles for purchase.

Then falls into blackness.

Down he falls. Down and down.

Luther doesn't see him hit the ground, but he hears it: a wet crunch; a long, chiming reverberation.

The strength leaves him. He staggers back to the walkway and sits. He dangles his feet over the edge.

He looks down. He can't see Madsen's body. But he looks down anyway.

He tries to think.

He's still there, trying to think, when the police arrive.

Acknowledgements

So here's how it's supposed to happen.

You're a novelist; you write a few books featuring a series character. You get lucky and the rights to your character are acquired by a production company; then someone else adapts your stories into a film or a TV series.

DCI John Luther, true to form, took the opposite path. Although I still think of myself primarily as a novelist, I write for the screen, too. *Luther* was a TV show before it became a book, which means the characters I introduced in screenplays were given greater substance, nuance and detail by the actors who went on to portray them.

I've said elsewhere that the moment Idris Elba put on that coat and strutted into the room — a big man with a big walk — it became unimaginable to me that anyone else might ever have played the role. Idris made Luther. I hope this novel does him justice.

I would like to thank Saskia Reeves, Stephen Mackintosh, Warren Brown, Dermot Crowley, Paul McGann and Indira Varma because the characters of Rose Teller, Ian Reed, Justin Ripley, Martin Schenk, Mark North and Zoe Luther belong as much to these fine actors as to me.

Katie Swinden has been my comrade-in-arms for years now. Nobody's got a better feel for story; many of this book's problems were disentangled during an epic walk we took across the unforgiving face of London early in January, 2011.

I would also like to thank Phillippa Giles, without whose zeal *Luther* wouldn't have existed in any form . . . and without whose friendship I might have lost my mind instead of just, y'know, temporarily mislaying it a few times.

I owe a debt to Simon Morgan, who points out my abundant procedural inaccuracies without ever laughing.

My gratitude also to Doreen Lally and Tracy Harwood for their procedural and medical insights. And for laughing like crazed mad-women.

Of the many sources I consulted, I'm particularly indebted to *Adoption: Uncharted Waters* by David Kirschner PhD (Juneau Press, 2006), Paul Talling's *Derelict London* (Random House Books, 2008) and *Edgelands* by Paul Farley and Michael Symmons Roberts (Jonathan Cape, 2011).

Much of Maggie Reilly's campaigning piece I lifted from Camilla Cavendish's *Times* article 'We Can't Just Trust Experts on the Risk to a Child' (November 10, 2010).

Vasile Sava's ardent defence of his misdeeds owes a great deal to Minette Martin's *Times* article 'Baby Trafficking May Not Be All Bad' (October 8, 2006).

Finally, my gratitude to Francesca Main and Gordon Wise, my publisher and literary agent respectively. I promised them a proper novel, and

I promised to deliver it on time.

I failed miserably at the latter: if this were a movie, there'd be someone hovering at my shoulder right now, impatiently waiting to grab this piece of paper the instant I rip it from the typewriter.

If it's a proper book, that's only because their conviction and occasional tough love kept me going.

As did the unwavering faith of my wife, Nadya, and the very existence of my joyous, excellent sons, Ethan and Finn. My greatest debt, as ever, is to them.

We do hope that you have enjoyed reading this large print book.

Did you know that all of our titles are available for purchase?

We publish a wide range of high quality large print books including:
Romances, Mysteries, Classics
General Fiction
Non Fiction and Westerns

Special interest titles available in large print are:
The Little Oxford Dictionary
Music Book
Song Book
Hymn Book
Service Book

Also available from us courtesy of Oxford University Press:
Young Readers' Dictionary
(large print edition)
Young Readers' Thesaurus
(large print edition)

For further information or a free brochure, please contact us at:
Ulverscroft Large Print Books Ltd.,
The Green, Bradgate Road, Anstey,
Leicester, LE7 7FU, England.
Tel: (00 44) 0116 236 4325
Fax: (00 44) 0116 234 0205

Other titles published by
The House of Ulverscroft:

BURIAL

Neil Cross

Nathan has never been able to forget the worst night of his life: the party that led to the sudden, shocking death of a young woman. Only he and Bob, an untrustworthy old acquaintance, know what really happened and they have resolved to keep it that way. But when, years later, Bob appears at Nathan's door with terrifying news, old wounds are reopened, threatening to tear Nathan's world apart. Because Nathan has his own secrets now. Secrets that could destroy everything he has fought to build. And maybe Bob doesn't realise just how far Nathan will go to protect them . . .

CAPTURED

Neil Cross

Although he is still young, Kenny has just weeks to live. Before he dies, he wants to find his childhood best friend Callie Barton and thank her for the kindness she showed him when they were at school together. But when Kenny begins his search, he discovers that Callie Barton has gone missing. Although her husband Jonathan was cleared of any involvement, he seems to be hiding something. Kenny has no choice but to take matters into his own hands. And knowing that time is running out on him, he's prepared to do whatever it takes . . .

NEVER KNOWING

Chevy Stevens

At thirty-four Sara Gallagher is finally happy with her life, but there is one big question that still haunts her — who are her birth parents? Finally ready to hear the truth, Sara discovers that some questions are better left unanswered: her biological father is an infamous serial killer, a wanted man who has been slaying women for over thirty years. And now he has a daughter. Sara soon realises that the only thing worse than finding out your real father is a killer is him finding about you . . .